A C

Prologue
January 2020

Vanessa took a deep, calming breath and surveyed the room.

Everything was ready. At least everything she could see. The wood-plank flooring was swept clean. The dozen tables—a funky and eclectic mix of sizes and shapes—were all wiped down. The two large sofas, one by the bay window, the other nestled in a little alcove which she and her staff had taken to calling "The Lover's Nook," both had their colorful throw cushions fluffed and arranged just so.

The pastry cooler, attached to the ordering counter, was stocked with pastries and plastic containers of diced fresh fruit. The coffee machines were turned on, emitting an intoxicating mix of the different blends brewing, and the espresso maker positively gleamed, the result of Vanessa's almost obsessive polishing the night before.

Yes, everything I can control is ready.

If there was a meteor hurtling towards Earth right this very minute to wipe out Carlsbad, California, she couldn't do anything about that. Same for the San Andreas fault if it decided to suddenly shift and throw the entire state into the Pacific. Nope; completely out of her hands.

All I can control is this coffeeshop and doing everything I can to make sure we're a hit.

Vanessa checked her watch. After thirty-five years on this planet, she was now only 10 minutes way from opening her very own coffeeshop, La Vida Mocha. Reaching into the pocket of her favorite black ripped jeans and extracting a hair tie, she pulled her long raven hair back into a ponytail, mindful of the fact that when she wears it down, she tends to look too fancy, *too* glamorous—at least that's what people always told her. *Like a goddamn supermodel on the red carpet*, one of her ex-girlfriends had told her.

The recall of that memory made Vanessa stop for a second. That had been Rebecca who'd made that comment. Rebecca, who was no slouch in the looks department herself but for some reason had terrible self-esteem and was intimidated by Vanessa's own startling beauty. It was that lack of self-esteem which had eventually led to their breakup when Rebecca left Vanessa for a slightly overweight blonde with bad skin.

Vanessa shook her head.

Women! Can't live with 'em; can't be straight.

In any case, ponytail it was. Relaxed, casual, fun. Because this was supposed to be a relaxed, casual and fun coffeeshop.

She took another deep breath and then said, "OK, we're ready. We're ready."

Chloë, one of Vanessa's two employees, looked up from the table she was nervously re-polishing. Her pixie-cut platinum hair caught the early sunlight streaming through the picture window.

"We're more than ready, Vanessa," Chloë said with a smile. "By the way, have you seen the line forming up outside?"

No, Vanessa hadn't seen, so focused had her attention been on the inside of her new business. But now she directed her gaze to the window and, sure enough, a line of about fifteen (hopefully future repeat!) customers was waiting. Something about the make-up of the line caused Vanessa to bite her bottom lip while she figured it out. When she did, she started laughing.

Chloë, needlessly polishing yet another table, looked up again. "What's up?"

Vanessa nodded towards the waiting people.

"They're all women," she said.

Chloë looked.

"Yeah, so?"

Vanessa was still laughing.

"Well, I mean...look! There's one...two...three...four!...couples holding hands and judging by the amount of flannel, I'm willing to bet the rest were last with a guy back in their experimental college years." She looked over at Chloë. "As much as I love the ladies, I didn't set out to open Carlsbad's premier lesbian coffeeshop."

Of course, it made sense, she considered. In the run-up to this grand opening, Vanessa and her cadre of friends had promoted La Vida Mocha by posting flyers in every lesbian bar from Oceanside to San Diego; by creating a Facebook page for the shop—and then linking it to just about every lesbian Facebook group in Southern California; by posting photos of the shop's transformation from empty former delicatessen to hip, So-Cal coffee hangout on Instagram and Twitter with the hashtags *#lesbianownedbusiness* and *#lesbiansrule* and by talking the shop up for the past three months to anyone they kissed, from significant others to one-night stands. Hell, even her only two employees were gay.

"Eh, who cares?" Chloë said. "The boys have plenty of their own places and the straights still rule the world. I wouldn't mind a chicks-only caffeine spot."

She came to stand by Vanessa, hooking her arm through hers. "It's finally about to happen, Vanessa," she told her boss with feeling. "You've been waiting a long time." She squeezed Vanessa's arm.

Vanessa was so grateful for Chloë's presence. The twenty-three-year-old may be a dozen years younger than herself but she had a good head on her shoulders and had been a calming influence for Vanessa when the rigors of opening a new business had gotten to be too much at times. The two had known each other since Chloë was still in high school and Vanessa had been her personal trainer, hired by Chloë's parents to help their daughter rehabilitate her knee from a mountain biking accident.

"Fuck!"

The exclamation startled both Vanessa and Chloë and they turned to see Luli, Vanessa's second employee, emerge from the back room, staring at her phone. Vanessa's heart thumped and her panicked eyes looked at her watch. Only five more minutes until opening! What the hell went wrong in the back? Did the walk-in fridge die? Did Luli discover rat droppings covering the sacks of coffee? Luli was looking at her phone...*was* there a meteor heading towards Carlsbad?

"Lu?" Vanessa asked, her voice a little shaky.

"Huh? Oh...sorry! Shit, we're not open yet, are we?" She quickly scanned the room to see if there were any customers that might have been offended at her outburst, then breathed a sigh relief upon only seeing Vanessa and Chloë.

Vanessa felt Chloë give her arm another squeeze, this time laced with meaning.

Breathe.

"Lu, what's wrong?" Chloë asked.

"My sister. She's trapped in China!"

"Oh no!" the other women exclaimed in unison.

Luli's sister, they knew, had left for China a month ago to visit relatives. She was due back any day.

"Yeah, they fucking closed China!" Luli continued. "China! Because of that virus! No one in or out. Including my sister!"

"Is she okay? I mean, does she have somewhere to stay and all that?" Vanessa asked. She and Chloë came to stand next to Luli and both looked down at her phone. It was open to the messaging app but all of the text was in Cantonese.

Luli nodded. "Yeah, she's fine. She'll just have to stay with our relatives. I mean, it's not bad; they own a string of electronics shops and are pretty well connected with the Party, so they're more than well off. Jia will be living in a mansion at least."

"Thank God," Vanessa said. "I'm sure she'll be fine and be able to come home soon. This corona thing will blow over in no time. It's not like China is a third-world country. They have the resources to fight this thing and contain it."

"Yeah, you're right." Luli shut off the phone, tucking it in her back pocket. "Anyway, my parents hate her boyfriend so Jia being trapped in the motherland is a blessing to them." She looked up at Vanessa. "OK, let's do this!"

Vanessa nodded. It was time. Well, a minute early but what the hell?

While Chloë and Luli took up stations behind the counter Vanessa smoothed down her fitted black tee (*relaxed, casual, fun*) and went to open the door. La Vida Mocha was open for business.

"Hi," she greeted the first person through. "Welcome to La Vida Mocha!"

Chapter 1
Six months later…

Megan decided she was done being nice.

One of her most dimwitted direct reports, Trevor, had just IM-ed her via Zoom for the sixth time today asking yet another stupid question, the answer to which was already supplied if Trevor would only do one of two things: look for it where he is supposed to look for it, or learn to read. What made it worse was that because he wasn't on top of things like he should be, his team was going to be late releasing a major deliverable.

Her lips pursed and her jaw tight, she typed out a reply in the chat box.

> *Trevor, I remember SPECIFICALLY, the answers to these questions being provided to us by Accounting in April during a meeting you attended. And now you're telling me that your team may be late with the release because somehow those answers did not make it to your developers?*
>
> *And why am I just hearing about this today? Why have you not brought this up during any of the release status meetings between April and now?*
>
> *Before you go log off today, I want you to set up a meeting with me, you, your lead devs and Andy for Monday morning. The release is still two weeks away. Your team WILL make the release date and on Monday we're going to figure out how you're going to do it.*

She clicked Send and then looked at her work laptop's clock. 2:41 p.m. She typically logged off at three but 2:41 was close enough, especially on a Friday. Sometime later tonight she'd log back in and make sure Trevor set up that meeting. If he didn't, there'd be hell to pay on Monday. No, scratch that…there'd be hell to pay tonight when she called him.

After shutting her laptop lid, she stood, stretched her five-six frame and then reached up and untied her auburn hair from the ponytail she'd had it in all day, shaking her head to loosen the curls. As she started walking out of the spare bedroom that she had had to turn into a home office she frowned when she noticed a tightness in her left hip. Sure, she had been sitting for two hours straight, stuck on boring conference calls, but certainly twenty-six-years-old was still too young to feel decrepit after sitting for a while?

Oh well. It was bound to happen eventually.

Unlike most of her friends, Megan had no qualms about aging. Besides, she was doing this whole approaching-thirty thing quite well. Slim and toned with youthful features that made people think she hadn't yet reached twenty-five, Megan knew she had no right to panic over her looks.

Just as she entered her bedroom her phone rang. The caller ID said *Abs*.

"Hey, Abby," Megan answered.

"Hey, what are you up to?"

"About to change out of my work clothes," Megan said. She put the phone on speaker, laid it on the bed and set about unbuttoning her slacks.

"Oh my God! You are such a dork!" Abby screeched. "You're *still* doing that?"

Megan laughed. When California went on lockdown a few months ago the company she worked for, BeachSoft, ordered all their employees to work from home until further notice. But even though this meant Megan no longer had to commute to BeachSoft's offices in Vista, she still awoke for work Monday through Friday at the same time *and* still got dressed in the mornings as if she was going to the office. Her rationale for keeping to that routine was that once things returned to normal and white-collar workers like her returned to the office it would be much easier to resume her old morning routines if she never stopped them in the first place.

Abby, on the other hand, used work from home as an excuse to sleep an extra hour each workday and to stay in her pajamas until bedtime, when she would change into different pajamas.

Megan now pulled off her navy striped blouse and went to her closet to determine what to wear now.

"Anyway, dork," Abby continued, "I want to make sure you haven't forgotten about tomorrow."

"Yeah, yeah, yeah," Megan replied. "Seven o'clock. I'm picking you up."

Their friends Angela and Desiree had just gotten engaged and were having a small party at their place here in Carlsbad. Not exactly Covid-19 protocol but Megan saw nothing wrong with it. She trusted Angela and Dee to use good judgment in their arrangements. Besides, it would be nice to get out of the house and see others because even she was starting to get a little crazy with all the forced isolation.

Giving up on choosing what to change into while Abby then chewed Megan's ear off about a "large and in charge" woman who had winked at her last night in the grocery store, Megan remained in her underwear until the call ended a few minutes later. When it did, Megan blew out a relieved breath.

Finally!

She loved Abby to bits, but her best friend was like a Chatty Cathy doll with a broken string.

And it was Friday! At this moment, Megan wanted nothing more than to change into some shorts and one of the cute yoga crop tops Amazon just delivered Wednesday and head out for a stroll along the seawall of Carlsbad State Beach and then find a nice quiet bench somewhere to sit and do some drawing.

***

An hour later, Megan was leaving the seawall after taking a good long walk south to the Cabrillo Power Plant before turning around to head back north to Carlsbad Village Drive. She was carrying her leather messenger bag that contained her iPad, wallet, phone and headphones. It was another perfect California day, sunny with a very slight breeze blowing in from the Pacific, tinged with salt and the scents of the ocean and beach, scents which always made Megan feel safe and at home. Despite the continuing lockdown there were plenty of folks out strolling, like her, all wearing face masks and trying their hardest to maintain some kind of distance between themselves and others. Megan found it funny how face masks had become a new fashion accessory and a form of personal expression. She herself wore a plain black one. Nonetheless, nowadays, when she went for one of her walks, she made a game out of trying to spot the most interesting mask. Today's winner (so far) had been a young girl of around ten whose mask depicted a cartoon mouth with its tongue sticking out.

As Megan waited for the light to change in order to cross Carlsbad Boulevard, she yawned...a huge one. The second one in as many minutes, in fact. God, why was she so tired? The idea of going back to her condo and taking a nap was seductively appealing but damn it, it was Friday! She was not going to waste this lovely early-evening at home in bed. Well, in bed alone, at least.

Coffee!

Coffee, after all, was the solution to a lot of life's problems. And when coffee failed, wine was always Plan B.

It was then that her eyes picked up on something across the street. She blinked to be sure it wasn't some kind of hopeful mirage because such a scene was now a rarity in this pandemic era. But...yes, it looked like...

On the corner was a coffeeshop, Brawn Brothers. That in itself was not unusual, coffeeshops were everywhere, but the fact that Brawn Brothers had a patio full of guests was odd! And from what she could see, there were guests inside too!

Were cafes now allowed to have sit-in guests? With all the changing rules in California about who could do what Megan supposed it was possible. Quite frankly, she had lost track. But hadn't she read that the Carlsbad/Oceanside region had recently experienced a surge in Covid cases after an earlier attempt at reopening the state?

Megan felt a tiny but hopeful pang of excitement. She hadn't enjoyed sitting in a coffeeshop working on her drawings since before everything shut down back in March. Unfortunately, that establishment, Your Best Shot, her absolute favorite, would never re-open, a permanent casualty of the pandemic.

Even though the light had changed and she could cross, Megan stayed on the curb, instead using her iPhone to find other nearby cafes. She had been such a loyal patron of Your Best Shot that she hadn't set foot into any other local places in at least three years. And Brawn Brothers was out. The place was obnoxious, she remembered, the customers too young and the vibe too frat house.

Wait...here was a place. And it was just up the street a bit on Grand Avenue. Four and a half stars on Yelp and Google. La Vida Mocha. Megan seemed to remember some of her friends mentioning it some time back when it first opened. And if they were open, really open, and she could sit and chill in a nice coffeehouse vibe...

Okay...why not?

Chapter 2

"Holy fuck," Vanessa said into the phone, not really caring that it was her mother on the other end. "Remind me again that we live in America."

Her mother tutted but did not reprimand her daughter's language.

"Still no luck?"

"Only in that I have now memorized every single word on the website because I only ever get to see this one page," Vanessa answered.

"Just keep trying."

Vanessa bit her tongue to stop a sarcastic comment from leaping out of her mouth. Moms were great, but why did they insist of offering such useless advice at times?

Instead, Vanessa said, "I will definitely keep trying, Mom. Look, I'd better go..."

"A customer?" her mother asked hopefully.

Vanessa decided to lie. "Yeah, a customer, Mom. Love to Dad, talk to you soon. Bye." And she tapped the red button on her phone's screen.

A customer. Yeah, right. She'd had three all day. None since...what, one-thirty-ish?

The thing about coffeeshops, Vanessa wanted to tell the State of California, was that customers wanted to spend *time* in them. Thus, magnanimously allowing coffeeshops to remain open only for take-out during the pandemic was kind of pointless because the only people who wanted to-go coffee were people heading to work. Yet the only workers willing to plunk down five bucks for an iced mocha or seven bucks for a caramel frappe were of the white-collar variety. But the white-collar variety workers were all working from home. Not only that but white-collar variety workers were typically smart enough to realize that it was possible in the twenty-first century (and the twentieth and the nineteenth, the eighteenth, the seventeenth—all the way back, Vanessa figured, to Neanderthal times) to make coffee at home. It was that kind of intelligence that allowed those people to become white-collar workers in the first place.

Coffeeshops were establishments people went to in order to be *away* from home, to get a caffeine fix while also indulging in being out in society—even if some people's idea of socializing was sitting at a table, eyes glued to a laptop, AirPods stuck in their ears. Most people just didn't bother going to a coffeeshop if once there they couldn't find a comfy spot to sit and enjoy being out.

So, while Vanessa was grateful to the good folks up in Sacramento for allowing her to earn a meager living by keeping her shop open for the handful of people each day who found themselves in need of coffee but unable to get home to make it themselves, she really wished they'd come up with another plan.

And she also really wished Washington would get their act together and fix the website for their newest loan program for small businesses. All week long, Vanessa had been trying to access the site to apply for some of that money the politicians were boasting about handing out only to end up feeling like she was living in Honduras or some other third-world country that didn't know how to build web pages.

She sighed. She had enough of that for the day. Closing the lid of her laptop she looked around at her empty shop.

La Vida Mocha had started off gangbusters. Sure, in a town the size of Carlsbad one could expect a new place to be busy for the first couple of weeks after opening, simply because the residents now had something different to try. But Vanessa's coffeeshop had sustained its popularity well after the novelty had worn off. This was helped by her choice of location. La Vida Mocha's spot on Grand Avenue was on a block in which Vanessa's only neighbors were an art gallery, a New Age crystal store, a dry cleaner and a place that sold beach clothes. Across the street was the Thirsty Lion, a British-style pub, and an antique bookseller. There wasn't another coffeeshop for a couple of blocks.

It also helped that La Vida Mocha served really good coffee. Vanessa had been very picky about where she sourced her coffee from, choosing a California supplier known for high-quality products. And because Vanessa had also worked for three years as a barista after leaving the corporate world, while running her personal trainer business as a side gig, she knew how to get the best results from her coffee and her equipment. The reviews of La Vida Mocha were phenomenal (even when Vanessa ignored the ones that were obviously written by her friends) and the coffeeshop had even gotten a favorable write-up in the *Orange County Times*.

But then March came.

California simply shut down.

Weeks went by when Vanessa could not even legally open La Vida Mocha's doors. She tried to apply for the first round of the Paycheck Protection Program but by the time she had gathered all the necessary information needed from her bank and the Small Business Administration and filled out the application, the program had run out of money—in thirteen days. Not surprising considering just about every small business in the country was trying for the same pot of money. And even though a second round of PPP funds had become available in April, by then it was pointless to apply for it because by then she had no more employees.

Chloë and Luli were gone, Vanessa unable to keep paying them. Chloë had landed on her feet; she had eventually snagged a job at an Amazon warehouse. Luli, however, had had to give up her apartment in nearby Oceanside and move back in with her parents in San Diego. There were no hard feelings from either of them; Vanessa even had plans to see Chloë tomorrow night. In any case, by the time March turned to April Vanessa was left alone with La Vida Mocha and the very real struggle of how to keep her business going.

Even when the state relaxed the shutdown a bit and allowed establishments like hers to open for takeout, it seemed too little too late. All of the shops surrounding La Vida Mocha were still closed, the art gallery permanently, a For Lease sign now occupying its window. And a lot of La Vida Mocha's patronage had come from folks shopping nearby, so all of those customers had vanished. People were staying home. Which meant their money was staying home with them.

One night in May, alone in bed and unable to sleep, Vanessa had the most terrible thought she had ever had in her life.

Thank God Nana died.

As soon as that statement crossed her mind Vanessa had sat up suddenly and spent a good ten minutes weeping, hating herself.

Oh my God, what the fuck is wrong with me?, she had chided herself, openly sobbing. *How could I think such a thing!*

But she knew how *could* think such a thing. After all, when Nana had died back in October of last year, Vanessa, the only grandchild, had inherited some money. Not a Bill Gates-like fortune but certainly more than Vanessa had ever seen at one time in her life.

It was the inheritance that allowed her to finally take the plunge and open up her own coffeeshop, a longtime dream. Vanessa had socked the money away in a savings account, secured a small business loan from Chase and figured that she could keep Nana's money mostly untouched while La Vida Mocha found its footing.

Yet now it was Nana's money that allowed Vanessa to keep opening La Vida Mocha each day.

Occasionally, she experienced a pang of guilt when she thought of Chloë and Luli, though. Nana's money could have kept them on the payroll even until now but the businesswoman in Vanessa couldn't justify that. Not in this day and age. Not when there was no sure way to know when (or if?) she could reopen normally, with actual sit-down guests. Not when she had the loan from Chase to repay. Not when she had rent for the coffeeshop to pay each month in addition to the myriad other regular expenses.

No, she had done the right thing, letting them go. But damn it, things had to get better soon. A vaccine, a cure...something! Because according to her very simple back-of-the-envelope calculations, the big wad of cash she had gotten from her beloved Nana would run out by January if things remained the same.

And it was at this point that the bell over the door dinged.

Vanessa reached for her face mask which she had taken off when the last customer had left, way back when the afternoon was still young. Expertly putting it on she looked up, feeling stupid when she realized she was smiling a welcome behind a mask that completely hid her mouth.

When she saw the woman who walked in, Vanessa's heart thumped. Boom!

Whoa!

Suddenly she was thankful for the mask because she realized that her mouth had dropped open in awe.

Her customer had long auburn hair pulled into a ponytail and was wearing skintight workout shorts that topped off a gorgeous pair of tanned legs. She was wearing the most adorable purple yoga crop top revealing a flat and toned midriff, which Vanessa appraised with her ex-personal trainer's eye. Jealously, Vanessa wondered where she got the top from but she also couldn't help noticing that the top accentuated a pair of wonderfully small breasts. Vanessa had a thing for small breasts, always had.

In this pandemic age, where you could often only see half a person's face, Vanessa nonetheless knew this woman was drop-dead beautiful based solely on her eyes—perfectly shaped and of such an intensely deep green Vanessa couldn't stop looking at them. Unless she had a classic Tom Selleck mustache under the mask, Vanessa was certain the woman would be stunning when her entire face was revealed.

Lucky woman who gets to see that. Of course, chances are it's probably a lucky guy.

"Um...hi! Welcome in!" Vanessa greeted her and then immediately cleared her throat. That had come out wobbly, like a teenager who finally found the courage to speak to her crush.

But...

Vanessa wasn't sure if she imagined it but did the woman's eyebrow slightly raise at the awkwardness of her greeting? And, also...well, the woman hadn't taken her eyes off Vanessa once since entering, and Vanessa was pretty sure the woman's eyes were telegraphing interest.

She seemed quite young, maybe—*maybe*—twenty-five?

"Are you *open* open?" the customer asked, her voice muffled slightly by the mask.

Vanessa shook her head. "Sorry, no. Just for takeout."

The woman's eyes transmitted disappointment as she looked around the shop.

"Damn," she muttered. She then pointed behind her, indicating outside. "I saw Brawn Brothers with customers inside and I just hoped."

God, Brawn Brothers!

"They got a citation from the police for doing that last Friday also," Vanessa told her. "Looks like they'll get another one this week too."

The woman shook her head. "That is just so irresponsible! Not the police, I mean; the coffeeshop! Didn't I hear there was a spike in Covid cases in our area?"

"I heard the same. And it's because of places like Brawn Brothers and their insensitive customers. They must all be Republicans. Heaven forbid Republicans actually believe in science, you know? I think most of them still believe the earth is flat and that early man had pet dinosaurs."

Vanessa colored.

Shit!

That was careless. She never Republican-bashed to a total stranger! Particularly a total stranger who had just entered her now-struggling coffeeshop with the intention of spending money. For all she knew, this auburn-haired beauty, who presumably had money somewhere in that cool retro leather satchel she carried, had a donkey tattooed on her ass.

I wouldn't mind determining if that's the case, of course…

Thankfully, though, the customer laughed and, goodness, how it lit up her eyes! So, she's either a normal person or at least a Republican with a sense of humor.

"Best laugh I've had all day." She looked around the coffeeshop again, the disappointment from before returning to her eyes. "I was hoping I could sit in here and do some drawing while having my coffee, but oh well."

"You're an artist?" Vanessa asked, genuinely interested.

The smile hidden by Miss Auburn's mask reached her eyes.

"Yeah. Well, it's not my day job but it's what I do when I'm not at my day job. I used to hang out at Your Best Shot and work on my art there."

"Gotcha. Yeah, I was sorry to see they closed down." Vanessa meant that. Technically they had been the competition, yes, but Margaret, the owner, had sent flowers to Vanessa on the day La Vida Mocha opened. *Welcome to the neighborhood!* the card had read. Margaret had even come to the shop herself later that opening week with some of her staff and insisted on paying for the round of coffee Vanessa offered on the house. She was good people.

The customer sighed.

"Well, I guess I'll just take an Americano to go, then. Large, please."

"Coming right up," Vanessa said, locking her gaze with the woman. There was definitely a flicker of interest being returned!

No. It's just been a long lonely day. You're seeing things.

"Hot or iced?" she managed to ask.

"Um…hot, like our ancestors drank it."

Laughing, Vanessa set about making the drink. Her customer, meanwhile, started looking around.

"This is a cool shop," she said. "I can't wait until this stupid lockdown ends. I may end up spending a lot of time here."

Softly; so softly that she barely heard it herself though it came from her own lips, Vanessa whispered, "Yes, please."

"What was that?" the customer asked.

Fuck! She caught that?

Vanessa felt flame coloring her cheeks. She forced herself to keep her eyes focused on the espresso machine. God, what was wrong with her? This wasn't normal. Obviously, it had been too long since she'd had sex. How long was it, anyway?

"Nothing," she said cheerily. "Just talking to this damn machine."

"Oh."

Why were Americanos so easy to make? Vanessa was just about done with the drink already. Then this vision of a woman would pay and skip on out of here. Why couldn't she have ordered Vanessa's signature drink, the triple chocolate caramel frappe with espresso and Godiva chips. That had nine ingredients and each one took five minutes to make. Of course, it also had about a bazillion calories and judging by the figure this customer had, she certainly did not overindulge much.

All too soon the to-go cup was filled. She turned back to the counter and waved the cup at her guest who had wandered away to continue her inspection of the shop.

"That's three-twenty," Vanessa said.

The woman unzipped the flap of her leather messenger bag.

"Cool bag!" Vanessa said.

That earned Vanessa another mask-hidden smile which nonetheless reached the other woman's eyes.

"Thanks! I got it in Singapore. Back in the Before Times when we could still travel the world." She extracted a wallet and then pulled a five out. "Keep the change," she said.

Damn!

Sure, Vanessa was grateful for the tip but it also meant she couldn't keep her visitor here just a few moments longer while she worked the register and got her change. An idea came to her.

"Um...why don't you just stay here and drink that? And work on your art?"

There went the eyebrow again. Vanessa's heart went boom. Like, *BOOM!*

The customer hesitated a moment.

"That's sweet but I don't want to get you in trouble."

Vanessa gave a little nonchalant wave.

"You won't, I'm sure. Look," and here Vanessa pointed to the sofa in Lover's Nook.

Seriously?

But there was no way the other woman knew that's what the little niche was called.

"Um...that sofa is out of view of the window. No one will see you. And on the off-chance that a cop comes in I'll tell them that you're one of my staff. Doing inventory."

The woman laughed and looked over at the couch. She still hesitated a moment but then she said, "If you're sure?"

"I am."

"Well, thanks. I'll definitely stay. On one condition..."

Chapter 3

Megan stated her condition.

"I'll feel weird if I'm over there drawing and you're here doing whatever. I mean, it's just the two of us in here. I'm sure you're busy and all but if you get a break would you come hang out with me a bit?"

Megan felt like a silly schoolgirl but she also realized that her happiness over the next few seconds was dependent on whether this gorgeous barista agreed to come chill with her on the couch.

Jesus, get a grip. You passed how many hot women along the seawall today without getting all flushed?

But this was different.

This barista with her long black hair made Megan's heart race a bit every time she stared at Megan with those eyes that were like deep pools of coffee.

Earlier, while the barista had busied herself making the Americano, Megan had wandered a bit from the counter. Sure, she wanted to check the place out, with its funky and eclectic mix of furnishings and industrial décor, but she had also taken the opportunity to check out the woman fixing her drink.

Black jeans that hung low on her hips, a tight cream-colored t-shirt that was sleeveless and showed incredible arms and hugged a bust that was…yummy. Hair that was as black as one of the evil queens in a Disney movie. Even her face mask was cute, displaying Darth Vader's grill.

A sci-fi nerd.

That thought made Megan happy, being into sci-fi herself.

And, of course, the most important thing about the barista: Megan's gaydar was pinging like there was a Russian sub dead ahead. *Ping! Ping! Ping!*

Then, surprisingly, the barista had invited her to stay!

Ping!

Megan raised an expectant eyebrow at the other woman as she waited for the answer to her invitation to hang out on the sofa.

The barista swallowed.

"What about your drawing?"

Megan *pshawed*.

"I got all night to do that. I'll work on it when I get home later."

"Okay, then; yeah, I'll join you. Just give me a sec."

"Excellent," Megan said, feeling like that silly schoolgirl again. It was as if the cheerleading captain had agreed to sit with her in the cafeteria. Alone. *So* cliché, Megan knew, but, well, cheerleaders...

She went over to the indicated sofa in its own little niche and sat down. Her Americano smelled fabulous. Reaching up to her face, a sudden thought struck her.

"Damn!" she exclaimed.

It caught the attention of the barista across the room. "Is something wrong?"

Megan looked over at her.

"I just realized that I'll have to remove my mask to drink my coffee and then *that* made me realize you might be uncomfortable about it, me being a perfect stranger and all."

The barista looked at her with a cocked eyebrow.

"*Are* you perfect?" she asked.

Megan's mouth dropped open and she blushed.

"You know what I meant," she replied with a laugh. Were they flirting?

"Well, have you been careful?"

"Totally," Megan said. "I've been working from home since March and I'm something of a hermit anyway so my house has been like my Fortress of Solitude." She snapped her fingers. "Oh, wait! There was that time I snuck into Wuhan and licked all the doorknobs! Shoot! I forgot about that!"

Laughing, the other woman started walking over, carrying her own cup of coffee. Megan's eyes automatically locked onto the movement of her hips. When she reached the sofa, she sat two cushions away from Megan and then raised her coffee mug.

"Looks like I'll have to take my mask off too," she said with a grin. "So we'll be sharing the risk. On three?"

"Cool," Megan said. She was digging this barista and her fun attitude. And she was digging those biceps, too. They were the perfect combination of strength and femininity and Megan could imagine how amazing it would be to feel enclosed by them in an embrace. Safe and...turned on.

"One...two...three!"

Simultaneously, both masks were pulled off. Megan's breath hitched as the barista's face was fully revealed showing a pert nose and full lips that were glossed with a purplish color. She was gorgeous. Like cover girl gorgeous. It took a moment before Megan realized that she had now spent several seconds staring at the barista's lips. She wrenched her eyes upwards only to discover that the barista was also staring at Megan's lips.

Megan had to cross her legs.

"I'm Megan, by the way," she said to get her mind off some rapidly developing lascivious ideas.

"Vanessa." The introduction was accompanied by a megawatt smile.

"Nice to meet you." Megan held up her mask. "You sure you don't mind...?"

"No, of course not. It's actually nice to see someone's entire face in here, you know?"

Megan nodded as she sipped her Americano. "Mmm...I know what you mean. Although, I think that maybe this pandemic is, like, reawakening some long-buried instincts we humans forgot we had."

Oh God, did I wake up today and decide to be Super Nerd?

But, surprisingly, Vanessa seemed interested. She even leaned forward a bit.

"Ooh, say more," she said.

Blushing at having revealed her nerdy super powers, Megan ploughed on.

"Um...I just mean that...well, for example, even though I just met you and even though I know nothing about you, I just *knew* somehow that I'd be perfectly safe sitting here without our masks on. That *we*—you and I—don't need masks to sit and talk. So, it's like this pandemic is causing a sense we didn't even know we had to reawaken. It's like—"

"It's like we're the zombies in *World War Z*!" Vanessa interrupted. "Able to sniff out a healthy host."

Megan's eyes went wide, totally getting the reference.

"Oh my God, I love that movie!"

"Me too! It's one of my comfort-food films," Vanessa said. Then, adorably, her cheeks flushed pink. "Jesus, was that, like, a super nerdy thing to say?"

Megan laughed. "Probably, yes. But I love sci-fi so you're lucky, you couldn't have a better audience."

Vanessa grinned. "Well, I figured I might be safe once you used Fortress of Solitude in a sentence."

Now it was Megan's turn to blush. "The funny part is, I don't even like superhero movies. I mean, the 1978 Superman is cool in a totally retro way. And Michael Keaton's Batman from eighty-nine was awesome, but all of these new ones..." She shook her head.

"I know what you mean. An ex-girlfriend of mine took me to one of the *Avengers* movies back when it came out. I didn't want to go because I hadn't seen any of the previous movies and so I was afraid I wouldn't be able to follow the plot, right? Turns out I shouldn't have worried. All you need is a fourth-grade education, so I was good."

Megan found herself laughing again. Vanessa had a great sense of humor.

And thanks for confirming my gaydar still works.

"Thanks for joining me," she told Vanessa. "I was totally prepared to spend the evening on my own, just me and my art, but I don't know, once we started talking, I guess I realized I wanted some kind of interaction. Anyway, I appreciate your company."

There was a moment which passed between them after Megan said that, she was sure of it. Vanessa's eyebrow had arched so imperceptibly that Megan at first thought she imagined it but no, she was sure it had happened. A flush that was nowhere near her face bloomed and spread. Suddenly feeling obvious, Megan looked around the coffeeshop while crossing her legs again.

"Are you sure your boss won't mind you sitting here? With me? A potentially contaminated customer?" she asked.

She noticed Vanessa's face color that adorable pink again as she smiled shyly.

"As it turns out, I'm the boss."

"No way!" Megan exclaimed. "Wait...like, manager or...?"

"Owner." The pink got deeper.

Oh my, she's modest. Could she get any hotter?

Vanessa shrugged and waved her arm, indicating the vacant shop.

"Yep, this is my bustling coffeeshop," she said. "Nice, huh?"

Without thinking, acting solely on instinct, Megan reached forward and placed her hand on top of the one Vanessa had draped on the back of the sofa. She gave the hand she was now covering a gentle squeeze. And though she had made the gesture to comfort Vanessa, Megan couldn't deny that the sensation of touching her sent thrilling shivers which quickened her pulse.

Chapter 4

Vanessa stared at the hand now on her own. And when Megan's hand squeezed hers, one thing filled Vanessa's mind.

Please keep it there. Just please keep it there.

Megan's fingernails were trimmed short and painted a soft almost-not-there bubblegum pink. The polish on her ring finger was chipped just a bit. For some reason, Vanessa wanted nothing more than to bring Megan's hand to her mouth and suck on that particular finger.

But then suddenly, Megan jerked her hand off.

"Oh my God! I am *soooo* sorry!" Megan said, a mortified look on her face. "I shouldn't have done that with all this virus shit going on! I had no right. I mean, you don't know me and I shouldn't have presumed to touch you! You don't know where my hands have been and—"

"Hey, hey!" Vanessa cut her off. "It's okay!"

"Oh my God, are you sure? You just seemed sad and I wanted to comfort you and—"

Vanessa cut her off again by scooching a few inches closer and reclaiming Megan's hand. The other woman then looked like she lost the power of speech.

"We're *World War Z* zombies, remember?" Vanessa said, smiling.

Megan smiled back.

"Right, we're zombies."

Vanessa took a chance and intertwined her fingers with Megan's. That Megan was a lesbian, Vanessa had no doubt, but she hoped Megan wouldn't freak out at the intimacy of the gesture.

"Thank you for wanting to comfort me."

Oh my God, her hands are so soft!

"Is everything okay?" Megan asked and then rolled her eyes. "No, of course everything isn't okay! You're a small business owner in the middle of the plague of the twenty-first century. Sorry."

Vanessa laughed. It felt good.

"Things aren't great, sure. But things aren't catastrophic yet either. I had to lay off my two employees and don't tell the three other customers I had today but I also had to switch to a cheaper brand of to-go cup. Hopefully they finished their coffees before the bottoms of their cups fell off."

Megan laughed.

"Sorry, but that was a funny image. Anyway, my lips are sealed," Megan promised. Then, "It seems so stupid and trite to say things are going to get better but they have to, right? I mean, this just can't keep going, right?"

"God, I hope not," Vanessa said with feeling. And she wanted to believe it; she needed to believe it. But it was getting harder to each day. When this whole pandemic thing started back in February, Vanessa couldn't imagine it lasting this long. Like many of her friends, she didn't think that this far into the twenty-first century, science wouldn't be able to quickly come up with a vaccine, if not a cure.

"I'm luckier than most, though," she continued. "I figure I could at least make it to the end of the year. Unless Cyberdyne Systems finally gets Skynet working and my espresso machines rise up and slay me."

Megan's eyes lit up. "Do you know I just read somewhere that most people think *Terminator 2* is the superior movie to the original?"

Vanessa put a serious look on her face.

"Yeah, I probably wrote that because *Terminator 2 is* superior to the original."

"What?! You can't be serious!"

"Um...hello! Liquid metal T-1000? Epic chase scene at the beginning that destroys most of L.A.? Killer special effects?"

"Um…hello! Better storytelling and no annoying twelve-year-old kid with a whiny voice in the original?" Megan rebutted.

Vanessa shook her head. "I can see you're going to be trouble," she said with mock gravity. "I need to check if anti-discriminatory laws apply to a person's movie tastes."

Megan stuck out her tongue. Vanessa's heart almost stopped.

"I'm sure they do," Megan said, "which means I'm free to come in here anytime with my pro-T1 mindset."

Vanessa laughed. Meanwhile, another thought was racing through her mind.

She's still holding my hand…

"So, what do you do for a living?" Vanessa asked her.

"Oh my God, my job is *too* boring to talk about!" Megan replied. "But since you asked, I work for BeachSoft. I'm their director of mobile app development."

"Sounds impressive, especially since you're, like, really young."

"I'm twenty-six and, yeah, I'm the youngest executive in the company but I think that's because my boss also knows that the original *Terminator* is vastly superior to the second *Terminator*."

"Whatever!" Vanessa said, breaking into another fit of laughter. She thought it was ridiculous how much she was enjoying this. Considering all the problems she was facing with keeping La Vida Mocha open, coupled with the frustrations of dealing with the federal government in the hopes of securing some kind of financial assistance, Vanessa hadn't been much for socializing or making small talk lately.

Christ, am I this lonely?

But loneliness wasn't the issue here, Vanessa knew. This was something else. Something hardly worth thinking about because she had no time for such things, despite what her heart was saying.

"Anyway, are you from here?"

Megan shook her head.

"La Jolla, originally. Then I went to New York for college. I probably would have stayed there after graduating but then BeachSoft recruited me and so I returned. They're in Vista and since I've always loved Carlsbad, I decided to buy a place here. You?"

"L.A.," Vanessa told her. "Then Oceanside after college. Did the corporate thing for a while with a side gig as a personal trainer. I also did some extra moonlighting as a barista just so I could learn the business. Then I settled here in Carlsbad and eventually decided I wanted to open this place, which I did in January."

Megan smiled. "This is awesome! We've only known each other for ten minutes and yet we've already caught up on each other's lives."

She looked like she was about to add more when her cellphone chirped. She held up a finger, instructing Vanessa to wait, and looked at the display. Vanessa saw a frown form on her face as Megan read what was obviously a text message.

"Everything okay?" Vanessa ventured.

"My ex," Megan answered. "For some reason, she apparently just *has* to see me now." She typed out a reply which almost instantly garnered a reply back. Then Megan's eyes got hard. She looked up from her phone and seemed to come to a decision. She released Vanessa's hand. Vanessa missed it instantly.

"Figures she'd ruin a perfectly good time I was having," Megan joked, standing and picking up her leather messenger bag.

"I just hope everything is okay," Vanessa said. She stood also. It was crazy how disappointed she felt. And maybe a little jealous.

I just met her.

But the instant the connection between their hands had been broken her spirit dropped a few notches.

"I'm sure it is," Megan said. "In fact, I'm sure it's something stupid like, 'Oh, I think I left my favorite bra under the bed.'"

The two women headed toward the door. Once there, Megan turned to face Vanessa and Vanessa was delighted to see an authentic smile on Megan's face.

"Are you opening tomorrow?" Megan asked.

"Of course. At eight."

"Cool. I am making it my mission to support a certain local business one Americano at a time."

Vanessa smiled. Megan was definitely flirting.

"And a certain local business would certainly appreciate it. Of course, if La Vida Mocha has to survive on one Americano at a time, I may have to start charging pandemic prices. I'm thinking five-thousand bucks for a small, maybe twelve-thousand for a large."

Megan narrowed her eyes. "Damn! I gotta remortgage my condo just for coffee now?"

"I'll throw in a blueberry muffin with each purchase, how's that?"

"And you're trying to make me fat! I see how you are! Anyway, sorry again about leaving so abruptly. Thanks for letting me stay and for chilling with me."

"Anytime," Vanessa assured her, opening the door for Megan who stepped through with a wave before heading west along Grand.

Vanessa couldn't help it. Leaning out from the doorway of the shop, she watched Megan walk away, her eyes fixating first on the bouncing of Megan's auburn ponytail as she moved and then fixating on those incredible legs. Impure thoughts of what Vanessa wanted to do between Megan's legs made her aware of a heat blooming between her own.

But those thoughts were suddenly interrupted when, at the corner of Grand and the next street, Megan turned to look back at Vanessa.

Fuck! Busted!

The heat between her legs transferred up to her face as she blushed.

She sheepishly waved to Megan who gave a wave back, and then Vanessa retreated to the sanctuary of her shop. Closing the door and leaning against it she couldn't help but start laughing at how embarrassing that was.

"Smooth, Vanessa. Real smooth."

Chapter 5

As she started her drive back to her neighborhood from downtown Carlsbad, Megan couldn't help but recall catching Vanessa watching her from La Vida Mocha's doorway. The implications caused goosebumps of excitement to spring up on her arms and she blew out a deep breath to re-center her focus. The idea that someone as heart-stoppingly stunning as Vanessa was interested in her, enough to watch her walk away, was...wow!

However, true to form, Megan also tried to see a more rational, if less exciting, side of things.

Perhaps she just wanted to make sure I was okay. I did leave kind of abruptly. So...don't read anything into it. Yet.

There was also something else to consider. New York.

Flirting—and possibly doing more—with Vanessa was fine, as long as it didn't lead to anything serious because of New York.

After almost running a stop sign because of thinking about Vanessa, Megan focused. Then, she gripped the steering wheel so tightly her knuckles turned white.

"Fucking Cindy!" she said out loud.

Cindy was Megan's ex. Megan had once had hopes she and Cindy would eventually marry. Though she hadn't proposed to Cindy yet, Megan had found herself staring in jewelry store windows or reading articles online about destination weddings or the *10 Best Places to Honeymoon.* Cindy was supposed to be Megan's forever. They had been together for two years and she was ready to take it to the next step.

And then Megan discovered Cindy had been cheating on her. With a man.

From the beginning, Cindy had told Megan that she had dated men in the past, the key phrase being *in the past.* And Megan hadn't raised an eyebrow. After all, it wasn't unusual in the lesbian community to meet women who currently identified as lesbian but who'd had relationships—even sexual relationships—with men. The reasons were varied, of course, but Cindy's story was a common one: in her teens and early twenties, Cindy had dated men as she came to grips with her sexuality, her Christian upbringing in Minnesota refusing to allow her to see that her attraction to women was perfectly normal and fine. But at twenty-five-years-old Cindy had finally embraced her attraction to women and by the time she had met Megan at a Pride barbecue Abby had dragged Megan to, Cindy had been exclusively dating women.

Then this past January, Megan discovered her potential wife was having an affair, with one of Cindy's co-workers. A male co-worker.

When Megan confronted Cindy about the infidelity—with a fury that Megan hoped she would never ever feel again—Cindy had turned into a blubbering mess. She begged Megan to not end things, insisting they could work it out. She begged Megan to understand that she had come to the realization that she was more bi than gay but that it didn't have to mean the end of everything they had built together. She promised Megan that Megan would always be her priority, that anything she ever did with a man would be just "scratching an itch."

For her part, Megan couldn't believe what she was hearing, especially when Cindy said she too had been hoping they would get married. That had just made Megan's jaw drop. Did Cindy actually believe that Megan would marry her *and* allow her to keep seeing men?

That night had been the hardest of Megan's life. At one point, as she coldly sat next to a sobbing Cindy on the couch in the living room, Megan saw the end of all her dreams of happiness vanishing like smoke in a breeze.

The betrayal was just too much. Megan viewed loyalty in a relationship as being as essential as sex and respect. She herself had had plenty of opportunities to cheat on Cindy if she had wanted to take them. One thing Southern California was not short on was lesbians and many of those lesbians were not too shy to let Megan know how attractive she was. But always—always—the thought of what she could lose by losing Cindy…it was never a risk she wanted to take.

But apparently Cindy hadn't seen things the same way. And Megan realized her trust in Cindy could never be restored.

And yes, it was worse that Cindy's infidelity had been with a man. Megan couldn't really articulate why; she had nothing against bisexual people; she had nothing against men, for that matter, except the usual complaints. But it didn't matter. Cindy had crossed a line that Megan hadn't even known was there.

So, she ordered Cindy out and while Cindy spent two weeks finding a new place to live and then moving, Megan spent those two weeks crying for hours in Abby's spare bedroom.

***

Megan felt her jaw clench when she saw Cindy's car parked on the curb in front of the condo. Megan pulled into her driveway but didn't open the garage. Cindy got out of her car the same time Megan got out of hers.

Cindy's hair was shorter, Megan noticed right away. And she'd had gold highlights added. Oddly, she was dressed in sweatpants and an old t-shirt from her alma mater that Megan recognized as being one of Cindy's favorites. But these were the kind of comfort clothes Cindy never wore out of the house.

Cindy stood in front of her car, staring at Megan, twisting her hands together like she did whenever she was nervous.

Megan just stared back at her realizing her clenched jaw was starting to give her a headache.

Eventually, Cindy gave a little wave.

"Hey," she said tentatively.

"Why are you here?" Megan asked, proud there was steel in her voice even though the truth of the matter was that seeing Cindy was like a hammer blow to her heart.

"Can we go inside and talk?"

Megan shook her head.

"No. Out here is fine, Cindy."

Cindy hung her head, biting her lip, her hand-twisting intensifying. When she looked up again, Megan was shocked to notice evidence that Cindy had been crying.

Megan's eyes softened and she dropped her armor.

"What's wrong?"

Cindy took a deep breath. "I didn't want to tell you this over the phone or in a text." She took another deep breath. "Mom's dead."

Megan gasped, her hands flying to her face. "Oh my God, no!" Without even thinking, she hurried to Cindy and pulled her into an embrace as her own tears started to fall. "Oh my God; I'm so sorry."

Cindy was nothing but sobs in Megan's arms and Megan rocked her gently while they stood there in the driveway. "Mom" was technically Cindy's Aunt Carole, but she was the woman who had raised Cindy when Cindy's parents died when she was four.

Megan knew that when Cindy had decided to finally identify as lesbian, Carole surprised her by being one-hundred percent supportive. She even went so far as to start displaying a rainbow flag in the front window of her house in Duluth.

Megan had come to know and love the woman also because Carole decided to retire to California, settling in a modest bungalow in Coachella. Visits with Carole were one of the most favorite things Megan enjoyed about being with Cindy, especially because the older woman deemed herself "Megan's Second Mom" the very first day Cindy brought Megan to meet her. It was such a touching gesture, with added meaning for Megan. She wasn't out to her own parents yet and so Carole's unconditional acceptance of Megan's relationship with her niece/adopted daughter, accompanied with motherly affection, was something Megan valued so much during the years she and Cindy were together.

"Come on, let's go inside," Megan whispered. Keeping her arm around Cindy's shoulders, Megan guided her into the condo. She sat Cindy down on the loveseat in the living room, told her she'd be right back and then went into the kitchen to start nuking water for tea. While the microwave did its thing, Megan thought of Carole, knowing she'd never see that wonderful woman again, and found herself wiping tears away with a napkin. In a couple of minutes, she returned to Cindy bearing a steaming mug of Earl Grey. Immediately, Megan was struck by how small Cindy seemed. The death of the woman who had taken her in at four-years-old and then became her mother had obviously taken a horrendous toll on her. Handing the tea to Cindy, Megan then sat next to her on the loveseat, putting her arm around Cindy's shoulders and pulling the other woman closer so Cindy could nestle her head against Megan's neck.

After a couple of sips of tea, Cindy revealed all.

It was cancer. And it had moved quickly, lethally. Even the doctors had seemed surprised.

"She died Tuesday," Cindy said. "I just got back from Coachella today but I need to go back to continue making arrangements. I just needed to come home and pack some more things. And then I thought I'd better stop and tell you. I know you hate me but it felt right to come tell you in person."

"Shh," Megan cooed. "Don't go down that path. I loved Carole, you know that, and you did the right thing coming here."

"Thank you. She loved you too, so much. She thought I was the biggest idiot for...Never mind." And Cindy started sobbing again.

For a good twenty minutes, Megan just let Cindy cry, stroking her hair and wondering at the Twilight Zone-esque quality of having Cindy Lawler, the woman she had wanted to marry and whom she had spent pretty much all this year so far hating, in her arms again. It would have taken a death to make this happen, she realized. But why did it have to be Carole?

"When is the funeral?" Megan eventually asked when Cindy seemed to have calmed down enough to perhaps speak normally.

"A week from today."

"In Minnesota?"

"No, in Coachella. Turns out Mom wanted to be buried there." She gave a dry little laugh. "I think she just didn't want to spend eternity in the frozen ground of Minnesota. Can't say I blame her."

Megan made a decision.

"May I come to the funeral?" she asked quietly.

Cindy pulled away just enough to be able to meet Megan's eyes. Her own eyes were red and watery and Megan thought it was a good thing Cindy wasn't wearing any makeup because by now she'd look like a raccoon.

"Of course you can come," Cindy said. "I would never deny you the chance to say goodbye to her." She swallowed and looked down at her hands. "I was hoping you'd come. But don't worry. You don't have to speak to me or even acknowledge me while you're there. I get it."

"Shut up about that for now," Megan ordered, pulling Cindy close again. "You're going through a horrible time in your life. Even I'm not that big of an asshole to try to make it about our breakup."

Cindy sniffled. "I honestly didn't think you would but...well, thanks."

After another while had passed, Cindy said, "Your plants are doing great," referring to Megan's impressive collection of houseplants in the room. "Where's the ficus, though?"

Megan took a deep breath before answering.

"I gave it to Mrs. Morton two doors down. You remember...she has, like, a jungle in her sewing room."

Megan felt Cindy stiffen.

"But I gave you that one. When you got that promotion."

Yeah, you gave me that one, but I dare you to find anything in this house anymore that would remind me of you.

Instead, she stroked Cindy's hair and said softly but firmly. "Hush. Priorities, remember? Stop thinking about stuff that isn't important. Now do what I say. Drink your tea and just sit here."

Chapter 6

"How long was she there?" Abby asked the next night, eyes that were wide as dinner plates on Megan as Megan drove east on the 78 towards Vista where Angela and Desiree lived.

"About an hour; maybe less."

She had just told her best friend about Cindy's visit the evening before.

"That's a long time!"

"What? Did you not hear me? I said it was about an hour!"

"But you *loathe* that woman! I *loathe* that woman! Five minutes is more than she deserves."

"Jesus, Abs, her Mom died! And Carole meant something to me too. You would have done the same thing."

Abby shrugged. "I guess." Then her brow creased as a thought came to her. She leaned forward against her seatbelt and examined Megan's face. "Tell me you did not have grief sex with her!"

Megan's startled reaction made her veer slightly into the next lane, earning her a honk from a minivan.

"What? Grief sex? Is that even a thing?"

"Um...hello! Of course it's a thing. It could even be considered an upside to someone dying. Remember Hannah? When her uncle died we had some incred—"

"I don't wanna know!" Megan said.

"Anyway, nice deflection, Miss Baldwin. Answer the question."

Megan rolled her eyes.

"No, we did not have grief sex, stupid. But..."

Abby leaned forward again. "But what?"

"I'm going to the funeral next week in Coachella."

Abby groaned. "Jesus, Megan!"

"I have to!" Megan defended herself. "You don't understand. Carole was more than just my girlfriend's mother. Spending time with her allowed me to imagine what it would be like to have a supportive mother figure that I'm out to."

"Which is something you still need to do. Just saying."

"Yeah, well, we're not having that conversation now."

They drove in silence for about a mile before Abby asked quietly.

"What if *he's* there?"

Megan didn't need to ask who *he* was. And Abby's question was one Megan had asked herself about a dozen times since telling Cindy she'd be at the funeral.

"I expect he will be there," she said, coming off the highway at their exit. "But that's not the point. The point is I need to say goodbye to Carole properly. I go to the funeral and I leave. I won't even stay for casserole and deviled eggs afterwards. Easy peasy."

"If you say so," Abby said.

"I do say so. Now, forget about that...Who all is coming to this shindig?"

"The usual lot plus one or two others you probably don't know because you're a Hermit Dork and don't come out with us all enough. Oh, my friend Chloë will be there, you haven't met her yet."

"Which one is that again?"

"You know, the barely legal little thing who walks my dogs and works the night shift at Amazon. Apparently, she knows Desiree from somewhere."

"Did you have a thing with her? Is this going to be awkward?"

"Nah, I don't think she goes for the butches." Abby looked Megan up and down. "You might be in trouble, though," she declared.

"Is she cute?"

"Adorable."

"Like, young Kate Jackson adorable?" A long time ago, Megan had discovered that she apparently had a thing for TV stars from the 1970s. Kate Jackson topped her list. Followed closely by Lindsey Wagner, Farrah and that woman who played Bailey Quarters on *WKRP in Cincinnati*. And, if asked, she preferred Janet over Chrissy.

"Who the hell is Kate Jackson?" Abby asked.

"Oh my God, you're a lesbian and you don't know who one of the original Charlie's Angels is?"

"No, I don't know who one of the original Charlie's Angels is but I do know you're a dork. But I love you."

Just five minutes after getting off the highway, Megan pulled up to a cute little green house on a quiet street in Vista. A few other cars were already parked in front of the house but Megan still found a prime spot. Before Abby had a chance to open her door, however, Megan put her hand on her arm, stopping her.

"Do me a favor," Megan began, "don't tell anyone about Cindy's visit."

"Yeah, yeah, don't worry."

"I'm serious, Abs," Megan warned. "I would have preferred never seeing her again and the last thing I need is her name coming up all night."

Abby put her hand over the one Megan had on her arm. "Okay, okay. Don't worry."

Satisfied, Megan reached into the back and retrieved the bottle of wine they had stopped off and bought on the way.

"Okay, let's go."

***

A couple of glasses of wine later and Megan was pleasantly buzzed and relaxed.

As promised, the party was very low-key. Soft jazz provided the background music, catered food in trays were set up on the dining room table and the small group of guests were encouraged to just eat whenever and wherever they felt like it. Naturally, being that they were in Southern California, just about everyone decided to congregate outside in the backyard where some small candle-lit tables had been arranged and a few folding chairs occupied the small lawn. Masks were optional, their hosts insisted, and so no one wore theirs.

As Abby said, there were a couple of women Megan didn't know but which Abby did. They had come as plus-ones of other friends, new girlfriends that Megan hadn't gotten around to meeting yet because the truth was, she *was* a Hermit Dork who preferred quiet nights in. But the newcomers were friendly and easy to get to know.

And Angela and Desiree were completely adorable as the couple of honor. Keeping with the whole low-key vibe they wanted, they were both dressed smart-casual in denim shorts with sandals and matching peasant tops.

"Oh God," Abby had faux-moaned when she first saw them. "Are you going to be all matchy-matchy from now on?"

Desiree, a statuesque African-American woman with a runner's body, giggled. "Maybe."

Angela, a freckled redhead, her arm around her fiancée's waist, added, "Besides, it shows who belongs to who."

About twenty minutes after Megan and Abby arrived, while Megan was finishing that second glass of wine, and telling herself it was the last one unless she planned on taking a Lyft home, the doorbell rang.

From her position in the kitchen, getting a bottle of cold water from the fridge, Megan heard Abby shout, "I'll get it!" and then a moment later, "Hey girl!"

"Hey, Abs! How's the mommy of my two favorite schnauzers?"

Megan smiled. That must be Chloë, the dog walker. She then heard Abby exclaim, "Vanessa! I didn't know you were coming! Awesome! Bring it in!"

Megan's eyebrows raised up. After taking a slug of water, she headed towards the front of the house to meet the new arrivals.

Wow, what a coincidence! Meeting two Vanessas in the space of twenty-four hours. Weird.

Chapter 7

Vanessa had barely finished giving Abby a hug hello when her eyes caught the movement of someone emerging from a room across the entry way. She couldn't help the gasp that escaped her lips when she recognized Megan, and she couldn't help a flutter of excitement in her chest when she noticed Megan's mouth drop open in recognition and her eyes go wide with obvious delight.

She let her eyes rake over Megan, who looked too adorable and scrumptious in a floral print sundress and sandals.

In short order, the two women rendezvoused in the middle of the living room.

"Oh my god, it's you!" Vanessa said with a laugh.

"Oh my god, it's *you!*" Megan replied.

There was then this moment of uncertainty of what to do next. In pre-Covid times, Vanessa would have given Megan a friendly embrace and she could tell that Megan was thinking the same thing. Finally, Vanessa chuckled to break the ice and said, "Fuck it. Zombies, right?"

Megan's smile grew wider.

"Zombies," she confirmed and then simultaneously two women moved forward for a hug.

Vanessa's eyes closed and she inhaled deeply as soon as she felt Megan's body pressed against hers. The woman smelled of vanilla and cherry blossoms and coconut and all Vanessa wanted to do now was get Megan somewhere private so she could determine from where on her body each scent was coming from.

I swear I am going to make that happen soon.

"You two know each other?" Abby asked, interrupting the reunion.

Separating from Megan, Vanessa answered, "Yeah. Megan here is supposed to single-handedly keep my coffeeshop afloat one Americano at a time."

"It's true," Megan said. "Gotta remortgage my house and everything. And we're fellow zombies."

Abby and Chloë shared a confused look between themselves and then Abby threw up her hands.

"You know what, whatever." She put her arm around Chloë. "Everyone else is out back, come on."

Walking through the house, Vanessa was pleased when Megan kind of naturally fell into step beside her as they followed Abby and Chloë.

"I'm, like, shocked to see you," Megan said. "What a coincidence!"

"Good coincidence or bad coincidence?" Vanessa asked, knowing which choice she herself would make.

"Hmm...I'm not sure," Megan drawled. "That whole *T2* is better than the original thing makes me suspicious of your sanity."

Vanessa scoffed.

"*My* sanity? I'm thinking of giving you the number of a licensed therapist."

Reaching the backyard, Vanessa was pleased to see that she knew most of the handful of women arrayed around the candlelit tables, many with wine glasses in their hands. The hosts, Angela and Desiree, she already knew from her personal trainer days and various social outings which had spawned from that, which in turn had led to her knowing several of the other ladies.

After she had been introduced to two women she didn't know, Vanessa turned to Megan.

"I don't get it...if this is your crew, why haven't we met before yesterday?"

"Because she's a Hermit Dork," Abby supplied, causing the group to laugh.

"Yeah," Melody, a forty-something blonde Vanessa knew from the lesbian bar scene agreed. "Megan is like one of those reclusive celebrities. She doesn't make a lot of public appearances and when she does it's front-page news."

Vanessa thought it was impossibly adorable the way Megan rolled her eyes and blushed. Oddly (and somewhat surprisingly), Vanessa felt a surge of protectiveness towards Megan. She wanted to put her arm around her and use herself as a human shield against all this good-natured ribbing.

Seriously, what is happening to me?

Desiree tapped Vanessa on the arm and indicated Megan with a nod.

"You might want to get a selfie with her, V," she said. "A selfie with Megan is worth about five-hundred likes on Instagram."

"Oh my God! You guys are so stupid!" Megan screeched, laughing. "And since no one else seems to be offering...," she turned to Vanessa, "...can I get you some wine?"

"That would be awesome," Vanessa said.

"Chloë?"

"None for me, thanks; I'm on a one-week cleanse," Chloë responded. She was crouched down and providing Angela and Desiree's pug, Barney, belly rubs.

"God, that sounds horrible," Milli, an African-American who was a regular at Vanessa's gym, back when gyms were still open, said. "And what are you, fifteen-years-old? What could you possibly need to cleanse out of your system?"

"This time? Lauren." Chloë said, standing up and ignoring Barney's doleful eyes that were pleading for the belly rubs to continue. "Every time I break up with a girl I go on a cleanse."

"And with Chloë's track record this means she hasn't eaten a decent meal in seven years," Vanessa quipped.

Megan caught Vanessa's eye.

"Wine's in the kitchen, wanna come with me?"

Vanessa had to bite her lip to keep a smirk from forming at the—most likely unintended—double entendre. Of course, that didn't stop her mind from going there.

Yes, I would like to come with you, Megan. Several times, if you can manage it.

And then, right there! Vanessa wasn't sure if it was real or if she had just imagined it, but she could have sworn Megan's right eyebrow arched just the tiniest bit. Suddenly Vanessa felt herself blushing, worried that somehow Megan had read her mind.

"Lead the way," she managed to croak.

In the kitchen Megan asked "Red or white?"

"White, please. Red gives me a headache."

"Me too! Something we have in common." Megan went to a wine cooler and opened the glass-fronted door. She asked, "Riesling, Pinot Grigio or gewürztraminer?"

Vanessa frowned.

"Guh-what?"

Megan laughed as she extracted a bottle. She took a wine glass from a collection on the counter and poured just a splash into it.

"Gewürztraminer," Megan repeated. "I brought it tonight; it's one of my favorites. This one is kinda dry, not overly sweet." She handed the glass to Vanessa. "Here, try a taste."

Vanessa did. However, instead of sucking the wine down like she normally would have done, with Megan sounding like an expert and watching her taste this Guhvertza-whatever, she felt compelled to do that swishing thing snooty wine people did.

"Hey, I like that," she declared after swallowing the small taste.

"Right? Isn't it different? More?"

"Please."

Megan did a full pour into Vanessa's glass and then poured herself one. "I wasn't going to have another one," Megan said. "But I can't have you drinking alone, can I?" She then clinked her glass to Vanessa's. "Cheers."

Vanessa was afraid that Megan would suggest they rejoin the others in the backyard. Being honest with herself, she really did not want that. It was so comfortably companionable to be alone in the kitchen with this incredible-looking woman with the auburn hair. Fortunately, Megan made no move towards the back door.

"So, are you some kind of wine expert?" Vanessa asked.

"God, no." Megan said after another sip. "No, I took the time to learn some things about the varieties I like—it helps me make better shopping choices. But that's only, like, a handful of whites. Reds I have categorized as Mild Headache, Bad Headache and Fuck Me, I Wanna Die."

Vanessa laughed. "You are too funny." All day long she had been hoping Megan would come into La Vida Mocha and had been disappointed when that hadn't happened. The pure surprise and pleasure of encountering her here was still making Vanessa feel buzzed, more so than this delicious but impossible-to-pronounce wine.

Then, because she really did not want to risk Megan deciding to rejoin the others, Vanessa walked into the living room, looking around, hoping Megan would follow, feeling rather happy when she did.

"I've known Angela and Dee for a while now but I've never been to their place," Vanessa said. "It's really cool."

"Yeah, the house is super cute and it's a great neighborhood," Megan said. But then she added in a conspiratorial whisper after making sure no one else was around, "It's a little busy in here, though, for my tastes."

"Oh, thank God!" Vanessa said with her own whisper. "I was thinking the same thing!"

The small living room was just full of stuff—not like hoarders lived here; it was all very neat and organized, and certainly cozy; but it was clear that two women with two distinct tastes had decided to create a mishmash of each other's interests and styles. The result was a room that looked like an over-caffeinated decorator had run rampant in it. Vanessa's eyes just didn't know where to go and it was a relief of sorts when she spotted a framed picture on one wall that arrested her attention.

"Oh my God, that is beautiful," she murmured, stepping around the furniture to stand in front of the picture. It was a poster-sized black-and-white image of a ballerina in a black leotard stretching at the barre. The picture did an excellent job of portraying not only the artistry of the dancer and her commitment to her craft but also the incredible musculature of her legs and torso.

"I love this," Vanessa whispered.

"Thank you," Megan said. She also came to stand in front of the picture.

Vanessa's head whipped to her right to look at Megan. Megan smiled shyly.

"I drew that," she said.

"No!" Vanessa stared at the ballerina again. "You *drew* this? Wait...are you sure?"

Megan laughed. She rocked back on her heels with her hands in the pockets of her dress.

"Of course I'm sure. It took me two months to draw this one, a couple of years ago. It's done in graphite. When I finished it and posted it on my website, Angela messaged me right away saying she wanted to buy it. Not a print, the original. I gave her a bit of a discount on the price because we're friends."

Vanessa stared at her and then made a decision. She just had to know more about this woman and she was no longer willing to leave it to chance. It wasn't just that she was beautiful—though the more time she spent with Megan the harder it was to take her eyes off her. It was that she was...compelling. That was the word she was looking for. Compelling. Vanessa wanted to know more about Megan's life and her art and why this interesting and...*compelling* woman appeared to be single. Also, she just flat-out *wanted* her.

"We should hang out sometime," Vanessa stated.

Megan turned her head to look at her, her face radiant with a smile.

"I'd like that," she said.

Then, at the exact same time, both Vanessa and Megan said, "But there's something I should tell you."

They both burst into wide-eyed laughter. Megan even reached out to place her hand briefly on Vanessa's arm. Vanessa thrilled at the touch.

"You first," Megan insisted.

"Okay." Vanessa took a moment before continuing. She had to make sure that what she was about to say didn't come off the wrong way. The last thing she wanted was to seem like some kind of female Casanova, only looking for a quick lay. But she also wanted to be honest with Megan. "We should totally hang out sometime but I should warn you that I'm hardly a candidate for a relationship."

Megan quirked an eyebrow.

Vanessa went on.

"You see, my coffeeshop literally keeps a roof over my head and it takes up a lot of my physical, mental and emotional energy. I mean, even when I'm not at La Vida Mocha, I'm *thinking* about La Vida Mocha. And with this fucking pandemic…" Vanessa shook her head.

"I totally get it," Megan said. Vanessa felt relieved because when Megan said she totally got it, she sounded like she totally got it, and not like she was just saying so.

"Are you sure?"

"Totally."

"So, what's your thing?" Vanessa inquired.

"My thing is that I'll be moving to New York soon."

Vanessa's mouth dropped open in shock. She hadn't expected that.

"When?"

Megan's brow furrowed.

"That's still an open question," she said. "BeachSoft plans to open an office there and I'm to head it up. It's actually a big promotion and I suppose if Covid wasn't around I would have moved there already. Anyway, the CEO of my company says she wants me there by the end of the year regardless, so, I'm not exactly looking for anything…"

"Lasting?" Vanessa offered.

Megan smiled.

"Exactly."

Vanessa sucked her bottom lip between her teeth. Was it really possible that this gorgeous creature standing in front of her was open to the casual, no-strings-attached type of fling that she herself wanted?

"Are you doing anything tomorrow?" Vanessa asked.

"Aren't you opening your shop tomorrow?"

Vanessa shook her head. "Not on Sundays anymore; at least until these stupid restrictions are lifted and I can hire staff again. It's bad enough I'm there six days a week."

"In that case, I'm free tomorrow."

"Excellent."

Before they had a chance to make more detailed plans, a new voice interrupted them.

"Did you guys go to fucking France for the wine? Jeez!"

It was Abby. While looking at Vanessa she pointed at Megan.

"She didn't trap you in a boring conversation about something like how one of those *Star Wars* movies would have been so much better without the Ewoks, did she?"

Vanessa turned to Megan.

"You don't like the Ewoks?" she asked in a wounded voice. "They're so cute!"

"They're fucking annoying!" Megan said with a laugh.

Abby just rolled her eyes.

Chapter 8

Megan had to admit she missed this feeling.

Driving back west on the 78 en route to Abby's place to drop her off, Megan was enjoying the excited butterflies in her stomach and that buzzing feeling of anticipation that was like a nervous energy coursing through her veins. Goodness, it had been too long.

She wasn't even aware she was humming to herself until Abby said, "God, you're making me sick!"

"Hmm? What?" Megan inquired.

"Are you even going to be able to keep yourself under control until your date with Vanessa tomorrow?"

"It's not a date," Megan corrected.

Abby looked at her, confused.

"Well, what is it, then?"

Megan shrugged.

"It's just…We're just getting together to hang out, that's all. But not like a date."

"Oh my God!" Abby gasped theatrically. "You little tramps! You're just using each other for sex!"

Megan took one hand off the steering wheel and smacked Abby's leg. Abby should be one to talk, the queen of one-night stands.

"It's not like that!" she protested.

But it most probably is.

Megan continued.

"Vanessa and I are probably just gonna hang out here and there occasionally but we're not putting labels on anything. Neither one of us wants a relationship. She's got a business to run and in case you've forgotten, I'm eventually moving to New York."

"No, I haven't forgotten," Abby said sullenly. "I'm still bummed about it."

This time Megan patted Abby's leg gently.

Last month, Lucy Whitaker, the CEO of BeachSoft, announced plans to open a New York City office. The company was growing incredibly fast and Lucy wanted to take advantage of the vast pool of I.T. talent in the Big Apple. And Lucy had personally asked Megan to head BeachSoft NY, as vice-president of operations. It would make Megan an incredibly powerful executive in a Fortune 500 company before her thirtieth birthday, and was the kind of career move most people twice her age could only dream of.

And Megan was super excited about the chance to live in New York again, a city she fell in love with when she attended NYU for four years. A drawback, of course, was leaving behind friends like Abby. She and Abby had grown up together in La Jolla and had been through all the tribulations of being gay teenagers together. Megan knew she was going to miss her friend terribly.

"Anyway, tell me something," Abby said. "What was all that talk you and Vanessa were doing about zombies and, what was it, T2 or something?"

Megan giggled.

"You never saw *World War Z*?"

"Does it have any car chases or badass female superheroes in it wearing skintight outfits?"

"Nope."

"Then no."

"Anyway," Megan continued, "in *World War Z* there are these zombies, right? And of course, it seems like the zombies attack everybody, but the zombies actually only attack healthy people; they can tell if someone is infected with a disease or something. So, when Vanessa and I met yesterday, we both said how we knew the other one wasn't sick with Covid and how that was like the zombies in *World War Z*. The T2 reference is because she thinks *Terminator 2* is better than the first *Terminator*, which is dumb, but she's super pretty so I can forgive her that."

Abby rolled her eyes.

"So, let me get this straight," Abby began. "Queen of the Dorks—that's you—discovers that there is in fact another Dork

Realm somewhere and that the queen of that realm not only lives in Carlsbad but is also gay."

"You know what's dorky? Using the word 'realm' more than once in a sentence."

"Not if that sentence is a sentence about dorks," Abby insisted. "Anyway, the point is, you found another lesbian who knows about zombies and Terminator robots and Ewoks. Why are you wasting time pretending that this isn't going to end with you both renting a U-Haul?"

"Shut up," Megan said, laughing. After a few moments, she asked, "So, what's her story?"

"Who? Vanessa? She's good people," Abby declared.

"Why is she single?"

Abby shrugged.

"Vanessa is one of those chicks who is, like, super focused on whatever it is they got going on. Chicks like that don't have time for relationships. I mean, she was involved with a girl named Rebecca for a while, but that didn't last too long."

"Well, I guess I'll find out more about her if she chooses to tell me," Megan said, not exactly feeling as nonchalant about it as she sounded. She *wanted* to know more about Vanessa. But then she scolded herself internally. "It doesn't matter anyway. It's not like our little fling is going to amount to anything."

"Except a trip to the U-Haul office," Abby said.

"Shut up."

Then, as if the gods were conspiring against Megan with her best friend, her car's touchscreen display chirped and a message appeared.

Text message from Vanessa.

Before Megan had a chance to tap the *Ignore* option on the screen, Abby cackled and tapped *Read*.

The car's robotic female voice spoke from the Bose speakers.

"Text message from Vanessa. It was great seeing you tonight. What a surprise! I can't wait until I see you tomorrow."

Abby was laughing.

"Oh my God! This is great!" Abby said, chuckling. "So, the cool thing about U-Haul is, you can use their website to set up everything. Like, the truck reservation, ordering supplies..."

"I swear to God, if you do not shut up!"

***

Once home, Megan went upstairs to her bedroom and changed into a comfy pair of pajama shorts and a white tank top and then, because she hadn't had a chance to do it yet, she sat on the edge of her bed and replied to Vanessa's text.

Sorry, I was driving and couldn't answer. Can't wait either. So excited! How does a walk along the seawall and maybe some ice cream sound?

That wasn't her first choice of a suggestion for tomorrow but Megan figured that flat-out asking Vanessa over so they could fuck each other's brains out was probably being a little too pushy.

She then headed downstairs but halfway down the steps her phone chirped and she stopped to read the newest message from Vanessa.

Sounds awesome! Text me tomorrow with details. Glad you made it home safely. I am heading to bed. Long day. See you tomorrow!

Megan smiled and replied that she hoped Vanessa slept well and then continued down the steps, the smile lingering on her face. Despite the three glasses of wine, Megan wasn't at all tired and so she decided that since it was Saturday and she didn't have to work tomorrow, she could stay up late getting some drawing done. She instructed Alexa to play the soundtrack from *The Empire Strikes*

Back and then she sat at her drawing table which was in a corner of her living room.

Her salary may come from her job working for a software company—and a great salary it was, soon to be made even greater once she made the move to New York—but Megan's true passion was her artwork. She first discovered she had a talent for it when she was a senior in high school during an elective art class. She also discovered then that when she drew it was like meditation for her—a calming exercise that also made her feel whole, as if that activity, more than any other, was what made Megan completely Megan.

Nonetheless, she left high school with no desire to pursue a career as a starving artist; hence college in New York for a degree in Information Technology before returning back to the west coast after being headhunted by Lucy Whitaker herself even before Megan had graduated due to her advanced course load and her leadership position in an BeachSoft-sponsored student club called "Women in I.T."

Still though, once she had turned twenty-five last year, Megan began realizing that if she could, she'd love nothing more than to be a full-time artist—just one with a steady paycheck.

And that was her problem. She liked what her BeachSoft salary had brought her so far: an upscale condo in hip Carlsbad, California; a nice car; the ability to have a savings account that grew each week and enough disposable income to treat herself to nice things pretty much whenever she wanted them while still keeping food in her kitchen and the lights on in her house. She'd also vacationed in Singapore, London, Amsterdam, Berlin and Paris.

No, she was fine keeping art as a hobby.

Settling herself at her art table, she picked up a pencil. She was working on a new piece depicting the legs of her friend Anastasia, who was a ballerina and who Megan had photographed in a studio back when the world was normal. She would readily admit to anyone that she had a thing for dancers, particularly ballerinas. They made Megan swoon. Cindy used to tease her about it, say that she was certain Megan was going to leave her the next time the Bolshoi blew into town.

As she resumed work on the drawing, Megan started thinking about her date tomorrow.

Whoa, whoa, whoa! Not a date!

Her *whatever* tomorrow.

A walk along the seawall and ice cream sounded perfect. Besides, even if she and Vanessa were really going to just be casual and have a bit of fun, Megan still wanted to get to know at least a little bit about Vanessa. No-strings-attached, fuck-buddy-type sex with a beautiful woman? No problem. But Megan still liked to at least know what the woman's favorite color is.

Still, though…

There were several times during the engagement party when Vanessa would touch Megan just so. On the elbow, the small of Megan's back, Megan's upper arm. At one point, Vanessa had reached up to tuck a strand of Megan's hair behind Megan's ear and with each touch, especially that last one, Megan's clit had pulsed.

At another point, Vanessa had offered to go back in the house to get Megan a bottle of water, and as she walked past Megan, she brushed her breasts against Megan's arm. It was the kind of contact that to an outside observer could easily have seemed accidental, but Megan knew it hadn't been. Vanessa had *pressed* her breasts against Megan, sending shivers down Megan's thighs and arousal out of her core so that she was left waiting for her bottled water in wet panties.

Vanessa wanted her.

Megan wanted Vanessa.

Seawall? Ice cream?

Megan groaned as her clit pulsed again.

"Fuck what her favorite color is," she said to herself.

Chapter 9

Vanessa was doing her normal early morning run, a ten-mile set that took her from her house in Carlsbad, up to the Oceanside pier and back. It was a good course on well-populated busy streets, even at 6 a.m., and which included a few inclines for that added bit of cardio. On any other day, Vanessa would return to her house, quickly shower and head to La Vida Mocha for opening. But this was Sunday and she had the day off, so she was actually setting a bit of a slower pace during her return leg.

A young man leaned his head out the passenger-side window of a car that had just zoomed past her on Carlsbad Boulevard, clearly wanting a lingering view of her front now that he'd had one of her back. His mouth was moving but with her AirPods in she couldn't hear whatever juvenile nonsense he was spewing.

Vanessa rolled her eyes.

So barking up the wrong tree, fella.

In another ten minutes she was home at her house on the outskirts of downtown Carlsbad.

Entering, she went into her bedroom, stripped, and got into the shower. Under the spray, Vanessa smiled. Today was her non-date with Megan and she couldn't wait. In truth, Vanessa hadn't been out with a woman she was interested in since late the year before, with a woman named Holly, an abortive relationship that didn't really have a chance to get off the ground because it was during that period when Vanessa, new bank loan in hand, was devoting most of her time and attention to bringing La Vida Mocha into being. Between then and now she'd had exactly two one-night stands, meaningless encounters that satisfied a need, but which Vanessa had had no intention of continuing. The coffeeshop was her priority, even more so now that a microscopic virus was threatening its very existence. Dating—actively trying to find a girlfriend—was just not something Vanessa had even thought about over the past several months.

But Megan seemed completely open to having a little fling, one with an expiration date, and the possibilities of what that could mean over the next few weeks or months or however long it lasted made Vanessa excited. She was fine being alone, sure, but the opportunity for sex with a great-looking woman like Megan was not to be passed up.

Her phone rang almost as soon as she stepped out of the shower, a towel wrapped around her wet hair. A part of her worried that it was Megan canceling their plans, and so she was relieved when she saw *William* on the caller ID.

"What up?" she answered.

"I love you," William replied, "but I'm going to cut right to the chase. I need an Operation Gandalf on Wednesday."

Vanessa put the phone on speaker mode so she could dress while talking.

"Again?" she asked, pulling a *Space: 1999* t-shirt off a hanger.

William was Vanessa's closest friend on the planet. They had met in college in L.A. and had been inseparable since freshman orientation. After college, they both moved south to Oceanside, living together for two years before Vanessa decided to buy her own place in neighboring Carlsbad.

In that freshman year of college, Vanessa came out to William the day before she did to her parents. At the moment, she had expected William to also come out to her, because it had been fairly obvious to Vanessa that her best friend was gay within an hour of first meeting him; but he didn't, and she didn't press. He finally did come out to her when school resumed the next year.

But he never came out to his parents or anyone else in his family. He tearfully had told her once that it would be too much. His parents, his brothers, his uncles, basically everyone important to him were extremely, extremely traditional and conservative when it came to gender roles and sexual identity. Coming out to even one person in his tightknit family would basically cause him to be shunned. Thus, Operation Gandalf, their name for when Vanessa was William's beard.

"I know, it's stupid," William said, "I don't know why they're visiting so much! They keep saying it's just because they miss me but then they keep asking me about housing prices and what the good neighborhoods in Oceanside are! I think they're planning on moving here!"

Vanessa pulled on a comfy pair of shorts and huffed loud enough for William to hear.

"If they do move here, you're gonna have to find yourself another beard, William. I'm serious."

"I don't even want to think about it!"

"Well," she said, "if it's Wednesday you need me, you're going to have to wait until I close the shop."

"That's fine," William said. "Gotta go! Loves and kisses! And thanks!"

***

At 10:30, Vanessa was trying to read a magazine in her living room but not really succeeding because her anticipation wouldn't allow her to concentrate.

It was annoying, really.

This isn't a date!

Yet here she was, unable to focus on the content of a silly fashion magazine because her anticipation was making her mind incapable of processing information.

Her phone chirped. A text from Megan.

Tick-tock! Ninety minutes and counting…

Vanessa smiled and tapped out a reply.

89 by the time you get this…

Megan's reply came almost instantly in the form of six straight smiley face emojis.

They had agreed that they would meet at noon at Magee Park, which was in downtown Carlsbad, just a block from the beach. She thought Megan's idea of a stroll along the seawall and then stopping for ice cream was a good one. The problem now was waiting ninety minutes. Well, eighty-eight or so…

Her phone pinged again. Another text from Megan.

So, listen…how about we meet at my place, maybe have a glass of wine and then drive to the beach together?

Vanessa's eyebrows shot up and she sucked her bottom lip between her teeth. Her insides got warm.

That sounds great! I never say no to a glass of wine.

The next message from Megan contained her address. Vanessa took a deep breath and suddenly decided she wanted to change her plans for getting ready and she quickly got up off the couch and speed-walked to her bedroom.

She had had a super casual outfit already chosen and laid out on the bed: stretch denim skinny jeans with frayed cuffs and a grey tank top. She had figured she'd complete the look with some slip-on Skechers. It was an outfit perfect for a couple of hours hanging out with someone by the beach. But now, Vanessa wanted to change tactics. She'd keep the grey tank (she knew she looked awesome in it) but the skinny jeans were out. Instead, she located one of her favorite black midi skirts in her closet and tossed that on the bed. She also decided that the Skechers would be replaced with an adorable pair of black ballerina flats that had elastic straps which crossed at her ankles. It was still a casual-look outfit perfect for taking a long walk by the shore, but it had that little something extra Vanessa wanted.

Thinking of being prepared, she went back to her dresser, opened the top drawer, rummaged around and found the matching black lace bra and panties she was looking for.

She knew that there was every reason to believe that Megan's invitation to come over for wine was just that: an invitation for wine and nothing else. They'd each drink a glass of white and then leave for the beach, nothing more than that.

But, fuck, I hope not!

Tossing the lingerie on the bed, she looked at the clock.

Seriously? Over an hour left?

Her hair was already dried and brushed; all she had to do was either pull it back into a ponytail or leave it down with maybe a cute hair band on top. Makeup would be light, mostly accentuating her eyes. In other words, it would only take her twenty minutes, tops, to get dressed, made up and then out the door.

She just had to kill time.

So far, that had proven harder than she thought possible, as her failure to even remember a single thing she had been reading in a magazine proved.

She went back into the living room, where she had left her phone, and called Chloë. Despite the differences in their ages, Chloë had become one of Vanessa's closest friends and she missed having Chloë around the coffeeshop every day. Her friend answered on the first ring.

"Hey," Chloë greeted.

Vanessa frowned. Chloë was usually far bubblier; more "Hey!!" with the two exclamation points audible.

"Hey, back," Vanessa said.

"So, what's up?"

"Are you okay? You sound off somehow."

"I'm good. What are you up to?"

"I'm meeting Megan in a little bit," Vanessa said, hoping the cheeriness in her voice would somehow transmit to Chloë wirelessly and perk her friend up. Instead, Vanessa swore she could hear Chloë sigh in irritation.

"Great," Chloë eventually replied. "Hope you and *Megan* have a great time."

"C'mon, out with it...what's wrong?" Vanessa insisted. This was too weird. Chloë was the proverbial duck from whose back water ran off; she never let things bother her, at least to the point where they manifested themselves in surly behavior.

"Look, nothing's wrong, Vanessa. I'm just...I don't know...I'm just not feeling chatty today, that's all. Sorry."

"Okay, fair enough," Vanessa assured her. Maybe it was just PMS, she thought. "Anyway, if it turns out there is something bothering you, just call me, okay?"

"I won't interrupt your perfect date with *Megan*, don't worry."

There! She did it again. The way she said Megan's name, kind of resentful like. Vanessa quickly reviewed the previous night's party at Angela and Desiree's. Had Megan said or did something to offend Chloë? Vanessa didn't think so. In fact, to the best of her recollection, Megan and Chloë had barely interacted.

Vanessa shrugged. Maybe Chloë was just a little out of sorts because she just had a breakup with—wait, what was her name? Lori? Lauren? It was hard to keep track of all the names with Chloë.

"Well, it's not a date," Vanessa corrected Chloë. "We're just hanging out for a bit today, that's all. Anyway, I guess I'll talk to you later?"

"Yeah, later," Chloë said with a sigh.

The call over, Vanessa tossed her phone on the empty sofa cushion next to her. So much for killing time that way. She reached for her TV remote.

Netflix it was.

Chapter 10

Megan checked her makeup in the bathroom mirror for the umpteenth time.

Stop it! You look fine!

She forced herself away from the mirror and checked the clock on the nightstand in her bedroom. It was 11:49. Then she noticed her bed.

Shit!

Earlier, Megan had agonized about what look to choose for this non-date, wanting something that had a relaxed sexiness to it; an outfit which said *I'm ready to chill at the beach or I'm ready for you to throw me on the bed and have your way with me. You pick.*

After trying on what seemed like countless combinations of items, she had finally decided on a pair of tight denim cut-off shorts and a light-olive green cami top that she could wear braless.

However, even though she had finally settled on an outfit, the search had left her bed looking like a delivery truck from Forever 21 had simply disgorged its contents onto it. To make matters worse, she now heard an engine just outside her condo. Going to the window and looking down, she spotted a red Jeep coming to a stop. That had to be Vanessa. Firstly, who else would be stopping in front of her condo? Secondly, Vanessa just seemed like a Jeep girl.

Shit!

In a panic, Megan began scooping up all the clothes on her bed and tossing them in the closet, not caring that the resultant heap of tops, dresses, jeans, shorts and skirts, not to mention their hangers, was going to take forever to sort through and put away later.

She had hurled the last armful of garments into the closet and shut the door when the doorbell rang.

"Hey!" Megan said downstairs when she opened the door.

"Hey, yourself," Vanessa greeted. "You look great!"

Megan warmed at the compliment but was finding it a little hard to speak.

Vanessa's grey tank had a scoop neck and Megan's eyes lingered on Vanessa's clavicle. Suddenly she wanted nothing more than to softly kiss the hollows there, wondering if that would be enough to get Vanessa to moan. And, good god, the tank was snug! The way it was practically glued to Vanessa's breasts…

Oh my God!

"You look great, too," Megan finally managed to say, feeling her center react.

So great.

Megan blinked, realizing Vanessa had said something else.

"Huh? I'm sorry, what?" Megan stammered, feeling the blush that started at her neck move its way up to color her face.

Vanessa smirked.

"I asked if I should come in." she said. "Or did you change your mind about the wine and just want to head straight to the beach?"

Fuck the beach.

"Yes, of course," Megan said, supremely embarrassed at forgetting her manners. She stood aside to let Vanessa enter.

"God, I love all the art!" Vanessa enthused, stepping into the living room and twirling around, looking at everything Megan had on display. "Are all of these yours?"

Happy that Vanessa seemed to like her place, Megan spent some time pointing out which works were her creations and which were prints of her favorite artists.

"Oh my God, these are *beautiful!*" Vanessa gushed when Megan pointed out a series of nudes she had drawn a couple of years ago. Vanessa spent several moments admiring them before looking at Megan with an arched eyebrow.

"Was this a girlfriend?" she asked.

Megan shook her head.

"Just a local model I hired," she answered. She opted to leave out the fact that she had wished Emily could be a girlfriend because Emily was stunning but, alas, straight.

"Let's get that wine," Megan said. She decided to be forward and took hold of Vanessa's hand as she led her into the kitchen. She didn't know about Vanessa, but the contact sent electric tingles up Megan's arm.

"Do you have any of that wine we had last night?" Vanessa asked.

"I do! I'm so glad you liked it!"

Megan opened her wine chiller, extracted a bottle of gewürztraminer and set about filling two wine glasses, annoyed that her hands were shaking, hoping that Vanessa didn't notice.

Calm down! Calm down! Calm down!

Easier said than done. She could smell Vanessa close to her. One of those ultra-sexy body lotion scents from Bath and Body Works which Megan liked.

Turning around, she found that Vanessa was very close. All Megan wanted to do was grab a handful of that impossibly black hair and pull the woman in for a deep kiss. Instead, she simply handed Vanessa a wine glass.

"Cheers," she said.

"Cheers," Vanessa replied, and they clinked glasses. After that first sip, Megan licked her lips and was gratified to see Vanessa's eyes follow the action of her tongue before Vanessa licked her own lips as well.

Megan made a decision.

Putting down her wine glass back on the counter, she then took Vanessa's glass away from her and did the same. Vanessa didn't protest. Then she looked straight into Vanessa's eyes as she reached to take hold of Vanessa's hips. She noticed Vanessa's breath hitch, but Vanessa didn't pull away and so Megan gently started pulling Vanessa closer until the space between them was erased and she could feel Vanessa's breasts pressed against her own, a sensation her clit took notice of.

Vanessa was slightly taller and so Megan had to tilt her head a bit to claim Vanessa's lips. They were soft and plump and slick with gloss and tasted of wine. Megan groaned and pulled Vanessa in tighter. Vanessa's kiss was receptive, yielding to Megan's lead and

Megan pressed her tongue forward, demanding entry, which Vanessa granted, and their tongues began dancing. When Megan heard Vanessa purr with pleasure, she felt arousal pooling between her legs.

After what seemed to Megan to be either two minutes or twenty, they parted, both somewhat breathless.

"What's your favorite color?" Megan asked.

Vanessa gave her a confused look. Megan couldn't blame her. Talk about a curveball.

"Um…orange," Vanessa said, puzzlement in her voice.

Megan made a face.

"Orange? No one says orange!"

"Yeah, I know, but I love it," Vanessa said. "I mean, I never wear it because orange looks terrible on me, but whenever I see the color, it makes me happy. Why on earth are you asking me about my favorite color?"

Megan smiled.

"Because I've kinda lost interest in going to the beach," she answered.

Chapter 11

Somehow, they ended up on the couch, Megan leaning forward, forcing Vanessa back until Vanessa was reclining against the sofa's cushioned arm. Megan's bottom lip was curled between her teeth as she stared down at Vanessa, who was suddenly feeling excitedly like captured prey.

"I like this aggressiveness of yours," Vanessa said.

"Do you now?" Megan asked. She swooped her head down and licked behind Vanessa's ear before nipping her earlobe.

Vanessa groaned and then said, "Yes."

"You like a woman who takes control?" Megan asked, ghosting Vanessa's lips with her own.

Vanessa was feeling dizzy. Yes, God, yes, she liked a woman who took control. She enjoyed being shown who was boss.

"Yes," Vanessa breathed. "Now, kiss me."

"Shh!"

Vanessa gasped in pleasure at having been shushed.

Megan pulled away just enough to flash Vanessa a wicked smile. Her eyes were like those of a huntress. She brought her head down again until her lips were brushing against Vanessa's ear.

"Ready to do what I say?" Megan whispered before again nipping the earlobe.

"Yes," Vanessa murmured.

"Are you wet?"

"Very."

"Good," Megan said softly. "Now, reach down and put two fingers inside yourself. Not one. Two."

Oh God, yes!

Vanessa reached her trembling right hand under the band of her skirt and then under the band of her panties. She gasped when she reached her wetness.

Soaked!

She gasped again as she felt how easily her middle and ring fingers slid inside, her palm resting against her clit. Automatically, out of habit, she started stroking the fingers in and out, but Megan suddenly grabbed Vanessa's wrist, stopping her.

"No. I didn't say move them. Did I say move them?"

If Megan kept talking like that, Vanessa wouldn't be able to stop moving them.

"No, you didn't," she moaned.

"Keep them in there until I say. And don't you dare fucking come."

"I'm so close already," Vanessa confessed.

"You won't be so close if I send you home, will you?"

Vanessa's eyes went wide. She sucked in an audible gasp of air.

She wouldn't do that! Would she?

But Megan's eyes were just daring Vanessa to challenge her, and Vanessa then knew Megan wasn't kidding. In all honesty, it wasn't helping bring Vanessa back from the brink of what was building up to be a massive orgasm.

Vanessa's mouth was then covered by Megan's in a long kiss with probing tongues. All the while, Vanessa concentrated on keeping her fingers still, even though her center was clutching at them, insisting on action.

"Pull them out," Megan finally ordered when the kiss broke. "Let me have them."

Vanessa obeyed, withdrawing her fingers from her center and from beneath her clothes. Megan took possession of Vanessa's hand and stared at the two fingers, shiny with Vanessa's arousal. Then Megan brought the fingers to her mouth and set to work sucking them clean.

"Oh, my fucking God!" Vanessa whimpered, watching her fingers disappear in Megan's mouth, feeling Megan's tongue swipe against them, thoroughly cleansing them of Vanessa's essence. Megan moaned as she worked.

"Oh my God," Vanessa whimpered again, feeling herself lose grip on reality.

Finally, Megan withdrew the fingers.

"So that's what I have to look forward to tasting," she murmured, licking some stray Vanessa from her lips.

Quickly, Megan got up off the couch and stood. She took Vanessa's hand.

"I need you upstairs. Now."

Vanessa could barely stand, her knees were so weak, but mostly through the force of Megan pulling her she managed the stairs and then let Megan continue pulling her until they reached the bedroom.

Inside, Megan wasted no time.

"Take off your shirt," she commanded, and when Vanessa had lifted the tank off, Megan pulled her in for a kiss while simultaneously yanking Vanessa's skirt down past her hips. Vanessa stepped out of the garment as soon as it fell to her ankles. Then, she started to pull down her panties but again Megan grabbed her wrist, pulled away from their kiss and stared at Vanessa.

"Did I tell you to do that?"

Vanessa could only shake her head. Damn, the woman was good at this control thing. Then she closed her eyes as Megan began kissing her neck, mixing in a few bites as well. Soon, Vanessa felt Megan's fingers sliding her bra straps off her shoulders and then her shoulders being kissed and nibbled. Then the bra was unhooked and allowed to fall.

"Oh my God, Vanessa." Megan exclaimed in a hoarse whisper. "You're so fucking beautiful!" Soon, Vanessa felt soft hands cupping her breasts and then felt one rock hard nipple being sucked. She moaned, whimpered, moaned some more as the sucking became bites with just the right amount of pressure to send electric currents to her clit. The visual of seeing Megan bent over, her mouth latched onto her nipple, pulling on it with her lips was driving Vanessa crazy.

Megan finally came up for air and kissed Vanessa while guiding her to the bed, where Megan then guided her down and then pinned her arms above her head while straddling her.

"God, I wanna fucking devour you," Megan said, nuzzling Vanessa's neck.

Vanessa entwined her fingers in Megan's hair.

"Please do! Just fuck me!" she growled.

That brought Megan's head up from Vanessa's neck. Vanessa saw that dominating intensity in her eyes again as she stared at her.

"I like how anxious you are." Megan said.

Megan released Vanessa's arms and still straddling Vanessa reached behind herself with one hand and lightly played her fingers along Vanessa's upper thigh. She teased a finger along the edge of the crotch of Vanessa's black panties. All Vanessa wanted was for that finger to slip inside her underwear, find her clit and make her come.

"But you're being a little bossy," Megan said, continuing her finger-tease. "Tell me something, would you rather be good, in which case I'll give you what you want somewhat quickly? Or would you rather I make this teasing last *hours?*"

Again, Vanessa saw the challenge in Megan's eyes. The dare. She meant it. Vanessa knew.

Holy fuck!

"I'll be good," she said.

"Promise me."

"I promise I'll be good."

Megan grinned.

"I doubt it," she said, arching her eyebrow. "But then again, that could be fun too."

Megan then bent down for a kiss and after that started kissing her way down Vanessa's body. She stopped at Vanessa's breasts and spent time on each nipple, and while she was sucking and biting one, she was pinching and kneading the other.

Eventually, she continued kissing and licking downwards. When she reached Vanessa's waist, Vanessa felt Megan's hands push her thighs further apart. Then Megan's head was between Vanessa's legs and Vanessa watched as Megan inhaled deeply, a rapturous expression coming over her face as she enjoyed Vanessa's scent. At that moment, Vanessa could have believed Megan was coming just from smelling her. She did it again, and then a third time, running her nose along the fabric of the panties; each time taking deep breaths that made her visibly shudder.

Finally, apparently even Megan couldn't take anymore. Vanessa's soaked panties were yanked off roughly, tossed who knows where, and then Megan's face was back between Vanessa's thighs.

Megan began pulling Vanessa's folds into her mouth, sucking softly on each one individually, moaning as she did so, that moaning turning Vanessa on even more, making her gasp and give startled cries of pleasure. Then Megan released the folds and started kissing around her opening, along the sides and then up on the landing strip of curls. But the woman was frustratingly avoiding Vanessa's clit. The tease was too much, Vanessa needed her clit touched.

She began moving her pelvis to guide her clit to Megan's mouth, but Megan kept avoiding her efforts.

Fuck!

So, Vanessa reached down and grabbed at Megan's hair, determined to guide that teasing mouth where Vanessa desperately needed it to go.

Megan took her mouth away from Vanessa's sex.

Vanessa looked down and saw Megan the huntress looking up at her. The younger woman held her gaze for a moment and then nodded to her left.

"Look at the clock," Megan said firmly.

"What?" Vanessa barely managed to breathe the word. Her entire center was throbbing.

Megan's eyes narrowed.

"Look. At. The. Clock."

Vanessa did as she was told. The digital display read 12:38 p.m. She looked back at Megan.

Again, Megan held her gaze with a laser focus.

"I know what you want," she told Vanessa, her breath caressing Vanessa's wetness, "But every time you misbehave, you're going to wait another five minutes."

Vanessa's mouth dropped open.

No!

Megan smiled slyly. "You'll get what you want at 12:43. Maybe."

"That's not fair!" Vanessa whined.

"12:48," Megan replied instantly.

Oh God, no!

Megan lowered her head and resumed kissing and sucking every bit between Vanessa's legs. Except her clit.

Vanessa's moans increased in octave when Megan's tongue darted its way inside her, exploring, lapping.

"Fuck, you taste good," Megan murmured. "I wanna drink you all day."

This was too much!

"Please," Vanessa begged.

Megan looked up again.

Oh no!

"The correct phrasing is 'Please, *Megan*.'" She kissed Vanessa's pubic hair. "12:53."

Fuck! This wasn't happening.

"But I didn't know!"

"'But I didn't know, *Megan*.' 12:58," Megan said before licking Vanessa's inner left thigh. "I've got all day, Vanessa."

Good God! No!

Yet this was turning Vanessa on even more. She had never, ever been this wet! She could feel it trickling out of her, pooling on the bed sheets now that it was no longer contained by her panties. And she moaned louder each time she felt Megan's tongue drinking the liquid arousal. But she needed her clit touched. It was pulsing so hard the tingles were felt in her toes. All she could do was moan for some kind of release—and she wondered if she'd be punished for that but, damn it, it couldn't be helped. Turns out, Megan was merciful after all. She let the moaning slide. Vanessa just had to not speak. And she had to keep her hands away from Megan's head. This was Megan's game. Those were the rules. Megan was the boss and she was ruthless. And it was the sexiest fucking thing on earth.

Vanessa gasped and arched her back as her labia were sucked again.

Don't speak! Don't speak!

She let out a breathy "Ohhhh!" as she felt a finger slip inside. It was glorious but insufficient, yet she now knew better than to beg for another. Instead, Vanessa bit the knuckle of her index finger to keep from saying a word. She might be too demanding or forget to say the name of her torturer. She couldn't bear another five-minute penalty. She just couldn't.

Apparently, she did good because after a minute or so another finger slipped in. The two digits were stroked slowly in and out while Megan's mouth nibbled Vanessa's thigh.

God in heaven...

A third finger. Vanessa whimpered. Completely unbidden by its owner Vanessa's center clutched at the three fingers. It now had a mind of its own. Just underneath her pubic bone the orgasm was still waiting, building up. Layers of unreleased pleasure kept stacking atop one another, yearning for the dam to break.

But Megan was unbelievably masterful at her ministrations. She knew exactly how much pressure to apply and where, and exactly the right speed to stroke Vanessa's insides with her fingers—all to keep Vanessa *close* to coming but nothing more.

Vanessa's hands clutched the sheets. Her toes were curling.

She wanted to look at the clock but didn't dare. She knew she would openly weep if she discovered there was even one more minute of this exquisite torture.

Finally, she felt Megan still her fingers. Vanessa whimpered, missing the stroking. But again, she had the presence of mind not to say anything.

Megan would punish her.

She felt Megan start kissing the top of her strip of curls and then move downward just a smidgen. Then downward again just a smidgen more.

Oh my God, please…

A smidgen more…

Pleasepleasepleasepleaseplease…

The tiniest bit more…that beautiful mouth was at the borderline now.

Vanessa mewled. This next one just had to be it!

She was right.

Suddenly Megan's mouth latched onto to her clit, her tongue swiping vigorously across it.

Everything below Vanessa's waist exploded.

"Oh fuck! Oh fuuuccckkk!" Vanessa screamed.

The orgasm shattered her with pleasure. Her hips were bucking, writhing uncontrollably, yet miraculously Megan's mouth remained hard-docked to her clit, sucking on it, pulling more of Vanessa's orgasm out through the tiny button. And Vanessa could feel her inner walls convulsing around those three fingers still inside her.

"Fuuuuccckkkk!" she screamed some more, even louder as the pulses wracked her, each stronger than the last, Vanessa's clit a prisoner in Megan's mouth.

Vanessa grabbed her own breasts, adding the sensation of pinching her nipples to the cataclysm happening between her legs. Eventually, she was incapable of forming words, her screams just guttural noises. She felt a muscle twinge because her back was arched like she was one of those circus performers. Finally, she fell back onto the bed, limp, as the orgasm spent itself but not before spreading through her extremities. Her feet tingled; her hands started shaking. And still her center convulsed, squeezing those amazing fingers still inside her, fingers she never wanted out of her.

"Good girl," Megan said before resuming licking Vanessa's clit gently, continuing Vanessa's climb into orbit.

Chapter 12

Right now, Megan believed she was the luckiest woman in the world.

She had just coaxed a second climax from Vanessa, her own center getting even wetter as Vanessa called Megan's name when the orgasm hit. As she took some final licks from Vanessa's still-contracting pussy, she couldn't help but remember the first time she had walked into that coffeeshop and seen this gorgeous woman. How could Megan have known then that just two days later she would be making that same woman come, screaming and tearing at her bedsheets?

Finally taking her mouth away from Vanessa, Megan got up on her knees and pulled off her top. She then lifted up her ass a bit to pull off her shorts and panties together. She looked down to find Vanessa staring at her.

"God, you're gorgeous," Vanessa whispered, her eyes roaming Megan's form. "You are so fucking gorgeous. Come here."

Megan laid down next to her, loving the way their nude bodies fit together. She felt Vanessa's leg separate her thighs and gasped when Vanessa pressed her knee against her wetness.

Megan cupped Vanessa's face in her hands.

"No more me being in control. I'm all yours. Do whatever the fuck you want with me. Please," she begged.

Vanessa's response was another deep kiss which Megan had to break away from to mewl, "Oh, fuck!" when Vanessa started rocking her leg against Megan's center, electrifying her clit.

"Fuck, you're so wet," Vanessa told her, nuzzling her throat.

Tell me something I don't know!

Megan had been wet since before Vanessa arrived. In fact, Megan had been wet since this morning, when Vanessa had responded favorably to Megan's text inviting her over for wine because Megan knew Vanessa was no dummy and would have seen right through Megan's little ploy to get Vanessa in her home.

Of course, she had also known that sex might not happen. Vanessa was older, after all—not by much, not even a decade;

nonetheless, Megan considered the possibility that Vanessa might want even this casual fling to evolve at a more sensible pace.

Happily, she was wrong, as the lingering taste of Vanessa on her lips proved.

And now, Vanessa was pinching one of Megan's nipples.

"Your breasts are so perfect," Vanessa whispered and then stopped speaking when she took the nipple into her mouth. Megan closed her eyes at the pleasure, marveling at that word *perfect*. She held onto Vanessa's hair, that gorgeous midnight hair which was now hers to touch, to grab, to entwine around her fingers as Vanessa now tentatively bit the nipple.

"Harder…" Megan murmured and then squeaked when the delicious jolt of pain/pleasure curled her toes.

Vanessa moved to the other breast and the process was repeated. First, gentle suckling, an expert tongue flicking the diamond-hard bud and then the surprise—*bam!* Teeth suddenly clamping down, the mix of pain and pleasure exactly what Megan was craving, making her wetter still.

After a few more moment, Vanessa shifted, her leg disappearing from between Megan's thighs. Megan's eyes went wide with shock and disappointment.

"Look at me," Vanessa ordered. Megan did. She felt fingers tracing her bottom lip and that incredible scent of Vanessa's pussy was still on them. Megan flared her nostrils to take in more of it.

"Same two fingers you were sucking on downstairs," Vanessa told her.

"I know," Megan breathed, "I can still smell you."

"You like my scent, don't you?"

"I'm not washing my hand tonight," Megan said, meaning it, and then sucked Vanessa's fingers into her mouth again, not breaking eye contact with Vanessa. She moaned when she realized Vanessa's fingers still tasted of what she first tasted downstairs.

"I'm going to fuck you with these two fingers now," Vanessa purred.

Megan felt her body warn her. Her eyes opened wider.

"I'm not gonna last long," she said hurriedly. "I'm so revved up, Vanessa, I'm probably gonna come so fast. I'm sorry."

Vanessa chuckled and then kissed her.

"Megan, who cares? I plan on making you come as many times as you'll let me."

Then, quick as a flash, her face was between Megan's legs. Megan drew her legs up, feet flat on the mattress, surrendering to her. Thankfully, Vanessa didn't seek revenge on Megan by teasing her also. Those fingers were inserted immediately, sliding inside with absolutely no friction, and Megan arched her back, calling out Vanessa's name, bearing down on the fingers, making them slide that much further in. And then her clit was being sucked, a tongue pressed firmly against it, swiping, while at the same time, Vanessa curled her fingers, hitting that magic spot.

Megan stuck the three fingers of her left hand in her mouth, the fingers that had been inside Vanessa and been absolutely coated when Vanessa had come. They still tasted of the woman who was now eating her out.

She was right...she didn't last long, and she plummeted over the edge.

"Oh, fuck! Oh, fuck, I'm coming!"

The waves of her climax surged through her entire body, the sensations heightened by the visual of Vanessa, her eyes closed, working her mouth on what now felt like the center of Megan's universe, her swollen and contracting pussy. The view lasted only a second because Megan then had no choice but to arch her neck, squeeze her eyes shut and let out a guttural scream, as a particularly intense wave of pleasure rocketed through her. More waves came, the potency of all of them reminders of how long it had been since she last masturbated.

Meanwhile, Vanessa coaxed her through it all with soft sucks on Megan's folds, gentle strokes of her fingers, quick darts of her tongue inside to capture Megan's come.

When she was spent, Megan went limp, feeling as if she would melt into the mattress. But apparently Vanessa wasn't quite done with her. The next thing Megan knew, Vanessa was straddling Megan's left thigh, pressing her wetness down on her flesh, and even though Megan had just come, the sensation of Vanessa's slickness revved her up again. Vanessa leaned forward, supporting herself on her arms as she started grinding her pussy against Megan's thigh.

"Oh God, that was so hot," Vanessa managed to squeak, her eyes squeezed shut. "You came so fucking fast!" She bore her center down harder on Megan's leg and now she leaned forward just a bit more until her nipples were grazing Megan's. "I just have to…" she gasped. "I just have to…Oh…fuck!"

Megan grabbed Vanessa's hips and pushed up with her thigh to provide her lover even more pressure. Vanessa riding her was the sexiest thing she had ever seen.

After a few more hip gyrations, Vanessa suddenly jerked, her body going taut as if she had just touched a live wire. Megan's eyes went wide, wanting to capture every visual moment of Vanessa's orgasm: the way her neck arched, the way her mouth opened, a few choked cries escaping, the way her perfect breasts with those dark nipples jutted forward.

Megan felt more of Vanessa's come trickling out onto her leg, running down the sides of her thigh just before Vanessa collapsed on the bed next to Megan, pulling her legs up into a fetal position as the climax had its way with her.

Megan looked at her thigh. A patch of her skin was slightly redder than the rest from Vanessa's rubbing and it was shiny and slick, coated with Vanessa's cream. Megan stared at it, burning the image into her mind because she never wanted to forget it. Her own sex was responding to the image also, her clit demanding attention, more arousal seeping from her folds. She reached out and dabbed at the spot on her thigh with the middle finger of her left hand, watching how a thin line of Vanessa's lubricant stretched between finger and leg as she slowly pulled her finger away, a process she repeated several times, playing with what Vanessa left her, loving how even more turned on it was making her.

Finally, she rolled onto her side and embraced the still-trembling Vanessa, whose back was to her. Megan helped ease her down from the orgasm by lightly kissing the back of her neck while reaching around her to take one of Vanessa's hands in hers, entwining their fingers, Vanessa making little whimpering sounds until finally she went still.

Megan wondered briefly if this was heaven.

Chapter 13

By two p.m., they needed a break.

A walk along the seawall? For her part, Vanessa wasn't sure she could walk across the room. Her legs were jelly, her center a non-stop tingling presence between them.

Megan's head was resting on Vanessa's chest as they lay in bed, recovering, and Vanessa was slowly twirling one of Megan's auburn locks with her finger.

"So, what's your favorite color?" Vanessa asked.

Megan giggled.

"Blue," she answered.

"What was up with that, anyway?"

"I just like to know at least one interesting factoid about a woman before I sleep with her," Megan replied.

"But you already knew some factoids about me," Vanessa said with a laugh. "I own a coffeeshop; I love *World War Z;* I have better taste in *Terminator* movies than you…"

Vanessa found herself under a tickle attack then as Megan started raking her fingers along Vanessa's left side. Fortunately, Megan showed mercy and stopped after a few seconds.

"Okay, okay," Vanessa said, still laughing from the tickling, "I won't bring up such a sore topic again."

"You'd better not," Megan said teasingly.

They fell into a comfortable silence then. Megan keeping her head on Vanessa's chest, one of her arms draped across Vanessa's middle while Vanessa continued playing with Megan's hair.

"So, tell me your life story," Megan eventually said.

"Oh God, are you ready to fall asleep?" Vanessa asked, "Seriously, you're talking to a plain vanilla white girl from L.A."

Megan purred, a sound that sent an electric thrill through Vanessa.

"Trust me, Vanessa," Megan began, "there is nothing plain vanilla about you. I've tasted, remember?"

How could I forget?

"Anyway, out with it," Megan ordered. "Why is your life story so plain vanilla?"

"Because I'm *soooo* California that sometimes I disgust myself."

Megan giggled.

"What do you mean?"

"I mean that, one, I grew up in Los Angeles, which you already knew," she ticked that off on a finger. "Two, I was on the freaking volleyball team all through high school. *Beach* volleyball." Another tick. "Three, I used to be personal trainer—and isn't that what people from, like, New York think all Californians are?"

"No," Megan said. "People from New York think all Californians are waitresses who are really actresses waiting for their big breaks."

"Gotcha," Vanessa said. "Well thank god I'm not one of those. And four, the vast majority of my wardrobe consists of clothes that would be perfect to wear on the beach at a moment's notice."

"And I personally see nothing wrong with that," Megan declared.

"Oh, you're just buttering me up because of that thing I did with my fingers a few minutes ago," Vanessa said slyly.

"Hmm…I don't remember what thing you're talking about."

Vanessa felt her heartrate pick up.

"You don't, huh?" she asked.

"Uh-uh. I'm drawing a complete blank," Megan answered. She rolled off Vanessa and lay face down on the bed. Vanessa watched as she slowly brought her legs towards her chest, raising her ass up.

"Refresh my memory," Megan instructed.

Vanessa licked her lips.

So much for taking a break.

***

"I'm starving!" Vanessa declared fifteen minutes later, propping herself up on her arms over a quivering and flushed Megan, who she had just brought to another climax.

It took a moment for Megan to catch her breath enough to speak.

"Me too. I'll cook something," she managed to whisper.

Vanessa was surprised.

"Really?"

Megan opened her eyes and met Vanessa's.

"Well, by *cook*, I mean place an order and have food delivered. I actually hate cooking."

Vanessa laughed.

"Me too! Absolutely loathe it!"

"Something else we have in common," Megan said, and as Vanessa looked down into Megan's eyes, she swore something passed between them and she was a little unnerved by the intensity of it.

Fling! Just a fling!

Vanessa's throat suddenly felt dry but she managed to say, "What shall we order?"

"Do you like pizza?" Megan asked. She reached up and wrapped her arms around Vanessa's shoulders. "Because if you don't, you can just get dressed and leave right now." She pulled Vanessa in for a quick kiss.

"I love pizza," Vanessa assured her.

"And I love tasting myself on your lips," Megan said, reaching up for another kiss.

After both women were out of bed and dressed, Megan used her phone to order a pizza be delivered from a local place she liked. As they headed downstairs to wait for the food to arrive, Vanessa made an observation.

"I see you've started packing," she said after noticing three large cardboard boxes placed against a wall near the top of the stairs. Each of the boxes was sealed with tape.

"Sort of," Megan replied. "Those are just some odds and ends I plan on storing at my parents' house in La Jolla when I leave for New York."

The mention of New York caused a pang to twinge in Vanessa's chest but she forced herself to ignore it. Yes, she was enjoying her time with Megan but this was all it was ever going to be: energetic bouts of sex followed by food.

"Wine?" Megan asked when they reached the first floor.

"Perfect."

"Are you close with them? Your parents?" Vanessa asked, while Megan poured two new glasses of the gewürztraminer. Vanessa made a mental note to pick up a couple of bottles of this stuff for her house because she really liked it.

"Sort of," Megan answered, leading the way into the living room. They took seats right next to each other on the couch. "I'm not very much like them, when it comes down to it. My sister, Molly, is, though; it's like she's some kind of dual clone of them both. But as far as I go…let's just say that there is a kind of unspoken agreement that certain topics are off-limits. I'm not even out to them yet. Pathetic, I know."

Vanessa reached over and put her hand on Megan's knee.

"Don't say that," she told Megan. "Coming out is a journey, a very personal one, one that you have to finish in your own time."

Placing her hand on top of Vanessa's, Megan said, "Thank you. And I get that, I do, but the older I get, the more like a coward I feel."

Before she knew what she was doing, Vanessa lifted Megan's hand to her lips and gave it soft kiss. The thought crossed her mind then of how intimate a gesture it was. And how un-fling-like.

Again, it was as if Megan was reading her mind.

"So, is all of this allowed with what we're doing?" Megan asked, peering at Vanessa over her wine glass. "I mean, all of this personal history talk?"

Vanessa smiled.

"Why not? This may just be a casual thing but I'd like to think we can still become friends."

Megan smiled.

"I'd like that."

"Besides, pretty soon you're about to be the only person I know in New York. That means I'll have someplace to crash the next time I travel there."

Lunch arrived about half an hour later. While they ate, though she managed to keep up a running conversation with Megan during which both women shared some more about themselves, Vanessa was also considering leaving. It wasn't that she wanted to leave; in fact, she was delighted to discover that she was enjoying spending the time with Megan outside of the bedroom as much as the time they had spent inside the bedroom. Well, almost.

But that was the problem. Vanessa could totally imagine spending the entire rest of the day with Megan doing nothing more than talking or even snuggling on the couch watching Netflix. Not only that, Vanessa could totally imagine going back upstairs and falling asleep with Megan. And what would be the point of that? Megan was leaving for New York eventually. Better to avoid any risk of forming an attachment.

After helping Megan clear away their lunch, Vanessa said, "So, can I see you again soon?"

Megan, who had been putting the leftover pizza in the refrigerator, turned to look at her, and Vanessa swore she saw a flash of disappointment on Megan's face.

"Oh! Are you leaving?" Megan asked.

"Yeah, it's my one day off and I usually try to cram laundry, housework and cleaning out my purse into it. I usually only get as far as cleaning out my purse, though."

"Totally get it," Megan said with a smile. "I guess I should probably get some chores done also."

"So…maybe later this week?"

Megan nodded.

"My life is boring. Text me anytime and chances are we can hang out."

"Count on it," Vanessa said. She came forward, snaked her arms around Megan's waist and pulled the other woman forward for a kiss. Vanessa had intended it to be just a quick see-you-later kiss, but once their lips touched, the kiss became long, slow and gentle; not at all the hungry, lustful kissing that had led them first to the couch and then the bedroom earlier. Instead, the kiss was that of two women who acted as if they had all the time in the world. Which they didn't, and when Vanessa reminded herself of that fact, she pulled away.

"Okay, then," Vanessa said, somewhat breathlessly. "I'm gonna go."

Megan walked her to the door and held it open for her.

"Seriously, text me later this week," Megan said as Vanessa stepped outside and started walking to her Jeep.

Vanessa doubted she could wait that long.

Chapter 14

It was like Abby had a sixth sense. Or, barring that, a set of surveillance cameras in Megan's house. Megan thought she might want to check if that was true.

As soon as Vanessa had left, Abby called.

"Tell me *everything!*" Abby greeted as soon as Megan answered.

Megan swallowed a laugh and concentrated to keep her voice level when she answered with, "About what? Vanessa came over and we ate pizza for lunch."

"You *fucking* liar!" Abby screamed. "Even you are not that much of a dork!"

"Okay, okay," Megan said, laughing. "Yes, a lot more than lunch happened."

"Details!"

"I am not giving you details, bitch! And, god, you called just after she left. How did you do that?"

"My spidey-sense was tingling, telling me my best friend just got laid. You see what I did there? I used a dorky comic book reference just because I love you. So, at least tell me if she was any good."

"Good" doesn't describe it.

Megan had to regain control of her thoughts because Abby's question had immediately made her recall all the things Vanessa had done to her. Megan's insides started swirling now.

"Beyond good," she confessed to Abby.

"Not a pillow princess? Because she looks like she could be a pillow princess."

"Fuck you, no she doesn't!" Megan said, and she was surprised at how defensive she sounded.

"Are you kidding me?" Abby returned. "Vanessa looks like she could just bring any woman to her bedroom, lay back, command that things be done to her and then tell the bitch to make her a grilled-cheese sandwich. When I first saw her, *I* wanted to make her a grilled-cheese sandwich!"

"God, you're a child sometimes!" Megan sighed, even as she knew Abby technically wasn't wrong. If Vanessa had asked for a grilled cheese sandwich earlier, Megan would have happily made her one.

"Vanessa isn't even your type," Megan added. Abby liked the butch ladies. In fact, some of the women Abby had been involved with over the years that Megan had met were more masculine than some men Megan knew.

Abby scoffed.

"Vanessa is *everyone's* type, dork! She may be a Barbie doll but I definitely would not turn her away."

"She is *not* a Barbie doll!" Megan said, surprised at how quickly she was jumping to Vanessa's defense.

"So, was this just a one-time thing?" Abby asked.

"No, we're planning on seeing each other again," Megan answered. At least she hoped that was the case. Abby may have made her point crudely but she did hit the nail on the head: Vanessa *could* literally have any woman she wanted, certainly any gay woman and probably her fair share of straights, and Megan wondered now if perhaps Vanessa would see no reason to continue seeing her since they'd already had sex. After all, Vanessa only wanted casual flings, and how many sexy and beautiful women came into Vanessa's coffeeshop each day who would give up their eye teeth for just one night with her? Hell, Vanessa was probably in her Jeep now talking to tonight's lucky woman.

Megan shook her head briskly to quell the rising jealousy she was now feeling. So what if Vanessa didn't spend tonight alone? She herself was going to New York soon to start a brand-new life, and once there she was bound to find plenty of attractive women to start a *real* relationship with.

"Ooh, another date?" Abby teased.

"Shut up! It won't be a date just like today wasn't a date. Vanessa and I are just having fun, whatever form that takes. I thought you'd be happy. Weren't you the one who kept bugging me to get over Cindy by getting under a woman?"

Abby laughed.

"Well, it's about time you listened to me," she said.

***

The next morning, Megan was sitting on her back patio at her round patio table with umbrella. Her feet were up on the table, her work laptop balanced on her thighs, a mug of coffee and a bowl of cashews within easy reach.

Her phone rang. It was her mother.

"Hi, darling," Audrey Baldwin greeted her daughter.

"Hi, Mom."

"How was your weekend?"

Pretty boring until I had amazing sex with a ravishing woman who I now can't stop thinking about, not that you would care.

"It was nice, Mom."

"Did you do anything fun?"

Megan rolled her eyes. She had learned that "fun" was her mother's euphemism for "go on a date."

A date with a man.

With a man she could marry and have kids with.

"No, nothing fun, Mom."

"We still on for lunch?"

Crap! Was that today? Has it been a month already?

"Of course, we are!" Megan answered. "My place, eleven-thirty?"

"Can't we go out somewhere?" Audrey asked.

"Well, no," Megan told her. "You do read the news, don't you? There's been a rise in Covid cases in the county and all the restaurants are back to doing take-out only for a while."

"Oh...right. But, can't we eat somewhere outside at least? It's such a nice day, after all."

After a moment's thinking, Megan said, "I suppose we can eat at Hidden Canyon Park; have a picnic."

"Perfect! See you then, darling." Audrey said and then hung up.

The entire conversation could have been conducted via texting, Megan realized. In fact, *most* of her conversations with her mother could be conducted via texting, but that wasn't Audrey's way.

Megan checked her watch. Just past ten-fifteen, and since she was already dressed as if she had been planning on being in the office, all she really had to do to get ready for her mother's arrival was call Vigilucci's for a to-go order and go pick it up.

***

At Hidden Canyon Park, Megan found an empty picnic table and rested the bag from Vigilucci's on it while waiting for her mother to arrive from La Jolla.

Her phone chimed. Megan frowned. A text from Cindy.

Thanks again for Friday. And thanks for being willing to come to the funeral. I think I'm going to need a normal person here to help because the Minnesota relatives have started to arrive and they're already driving me crazy.

Megan's frown deepened. Cindy *had* often talked about her Minnesota family, that they were basically good and decent people, just also sort of wacky in that small-town, Midwestern-caricature kind of way that someone like Penny Marshall would direct a movie about. But what was confusing Megan now was, why wasn't Cindy's man—the one Cindy left Megan for—helping Cindy cope with any craziness surrounding Carole's funeral?

What was the fucker's name again? Donald? Ronald?

Megan quickly typed a reply.

Just focus on what's important but let them help if they can. Don't try to do everything on your own like you normally do! This is hard enough for you, don't overdo it and end up making yourself more miserable than you already are. I'll be there Thursday but I don't know what time yet.

She swallowed, feeling her hand going clammy. She didn't ask about Donald or Ronald but if Megan had to show up in Coachella and run interference for Cindy during this difficult time, Megan was going to be sure to give Donald or Ronald an earful about him being a useless twat.

Her phone chimed again with a reply from Cindy.

Thanks for caring, I mean that. And you're right about what I normally do. I'll be sure to step back at times. See you Thursday.

It was almost normal, Megan considered, the two of them texting like this. No hateful words being sent by Megan. No pleading for forgiveness and understanding coming from Cindy. No mention of a home-wrecking Donald or Ronald. Normal. Like they were still together…

No! Don't do that!

The only—absolute only—reason Megan wasn't texting hellfire to Cindy was because Carole had just died. Megan would help get Cindy through the funeral, but once the service was done and Carole interred, Megan would hop back in her car and leave Cindy in the rearview mirror of her life once more.

Again, her phone chimed.

"Jesus Christ, Cindy!" Megan muttered under her breath. But then she saw Vanessa's name and Megan's heart started racing.

I fell asleep watching world war z last night. :-)

Megan smiled; Cindy now pushed out of her mind.

I myself drifted off while watching Star Trek the Motion Picture :-) It's free on Prime now.

Vanessa replied:

An underrated classic! (And Ilia can navigate my starship any day!)

Oh, do bald women do it for you? Shall I shave my head before I see you again?

Only if you wear the uniform also! ;-)

"Who are you so busy texting?"

Megan hadn't noticed her mother approaching the picnic table.

"No one!" Megan said. "I mean, no one you know." She put her phone face down on the table. "It's nice to see you, Mom."

"You too, darling! You look beautiful, still in shape."

Megan bit the inside of her cheek to keep a sarcastic comment from leaping forth. Heaven forbid one of Audrey Baldwin's daughters get out of shape. Of course, Audrey, even at fifty-six, looked phenomenal, with platinum blonde hair expertly styled and a figure that most twenty-something women would want. As usual, she was dressed in understated elegance, today wearing a tank-style floral print maxi dress with fitted waist.

After Megan took their lunch orders out of the Vigilucci's bag—the *insalata di cesare* for Audrey and the *spaghetti carbonara* for Megan—they sat at the picnic table. Mother and daughter then began catching up. Megan filled her in on work and the latest on her transfer to New York. There wasn't much to tell on that score, except to say that Lucy Whitaker had promised Megan that she'd be relocating there before year's end.

Audrey, after telling Megan that her father sends his love and was finally considering retiring from the investment bank he worked for, naturally wanted to talk about her current favorite topic: Megan's sister's wedding.

"Molly has chosen the most *darling* invitations." Audrey said. "Just wait until you get yours; you're going to love it."

"Does Molly really have to send me one, Mom?" Megan asked. "I thought maybe the combination of being her sister *and* being in the wedding party would be invitation enough."

Audrey *tsked*.

"It's tradition, sweetheart. Besides, it'll be a memento of the big day."

"It's a waste of paper, Mom, not to mention a stamp." Megan leaned forward. "Listen, Mom...is Molly sure she doesn't want to postpone the wedding until all this Covid stuff has calmed down and things have somewhat gotten back to normal?"

"She doesn't see a need to postpone, darling, and neither do I. It's six months away yet."

Megan took a breath before responding, mindful of who she was talking to.

"Buuut...the coronavirus doesn't exactly follow a schedule, Mom. I mean, six months ago, people—myself included—didn't think we'd be still be wearing face masks and still having to order take-out lunches now."

As expected, Audrey dismissed Megan's concern with a wave of her hand.

"It'll be fine, darling. In six months, this will all be a memory to laugh at."

Megan shrugged and dropped it. There was a time when she would have pressed her point, but she'd long ago learned her lesson about the futility of such actions. If her mother and Molly wanted to keep planning a wedding during a pandemic, they could knock themselves out as far as Megan was concerned. And when Molly got her wedding photos back and they all showed a bunch of people who looked like they were about to rob a stagecoach, maybe then Molly would question her decision.

They talked about other things for a while as they ate; or, rather, Audrey talked and Megan listened; at least, she pretended to listen. She actually spent most of Audrey's monologue thinking about Vanessa and about how she had wished Vanessa had spent the night last night.

It was silly, of course. Their arrangement, or whatever it was, certainly did not mandate going to sleep and waking up together. Nonetheless, when Vanessa had told Megan yesterday afternoon that she was leaving, Megan had been disappointed. But she certainly wouldn't have admitted that to Abby when Abby had called.

I'm just lonely, that's all.

It made sense. The last woman Megan woke up with was Cindy, and they had been split up since January.

Still though…as she lay in bed last night before finally succumbing to sleep, Megan had imagined how nice it would have been to have Vanessa there next to her. Not having sex, just *there*.

Megan realized her mother had stopped talking and she forced her mind back to the here and now to find Audrey shaking her head in that disapproving way of hers and staring at something over Megan's shoulder.

"Such a shame," Audrey murmured with a cluck of her tongue.

Confused, Megan turned to look behind her.

Considering how nice the weather was, the park was surprisingly empty. The only thing Megan could see was two young women about her age walking hand in hand, their heads close together as they talked. The taller of the two, a redhead, said something which made her companion laugh.

Other than that, there was nothing that Megan could see that would—

She felt her cheeks flush with anger as she turned back around to look at her mother. Sure enough, it was those two women that Audrey was focused on.

"What's a shame, Mom?"

In a whisper, even though there was no one close enough to eavesdrop, Audrey said, "You saw. Those two girls. Such a shame they can't find men to spend the afternoon with."

Is she for real?

But, of course, Megan knew she was for real. This was typical Audrey Baldwin.

"For goodness sakes, Mom. It's obvious they're gay. They're not *looking* for men to spend the afternoon with."

Audrey waved that off as if it was the most ridiculous thing Megan had ever said.

"They're just not trying hard enough to be with men," Audrey stated as if, to her, it was the same as saying the sky is blue.

"And I suppose Black people just aren't trying hard enough to be white, right?" Megan snapped.

"Oh, don't be ridiculous! It's not the same thing."

"It is too the same thing!" Megan, with a dry and humorless chuckle, said. She subtly indicated the two lesbians with a tilt of her head in their direction. "You're expecting them to somehow change into something they're not!"

"I'm expecting them to accept that the natural order of things is for a woman to be with a man. Otherwise, we all wouldn't be here, would we?"

Not too long ago, Megan would have allowed this argument to continue, both her and her mother growing more and more exasperated and heated as it did; but Megan had finally learned that it was useless and not worth the aggravation. So, she just sighed, threw her hands up and set about packing up the detritus of their lunch.

"Are we leaving?" Audrey asked.

"Well, I am," Megan said, standing. "I have a meeting soon." Her meeting was still more than ninety minutes away but Megan forgave herself the little lie. "Sorry, I should have mentioned it earlier; hopefully you don't feel like you drove up here for nothing."

"Don't be silly," Audrey said, also standing and picking up her purse. "Seeing my oldest daughter is never a waste of time. Of course, if said oldest daughter would come visit her parents in La Jolla more often, that would be nice also."

Of course, if the parents of said oldest daughter weren't homophobic throwbacks to the 1950s, said oldest daughter might visit La Jolla more often.

After Megan dumped the trash in a nearby receptacle, she walked with Audrey back to the parking lot. Megan escorted her mother to her silver Lexus and gave her a hug goodbye. Over her mother's shoulder, Megan spied the two gay women approaching a vehicle two spots away from Audrey's car.

Before Audrey could see them and say something else outrageous, Megan ended the hug, said a quick goodbye and hurried to her own car. Once she started the engine, she pulled out of the parking spot without even taking the time to fasten her seatbelt. At this point, she just wanted to get as far from her mother as quickly as possible.

At the first stop sign on Vancouver Street, Megan put on her seatbelt, silencing the insistent pinging noise her car was making, as if asking her if she was out of her mind for driving so recklessly. She then considered her next moves.

She could go home and log back in to work but the fact of the matter was that her next important obligation wasn't until that estimation meeting at two o'clock.

Megan chewed on her bottom lip, thinking.

The estimation meeting was sure to be boring. All estimation meetings were boring. Thus, it would help if she had some coffee to keep herself awake. She had coffee at home, of course, and a great coffee maker. But...

There was another place where she knew she can get a great cup of coffee...

She signaled right and headed towards downtown Carlsbad.

Chapter 15

"We should definitely go on a double date," William told Vanessa. They were on the phone while Vanessa was behind the counter in La Vida Mocha, working on a crossword puzzle from a puzzle book she had found at home. She had nothing better to do; La Vida Mocha was currently sans customers.

"The problem with that idea," Vanessa began, "is that Megan and I are not dating."

"So what?" William crowed. "You mean you and Megan can't just meet up with me and Tyrone for drinks or something?"

Vanessa thought about that. She supposed that, technically, there was nothing preventing her and Megan from meeting up with friends for drinks or a night of playing board games or whatever. People in casual flings did stuff like that all the time. Unless, of course, Megan wanted to restrict their time together to the bedroom...

And I have no problem with that.

"I think I'd better spend some more time with her first before I subject Megan to the craziness that is William, sweetie. I like this woman, after all, temporary though she is."

"You can't see me, but I'm giving you the finger, honey," William said. "But listen, if you like this woman, you *need* to introduce her to me so that I can tell her how fabulous you are—you know, basically *lie*—and then she'll fall in love with you, forget all about moving to New York, and then you and her can have a destination wedding in Tahiti!"

"Jesus! No one is getting married!" Vanessa laughed.

"Don't sell yourself short, honey! You're a catch! If I were straight, I would have already popped the question."

"If you were straight, all the gay bars in Southern California wouldn't need as many security guards," Vanessa said.

"Once again, I am giving you the finger."

"Anyway, speaking of you being gay, not straight, what are the plans for Wednesday night?"

"What time do you close the shop again?"

"Seven. Although the way things have been going lately, I can just put a cardboard cut-out of myself behind the counter after six o'clock and sell as much coffee."

"Aww, I'm sorry. Anyway, my place, at seven-thirty," William told her. "My mom is cooking."

Vanessa groaned inwardly. It wasn't that William's mom wasn't a good cook; she was. It's that the woman tended to overdo it a bit with the spices. Vanessa made a mental note to put her bottle of Pepto-Bismol in her purse that night.

"You know, I've always wondered something," Vanessa said. "What does darling Tyrone think of all this nonsense you pull just to keep your parents in the dark?"

William blew out an unconcerned breath.

"Please. He's not out yet either, so he gets it. Whenever my folks come by, he just hides out in his apartment two floors down; then, when my folks go to sleep, I sneak out and spend the night with him."

"It's the classic gay love story, isn't it? Why do you think Disney hasn't made a cartoon out of it yet?"

"Once again, the finger."

"Anyway, I need to go. I'm a busy and important woman with things to do."

Like coming up with a six-letter word for "Zen enlightenment."

"Fine," William said. "See you Wednesday."

And with that, they hung up.

Ugh! Fuck Zen enlightenment!

Needing a break from the crossword, Vanessa decided to finally get around to reading the day's news. Opening the site of the local paper on her tablet, she immediately discovered an item about how the San Diego County supervisors were considering allowing places like restaurants and coffeeshops to reopen for customers again provided the amount of new Covid cases did not exceed a certain threshold by Friday and that establishments continued following health protocols by limiting the amount of customers in their places at one time and enforcing social distancing of their patrons.

No way!

Just below that piece, was another one stating that Brawn Brothers, the coffeeshop a few blocks away from La Vida Mocha, had not only been heavily fined again for continuing to allow large groups of guests to congregate on their patio as well as inside their establishment, but had also been ordered to shut down until a hearing before the Carlsbad City Council during which their license to operate would be up for discussion.

The news had made Vanessa to do a little happy dance and yell out, "Ha! Ha! Suck it, Brawn Brothers!"

It occurred to her that this explained why La Vida Mocha's morning had been so busy; far more so than it had been in long time. Apparently, all those former Brawn Brothers customers still needed their caffeine fix. That sudden onslaught had run Vanessa ragged, and more than once she had wished for Chloë's presence, but it was worth it. La Vida Mocha's morning receipts were quite healthy.

Now, nearing one o'clock, things had been still for a while. She'd had a few more lunchtime visitors but that was it. If things stayed true to pandemic form, she wouldn't see her next round of customers until three o'clock or so.

Just then, the bell over the door dinged.

Spoke too soon...

Looking up, she expected to see another random stranger just popping in for a whatever to go, but was left breathless when she saw Megan.

"Oh my God!" Vanessa said, coming around the counter to the seating area. She met Megan near one of the empty tables. Being this close to her again was making Vanessa's heart palpitate, especially when Megan's scent of vanilla and cherry blossoms reached her nostrils.

"How are you?" Vanessa asked.

Megan rolled her eyes, a habit Vanessa was learning she liked because she did it so theatrically.

"Just had lunch with my mom," she said. "I ended it when she told me that a lesbian couple we saw really should try harder to find some men."

"No!" Vanessa was laughing. "Awkward."

"So, I'm here wondering if you have any available men for me to choose from?" Megan made a show of looking around. "Hmm...nope, no men; guess I'll remain gay."

Vanessa laughed.

"Anyway, I have a boring meeting this afternoon and will definitely need some caffeine; so, here I am."

"Then it's a good thing I'm allowed to legally peddle what probably should be considered a controlled substance by now," Vanessa joked.

"I have a confession," Megan said. "Halfway here I debated on whether to stop by so soon after yesterday. I didn't want to seem stalker-ish."

Vanessa wanted to tell Megan that if she could hand-pick a stalker, it would be her.

Instead, she said, "Are you kidding? I'm glad you're here." That last sentence came out throatier than Vanessa intended, hungrier, and she blushed a bit, hoping Megan didn't notice. "Besides, you're expected to keep my business afloat with all those Americanos, remember?"

"I haven't forgotten! I cleared out my savings account to afford your exorbitant prices, madam, so start brewing, please." She paused and held Vanessa's gaze. "But I have another confession. I would have come by here even if you sold hubcaps, just so I could see you and say hello."

Vanessa felt her breath hitch.

"Well, it's good to know that if I lose the coffeeshop I can still lure you with hubcaps," she said. "And on a day full of good news so far, the fact that you wanted to see me so soon is the best news I've gotten."

"It better be!" Megan said teasingly.

"So, do you really need an Americano?"

"I'm afraid I do," Megan said. "I have what is sure to be an ass-numbingly dull afternoon and I could really use a jolt."

"Come on over," Vanessa instructed, leading the way back to the counter.

While she set about preparing Megan's drink, Megan asked what all the other good news was, and Vanessa told her about the items in the news.

"You missed my happy dance," Vanessa said.

"Oh, I bet *that* was a sight!" Megan stated. "But this is fantastic news. I am so happy for you! This means things could start looking up, right?"

"Well, I want to say yes, but it all depends on the customers and their willingness to come out again."

"They will," Megan declared. "As a customer, I can tell you that the people of my tribe are ready to get the fuck out of our houses, so please open up!"

In another few moments, Vanessa delivered the drink to Megan.

"On the house," she said.

Megan's mouth fell open.

"Oh no, please, let me pay," she said earnestly, reaching into her bag.

"No, really, it's fine," Vanessa tried assuring her.

"No, really, it's not," Megan insisted, pulling out her wallet.

"Megan, really—"

But Vanessa was silenced when Megan's eyes captured hers.

"Vanessa, hear me out, okay?" Megan said in a pleading tone. "I know we're just…temporary. But I really like you, and I hope I can see lots more of you for however long this whatever-it-is between us lasts. But the thing is, if you give me free coffee today then you might think you have to give me free coffee tomorrow and the day after and so on, and I don't want you ever thinking that every time I come in here, I expect free coffee. Or free hubcaps, if you decide to diversify. The reality is, if I come in here, it's not for freebies, it's because I want to see you and I want you to always know that."

Vanessa's breath hitched again. She was realizing this woman had a power to cast spells and she was alarmingly finding herself so super willing to be enchanted.

"Stay right there," she instructed Megan. Vanessa then came back around the counter and stood in front of Megan. They were inches apart and Vanessa would swear that Megan could hear her heartbeat.

Vanessa reached out and placed both hands on Megan's hips. She felt electricity shoot through her veins as Megan mirrored the movement, but instead of grabbing Vanessa's hips, Megan used her fingers to take hold of the front pockets of Vanessa's skinny jeans. Vanessa's knees quivered as she realized what Megan's fingers were close to, only the thin fabric of the inside of the pockets separating them from Vanessa's flesh. And then Megan pulled Vanessa to her, using her grip on those pockets until the space between them disappeared.

Feeling Megan's breasts pressed against her own made Vanessa stare down at the slightly shorter Megan hungrily. And when Megan continued pulling on Vanessa's pockets, until Vanessa's groin was pressed against her own, Vanessa couldn't wait any longer. The shop was still empty and she wanted to kiss this woman, so she brought her lips down to meet Megan's.

As the kiss deepened in intensity, Vanessa reached her hands up Megan's back, her fingers playing with the so-soft curls at the nape of her neck. The moaning Megan did in response to this was making Vanessa that much wetter and she suddenly pulled away, trembling, wanting to stop before she started doing certain things to Megan right here in La Vida Mocha.

They stood there, panting, foreheads touching.

"I could have made coffee at home," Megan whispered.

"I figured," Vanessa said. "You seem sufficiently affluent to own a coffeemaker."

Megan giggled.

"I am," she murmured. Then, Vanessa felt Megan's left hand move down and start rubbing Vanessa's jeans at her inner thigh. Vanessa's nipples hardened and her clit pulsed.

"Pretty soon I'm going to make you pay for that coffee some other way," she purred. "In fact, I—Oh my God!" Vanessa suddenly exclaimed, jumping away from Megan, her hands flying to her face as she stared across the room.

She had happened to look up as she was speaking to Megan and saw that they were no longer alone. Standing just inside the doorway of La Vida Mocha was a little old lady who Vanessa thought was at least eighty if she was a day. The lady just stood there, purse clutched before her in two hands, her sensible brown dress with a high collar immaculately pressed.

Megan turned to see what had startled Vanessa and then she also threw her hands to her face in embarrassment.

"Oh fuck!" she sputtered.

The old woman grinned at the two women, patiently looking at them with eyes made bigger by the Mister Magoo glasses she was wearing. She seemed as if she was pleasantly willing to wait all day.

"Oh my God, ma'am, I am so sorry!" Vanessa said, the heat of her blush making her feel like she had contracted a fever. She hurriedly reached into her pocket for her face mask and put it on. Jesus, how had she not heard the bell over the door?

Because I was lost in Megan's kiss, that's why.

Vanessa silently thanked her goddesses that she hadn't started fondling Megan's breasts; something she *had* been about to do. She wondered what kind of Yelp review *that* would have garnered from the elderly woman.

"No problem, sweetheart," the lady said. "I didn't mean to interrupt."

"God, no, don't apologize! Um…what can I help you with?" She left Megan's side to take her position behind the counter.

The customer came forward, Megan giving her a sheepish grin as she passed by.

"I was hoping to get an iced coffee, please. It's rather warm out today, isn't it?"

Vanessa smiled. "I wish I knew. I've been stuck inside here since I opened. Is that regular or decaf?"

"Fully leaded, please," the old lady said, and then she leaned closer and whispered conspiratorially, "Don't tell my doctor. She would already yell at me for being out without a mask on." She then moved her eyes back and forth between Vanessa and Megan before resettling on the barista. "So, have you two been together long?"

The abrupt shift in topic made Vanessa blush again as she prepared the iced coffee. She stole a glance at Megan and could tell from the crinkle around her eyes that she was stifling a laugh.

"We just met a couple of days ago," Megan answered.

"So, is this is your second date?"

"No," Megan corrected. "I just came in to say hello and get some coffee, that's all."

The old lady waved a dismissive hand.

"If there was a kiss, it counts as a date," she said in a firm voice that would brook no argument. "That's what I told my husband sixty-three years ago; although, I said that as a way to shorten the amount of time it was going to take to get us to the altar. Thank you," she said when Vanessa handed her the iced coffee.

Still embarrassed by the whole kissing thing, Vanessa tried to insist her customer take the coffee on the house.

"Nonsense!" Again, the voice used indicated no argument would be tolerated. Vanessa wondered briefly if she had been schoolteacher. For juvenile delinquents. The lady pulled a ten from her purse and plunked it down on the counter. "Keep the change," she ordered and then hooked a thumb in Megan's direction. "Use it to help take her on your third date." She then winked, nodded goodbye to Megan and left the shop.

As soon as the door shut behind her, Vanessa and Megan burst into laughter.

"Okay…that was, um, memorable," Vanessa said, leaning with her arms on the counter and looking up at Megan.

"If she thinks kissing equals a date, I wonder what she thinks going down on a woman equals?" Megan asked, eyes alight with mischief. She leaned with her arms on the counter also so that her face was just inches from Vanessa's. She then picked at the edge of Vanessa's mask.

"This has to come off," Megan commanded, and Vanessa felt drunk with how her body responded to Megan's directness. She pulled off her mask and then their lips were together again. During the kiss, Megan reached up with one hand and took possession of the back of Vanessa's neck and she knew by the insistent yet gentle pressure of the other woman's fingers that this kiss was not going to end until Megan decided it was going to end. The realization made Vanessa groan as she felt a certain part of her body respond.

Finally, Megan released her.

"This was a bad idea," Megan groaned. "I have a meeting and you have a coffeeshop to run."

"You started it," Vanessa teased.

"Hello? I did not! You're the one who started kissing me."

"Buuut, you're the one who showed up here wanting the best Americano in Carlsbad, instead of making a cup of Sanka at home."

Megan pouted.

"I will have you know that I do *not* drink Sanka at home! I buy very expensive Ethiopian beans from Whole Foods which I then grind in the store using that grindy thingy that they have."

"You're too cute," Vanessa said, resisting the urge to kiss Megan again. Nonetheless, she couldn't help reaching out and running her thumb along Megan's lower lip. Megan's tongue flicked out once and poked at it.

"Do you want to come back over tonight?" Megan asked.

Vanessa sighed.

"Yes and no," she said, and before Megan could ask for an explanation, she went on. "I want to, but I don't close until seven. By the time I've cleaned the shop, counted the receipts and locked up, it's eight o'clock. By the time I get home, shower, change, have something to eat and get to your place, it's nine or nine-thirty."

"That's still early," Megan said petulantly.

"No, it's not," Vanessa said. "You know that we're going to keep each other up past midnight having sex, but I have to wake up super early tomorrow to come here and do all this again." She spread her arms, indicating the whole of La Vida Mocha.

Now Megan sighed.

"Ugh!" she groaned.

"I know," Vanessa said. She was frustrated too. It was tempting to say *fuck it* and spend all night tonight doing all the pornographic things running through her mind that she wanted to do to Megan, but she also knew what a slippery slope that was. One night of unbelievable pleasure would turn into two nights of unbelievable pleasure which would turn into three nights…Before long, Vanessa would find herself never getting enough rest and struggling each day to function here at La Vida Mocha. But La Vida Mocha was too important for Vanessa to let that happen.

But then again…

Eventually, Megan would be gone. Gone from Carlsbad, gone from California, gone from Vanessa's life. Vanessa wondered: Did she really want to be on her death bed decades from now remembering that she passed up even one night of amazing sex with this woman?

Fuck it.

"I'll text you when I'm on my way," she told Megan.

Chapter 16

Megan watched as Vanessa pulled on her black yoga shorts, remembering the thrill she had had peeling those off Vanessa only an hour and a half ago.

Megan was still laying in her bed, naked and content, while Vanessa prepared herself to leave. If their situation had been different, Megan realized, she would probably be a little offended at Vanessa leaving so soon after they'd had sex, but this was their reality.

Alarmingly, though, Megan had been on the verge of suggesting that Vanessa stay the night. She had even typed the words "Why don't you plan on spending the night?" into a text message earlier, before Vanessa arrived, but had simply hovered her thumb over the Send button for a few moments before finally deleting the message.

It had been a long time since Megan had slept—actually slept—with another woman beside her, and she could easily imagine how nice it would be to fall asleep spooning Vanessa and then waking up in the morning to find Vanessa curled up next to her. But such scenarios could not possibly lead to good things, not when this thing with Vanessa had a shelf life.

"Okay, I'm off," Vanessa said, fully dressed now, coming to the bed to lean down and give Megan a kiss.

Once again, the urge to say *Stay the night* came over Megan but she maintained control. Other urges came over her as well as she kissed Vanessa. In fact, she was pretty sure she could make Vanessa stay the night by default if she just reached up now and began stroking Vanessa's center through those tight yoga pants. But, again, she maintained control. She needed to be respectful of Vanessa's priorities, of which she was not one.

"Try not to have lunch with relatives who upset you tomorrow," Vanessa said jokingly. She started to leave the bedroom. "And be sure to get out of bed and lock the front door behind me, please."

Megan felt a surge of warmth come over her at Vanessa's concern.

And she said "please."

"Yes, ma'am," Megan said, settling deeper under her comforter.

Vanessa looked at her.

"Do you promise?"

"I promise; I promise."

Vanessa crossed her arms and stood defiantly.

"Get out of bed now and come with me downstairs and do it," she ordered.

Megan sighed but did as she was told. She wasn't going to admit it to Vanessa right now, but, damn, that turned her on! She located her t-shirt on the floor and slipped it on, not caring that it was inside out.

"Don't trust me?" she asked Vanessa as they left the bedroom together.

"Just looking out for you, is all, woman to woman," Vanessa said. "Besides, your bed is super comfy; I know how hard it is to get out of it."

"No one was saying you had to leave," Megan grumbled and then clamped her hand over her mouth.

Shit!

They reached the bottom of the stairs and stood in front of the still-closed front door.

"Sorry," Megan said. "I didn't mean to say that out loud."

Vanessa laughed.

"No need to apologize. We probably should have a talk about…" She turned her eyes skyward, as if searching for the right word.

"Sleepovers?" Megan offered.

"Right! And other things. It might be good to set some parameters on this." She waved her hand between the two of them. "But not tonight. Tonight, I am going home to get some sleep because I have a business to run and I have to be lucid enough tomorrow to make correct change."

An idea came to Megan. She chewed on it mentally for a second before saying, "Well, I want to have this talk sooner rather than later. How about I bring you lunch tomorrow at the coffeeshop?"

Vanessa beamed a thousand-watt smile.

"I love it! My lunches at the coffeeshop are always kind of sad. Usually, I'm scarfing a salad or some fruit behind the counter all by myself. I should warn you, though, even nowadays I sometimes get a bunch people coming in during lunchtime…"

"No problem! Ooh, maybe I can help!"

Vanessa quirked an eyebrow. "Seriously?"

"Why not?" Megan asked enthusiastically. "My job is *soooo* boring; being at the shop might be fun."

"Okay, you're on," Vanessa said. She put her arms on Megan's shoulders. "Hmm, I wonder if I should make you wear a uniform?"

Megan grinned.

"Let me guess," she began, "plunging neckline and micro-mini skirt?"

Vanessa shook her head.

"I was thinking more like latex-clad dom."

Megan gasped. Her nipples had just turned to marble under her shirt.

"You need to leave now," she said. "Or you won't be leaving at all."

***

"So that is six-forty, please," Megan said to the cute brunette with a bob cut who had ordered a cold brew vanilla and caramel. The customer took out a card and Megan's face scrunched up, trying to recall Vanessa's tutorial.

"Is that debit or credit?" she asked.

"Debit," was the answer.

"So that means I tap this button," Megan said to herself, tapping an icon on the register's touchscreen. "Now you put the card in that thingy there...and now I tap this button." She breathed a sigh of relief when a moment later the transaction approval appeared on the screen. "Yay!" She looked up at the brunette and smiled, quite pleased with herself. "You're all set!"

"Receipt?" Vanessa whispered as she passed by to another station to continue preparing the cold brew drink.

"Oh, right! Damn!" Megan exclaimed. She looked back up at the customer. "Sorry! Do you want a receipt?"

"No, I'm good," was the answer. The brunette gave Megan a flirty smile and her eyes were telegraphing interest. "Thanks for your help."

Megan blushed.

"Anytime. Um...Vanessa will have your drink waiting for you over there."

That was the last of four customers that had all come in almost back to back and Megan blew out a relieved breath.

Earlier, Vanessa had insisted it was her turn to buy lunch and so all Megan had to do was pick up the order Vanessa had called in to a salad place near the shopping mall. When she had arrived at La Vida Mocha about half an hour ago, Vanessa was finishing helping a customer and there was another one waiting, dutifully standing on one of a series of floor decals that were each placed six feet apart. When Vanessa saw Megan enter, she smiled and gestured for her to come behind the counter.

"I'll be done in a sec," Vanessa had told her. "Why don't you put the food back there and I'll come find you."

So, Megan had waited in the back, in a room crammed with boxes, sacks of organic coffee beans, stacks of supplies and a small folding table on which sat Vanessa's hobo purse. The hum of the huge walk-in refrigerator was the dominant noise in the confined space, kind of like being on an airplane. There was so much to touch and explore but Megan didn't have a chance. Vanessa came in a couple of minutes later and leaned against the door frame, her eyebrow cocked.

A thrill had shot through Megan, thinking that Vanessa wanted another make-out session.

Vanessa said, "You ready for this?"

For your hands all over me and your tongue down my throat? Yes!

She bit her bottom lip seductively and purred, "I am ready for anything."

"Good, come with me!" And Vanessa went back out to the front. Perplexed, Megan had followed and then pouted when she realized what Vanessa had in mind.

Checking her watch, Vanessa had said, "It's a good chance we'll get somewhat busy in about twenty minutes. Let me give you a rundown on the POS."

"The POS?" Megan had asked.

"Yeah, this..." Vanessa tapped the device in front of her which was dominated by a large touchscreen.

Megan had frowned. "You mean the cash register?"

Vanessa laughed.

"We call it a POS in the twenty-first century, Luddite. Point of sale system."

Thus began Megan's tutorial, and just in time, because they had indeed gotten several customers at around noon. But now, with the flirty brunette served—who gave a little wave to Megan as she walked out with her drink—Megan finally realized that she and Vanessa hadn't yet eaten.

"You know," Megan said, as she watched the brunette head off, "I think you get a lot of lesbians in here. That one, for sure, and there were a couple of others my gaydar pinged on earlier."

Laughing, Vanessa told her that back before the pandemic, La Vida Mocha had had quite a sizable lesbian and queer clientele. Her eyes narrowed. "And yet, I don't remember seeing you in here."

Megan shrugged. "To be honest, even if I had known this was the quote-unquote lesbian spot for coffee, that probably would've made me avoid it."

Vanessa gasped in mock indignation and put a faux injured look on her face, making Megan laugh.

"You gotta understand," Megan continued. "When I go out to draw, that's what I want to do...draw. I want to sit somewhere that's not my living room and focus on my art. I want to be somewhere there's people, but I don't want to socialize, if that makes sense—and I certainly don't want to bother with getting hit on. That's why I bought huge and expensive Beats headphones. They say, 'Yes, I'm cute, but leave me alone!'"

Vanessa stepped closer. Megan's pulse thrummed when she felt Vanessa's hands on her hips.

"You didn't have a problem socializing with me the first time you came in here, as I recall," Vanessa murmured.

After licking her lips, Megan said, "No, I didn't."

Megan shivered slightly as Vanessa brought her head closer. She parted her lips, eager for Vanessa's kiss, but was surprised when Vanessa instead brought her mouth to the side of Megan's head and started ghosting her ear with her lips. Megan hummed and her clit pulsed once.

"Why?" Vanessa whispered, then nibbled on Megan's earlobe. Megan brought her arms up to encircle Vanessa's back, entrapping her. It took a moment for Megan to be able to speak.

"Because as soon as I saw you, I was hoping for moments like this," she purred. She nuzzled Vanessa's neck and was rewarded with feeling Vanessa's fingers tighten on her hips.

The woman smelled amazing and Megan flared her nostrils to drink it in. Lavender and coffee.

Thank god she doesn't work at a pig farm.

She couldn't take it anymore. Pulling her face away from her neck, Megan found Vanessa's lips and initiated a passionate kiss, instantly inserting Vanessa with her tongue. Her clit pulsed twice. Then, emboldened by the slickness her center was producing, Megan decided to be devilish. Using one of the hands she had on Vanessa's back, she moved along Vanessa's bra strap until she felt the catch under the fabric of the yellow t-shirt Vanessa had on; then, she hooked her thumb underneath it, pulling it away slightly from Vanessa's skin, as if she was about to unhook it.

It had the desired effect. Vanessa whimpered and even sagged a bit and then deepened her kiss.

Megan's clit pulsed three times.

This time it was Megan who forced herself away when her stomach rumbled loudly.

"We still haven't eaten," she said.

Vanessa smiled. "I know. Sorry our lunch together has been mostly doing work. Let's eat out here so we can see any customers coming in. I'll go get our food."

***

"When do you have to leave?" Vanessa asked a few minutes later. She and Megan were enjoying their lunches at one of the out-of-the-way tables near the hallway that led to the restrooms in the back.

"Soon," Megan replied. "I have a one-thirty. And I *have* to keep my second job because of the crap wages you pay me," she added teasingly, rolling her eyes dramatically. She was trying not to shovel salad into her mouth because the truth was, she was starving. "So…let's talk. I believe the first topic is sleepovers?"

Vanessa grinned. "Right."

"Well, let me get the ball rolling by saying that going forward, I think it's silly for you to leave my house at nearly eleven o'clock at night only to go home and go to bed."

Nodding, Vanessa said, "Okay, that makes sense. So, how about this: If one of us is over at the other's house past a certain time, she spends the night." She held up a finger. "But only past a certain time."

"And what time should that be?" Megan asked, realizing she was hoping Vanessa would say nine p.m.

"Let's say eleven?"

Crap!

"Deal," Megan said, disappointed but not wanting to be pushy by suggesting ten o'clock. "And if one of us doesn't want to spend the night, the other one can't get bent out of shape about it."

"Of course," Vanessa said.

"What else?"

"Well," Vanessa began, "I think we need to set some ground rules."

"Like?"

"Like, maybe we should limit how often we see each other."

Megan frowned.

Hell no.

She was going to be moving to New York in the near future and the woman responsible for the best sex of her life was telling her that they should *limit* their time together? She wasn't going to accept that.

"I don't agree," she stated.

Vanessa blinked.

"What?"

"No, Vanessa. I may be leaving California at the end of the year or at the end of the month, for all I know. Either way, I see nothing wrong with both of us having as much fun together as humanly possible. And for the record, when I say 'fun' I mean sex."

Vanessa chuckled.

"Yeah, I kind of figured that's what you meant," she said. "Okay, then, we at least need to limit things like what we're doing now."

"Eating?"

"Yeah, eating. Together. Out. I mean, ordering a pizza after sex is one thing, but meeting up for meals should be a no-no because that's a date."

Megan thought about that. That rule felt weird for her but that was only because she was new to this fling thing. But it made sense given their circumstances and so she said, "Deal."

"Oh, one more thing!" Vanessa said.

Damn, this woman has a lot of rules!

"And that is?" Megan prodded.

"Well, neither one of us should get possessive about the other's time. If you don't want to, or can't, see me one night, for example, I need to be okay with that. Same for you."

Megan nodded.

"Deal," she said firmly.

"Good," Vanessa said, and then smiled slyly, "because I can't see you tomorrow night. I have plans."

Megan felt a jolt of jealousy charge through her, though she tried to squash it immediately. Jealousy should *not* be a factor in anything her and Vanessa did. But, alarmingly, there it was.

Plans? With a woman?

Megan toyed with the remnants of her salad in a way that she hoped looked indifferent.

"What kind of plans?" she asked.

"Dinner with my best friend William and his parents. He's gay but not out and I pretend to be his girlfriend whenever his parents stop by."

Megan giggled, partly in relief. *William.* A guy.

"Seriously?" She was elated Vanessa's plans weren't with another woman.

"Yeah, it's stupid, I know; but I love the idiot."

"Well, just so you know, if we can't get together tomorrow then we most likely can't get together until Friday or Saturday, because I leave for Coachella on Thursday."

Vanessa swallowed a bite of salad.

"Coachella? Is it work related?"

Megan noticed a change in Vanessa's voice when that question was asked.

Wait! Was Vanessa jealous about what my plans might be?

"A funeral," Megan told her.

Vanessa's hands flew to her face. "Oh my God! I'm so sorry! Was it a family member?"

"No, no," Megan said with assurance. "No, thank God. It's the mother of my ex. But I felt very close to her also. I may hate Cindy and wish the hounds of hell would come up and devour her bit by bit, but I do want to pay my respects to Carole."

"That's sweet," Vanessa said. "Well, except for the hounds of hell part. Maybe leave that out if you're asked to say a few words."

Vanessa then leaned forward until her face was only an inch from Megan's. Megan licked her lips and then gasped when she felt Vanessa's hand on her thigh under the table.

"So," Vanessa murmured, "since we have a couple of days off from each other this week, I expect we'll be together tonight?"

As if believing Megan needed convincing, Megan felt Vanessa's fingers graze the zipper of her jeans. Megan couldn't help the little moan which escaped her lips as she felt her panties, already damp from their quick make-out session earlier, get even wetter.

"Yes, please," Megan breathed, but that was all Vanessa allowed her to say before her lips found Megan's for a passionate kiss that might have lasted five minutes or might have lasted ten, Megan didn't know. All the while, Vanessa continued stroking the crotch of Megan's jeans.

When they parted, Megan felt supremely satisfied with the desire evident in Vanessa's eyes.

"I'll text you when I'm on my way," Vanessa said. "I should be there by—Oh my God!"

Vanessa bolted up to stand as if her chair had suddenly caught fire. With her hands over her mouth, she was staring at something over Megan's shoulder. Megan turned.

The little old lady from yesterday was standing there again, this time in tiny tan slacks and a floral blouse, her purse still clutched primly in front of her, her eyes like saucers behind those incredibly strong glasses.

"Jesus, are you a ninja?" Megan exclaimed, getting up and standing by Vanessa, her right hand over her heart, which was thudding.

The old lady smiled.

"I enjoyed yesterday's iced coffee so much, I thought I'd have another," she said. She then looked from Megan to Vanessa. "I see your third date is going well!"

Chapter 17

The next night, at seven, Vanessa made sure the front doors of La Vida Mocha were locked and the neon *Open* sign in the window switched off. In the back room, she gathered up her purse as well as a small bag containing two cranberry-nut muffins that she hadn't sold today, figuring William's parents would like them. After setting the alarm, she left the coffeeshop out the back door which opened onto the parking lot where her Jeep was waiting.

It had been a busy day in La Vida Mocha. News of the pending reopening of places like coffeeshops had spread. Some of the customers today were familiar faces Vanessa hadn't seen in a while who had come in just to ask her if it was true that they'd be able to once again order coffee and *stay*. It was so gratifying that Vanessa had spent the day feeling a happy buzz.

Before she got in her Jeep, Vanessa took her phone out of her purse. It occurred to her that Megan would have liked today's outfit: a boho casual short-sleeved dress with a brown tie-dye pattern that she had combined with a pair of brown suede ankle boots. Standing in front of the closed back door of La Vida Mocha, Vanessa posed and snapped a selfie which she then fired off in a text to Megan.

Almost as soon as Vanessa started her Jeep and began pulling out of her parking spot, her phone rang, the display on her dashboard telling her it was Chloë.

"Hey!" Vanessa greeted.

"Hey!! So, seriously, I can come back?" Chloë asked.

Earlier, Vanessa had sent a text to her young friend with a link to the online article about the loosening of restrictions and asking if Chloë would be willing to return to La Vida Mocha on Saturday.

"Yeah, of course! I fucking need you!" Vanessa told her. "But, listen…I don't know how long this is gonna last. Hopefully indefinitely but I don't know if you should quit Amazon just yet. I mean, right now that's steady work and I know you got bills to pay."

"Whatever," Chloë said. "If they can't be flexible on my schedule there are other jobs."

Ah, to be young and carefree again!

Vanessa decided not to press it. Chloë was a grown woman who already had two parents; she didn't need a third. Instead, she decided to ask about something else.

"Listen, are we good?" she asked, turning onto Carlsbad Boulevard. "It's just that the other day, you seemed upset. Like, upset with me. Am I wrong?"

Chloë sighed.

"No…I mean…no…"

"Out with it," Vanessa said.

"It's so stupid, though," Chloë whined, sounding like the teenager she was when Vanessa first met her.

"Come on."

Another sigh, and then Chloë said, "Look, I was just a little bent out of shape because of that chick Megan. When I met her on Saturday, I thought she was hot. Then I find out Megan is into you and I'm like, 'Of course Megan is into Vanessa because Vanessa can have whoever she wants, so why wouldn't a cool chick like Megan *not* be into Vanessa? Why would a cool chick like Megan even think about being into me?' And it just fucked with me."

"Oh, sweetheart," Vanessa said. She had no idea Chloë thought that way about her, especially that she could have anyone she wanted. And in all of the various social settings that she and Chloë had been in together over the years, from backyard parties like Saturday's to pride parades to lesbian bars, Vanessa had never had any inkling that Chloë considered her to be competition. Chloë's tastes and Vanessa's tastes in women seemed, up until this point, totally different. Megan didn't seem even close to what Chloë usually went for.

"Anyway, I'm over it," Chloë said off-handedly. "Sorry if I was a bitch the other day."

"No worries, really. I just wanted to make sure you were okay. And, look, Chloë…I can't just have anyone I want…"

"Oh, please, Vanessa, you're a goddess. Everyone thinks so. If I could have sex with just half the women who come into La Vida Mocha and practically throw themselves at you, I wouldn't have time for job."

Vanessa's mouth dropped open. Is that really what her friends thought of her?

"Um…well, it's not like you're a slouch in the looks department, Chloë," she said, trying to gather her mind back together.

"Yeah, fine, I'm really pretty, I know that," Chloë said. "But I'm not *your* level of pretty. When you're in the room anytime there's a Megan-level lesbian around, I may as well be a dude."

"C'mon, Chloë…"

"Vanessa, I'm fine. Anyway, do you want me there to help you open on Saturday?" Chloë asked.

Vanessa thought a moment, still not happy with ending the previous topic of conversation.

"No, I can handle opening. Can you show up at eight, maybe?"

"Perfect! I'm so excited to be back at the shop! Amazon pays well, but, ugh! The work is dull!"

"I'm excited to have you back! Let's just hope now it's forever."

***

The drive to William's apartment building in Oceanside took only a few minutes and Vanessa found a spot on the street not far from the entrance. He lived in a six-story, mid-century structure called, optimistically, *The Luxe,* though its luxe days were far behind. Waiting for the elevator, Vanessa's phone dinged.

Lovelovelovelove, the dress! Promise you'll wear it over one night just so I can take it off you!

I promise. I just arrived at William's building. I'll text you later.

***

Vanessa honestly, for the life of her, could not understand—at all—how William's parents did not know he was gay.

She just didn't get it. They didn't seem like particularly stupid people, so she just couldn't understand it.

William answered the door wearing a tan blazer over a black fishnet shirt, artfully torn jeans and actual penny loafers, which Vanessa didn't think anyone still made. As usual, he looked very handsome, a day's growth of stubble on his square jaw, ocean blue eyes behind frameless glasses, his brown curly hair gelled just so.

"Um…nice shirt, sweetie?" Vanessa said, pointedly. She may be a lesbian, but even she knew fishnet shirts were not in most straight men's wardrobes.

"Isn't it? I lost five pounds this week and thought I'd celebrate by pulling one of my favorites out of the closet. But forget about me…I *love* this dress, honey! Where did you get this?" He then started circling her, examining her dress by touching it, running the fabric through his fingers, appraising the stitching and hems, evaluating the fit. He was like Zac Posen on an episode of *Project Runway,* checking out the creation of one of the contestants.

Meanwhile, Vanessa could see William's parents a mere few yards away in the living room, wine glasses in hand. They waved at her when she caught their eyes.

"Twirl," he finally ordered, circling the air with his index finger.

"I am *not* twirling!" Vanessa hissed, just loud enough for William—and only William—to hear. "Straight men do not ask their girlfriends to twirl, you idiot! Even I know that!"

"Oh, right," William whispered. "Good point."

The dinner might have been delicious, but, honestly, Vanessa just couldn't tell. Once again, Mrs. Heller, who was half-Mexican, used a heavy hand with the spices and after the first three or four bites all Vanessa's mouth could feel was heat. Naturally, she had forgotten to put the Pepto-Bismol in her purse, which meant her heartburn was going to be acting up until she swallowed half the bottle she had left at home. She blamed it on being distracted by thoughts of Megan, thoughts that were becoming alarmingly frequent and always erotic.

Mr. Heller asked her how her business was running, especially in the Covid era. He had also owned a small shop years ago, a haberdashery, a word Vanessa had had to look up when Mr. Heller had first told her about his establishment back when they first met. She had then been amazed he had kept it going for twenty years before it folded, seeing how everything a haberdasher sells could be found at Walmart.

"Monica and I will be sure to stop by soon," Mr. Heller promised her. He looked over at his wife, who gave him a slight nod. "In fact, since we're moving to Oceanside, we may stop by sooner than you think," he added with a twinkle in his eye.

Vanessa, eyes wide with shock, looked at William, who had paled a couple of shades.

"So, you've decided, then?" William finally managed to ask.

"L.A. is just no longer for us," Mrs. Heller said. "And I've wanted to live closer to the beach for a long time. Right now, we can sell our place in L.A. and have enough to buy a new place here in Oceanside and be within walking distance of the beach."

"That is so great," William drawled. He looked across the table at Vanessa. "Is that great, honey?"

"So great," Vanessa said with forced cheeriness, staring back at him.

After dinner, while William's parents were enjoying some more wine out on his balcony, and she and William were loading his dishwasher in the kitchen, Vanessa said, "After this dinner, we need to break up."

"What? Why?"

"Why? It's one thing playacting when your folks live up in L.A. and only drive down every few months; quite another when they're going to be living down the street! I don't have time for this anymore, sweetie. I have a business to run! It's bad enough I can't even have more than a sexual relationship with someone like Megan."

Forgetting about the dishes, William leaned against the kitchen counter.

"Speaking of which, how's that going?" he asked, switching into gossip mode.

"Good, so far. She's cool. We have an understanding."

"Is she good in bed?"

"Remarkably so," Vanessa confessed. "And...I *like* her, William. Like, beyond sex. I feel this connection with her which I'm not sure I've ever actually felt before. It's a good thing she's moving to New York otherwise I might be in real trouble."

William pouted.

"But that's a shame," he whined. "If you two get along well you should have a chance at making a go at it."

"William, I'm barely holding onto things as it is," Vanessa stated. "La Vida Mocha is bleeding money because of this fucking pandemic." She refilled her wine glass from the bottle of white that was on the counter. "I've got a billion things to stress about each day, the last thing I need is a girlfriend who's expecting me to leave little love notes for her on the refrigerator or wondering why I seem so emotionally distant all the time."

She took a long sip of wine.

"No, things with Megan are perfect the way they are. I see her, we fuck. At least I don't have to add sexual frustration to my list of problems. For now, anyway." She pointed at William with her wine glass. "Besides, just because her and I have great sex and I *maybe* feel a connection doesn't mean we'd be good as a couple."

But as soon as she said that, Vanessa realized that she didn't actually didn't believe it.

She had had plenty of flings before. Virtually all of them were with women Vanessa knew she couldn't possibly develop a romantic interest in. But wasn't that the purpose of flings? To have a bit of meaningless fun with a woman who wasn't your type?

The problem was, Megan *was* her type, Vanessa had known that since she first laid eyes on her and she had felt a *boom* in her heart. And even though they had only spent a short time together, Vanessa also knew that if she and Megan did have a chance, they'd be fantastic as a couple.

She noticed William giving her *that* look; the one he gave her when he knew she was bullshitting. Damn him for knowing her so well.

"Looks like someone is kidding herself," William said in a singsong voice.

Vanessa sighed.

"Okay, fine; we probably *would* be good as a couple, but Megan certainly isn't going to give up a big-time job promotion, and I'm certainly not moving to New York."

"No problem," William said, putting his hands on her shoulders. "I'll take care of it."

Vanessa looked at him, confused.

"What do you mean?" she asked.

"Simple. I'll start smearing her on social media," William answered. "Lies, innuendo, rumors…by the time I get done with her, she'll be fired from her job and will have to come work for you at La Vida Mocha."

Vanessa laughed and pulled William in for a hug.

"Why don't we call that Plan B?" she told him.

Chapter 18

The bell over the door to La Vida Mocha dinged as Megan pushed through at a little past one in the afternoon the next day. She briefly wondered if that bell's sound was eventually going to become Pavlovian to her, triggering her to salivate every time she heard it because of the association between coming in here and kissing Vanessa.

Actually, if she was honest with herself, the smell of coffee was already having that effect on her. This morning, as she brewed some at home in her kitchen, the aroma made her drift off into la-la land recalling the feel of Vanessa's lips and tongue. It had made her incredibly horny.

Speaking of Vanessa...

"Hey, you," Vanessa called out from behind the counter. "Are you on your way out of town?"

"I am," Megan said, approaching. "I wanna beat the traffic."

"Good idea."

"Want one for the road?" Vanessa inquired, nodding her head toward all the coffee-making apparatus behind her.

"I do, make it a large, please."

And then lock the doors, turn off the lights and let me take you right here in your coffeeshop, please!

"So, since I worked here the other day, does that mean I get to come behind the counter like a VIP?" Megan asked.

Vanessa gestured with her arm in a *come on through* motion and Megan came around. Once she did, she couldn't help her eyes raking over Vanessa's legs that were on display because Vanessa was wearing a short skirt. Megan scanned the coffeeshop. It was empty.

"How is your ex doing?" Vanessa asked, prepping the espresso for the Americano.

"Hmm?"

Cindy? Why was she asking about Cindy?

"Your ex, whose Mom died?"

"Oh! Um...about as well as could be expected, I guess. Some of her family from Minnesota are here and so she has some support."

"Well, it's nice that you're going also. Family is great and all, but I've learned that sometimes friends are a bit more stabilizing when it comes to stressful things like funerals, you know?"

"True," Megan agreed, wondering what Vanessa would say if Megan told her that at one point, she had wanted to marry this particular ex. Were her and Vanessa allowed to talk about things like that? Would Vanessa want to hear how shattered Megan had been upon discovering that Cindy had been having an affair with a man? Would Vanessa be sympathetic hearing Megan tell her how she had cried herself to sleep every night for two whole weeks? Or were such topics of discussion not allowed between two people having a fling?

"You okay?"

"Hmm?" Megan snapped out of her reverie.

"You okay? You looked like you spaced out there for a moment," Vanessa said.

Megan smiled.

"Just thinking about this drive, that's all. Honestly, if I could afford it, I think I'd helicopter everywhere. Even here to your shop." She took the coffee Vanessa now had ready and in a to-go cup.

"On the house," Vanessa told her. "And shut up. It's on the house."

Megan took another look around the coffeeshop, just to confirm that she hadn't, in fact, missed anyone when she checked earlier. Nope. Still empty.

"No, I want to pay you," she told Vanessa, placing the to-go cup down next to the espresso machine.

"Seriously," Vanessa began, "I want you to have—"

Megan silenced her with a kiss. She used her body to pin Vanessa against the counter as she hungrily deepened the kiss and used her tongue to duel with Vanessa's.

"Turn around," Megan ordered when she pulled away. "Now."

Vanessa's mouth dropped open but Megan was glad that she obeyed instantly.

"Put your hands on the counter," Megan instructed, and when Vanessa did so, added, "Keep them there."

Megan didn't want to waste time. A customer could come in at any moment. She grabbed the hem of Vanessa's skirt and pulled it up until it was around Vanessa's waist.

"Megan!" Vanessa exclaimed, worry in her voice.

Megan cut her off.

"One more word and this turns into a spanking," she told her, getting turned on even more when Vanessa closed her eyes and groaned.

"Mm," she hummed in Vanessa's ear. "Sounds to me like I'll have to keep that in mind for next time."

Vanessa nodded, biting her bottom lip.

Megan took hold of Vanessa's pink panties and yanked them down until they fell to Vanessa's ankles.

"Step out of them."

Vanessa did.

"Open your legs."

Vanessa did that too.

Megan ran her right hand over Vanessa's perfect ass and then slid her fingers between Vanessa's thighs, delighted to find Vanessa's sex already wet, primed for two fingers to be inserted, which Megan did without hesitation. Vanessa pushed her ass back, driving the fingers in deeper and almost instantly the two women found their rhythm, Vanessa uttering stifled moans as Megan fucked her. Eventually, through all the arousal flooding Vanessa's insides, Megan could feel the fluttering of her walls. Vanessa was close. Time to push her over the edge.

Reaching around Vanessa's front with her left hand, Megan zeroed in on Vanessa's clit and began rubbing the tiny bud.

Vanessa's stifled moans turned into stifled squeals.

Megan began whispering into Vanessa's ear.

"Somebody could walk in at any time, Vanessa. They could see me fucking you and hear how wet you are."

"Oh God, Megan," Vanessa whimpered, her eyes squeezed shut.

Megan watched as a young woman walked past the picture window of the shop, her eyes on her phone.

"Somebody just walked past," Megan told Vanessa. "A pretty young woman who had no idea you're being fucked right in front of a window."

"Megan, I'm so close."

"She could have walked right in and caught us."

"Yes…"

"And I think you would have liked that."

"Oh fuck, I'm gonna come…"

"No one is here," Megan whispered into Vanessa's ear. "Let me hear you come. Let me hear you."

Vanessa came undone with a cry, slamming her ass back against Megan, driving those fingers in as far as they could go. She cried out again and Megan was sure it could be heard out on the street. But she didn't care. She was on the verge of orgasming herself at the thought of some random passerby learning what Vanessa sounded like when she came.

Megan kept her fingers inside Vanessa until the climax ran its course and then slowly withdrew them. She instantly brought them to her mouth and sucked them clean, realizing how much she had missed this taste after going only one night without it.

"Wow!" Vanessa said shakily, her hands still on the counter as she caught her breath.

"Yeah, wow," Megan agreed, feeling deliriously pleased with herself. "And with that, I have to go."

Vanessa turned around and pulled her in for a quick kiss.

"If that's the payment I get for a stupid Americano," Vanessa began, "I can't wait to see what a cappuccino is worth to you."

***

On the drive out of town, her car's touchscreen told her that her sister, Molly, was calling.

Rolling her eyes, Megan tapped *Answer*.

"Hey, sis," she greeted cheerily. It was possible—barely possible—that Molly was calling just to shoot the breeze with her big sister.

"Mom thinks you're upset with her because of some gay women in the park the other day?" Molly replied.

So much for that idea.

"Of course, I'm upset with her," Megan answered. "I always get upset around narrow-minded bigots."

"Jesus, Megan! A little harsh!"

"Not harsh enough," Megan insisted.

"Mom and Dad are just…that way," Molly added.

"Molly, why are you defending her? Oh, wait, never mind...I forgot who I'm talking to. Mini Mom."

Megan almost regretted how spitefully that came out, especially as she knew that that particular jibe irked Molly to no end, but the truth was the truth. Molly had always been her parents' apologist.

"You know I hate it when you call me that!" Molly said in a high-pitched voice, and suddenly it was if Megan was talking to her sixteen-year-old baby sis rather than a grown woman of twenty-two about to get married.

"I'm sorry," Megan said, only half meaning it.

"Why is it such a big deal to you anyway?" Molly asked. "So Mom went off about some lesbians. Who cares? Did she confront them? Attack them? No. It's just how she is."

Megan gripped the steering wheel so tightly her knuckles lost all color.

Why was it a big deal? Did she seriously ask that?

"It's a big deal, Molls, because even though people like Mom may not physically attack gay people, they still allow hatred to exist by not keeping their outdated and stupid opinions to themselves and by not even trying to view things differently. And by even just voicing their bigoted opinions, they give other small-minded people justification for actually attacking gays. Why do I have to tell you this? God, did you grow up in the 1850s also?"

"Shut up!"

"No, you shut up!"

Yep, just like they were teenagers again.

They stayed silent for at least half a mile, Megan finding herself needing to concentrate really hard on not rear-ending the vehicle in front of her because she was so upset.

"Anyway, look, I gotta go," Molly finally said. "I have one more online class before I'm done for the day."

Megan knew that as the older sister, she shouldn't allow the conversation to end this way, but she was also not wanting to deal with this while driving.

"Right. Talk to you later."

Before anything else could be said, she jabbed the disconnect button on the steering wheel.

She sighed.

How much longer did she want to have conversations like this with her family? Conversations wherein she deftly avoided giving away any clue that she was a lesbian.

A couple of years ago, Megan had promised Cindy that she would come out to her family before she was thirty. And sure, now Cindy was gone but Megan was still planning on holding herself to that promise. But the clock was ticking. Her next birthday, which was less than two weeks away now, was number twenty-seven, but wasn't it just yesterday she turned twenty-six?

Fuck, time flies when you're adulting!

And what would happen when she moved to New York, got settled in and started meeting women? Presumably, she'd eventually meet and fall in love with someone there.

What if that happened before Molly's wedding next year?

She chewed her bottom lip thinking about this.

Coming out before the wedding meant risking being *uninvited* to the wedding. It was positively medieval, Megan thought, but true. Her parents' minds were stuck in some prior century. Molly wasn't *as* bad, but of the two sisters, Molly had been influenced far more by Mom and Dad than Megan had. Megan didn't know exactly how deeply that influence ran, but what scared her now was that if she came out before the wedding and created a rift in the family, it would ruin Molly's big day. Megan loved her sister, and when the knucklehead wasn't acting like a miniature Audrey Baldwin, they actually got along. The last thing Megan would want now was to take Molly's wedding and make it all about Megan.

But waiting to come out until sometime after the wedding created an unpleasing potential scenario, Megan realized, because suppose she did have a girlfriend when the date of the wedding arrived?

"What am I supposed to do?" Megan asked herself out loud in the car. "Say to her, 'Can't meet up with you today, babe, because I have to fly to California to attend this very important family function that I can't bring you to? Call you when I land?'"

Megan smacked the steering wheel in frustration.

"Fuck!"

She wanted something happy to think about and so she brought the fingers she had fucked Vanessa with up to her face. They still smelled liked her and Megan wanted nothing more than to close her eyes as she inhaled the scent but, of course, driving at eighty miles an hour made that imprudent.

***

Megan made good time, arriving at the Indian Palms Country Club in Indio, just outside Coachella, a little before four o'clock. Even though she was only staying one night, Megan preferred spending the extra money on nicer hotels. As a woman traveling alone, cheap motels, no matter how nice the neighborhood they were in, never made her feel safe.

She toed off her flats as soon as she entered her second-floor room, dropped her overnight bag on the floor near the closet and then flopped backwards onto the bed, luxuriating in how the tension of the drive just melted away. Remembering she had promised Vanessa to text her that she had made it safely, she picked up her phone.

Made it. :-) Safe and sound in my hotel.

Now, she had to figure out what to do with the rest of the day. Coachella, being a desert town, was far hotter than Carlsbad. Her car's display had read 103-degrees when she arrived. Ugh! She was a coastal California girl, not bred for high heat. She had hated the summers in New York City, where, although the mercury hardly ever reached triple-digits, the humidity made even a 90-degree day feel suffocating. She had spent summers in the Big Apple hiding from the sticky and oppressive air in museums, art galleries, matinees on Broadway, antique shops and shady spots in Central Park. But Coachella was not New York.

No bother. Her room here was nice—and air-conditioned; she was not averse to remaining in here until dinnertime when she would most likely just have UberEats bring something by. After dinner, it should be cool enough to go for a walk. In the meantime, she could take out her iPad and do some drawing while watching a movie.

Her phone chimed. Thinking it was Vanessa, she eagerly snatched it up.

Cindy.

When do you get to town?

I got here a little while ago.

Oh.

Megan rolled her eyes. She knew Cindy well enough to read the meaning behind that one word *Oh*. She was actually saying, "Oh, why you didn't tell me?"
"Sorry, Cindy," Megan said aloud. "You're not on a need-to-know basis anymore."

Do you want to maybe meet for coffee?

Frowning, Megan re-read the text, buying time. On the one hand, she had gotten herself pretty stoked about doing her hermit dork thing and staying in her room. It meant she got to take off her bra, change into some comfy clothes…
On the other hand, she *did* come all the way to Coachella to lend some sort of emotional support to Cindy.
"God damn it," Megan muttered, typing.

Sure. But I'm done with driving for the day. I'm at the Indian Palms in Indio. There's a coffeeshop downstairs.

Cool! In 30?

30. See you then.

***

"You look better rested," Megan told Cindy, after Cindy sat down at the table Megan had secured in the hotel's cafe ten minutes earlier. Megan had ordered already for both of them. Cindy only ever drank black coffee and so Megan had a large one of those waiting for her ex while she had her usual Americano.

Cindy did look better than she had a few days ago. The bags under her eyes were gone, her skin looked fresh, and her hair was washed and pulled into a messy bun. She was dressed all in black, but not in a mourning kind of way: black skinny jeans, black flip-flops and a black V-neck halter top with an open back. Megan wondered if Cindy had chosen that top on purpose. When they had been together, that top had been Megan's favorite to see on her girlfriend…

"I took your advice," Cindy said after thanking Megan for the coffee. "I let go of carrying the burden solo and let my family help me. It's been a relief."

"I sense a 'but' coming," Megan prodded.

The tips of Cindy's lips curled upward in a tentative smile.

"*Buuut*, there's been a lot to do, you know? And even though they're helping…" she used air quotes to mark the word *helping* "…I keep having to double-check the stuff they're helping me with. Oh, and don't even get me started on keeping them out of the bungalow."

"What do you mean?"

"Oh my God, Megs," Cindy began with a sigh, and the use of her pet name for Megan felt oddly comfortable, but Megan had no time to unpack that and, shaking her head, she kept it at bay.

"They were like vultures," Cindy continued. "From the first day they were here, it was all about pointing to Mom's possessions and saying, 'I want this!' and 'Oh, Carole said I could have this!' and 'Can I take this back home with me?'"

"No!" and Megan felt real anger bubbling up inside her.

"Yeah! I couldn't believe it!"

Megan could see Cindy's eyes watering, though no tears fell yet. Her hand flinched, wanting, seemingly on its own accord, to reach for Cindy's hand. Megan had overridden the impulse but then remembered why she was here, and so she let her hand take Cindy's and give a comforting squeeze.

For a moment, Cindy said nothing, just stared at Megan's hand in her own. Then she seemed to gather herself and said, "Fortunately, I have the law on my side. Mom left a will. I met with the lawyer on Tuesday and turns out she left everything to me: the bungalow, the contents, everything. And since I have the only key to the place, I've managed to keep everyone else out easily enough. Still, though…it's just one more thing."

"Is there anything I can do?" Megan asked.

Cindy smiled and squeezed Megan's hand.

"You're already doing it," Cindy answered. "This is all I need you for now, providing an escape from the madness." She lifted her coffee. "And more caffeine."

Megan gently disengaged her hand from Cindy's.

"What's wrong?" Cindy asked.

Megan took a deep breath before saying, "What I want to know is, where is your man in all this? Why isn't he helping you deal with…well, *everything*? You haven't mentioned him once and it's pissing me off that you've apparently been abandoned to handle all of this alone." Her voice took on a steely edge. "What was his name? Donald? Ronald?"

"Brian," Cindy murmured, barely audible, as she stared down at the table.

Brian?

"Well, whatever his name is," Megan continued through clenched teeth, "where the fuck is he? I mean, you *left* me for this…*man,* so why isn't he *manning* up and doing what it takes to get you through the death and burial of your mother?"

Megan suddenly shut her eyes and breathed in deeply through her nose. She realized she was now shaking. She hadn't expected to have an outburst like that; she hadn't expected to *care* this much about the fact that Cindy was apparently going through all this alone, without any assistance from that prick Brian. What did it matter to her?

But evidently, it *did* matter to her, and Megan hated that even more than she had hated the thrill which she had felt when Cindy had squeezed her hand a few moments ago. Cindy was dead to her, at least that was the narrative that had been playing in Megan's head since January. So why did any of this matter?

All she wanted now was to go back upstairs to her room and be a hermit dork. She wanted tomorrow to hurry up and come so she could go to Carole's funeral, say goodbye to that wonderful woman and then get back in her car to drive to Carlsbad.

When she felt calm enough to speak again without clenching her teeth, Megan opened her eyes and said, "Sorry. Um…none of my business. I didn't mean to get hostile."

"Brian is no longer around," Cindy said. She was still looking down at the table.

Megan's mouth fell open.

"Hasn't been for a while, in fact," Cindy continued with a mirthless chuckle. "I, um, ended things with him maybe three weeks after you and I…well, you know." She took a deep breath. "Turns out, if you give up everything for somebody, that somebody had better be worth everything." She looked up and met Megan's eyes. "He wasn't worth what I gave up," she whispered.

Megan had no idea how to respond to this. In fact, she was starting to feel a little dizzy.

Three weeks?

Cindy had thrown away their *two years* together for a man she then left after three weeks? So what the fuck had their two years meant?

And why was Megan just now hearing about this? Why hadn't Cindy told her that she had ditched Brian upon discovering that Brian wasn't worth it?

As if reading her mind, Cindy said, "I wanted to tell you. I wanted to…run back to you and continue begging you to forgive me. But I knew you wouldn't. Besides, I had to sort out why I did what I did before I could ever really hope you'd be able to…let me back in."

"We can't talk about this right now!" Megan blurted out, fresh anger threatening to burst out. This new intel meant that Cindy could go to hell and all Megan wanted to do now was run, not walk, to the safety of her room upstairs. "Your mom just died. I'm not here to rehash what happened with us. So drop it."

Mercifully, her phone chimed.

Soooo sorry for taking so long! Typical woman (at least according to my dad) I forgot to charge my phone last night and it died. I have it on the charger now and got it up to 5 percent, just enough to send this. Thank you for letting me know ur safe!

Megan smiled. Then another text from Vanessa arrived.

BTW, I have never been fucked in my shop before! That was hot! I'm still so wet! And I've decided to double the price of my Americanos so expect to "pay" more the next time you want one.

Smiling, Megan re-read the message, and then read it a third time.

"Good news from someone important?" Cindy interrupted Megan's reverie. The question was asked casually but, again, Megan knew the woman who asked it too well. She sighed.

"Nothing you need to know about," Megan said, hoping it was direct enough to shut Cindy down from further questions.

Chapter 19

Vanessa sighed, exhausted.

But it was a happy exhaustion. It was an *I-finished-another-half-marathon* exhaustion or *I-just-spent-all-night-fucking-a-hot-woman* exhaustion. Exhaustion mixed with elation.

The reopening had been a success. Someone had even been waiting outside the door when Vanessa unlocked it at eight a.m. on Saturday, a young woman named Amy who had been a regular before the shutdown. She walked into La Vida Mocha with a laptop bag, saying "Thank God!" as she did so, promptly ordered a chai latte with coconut milk and then claimed one of the easy chairs near the window. She then set up camp. Out came the laptop, on came the headphones and she stayed there typing away, nursing her latte, until lunchtime.

Chloë apparently couldn't wait to get back to work. Despite Vanessa telling her she should show up about an hour after opening, Chloë was there only thirty minutes after La Vida Mocha opened for the day. Vanessa didn't mind. Chloë's presence was a godsend, making Vanessa realize how much she had missed her. Throughout the day, her young friend was seemingly everywhere at once, and thankfully, Chloë didn't need any refreshers on where everything was or on operating the coffee machines or the POS. She resumed her duties as if she had never left.

At noon, Vanessa used DoorDash to order lunch for herself and Chloë, each woman taking turns in the back room scarfing down their food while the other manned the front. When it was her turn for lunch, Vanessa used the time to finally scan her texts. Most of her friends had sent good luck messages, promising to come by and see how it was going. Her mom had also written, offering to come down from L.A. and spend next week in Carlsbad to help with the shop. Vanessa briefly considered it—free labor—but…ugh! Her mom was too young to die, and chances were that with Mom in her house *and* in the shop, a murder would occur.

Besides, there was Megan…

Vanessa had made up her mind on Thursday afternoon, after Megan had fucked her behind the counter, that as much as possible, when she wasn't in La Vida Mocha, she wanted to spend her free time with the woman.

Thinking of whom...there had also been a text from Megan.

You're probably super busy so I don't expect you to answer. I just wanted to say I hope things go well today. I'm also probably not going to stop by. Since now I know you get a lot of lesbians in La Vida Mocha, I will probably get into a fight the first time I see one giving you fuck me eyes. Just saying. Will I see you tonight?

Vanessa raised her eyebrows in surprise. It sounded like Megan was claiming her territory, at least that was one interpretation. And Vanessa liked it.

She had fired off a quick text, telling Megan she'd definitely come by tonight.

But only for an hour or so! I'm opening LVM tomorrow and need to be sure to get some extra sleep.

She had decided that La Vida Mocha would once again open on Sundays, and Chloë was game. It meant giving up a much-needed day off, but under the circumstances her business needed to be open as much as possible. Who knew how long this reopening phase would last?

I thought you were closed on Sundays? Megan had written back.

I'll explain later. Anyway, an hour or two tonight. Tops.

There had been no reply for a few minutes, allowing Vanessa to take some more bites of her lunch. Then, her phone pinged.

Vanessa, just pack a bag and stay for once.

Vanessa blinked.
Another text arrived:

It won't mean we're married.

Vanessa chuckled and then bit her lip, considering.

It *would* be a lot more convenient to spend the night. Besides, her and Megan hadn't gotten together yesterday, Friday, because Megan had got back from the funeral in Coachella later than anticipated. The result was that Vanessa was pretty horny; too horny, she knew, to get satisfied in just an hour or two.

***

At closing time Vanessa was exhausted, but she had to do it all again tomorrow.

Chloë seemed intent on continuing to work at La Vida Mocha, which meant Vanessa could once again make her the assistant manager; then, if things continued going well next week, maybe she could find out if Luli was interested in coming back. If not, it wasn't as if there was a shortage of people looking for jobs. With three people on staff, including herself, Vanessa could arrange their schedules so that there would always be at least two people in the shop each day, and her and Chloë could alternate Saturdays and Sundays off.

Vanessa and Chloë spent forty-five minutes closing down the shop, Chloë doing most of the cleaning and prep work for tomorrow while Vanessa counted the receipts and bagged the cash for depositing at the Chase bank one block over.

As they walked out of the shop together once the place was buttoned down, Vanessa put her arm around Chloë's shoulders.

"I can't tell you how important it is to me that you're here, sweetie," Vanessa said with feeling, pulling her friend in closer. "I'm serious; I can't imagine anyone else I'd rather be doing this with."

Chloë put her own arm around Vanessa's waist and squeezed.

"Honestly? This is what I want to do, Vanessa, and where I want to be. I can't abandon you; you're the best boss on the planet."

***

At home, Vanessa sent a text to Megan as soon as she walked in the door.

Just got home! Give me 30 minutes and I'll head right over!

So far, they'd only made use of Megan's condo for their trysts, which suited Vanessa just fine. To begin with, Megan didn't live that far away; door to door it was five minutes. But, also, in the past, whenever Vanessa had had casual flings with women, she preferred to keep them out of her home as much as possible. It meant less chance that Vanessa would ever associate her sanctuary with a woman who was never going to be a permanent fixture there.

In her bedroom, she quickly stripped and got in the shower, making it extra hot, loving how the spray invigorated her, the steam helping to revive her. As she washed, she couldn't help but consider the possibilities of tonight. It was all she could do to keep her fingers from playing between her legs at the thoughts running through her mind.

Once showered and dried, Vanessa then took essential items like her wallet, car keys and phone charger out of the hobo bag she carried every day and transferred them to a larger Coach handbag, spacious enough to hold a change of clothes and toiletries, all of which she now spent a few minutes packing in the bag.

She then dressed quickly in a skater skirt and cotton tee.

Her phone beeped.

22 minutes since you texted. I'm assuming in 8 minutes I will get another text telling me that you're locking your door, right? Every minute you're late is a minute I take away from my kiss hello.

Vanessa gasped.
Oh, really?
And then...
Fuck, that's hot!
Not wanting to be denied any extra time kissing that gorgeous woman, Vanessa hurried, slipping on some super comfy flats and checking her appearance one last time.

Locking my door! 2 minutes to spare I might add!

***

It was near one in the morning when they were finally done with each other, two women exhausted and spent. It was Vanessa who surrendered to sleep first, soon after she had licked Megan to another orgasm. The fourth? The fifth? The last thing she remembered before the blackness overcame her was Megan holding onto her tightly.

When Vanessa next opened her eyes, the room was dark. There were a few seconds of disorientation while her mind tried to make sense of the different feel of the bed she was lying in, the different sounds of the room, the weight of a body next to hers.

Where am I?

And then she remembered and smiled with contentment. Her and Megan had had a fun night.

She took a look at the clock on the nightstand. Would she ever be able to look at that clock again and *not* get wet? It said *3:57 a.m.*

Vanessa turned her head to her left and was able to make out Megan's sleeping form next to her in the darkness. She was laying on her side, her back to Vanessa.

Vanessa smiled and moved herself so she was pressed against Megan, putting her right arm over her. In her sleep, Megan reached for Vanessa's hand and held it and then resumed softly snoring. Vanessa clung a little tighter. Then she closed her eyes again and was back asleep in a couple of minutes.

When Vanessa woke next it was because the alarm on her phone was ringing. A pleasant yellow California daylight was beginning to shine through the blinds. 6 a.m.

After silencing the alarm, she realized she was alone in the bed but she smelled coffee and figured Megan was in the kitchen.

After peeing and using some mouthwash, Vanessa spotted her Coach bag on the floor near the closet. She didn't recall bringing it upstairs last night and so figured Megan must have. It was a simple and thoughtful gesture and it made Vanessa smile.

Retrieving the clothes from the bag, she dressed quickly. She wanted to reach La Vida Mocha no later than 6:45 in order to have plenty of time to open.

God, I wish I didn't have to open today!

Suddenly, she froze as she brushed her hair in front of the full-length mirror in Megan's bedroom.

Just a week ago, Vanessa would have given her right arm for the chance to once again open La Vida Mocha on a Sunday. Now, she almost wished the stricter pandemic rules were still in effect.

Have I missed regular sex that much?

That was part of it, she knew. But she also knew that it was who she was having regular sex with.

She shook her head.

Nope! Not going there!

Turns out Megan wasn't downstairs. As Vanessa was about to descend the steps, a voice called out from one of the other upstairs rooms.

"Hey!"

Vanessa looked up and saw Megan sitting on a loveseat in a room two doors down from her bedroom, a steaming mug of coffee on a small table in front of her. She was dressed in a pair of pajama shorts and a tank top. Vanessa went to join her.

"You're an early riser," she said, leaning over to give Megan a kiss before dropping down on the seat next to her. Megan put down her Kindle and scooched closer to Vanessa.

"Oh my God, I know, right? I can't help it! Even on the weekends I still get up at the ass-crack." She snuggled Vanessa's neck, and it felt so good Vanessa could already tell she was going to need every iota of willpower during the next twenty minutes or so.

When Megan's hand slid up from Vanessa's waist and encountered Vanessa's bra under the fabric of her shirt, she pulled away, a confused look on her face.

"Wow, you're *dressed* dressed," Megan said. "What time do you need to be there?"

"No later than quarter to seven."

Megan pouted. Vanessa had to bite her cheek to keep from laughing, it was so adorable.

"Sweetie, I have to take advantage of this weekend trade while I can during this reopening. Before the pandemic, La Vida Mocha was open on Sundays, but back then I had two other girls working for me and I could take a Saturday or Sunday off. Now, it's just Chloë and me."

"Can't you hire more people?" Megan asked, resuming her snuggling, her breath finding its way down Vanessa's shirt to caress her cleavage.

Yep, willpower will definitely be tested.

"Hopefully," she said, stroking the back of Megan's head. "I need to see first if this reopening lasts. Right now, it's just me and Chloë, but that can't go on long because we'll drop dead from exhaustion. But, if business picks up again during this next week, I'll see about bringing someone else on."

Even—heaven help me—Mom.

She pulled away because somehow—Vanessa hadn't even been aware of it—Megan's hand had found its way under Vanessa shirt...

How the hell did she do that?!

...and Megan had started running her thumb over Vanessa's nipple through her bra. Vanessa couldn't stop the groan which escaped her lips as her nipple hardened.

"It's a ten-minute drive and it's not even six-twenty," Megan pleaded.

Vanessa summoned reserves of self-control she wasn't aware she had and gently grasped Megan's wrist, pulling the younger woman's hand from her breast. This time, Megan groaned.

"I know it's only six-twenty but I still have to stop somewhere and pick up breakfast."

But Megan pounced. Suddenly, Vanessa was pinned against the arm of her loveseat, just as Megan had pinned her downstairs on the couch the first night they'd had sex. It was déjà vu. Vanessa's heartrate picked up.

"Quick, what do you eat for breakfast?" Megan demanded.

"Yogurt and some fruit, usually," Vanessa whispered, unable to tear her gaze from Megan's lips.

Megan rolled her eyes.

"Oh, my God! And you call yourself Californian? Don't you realize by now that *every* woman in this state has those two things in their fridge?"

Megan got up off Vanessa and the loveseat.

"Come on," Megan said, holding out her hand, evidently meaning Vanessa to take it to help herself up.

Vanessa took Megan's hand and the two of them left the room and headed towards the stairs. As she walked, Vanessa was surprised at how damp her panties were. And her and Megan hadn't even really done anything just now! But that brief fondle of her breast which Megan had done combined with Megan topping her on the loveseat had been enough. She sighed. Apparently, she was going to have to resign herself to being wet all the time whenever Megan was around. And if Megan kept showing up at the shop for brief make out sessions, Vanessa knew she was going to also have to start keeping spare—meaning dry—underwear available in La Vida Mocha to change into.

The aroma of coffee was strongest in the kitchen.

"Fuck, I need some of that," Vanessa said.

Megan gave her a peck on the cheek. "I'll get you a travel mug. Why don't you raid my fridge? I have, like, twelve different flavors of Chobani in there as well as some diced fruit. Take what you want. I'll get you a bag for it."

"Are you sure?"

Megan *tsked*.

"I'm not sending you off to buy breakfast who knows where. By the way, I feel a little self-conscious giving you some of my coffee," Megan said, pouring from the coffeemaker's carafe into a travel mug. "I mean, you're a coffee expert but all I have are some ground beans from Whole Foods that I bought because they smelled good and were two bucks cheaper than some other beans that I also thought smelled good. I didn't even really measure them when I put them in the machine this morning. By the way, how do you take it?"

"If you have Splenda, two, please; if not, sugar will be fine. And when I'm in a rush, I'll even drink coffee from a gas station." Vanessa took two Chobanis and a small container of diced mixed fruit from the refrigerator.

Megan provided a small canvas tote for Vanessa to carry the food in, and then handed over the coffee.

"Two Splendas."

Vanessa arched an eyebrow.

"I should give you a job," she said with a smile. Then, before she could stop herself, added, "Hey, why don't you come by the shop today?"

Megan looked at her for a moment.

"You sure? Doesn't it violate rule number two?"

Vanessa smiled.

"As long as we don't share a meal, it's allowed. You could draw," Vanessa suggested.

Plus, I can just look at you!

"Deal," Megan said. "Now, go before I drag you upstairs and tie you to the bed."

Vanessa bit her bottom lip.

"Save that thought for another time," she said. "Please."

***

Pulling into the parking lot behind La Vida Mocha, Vanessa spotted Chloë's blue PT Cruiser already parked.

Inside, Chloë—bless her—had the coffeeshop well on the way to being open-ready.

"You're an angel!" Vanessa greeted her.

"Pastries just got dropped off," Chloë returned. "I was surprised I beat you here today. What kept you?"

Vanessa hesitated. After the conversation she and Chloë had had a few days ago, when Chloë admitted to having wanted Megan for herself at the engagement party, the last thing Vanessa wanted to do was reveal that the reason she was a little late today was because she had spent last night fucking that very same Megan and getting fucked senseless by her in return. And she *certainly* wasn't going to tell Chloë the story of the clock and the five-minute penalties from her and Megan's first time together, a story which ends with Vanessa having been given the most intense, soul-shattering orgasm of her life, by a woman closer to Chloë's age than her own.

"Didn't you see that chick Megan last night?" Chloë prodded.

"Um…yeah, I did. I went over to her place." A thought suddenly popped into Vanessa's head. "Um…she said she might come by here later today, by the way."

And please don't be all awkward about it.

Chloë looked up from arranging blueberry muffins on a plate in the pastry display counter.

"Cool," she said. "I'm assuming she's VIP, right; just so I know in case you're busy?"

Vanessa smiled.

"No, actually. She wants to keeps paying for her coffees."

Usually with cash, but sometimes by making me come.

Vanessa blew out a breath. No need to be thinking about *that* right now when there is so much to do. Besides, she was wet enough.

Chloë scoffed.

"What is the point of having a girlfriend who owns a coffeeshop if you don't get free coffee?" she asked, continuing to place muffins. She looked up again. "Oh, wait…are you guys not yet at the girlfriend-label stage?"

Vanessa was wiping down the espresso machine after spraying its top with some cleanser.

"We won't be getting to the girlfriend-label stage," she answered. "Megan and I are just having a little fling."

Chloë scoffed again. "Okay, fine, I get that. But still, a fuck-buddy with a coffeeshop means free coffee," she stated, as if it was a fact on par with *the Earth is round.*

Vanessa said, "I think it's kind of sweet. She knows how bad business has been during this Covid thing and she doesn't want to take advantage."

Chloë appeared to consider that for a moment.

"Yeah, I guess that is kinda cool of her." She paused for a moment, and stole a glance at Vanessa. "Can I ask you something?"

"Of course," Vanessa said, placing the dishrag she had used in the laundry bag just inside the entrance to the back room.

Chloë wouldn't look at her. Instead, she busied herself with pretending to inspect her fingernails.

"How come you and I never…you know."

What the fuck?

"Um…because it would have been a felony when I first met you?" Vanessa declared.

Chloë gave an exasperated *Ugh* sound.

"No shit," she said. "But I've obviously grown up."

Vanessa couldn't deny that. When she had met Chloë, to help her rebuild leg strength following a mountain biking accident, the then teenager had been this tomboyish waif of a girl with a taste for the grunge fashions of the nineties. Now, at twenty-three, Chloë had left her tomboy phase well behind and developed into this strikingly feminine woman whose most distinctive feature was her platinum-dyed pixie hairstyle and who virtually always wore really cute dresses that showed off fabulously long legs.

Swallowing, Vanessa asked, "What's this about?" She was almost afraid to hear the answer.

Chloë took a moment.

"Well, other than my recent brief interest in that chick Megan, primarily because she's fucking hot…" Chloë looked up at Vanessa then, an expression of horror on her face. "Shit! Sorry!"

Vanessa laughed. "Don't worry about it."

"Well, other than that," Chloë continued, "I'm kind of thinking I'm into older women."

"Oh."

"Not like grandma old, but your level of old."

"Great," Vanessa muttered under her breath.

"But every time I get a chance to flirt with a woman in her thirties or forties, it's like they're flattered but it's also like, 'Go away, kid,' you know? So, I'm kind of wondering, with you being an older woman, why you and I never…"

Vanessa took a few seconds to compose her thoughts. This wasn't how she expected her day at work to start.

"Look, sweetie, by the time you turned eighteen I already thought of you as a little sister. Even when we were all in Vegas for your twenty-first, you were still that sixteen-year-old kid with a busted knee in my mind." She reached out and touched Chloë's hand. "The timing just wasn't right for anything to develop between us."

"But it might have?" Chloë asked, hopefully.

This is too weird!

"I don't know. Maybe? If we had met at a bar or something one night? Who knows?"

Seriously? Would I have?

She decided to get hers and Chloë's mind off that particular track.

"What you gotta understand is that women my age are typically a bit more careful when it comes to getting involved with younger women. At least I am." She cringed inwardly at the use of the phrase, *women my age*.

"*Buuuut* you're with Megan, and she's practically my age."

Shit, good point!

Vanessa sighed.

"True," she conceded. "But Megan and I aren't going anywhere, trust me. Maybe if there was a chance that her and I could, I would question the wisdom of getting involved with someone as young as her."

Jesus, what was she on about? She had no idea why she was saying what she was saying because she knew damn well that if there was a possibility of having a normal *girlfriend-label* relationship with Megan she would take it, despite the age difference. She had known that the first time she had laid eyes on Megan. And it was especially true now knowing how good their sexual chemistry was.

She wasn't going to tell Chloë what else she was thinking. That Chloë's problem pulling these older women might have to do with the fact that Chloë kind of presented herself as a direction-less party girl who was perfectly content being an assistant manager at a coffeeshop, a professional dog-walker or a whatever-the-hell-she-was at an Amazon warehouse. Megan, on the other hand, had a white-collar job, certainly a 401k, owned a condo and her car wasn't a hand-me-down from her parents. In other words, Megan at twenty-six was doing some higher-level adulting than Chloë at twenty-three was.

But Vanessa didn't want to tell Chloë all that. It was bad enough they were in the middle of a conversation brought about because Vanessa was apparently now the ambassador for all older women on planet Earth. Let LeeAnne, Chloë's mother deal with the mom-type stuff.

"Just be careful, okay?" she said, putting her hand over Chloë's again. "A lot of women my age might only look at a twenty-three-year-old as a temporary plaything. I don't want to see you getting hurt. Now, can we please stop talking about how old I am and why you and I never hooked up?"

Chapter 20

Megan spent the morning in the same shorts and tank that she'd had on when Vanessa left. She did some housework, continued work on her graphite drawing and then made herself scrambled eggs for lunch, which she accompanied with a pear. At one o'clock she decided to head to La Vida Mocha.

She opted for wearing a cute sundress and equally cute ballet flats that were awesomely comfortable. The thought did cross her mind that she was more dressed up than usual for a trip out to a coffeeshop. Normally, shorts or yoga pants with a simple tee or cami top was more her speed for such an outing, but today she just felt like she wanted to look special.

When she stepped into La Vida Mocha, carrying her leather messenger satchel, she instantly felt nervous. Abby's friend, Chloë, was working the counter wearing a polka-dot mask, helping two teenage girls. Vanessa was nowhere to be seen.

Should have texted to tell her I was coming!

Megan didn't know if what Abby had told her was true, that Chloë had been "crushing" on her at the engagement party, but if it *was* true, Megan didn't know what to do if Chloë started flirting with her. But Chloë was one of Vanessa's good friends, right? So presumably, Chloë knew Vanessa was involved with Megan. But what if Chloë was the type of girl who didn't care about such boundaries and flirted with her anyway?

Seriously, I should've texted!

Megan considered retreating to an open corner table she saw until Vanessa made an appearance, but Chloë had already spotted her, apparently recognizing Megan despite Megan's mask and tilting her head up in a nod of greeting before continuing to help the two young women. So, Megan blew out a breath and approached the counter just as the teenagers stepped away with their drinks.

"Hey," Chloë greeted her. The smile that was hidden behind her mask reached her eyes.

"Hey," Megan replied. "It's nice to see you again."

"You too. It's good to be back here; I wasn't digging the warehouse work."

Right. Abby had mentioned something about Chloë working in a warehouse. Was it for Amazon, or Walmart, or…?

"Yeah, bills suck," Megan said instead.

"Vanessa is in the back, by the way, just doing some paperwork. She should be out in a sec."

"Oh, sure…whenever," Megan said in what she hoped was a nonchalant manner. "I'm just here to chill out and do some drawing anyway."

"No way, you're an artist?" Chloë asked excitedly. "That is so cool! Can I sit with you later to see your stuff?"

That didn't seem flirty. "Of course! I'd like that," Megan answered.

"Awesome! Anyway, what can I get you?"

"Large Americano, please. Iced."

"Sure," Chloë said, tapping the POS screen. Megan tried to remember her crash course from a few days ago.

Let's see…an Americano would be: Tap Espresso Drinks, tap Americano, tap Large, tap Iced. Ignore the add-ons menu, ask if there was anything else the customer wanted…

"Anything else?" Chloë asked.

Yay!

"Um…yeah. I wouldn't mind a white chocolate chip cookie, please."

Tap Food, tap Cookies, tap White Choc Chip, tap Add to Order.

"Awesome," Chloë said. Then, "By the way, the boss says you want to keep paying for your coffee?"

Megan nodded, already opening her bag to get her wallet.

"Absolutely! This is, like, the worst time ever to be accepting freebies from a small business. I wouldn't be able to sleep at night."

"Pretty cool," Chloë responded, and Megan thought she could detect just the slightest hint of respect in her voice.

Megan paid with a ten and told Chloë to keep the change. The Americano and cookie were handed over quickly. One of the reasons Megan liked Americanos was because they were so easy to make. Even if a coffeeshop was super busy, Megan's order was often ready and given to her before the orders of customers who had been waiting longer.

"Come by my table when you get a break," Megan invited Chloë.

"Cool, I will," Chloë said, the smile again reaching her eyes.

Ten minutes later, Megan was sitting at her table, eyes focused on her iPad as she used her Apple Pencil to add some fine details to the picture she was drawing when an odd tingling came over her suddenly which raised goosebumps on her arms.

Vanessa.

Looking up, she saw she was right. Vanessa was just emerging from the back room.

Megan's mouth dropped open.

How did that happen?

But there was no time to analyze it because Vanessa had already spotted Megan. She gave a little wave and then said a few words to Chloë before coming from behind the counter to approach Megan's table.

Megan stood up to hug her.

"You're here!" Vanessa said, squeezing Megan tight. "And you look super-cute! I love this dress! I might borrow it."

Megan almost laughed at the idea of Vanessa trying to fit her much larger boobs into the bust of this dress.

Vanessa continued. "Sorry, I was back there doing business owner stuff on my laptop since we had a lull."

"No worries. It looks like things are going great, though," Megan said, glancing around the shop.

"We got slammed this morning, and then lunchtime was wicked also, but that's a good sign. Fingers crossed it will keep up. Let's sit so I can take off this damn mask."

Megan couldn't help notice that as soon as Vanessa removed her mask, she pinched the bridge of her nose and let out a small groan.

"Is everything okay?" Megan asked.

Vanessa rewarded her with a small smile.

"It's good, I'm just tired. Actually, that reminds me." She took a breath before continuing. "So…I want to see you tonight."

Megan smiled and reached for Vanessa's hand.

"I want to see you too," she said, stroking the top of Vanessa's hand with her thumb, forcing herself to ignore the question now nagging her in her head of whether such a gesture of intimacy was allowed. Vanessa didn't seem bothered by it, though…

"But I really need to just go home, veg out and then crash early," Vanessa declared.

"Oh." Megan knew her disappointment was evident on her face and she mentally kicked herself for being so obvious. It went against the rules of a fling, after all.

"I know," Vanessa began, making Megan feel worse. "And I hate to sound like I'm seventy-years-old but I just can't do these super-late nights anymore when I've got to open this shop the next day. And I wouldn't be much company anyway."

"Totally understand!" Megan said, hoping she sounded like someone who understood. So Vanessa couldn't see her tonight, no big deal. They definitely had stayed up late last night doing wonderful things to each other. Of course Vanessa is tired. Probably exhausted. No big deal.

So why did it feel like one?

Don't go there! Don't go there! Don't go there!

"Are you sure?" Vanessa asked. "I'm worried I'm disappointing you."

Megan opened her mouth, closed it again, opened it once more and then frowned.

"Am I allowed to be disappointed?" she finally asked.

Vanessa blinked.

"What do you mean?"

Megan blushed, feeling foolish. She covered her face with her hands.

"I don't know!" she whined. She put her hands down and looked at Vanessa. "Does it violate the rules of our casual fling to be disappointed I won't see you on any given night? Or does my feeling disappointed make you feel like I'm getting too attached? I don't know!"

Vanessa laughed. This time, she reached for Megan's hand and Megan's heart did a little flutter.

"No rules have been broken. You're not acting like a bitch about it which *would* break the rules. Besides, I like that you're disappointed," Vanessa added. "Actually, all of this is my fault." A sly smile appeared on her lips, and she leaned forward, closer to Megan's head. "I should have obeyed you faster last night. Then perhaps I could have gotten more sleep. But I was having so much fun being disobedient."

Megan's insides reacted to that and she gasped.

"That's not fair!" she said, eyes wide.

Vanessa leaned back, a smirk on her face.

"Too bad you won't be able to do anything about it tonight, though," she said. She leaned forward again and picked up Megan's iPad Pro. "So, you can actually draw on this thing?"

It took a while for Megan to be able to respond because her center was now controlling her mind. Eventually, she became aware of Vanessa waving a hand in front of her face.

"Earth to Megan," Vanessa was saying.

Megan shook her head.

"Um…what?" she stammered. And why was Vanessa holding her iPad?

Vanessa was laughing.

"I asked if you could show me how you draw on this thing."

"Oh! Um…yeah. Here, let me show you," Megan said, taking the device back and unlocking it, grateful to be distracted from what was happening between her legs. She angled the screen so Vanessa could see it.

Before Vanessa had joined her, Megan had been continuing work on a portrait she had been laboring on for the past couple of months.

"Get out of here!" Vanessa exclaimed. "This is incredible!"

Megan felt herself blushing.

"Thanks. That's my friend Carina."

"She's beautiful," Vanessa said, giving Megan a pointed look that Megan wanted to believe was jealousy. But it couldn't be. Could it?

Megan laughed. "Very beautiful, but very straight."

Vanessa looked around the shop. "It's slow. Come with me!" she said, rising, taking Megan's hand.

"What about my stuff?" Megan asked.

Vanessa approached a cute young woman sitting alone at a table not far from Megan's.

"Amy, do you mind watching her stuff for about a minute?"

"Sure, no problem," Amy said with a smile that was more than polite.

Vanessa then called out to Chloë, saying she'd be back in two seconds and the next thing Megan knew, she was being escorted out of La Vida Mocha.

"Where are we going?" she asked when they were outside. "And who's Amy?"

Fuck! Why did I ask that?

Vanessa turned to her, stopping.

"Ooh, jealous little thing, aren't you?"

Megan got nervous. The truth was, she actually *had* felt a little jealous. It was stupid, she knew, and *totally* against the rules. But, dammit, Amy was pretty and Vanessa obviously knew her...

"No," Megan answered, somewhat defensively.

Vanessa laughed and took hold of Megan's hips.

"Maybe I like it," she said, holding Megan's eyes with her own.

Megan forgot how to breathe for a moment. She had to lick her lips before being able to speak.

"Jealousy doesn't sound like it would be one of the rules," she whispered.

Vanessa shrugged.

"Until you leave for New York, I'm not going to mind if you keep reminding me who I belong to," she said. She pulled Megan a little closer, and her eyes darkened. Her voice became husky when she then said, "Seriously, when we're in bed, keep telling me who I belong to."

Megan gulped. There were evidently layers of Vanessa that she hadn't even begun to reveal.

"You are being so unfair!" she whined.

But Vanessa just laughed and released her.

"I know, but trust me, you wouldn't want me tonight anyway. The first time I have a chance to get horizontal I will pass the fuck out. Imagine if I did that with your head between my legs. Anyway, Amy is a regular, that's all. But forget about her. This is what I wanted to show you."

Megan looked around. They hadn't gone more than ten steps from La Vida Mocha's door. What was she supposed to be looking at?

"What?" she asked, and when Vanessa pointed, said, "This?"

This was the empty storefront right next to La Vida Mocha, where, pre-pandemic, an art gallery had been. Now, of course, the display windows were empty, save for a "For Lease" sign. Through the windows, she could see the equally barren space inside, littered with a couple of empty moving boxes. Megan had never visited the gallery when it was still around. That was due solely to the fact that the gallery sold nothing but tacky beach scene paintings, some of them done on velvet. Velvet! Megan had always thought it less an art gallery and more of a souvenir shop catering to the lowest common denominator of the tourist crowd.

"This would be an awesome spot for your art gallery," Vanessa said, peering through the dusty window.

Megan scoffed.

"Art gallery?" What was this woman talking about? "Did you forget I'm moving to New York?"

Vanessa smiled.

"I know, I know; I'm just kidding. But do you remember what was here before? Those fucking velvet paintings? It would be nice if a real artist like you had this space."

Megan glowed at the compliment.

"With my luck," Vanessa continued, "they'll open a Jehovah's Witness Kingdom Hall or the regional headquarters of the RNC in this space."

Megan shuddered.

"I don't know which would be worse," she said. She stared at the empty storefront. This *would* be an awesome spot for a gallery of her own. Downtown. Within walking distance of the beach. Next door to a coffeeshop. A coffeeshop owned by the sexiest barista in San Diego Country. A sexy barista who thought Megan was a super talented artist.

Megan turned Vanessa to face her and then took Vanessa's chin in her hand and moved in for a deep kiss. She didn't care that they were out in public. Her tongue ran along Vanessa's lip, demanding entrance, and Vanessa obliged, surrendering her tongue to dance with Megan's.

"You're freaking awesome," Megan murmured, when she pulled away. "Are you sure there isn't—Oh my God!" she yelped, jumping away from Vanessa. When Vanessa turned to see what Megan was staring at, she yelped too.

That old lady had materialized again, same purse clutched in her tiny hands, same Mister Magoo glasses, same serene smile on her thin lips.

"Hello, dears," she said.

"Jesus, you're like a genie!" Megan exclaimed, her hand over her heart, trying to calm down from being startled like that.

"Are you thinking of leasing this space also?" the old woman asked Vanessa.

"No, ma'am." Vanessa answered. She nodded towards Megan. "I wish she was able to, though. She's an artist and I think this would make a great gallery for her."

"Oh, what a wonderful idea!" the lady said. "It would be so nice to have another art gallery in town! You should do it!"

Megan blushed.

"Unfortunately, I'm moving to New York."

The old lady frowned.

"That's hardly a reason not to do it nowadays. Here's what you do: You hire someone local you trust to man the place while you run the entire thing remotely from New York. The secret, I've learned, is to have a good VPN. You know, for all the encryption security."

Megan's mouth dropped open. She didn't know which surprised her more: that this elderly lady knew what a VPN was, or that she had accurately described the advantages of using it. She shared a look with Vanessa who was apparently only just keeping her laughter in check.

"Anyway, dear, you think about it," the lady told Megan before turning to Vanessa and looping her arm around hers. She started leading Vanessa back to La Vida Mocha. "Now that that's settled," she said as they walked, "I find myself in the mood for one of your iced coffees, please; but this time, I am going to go a little wild. I'd like you to add a shot of vanilla to it!"

Megan, trying not to laugh, gave Vanessa a little shrug when Vanessa turned back to look at her as she was being led away.

Chapter 21

Vanessa was so tired, her eyes hurt.

As soon as she stepped through the front door of her house at a little after six p.m., she dropped her bag on the floor, toed off her shoes, went straight to her living room and fell face first on her overstuffed couch, her feet hanging off the edge of one of the couch's arms.

"Oh my God, this feels so fucking good!" she said into the cushion her face was currently half-buried in. She had no intention of moving. Sure, she needed a shower, she should probably have dinner and, if she was honest with herself, despite being in excellent shape, if she laid here like this for more than ten minutes her thirty-five-year-old back would make her regret it. But she didn't care. Right now, this was feeling so good she wanted to stay here until morning.

Naturally, her back pocket started ringing and vibrating.

"Aargh!" she moaned, reaching behind her and extracting her iPhone from her jeans pocket. She had no intention of answering the call, whoever it was. All she wanted to do was set the phone to silent. Even if it was Megan calling, Vanessa would just text her later. But it was William's name on the screen, and she and William had a ride-or-die pact, something Vanessa took very seriously because they were both gay people in a still rather homophobic world.

"Are you being chased by Republicans?" Vanessa groaned by way of greeting.

"Not today, so far," William answered. "Wait, is *she* there? I'm not interrupting whatever it is girls do to pleasure each other, am I?"

"No, she is not here."

"What? Why not? First rule of new relationships, honey: the first six months are just one long sex-fest."

"I'm not in a relationship, for the millionth time. And Megan and I had a sex-fest last night, that's why I'm exhausted today, and that's why she's not here."

"So? She could still hang out with you. She could give you a foot rub or wash your hair or just let you fall asleep on her lap while watching Netflix."

"Sweetie, her and I are just about the sex, remember? And even if she was my girlfriend, in the sapphic universe it's a little too early for the 'come hang-out with me while I completely ignore you and try to sleep' phase."

"Why does your voice sound so funny?"

"Because my face is half-buried in a sofa cushion and I'm too tired to move it."

William huffed. "Okay, fine. I can tell you're not going to be any fun today."

"Then I will respectfully request that you let me pass out in blissful slumber. But call me if Republicans start chasing you. Love you. Bye."

And Vanessa hung up. She sighed. Passing out in blissful slumber sounded heavenly, and it was so tempting to continue laying where she was, but she knew it was borderline irresponsible. If she fell asleep now, there was a risk she'd wake up in a couple of hours, unable to then fall back to sleep later and get the good night's rest she desperately needed.

Groaning, she reluctantly pushed herself up to a sitting position and rubbed her eyes. She made up her mind to shower, eat a light dinner and then get to bed by nine o'clock. If she did that, she'd be able to wake up tomorrow, go for her morning jog—something she missed doing this morning after waking up at Megan's—and open the shop on time.

Half an hour later, Vanessa came out of the master bedroom, hair still damp from her shower, and wearing a favorite pair of old soccer shorts and a blue tank. Returning to the couch, she then started applying lotion to her legs, starting at her thighs and working it down onto her feet as well. She briefly wondered if Megan would enjoy getting a pedicure with her one day if the nail salons reopened soon. A simple act of pampering like that, Vanessa thought, would feel wonderful.

She suddenly stopped applying lotion and just sat there, considering.

Getting a pedicure with Megan sounded fun.

Doing a lot of everyday kind of things with Megan sounded fun. Shopping. Hanging out at the beach. Even just sitting here at home watching movies. Because the truth was, Vanessa was realizing, she enjoyed simply being with Megan. Turns out, they had a chemistry that extended beyond sex and throughout any given day over the past week, Vanessa had found herself daydreaming about a different kind of relationship with Megan. One that could include pedicures, shopping, hanging out at the beach or bingeing Netflix. And when she found herself daydreaming like that, Vanessa would force herself to stop, and that's what she did now.

Shaking her head in order to force out ridiculous fantasies of a relationship that could never be, Vanessa finished applying lotion to her legs and then considered her next move.

She still felt exhausted but the shower had at least energized her enough to consider eating. On bare feet, she headed into her kitchen, grabbed some leftover pasta salad from the fridge, poured a glass of white wine and returned to the couch.

As she ate, she used her phone to scroll through La Vida Mocha's social media accounts, gratified to see that customers were posting pictures and tagging the shop on the Big Three: Facebook, Twitter and Instagram. Amy had even posted a selfie on IG, holding her cappuccino.

Soooooooooooo glad my favorite coffeeshop is open again on Sundays! I've missed this awesome place!!!! #lavidamocha #lesbianownedbusiness #coffeeaddict #supportlocalbusiness

Smiling, Vanessa liked the post and tapped out a reply.

@amycoffeeaddict So great to see your gorgeous self again! We've missed you too. Can't wait to see more of you!

She read a few more posts and then decided to get down to the business of unwinding. She put the phone down but within reach on the coffee table, fluffed up one of the colorful throw cushions on the sofa and laid her head down on it, drawing her legs up to her chest as she turned on the TV.

She decided to watch *World War Z*. She'd lost count of how many times she'd seen it, but at times like this, when her mind just wasn't capable of following the characters and plot of a new movie, old favorites like this Brad Pitt zombie flick were what Vanessa turned to.

As she settled in to watch the film, she couldn't help but think of things at La Vida Mocha. She knew that her and Chloë couldn't keep going like this. And she also knew that it was too risky to stagger their shift times too drastically, say, with Vanessa opening and Chloë coming three hours later or so, and then Vanessa leaving a couple of hours before closing time. One person couldn't man La Vida Mocha for an extended period, not when the general population was eager to get out of their houses and resume their normal pastimes, like visiting coffeeshops. Besides, there were safety issues with having only one person in the shop. During the lockdown, when she had been in the shop all by herself all day, Vanessa always had pepper spray on her person and a stun gun under the counter. But she had never felt threatened. Customers had been few and far between then, with only the occasional rush of people.

So, she definitely needed to bring at least one more person on; but despite what she had told Megan this morning, about possibly hiring more staff as early as next week, Vanessa was now thinking it would be more realistic to wait awhile before deciding to bring someone else on. What was the point of hiring Luli back or training a new person if California went into lockdown-mode again sometime next week or even the week after?

Of course, there was her mother and her disturbing offer to come work at the shop. The only—only!—advantage Vanessa saw in that option was that her mother would work for free.

Well, not exactly free...

Vanessa knew her mother would expect to be repaid in time spent with Vanessa doing all sorts of mother-daughter bonding. And, of course, her mother would expect to stay at Vanessa's house. Vanessa loved her mother endlessly, but having that woman around all day at the shop *and* all night at home? Vanessa would rather kiss a man.

Besides, the last thing she needed was a clingy parent around when she had an eager and oh-so-skilled lover named Megan that she had limited time with.

The thought of Megan made Vanessa reach for her phone. She knew she probably shouldn't, but it was almost a compulsion. She sent a text to Megan.

Hey!

Hey back! I figured you'd be passed out by now!

Trust me I want to but trying to stay up until a more bedtime-y time

OMG, I love that phrase "bedtime-y!" Totally stealing it! So, what are you doing?

Watching world war z for millionth time

My zombie is watching zombies. How perfect!

ur silly but I like it
Tell me something new I don't know about you

Why was she doing this? What was the point?

Like?

What were you like as a kid?

Like, little kid? You won't believe it, but I was something of a tomboy! I even played Little League!

Vanessa's eyebrows raised.

Ur right I don't believe you

It's true! You should be proud to know that you are texting the girl who hit the game-winning double in the season finale, earning the La Jolla Sharks the district trophy.

Still don't believe u. I want video evidence.

Bite me! I'll get it too! What about you?

I was a TOTAL girly-girl as a kid! Played with dolls and everything! I didn't start getting all athletic until middle school.

Okay, my turn…Name of first girl you kissed? I mean, REALLY kissed.

Grinning, Vanessa typed the name *Shobana Sadachapakam*, and then laughed out loud when Megan wrote back:

Holy fuck! That's a mouthful! I expected a name like "Julie" or "Natalie."

Nope. Shobana. Gorgeous north Indian girl I went to high school with. Totally into each other. You?

Julie! Followed by Natalie.

Laughing, Vanessa sent:

I wish I wasn't so tired. I really wanted to see you tonight.

I know. Me too. But you need rest. Can we see each other tomorrow, or will that also be an exhausting day? (I'm totally OK if that's the case.)

I want to see you tomorrow for sure! Do you want to come over? I'll cook for you.

Cook?

As in order Chinese food.

Sweet! I can't wait!!!

***

Vanessa awoke the next morning still on the couch, her cell phone's alarm ringing. She didn't even remember falling asleep.

Thank goodness she had splurged for a decent couch because the occasional times she did sleep on it, she always slept like a log, and last night was no different. She felt completely refreshed, even energized enough for a morning jog.

Fifteen minutes later, as she was out running, she realized how good the jog felt, how normal it felt. The act of running after such a good night's rest was allowing her to think and make some big decisions, and when she arrived at La Vida Mocha later, she was glad to see that Chloë was just arriving also, stepping out of her PT Cruiser as Vanessa pulled into the spot next to her.

"Hey," Vanessa greeted her. "Have a good night?"

Chloë shrugged. "Eh, it was a swipe left kind of night."

Vanessa unlocked the back door of La Vida Mocha. She gave a visible shudder.

"God, I don't know how you can put up with online dating!" she said, holding the door open for the younger woman. "And how do you even do online dating during a pandemic! Are you being careful?"

Chloë smiled. "Relax. I don't know about anybody else, but I just go on the app now to see who's checking me out and maybe do some flirting. I have zero plans to actually hook up with anyone during this mess, unless I get to know them first."

"Good!"

Inside, Chloë set her backpack down on the small table in the back room.

"Before you get started, we need to talk," Vanessa said. She indicated that Chloë should sit and when Chloë did so, Vanessa took the chair opposite her.

"What's up?" Chloë asked.

"I've decided to change our operating hours, and I need to go over them with you," Vanessa started. "But I need this to be a *conversation*, Chloë, not just you listening and agreeing, okay? Because it affects you."

"Okay."

"Also, this change is just temporary; just until I feel like this reopening phase is going to stick. And if I do feel that's the case, then you and I together will work on finding at least one other person to work here, maybe two, and we'll go back to our usual operating hours."

"Okay," Chloë said again.

"Plan A is this: Monday through Thursday, we'll close at ten. That's ten a.m." Vanessa held up a hand when Chloë's eyes widened to keep her silent for now. "Friday and Saturday, we won't open until noon and we'll stay open until eight."

"What about Sunday?"

Vanessa took a breath. She had wrangled mentally with this last one quite a bit during her jog earlier.

"Sunday we're closed," she said.

Chloë raised her eyebrows again but this time added a whistle.

"I know, I know," Vanessa went on, "but we need a day off, Chloë. I love that you're willing to work practically around the clock here but you just can't. Anyway, I did the math at home, and these new hours will add up to an even forty for you, plus tips. The only problem is, it means you working six days a week."

Chloë nodded. "Yeah, but it's not like six *full* days. Fridays and Saturdays would be the only long ones." She chewed her bottom lip for a moment. "You said this is Plan A. What's Plan B?"

"Plan B is you only work five days a week, but we close on Sundays and Mondays."

"No!" Chloë said, and the force of the statement surprised Vanessa. "I won't let the shop be closed two days. I know you said this was only temporary but I'm worried we'll lose too much money by being closed like that."

Vanessa felt her heart warm. From the beginning, even before La Vida Mocha's grand opening, she had noticed how enthusiastic, committed to and even protective her friend was about the place, traits which only seemed to intensify once the shop was open for business. What's more, it had been Chloë, not Luli, who had shown a genuine interest in learning about the business of running a coffeeshop, asking Vanessa tons of questions about even the most mundane aspects of the operation.

Vanessa reached across the table and took Chloë's hands in her own.

"Sweetie, I need you to be sure, and be honest," she said, making eye contact with Chloë.

"I am being honest," Chloë insisted. "I honestly don't mind coming in six days temporarily, especially when most of those days are half-days. I just want the shop to be okay."

Vanessa felt a lump in her throat and she took a deep breath to hold some tears at bay. She squeezed Chloë's hands.

"Okay. Thank you," she said.

"So, how long were you thinking?"

"I've decided I'm going to wait at least three weeks, then we'll revisit it."

Chloë released Vanessa's hands and then leaned back in her seat, the very picture of casualness.

"*Pfft!* I can do three weeks of this standing on my head."

Vanessa laughed and then leaned forward, resting her arms on the table.

"Hey, listen," she started, "have you ever considered taking any business courses, maybe at the community college?" Vanessa hoped she wasn't sounding parental. She was sure that Chloë probably heard enough about her somewhat unmoored lifestyle from her folks at home.

"I actually have lately," Chloë said, almost as if she was embarrassed by the confession. "Do *you* think it's a good idea?" Chloë asked.

"Sure! You seem interested in learning how this place runs."

Vanessa saw Chloë's lips quirk upwards in a small smile.

"I am interested. I might want to have my own place one day. So, yeah, I guess I can look into it some more."

"You should! Besides, all of those beautiful older women you want to seduce will be impressed."

Chloë blushed.

"Shut up," she said with a smile.

"Anyway, do me a favor," Vanessa said, standing up, back to boss mode. "Use my laptop and print up signs showing our new hours. Make three of them; one for the door, one for the window, and we'll tape the third to the serving counter. While you do that, I'll handle getting the first batch of coffee brewing."

Chapter 22

Megan stared at the text message, confused.

Dinner at 6? it read, from Vanessa.

But La Vida Mocha was open until seven, Megan knew. She decided to have some fun with her reply.

You totally don't have to close La Vida Mocha early just to have dinner with little ol' me!

The reply came thirty seconds later.

LOL! Actually, LVM has been closed since 10. Will explain later. BTW I usually order from Lotus Garden. The menu is online. Tell me what you want and I will order it. Here is my address...

Since 10!
Megan hoped everything was okay at the shop, and all she wanted to do now was fire off text after text to get the scoop, but Vanessa said she'd explain later, aaaand…the tone of her text was breezy and light, suggesting no problems at all. Maybe Vanessa was one of those people who preferred actually talking about certain things rather than wearing out their thumbs texting about them. So, Megan forced herself to be patient. She checked the clock on the wall above her TV. It was just past 3:15.

Post work, Megan had decided to spend some time catching up on some reading, but she had also hoped to drive down to the seawall later and take a long walk before heading back and preparing for her tryst with Vanessa. But that was when she figured she wouldn't be meeting Vanessa until after eight o'clock. But now that the timeline was compressed, she decided to scrap the seawall plans. Instead, she'd just take a walk around her neighborhood, and she'd leave now.

After using her iPad to view Lotus Garden's menu and then texting *Egg foo young with shrimp, pretty please* to Vanessa, she went upstairs to change. Catching sight of herself in the full-length mirror in her bedroom, Megan once again thought it was a shame that her co-workers never got to see her work outfits anymore. Today, she felt she looked particularly cute in the blue pencil skirt and cream-colored blouse with bell sleeves she had chosen. Turning this way and that in front of the mirror, Megan made a mental note to wear this skirt around Vanessa one day. It hugged her in all the right places and Vanessa seemed to have a thing about her legs. It certainly hadn't escaped her notice how much time Vanessa licking, kissing and nibbling them up and down.

Vanessa also seemed to have a thing about her breasts, Megan considered. Anytime they had sex it certainly seemed as if Vanessa couldn't get enough of them. And Vanessa had even called them *perfect* at one point! Megan herself had always been a little self-conscious about her breasts, always wishing they were larger than B-cups. But Vanessa…she certainly didn't seem to mind their size, and quite frankly, Megan didn't know what to make of that.

Don't make anything of it! Just enjoy it for what it is, damn!

Megan sighed. She really had to get past these insecurities of hers. Less than forty-eight hours ago, she had had sex with a heart-stoppingly beautiful woman who was, by all accounts, totally into her. In other words, Megan chastised herself, she had nothing to complain about.

No sooner had she swapped the skirt and blouse for a pair of black leggings and white racerback sport top than Molly called. Megan answered it as she trotted downstairs.

"Hey, Molls."

What was this about now?

"Hey, what are you doing?"

"Leaving my place to go for a walk. Yes, I still believe in gay rights. Yes, I still believe in a woman's right to choose. Yes, I believe Black lives matter. How are things in the seventeenth-century? Have our parents burned any witches lately?" Megan opened the front door, stepped outside, locked the door and began walking along one of the pedestrian paths which meandered through her condo community.

"God, you can just chill?" Molly said.

"Why are you calling? And don't tell me it's because you missed talking to your sister."

She heard Molly clear her throat.

"Um…I actually *am* calling on behalf of Mom," Molly said.

"A-ha!" Megan exulted.

"But it's not what you think!" Molly replied. "I'm calling as her ambassador."

"What are you talking about?

"Your birthday, dum-dum."

Birthday? Oh, shit, that's right…

In all the excitement of the past several days: meeting Vanessa, Carole's funeral, unbelievable sex with Vanessa, dreams about Vanessa, more unbelievable sex with Vanessa, just plain Vanessa, Megan had forgotten all about her impending birthday, which was in…

Fuck! Ten days!

"What about it?" Megan asked.

"Marcano's?" Molly said, as if answering the dumbest question in the world. "Mom wants to know if we're doing it again? Apparently, they're open and Mom wants to make reservations, but she was too afraid to ask you herself because she figures you're still pissed about the lesbians in the park."

"Correction, Molls. *I* had no problem with the lesbians in the park because I'm a decent human being."

Not to mention a lesbian myself.

"What I had a problem with was Mom's reaction to the lesbians in the park."

She heard Molly sigh.

"You know what I meant," her sister said.

"Hmm, I couldn't be sure," Megan replied. "After all, you—"

"Do not call me mini Mom!" Molly ordered.

Megan smiled because that was exactly what she was about to do.

"So, what do I tell her?" Molly prompted. "Yes to Marcano's, or no?"

"Tell her yes. It might be the last time we get to do that for a while. I can't promise that once I move to New York I'll be able to come back each year for my birthday. But since you're playing Miss U.N. Ambassador, tell Mom that if there are any gay people in the restaurant and she makes one comment, I will leave."

***

Later, after showering, Megan, wrapped in a towel, opened her walk-in closet and scrutinized her collection of handbags hung neatly on hooks in one corner.

Even though her plans with Vanessa were for early in the night, Megan figured there was a possibility that she could end up spending the night if she stayed late enough. And there was a very good chance she would stay late enough. Her and Vanessa were like machines in bed, both of them often surprised at how much time had passed when they finally stopped for rest. Megan had never had anything like this before. Sex with Cindy had been good; sex with a lot of Megan's past lovers had been good, but this was next level stuff.

Now, Megan knew she needed a *what if* bag, having had no need for one during the two years she was with Cindy. The selection was crucial. It had to present as just an ordinary handbag but be large enough to accommodate a change of clothes and necessary toiletries, without seeming like Megan had packed a suitcase.

She was actually hoping she would end up spending the night, though. No, scratch that, she *wanted* to spend the night.

Waking up next to Vanessa on Sunday morning had felt wonderful, blissful. And Megan realized that she had actually slept better than she had since her breakup with Cindy. After opening her eyes, she had laid there, staring at Vanessa sleeping. At one point, she had reached out to tuck a loose lock of hair behind Vanessa's ear, happy that she had done so without disturbing her because the sight of Vanessa asleep in her bed was an image Megan had wanted to hold onto.

After a few moments of consideration, Megan settled on a yellow Kate Spade tote she had bought herself *just because* one day and set about filling it with the items she thought she'd need tomorrow morning.

The thought thrilled her but she also knew she had better prepare herself mentally and emotionally to be sent back home tonight. After all, this wasn't a sleepover kind of relationship.

But in an attempt to sway Vanessa the other way, Megan found another pencil skirt in her closet, this one a bit shorter than the one she had worn during work hours today, stopping just above her knees. She paired it with a cute spaghetti strap cami top in black that she couldn't possibly wear a bra with. If Vanessa really like Megan's girls as much as she seemed to, this top should make her think of little else.

In half an hour, she was ready. She texted Vanessa that she was on her way, receiving three smiley-face emojis in return.

Turns out, Vanessa's house was less than a five-minute drive away, on one of the side streets which branched off of Carlsbad Village Drive. Megan had to chuckle at the absurdity of Fate, that even in a small town like Carlsbad, a woman she'd never laid eyes on before but who now made Megan's heart flutter each time she thought of her, lived within walking distance of her condo.

"Oh, this is nice," Megan commented to herself, looking at the single-level ranch-style house with manicured front lawn as she pulled into the driveway. She checked her appearance one last time in the visor mirror, did a quick finger-fluff of her bangs and then deemed herself ready to exit the car.

***

When Vanessa opened the door, Megan instantly felt her body respond. And it wasn't because Vanessa looked stunning—she did, but this time it was because as soon as Vanessa opened her front door and caught sight of Megan, Megan heard her gasp and then watched as Vanessa's eyes drank her in. Every time Vanessa's eyes lingered—first on Megan's chest, then on Megan's legs, Megan felt her center getting slicker.

"Um…come in," Vanessa finally managed to say, licking her lips.

"Thank you." Megan stepped into Vanessa's foyer.

"Food will be here in about ten minutes," Vanessa informed her, eyes telegraphing desire as she reached for Megan's hips.

"Great. I'm starving," Megan said, allowing Vanessa to pull her closer. Then, with one firm tug, Vanessa removed the distance between them and covered Megan's mouth with her own. Megan dropped her Kate Spade bag and brought her hands up to wrap around Vanessa's back.

Vanessa's grip on her hips tightened and then Megan felt herself shoved against the closed front door. The control Vanessa was exhibiting was driving Megan wild and she moved her hands up to entwine her fingers in Vanessa's hair, pulling the brunette in closer so she could deepen the kiss. But Vanessa clearly had other ideas. Vanessa's hands slid up Megan's sides until they were at Megan's shoulders. Forcefully, Megan's arms were brought down to her sides and before she knew what was happening, Vanessa pulled the spaghetti straps of her top down off her shoulders, and yanked the garment down, exposing Megan's breasts. Hot desire pooled between Megan's legs when she felt Vanessa's hand cup one of her breasts, squeezing it, flicking her thumb over an already rock-hard nipple.

Megan whined in protest when their kiss was broken by Vanessa pulling away but that whine morphed into a moan when a nipple was sucked into Vanessa's mouth.

"God, Vanessa!"

Then…

"Oh, fuck!" as the nipple was then bitten hard, with just the right amount of pressure. Megan blindly grabbed for the doorknob to help support herself.

Vanessa repeated her ministrations to Megan's other breast and each time her nipple was bitten, Megan's clit throbbed as if the two were connected and all thoughts of how hungry she was and eating Chinese food left Megan's mind.

Eventually, Vanessa brought her head away from Megan's chest and began nuzzling Megan's neck.

"Is this okay?" she asked.

Because of the delicious tingling still radiating out from both her nipples, Megan could only nod dumbly at first, but then she regained the ability to form words.

"Yes, baby, more than okay."

"Promise?"

"I promise."

Vanessa licked an ear lobe and Megan melted.

"God, I wanted you last night," Vanessa murmured, still nuzzling.

"Me too," Megan squeaked. She decided to confess something. "I was playing with myself while we were texting last night."

Vanessa's fingers now had a grip on the waistband of Megan's skirt and was slowing inching it down.

"Is this okay, too?" she prompted.

"Mm-hmm," Megan groaned, biting her bottom lip. Vanessa's fingers also took hold of Megan's panties and in one motion, Vanessa yanked both past Megan's hips. Megan let them fall to her ankles.

"Keep telling me about playing with yourself while texting me," Vanessa ordered, pressing Megan more firmly against the door.

Vanessa was sliding her hands along the sides of Megan's thighs.

"I-I was rubbing my clit. I kept thinking about how much I wanted to be with you last night. Oh, God, Vanessa..."

Vanessa had grabbed Megan's ass with both hands, squeezing the soft flesh, the tips of her fingers tantalizingly close to Megan's center. Megan had to hold onto Vanessa's shoulders to keep from collapsing because her knees suddenly felt too week to support her.

"Keep telling me," Vanessa whispered. "Did you come while we were texting?"

"No, it was after."

"What made you come?"

"Remembering fucking you in La Vida Mocha," Megan gasped. "I came so hard."

So fucking hard! Even now, Megan could recall how her hips had bucked and her toes had curled.

Vanessa slid her right hand between Megan's legs and began sliding her fingers through the arousal that was coating Megan's swollen lips. Megan moaned and thrust her hips forward to make more contact with the hand playing with her pussy.

"Did you say my name when you came?" Vanessa demanded.

"Yes."

"You're lying."

"No, I swear I'm not. I said 'Oh God, Vanessa.'" Megan's head fell back against the door as Vanessa's fingers teased her opening. "Please don't stop! Please fuck me, Vanessa!"

"I'm going to, sweetie," Vanessa whispered against the shell of Megan's ear. "I want you to come hard again like you did last night."

No problem!

Megan then felt two fingers stretching her open and entering her and then Vanessa starting thrusting in and out, Megan trying to push down with her hips to take the fingers in deeper, finding and matching Vanessa's rhythm.

"You're so fucking tight!" Vanessa moaned. "And so fucking wet!"

The way Vanessa was so obviously turned on by Megan was bringing Megan that much closer to her release.

"I wanted you over here last night," Vanessa groaned. "I wanted you to lick me until I passed out."

"Vanessa! Oh, fuck…"

"I wanted to see your pretty little face eating me out and licking my come over and over again."

"Vanessa!"

"Come on, sweetie…that's it…" Vanessa gently urged.

Megan felt her walls clutching rapidly at the fingers pumping her. She was so close now.

"Oh fuck!"

Vanessa's thrusts became more forceful and then Megan felt Vanessa's thumb press against her clit just a moment before Vanessa curled her fingers inside, stroking hidden spots inside Megan's center.

"All of this is mine, sweetie," Vanessa growled.

"Yes…"

Megan wanted to be this woman's possession.

"Then say it!" Vanessa ordered.

"It's…it's yours. All of it is yours! Fuck, Vanessa!"

"Say it again."

"Yours…all yours," Megan whimpered.

"Now, say my name when you come!"

That sent Megan over the edge.

"Oh *fuuuck! Vanessaaaa!*" Megan screamed as the orgasm tore through her and her pussy spasmed around Vanessa's fingers, coating them with even more lubrication. Megan shuddered and screamed again, this time with her face buried in Vanessa's shoulder. And still Vanessa kept pressing on her clit, still she kept curling and uncurling the fingers she had buried inside Megan, and Megan's eyes shot open as she realized another orgasm was right behind this first one.

No fucking way!

Megan uttered a high-pitched squeal just a second before her sex exploded with even more intense throbs of pleasure even as it was still vibrating from the first climax. When this one hit, she let out more screams, trying to say Vanessa's name but not being able to form anything coherent. She clung onto Vanessa tightly, needing the other woman to support her, otherwise she was going to collapse because she could no longer feel her legs.

The doorbell rang. Megan jerked at the sound but by pressing even more firmly against her, Vanessa indicated that Megan wasn't to go anywhere. Instead, Vanessa slowed her fingers and Megan just held on to her as the spasms of her overlapping orgasms had their way with her, the strongest ones making her flinch, gasp, whimper. Finally, Megan felt the fingers being carefully withdrawn and then Vanessa's mouth was on hers for a deep kiss.

"I-I think the delivery guy probably wants to be paid," Megan eventually said when the kiss ended.

Vanessa smirked.

"I chose a no-contact delivery," she said. "He should have left the food by the door." Her smirk grew wider. "Perks of a pandemic. Though I'm pretty sure he got an earful of a certain young lady having a pretty good time in here."

Megan blushed.

With a tilt of her head, Vanessa indicated the hallway to Megan's right.

"That way, to the end and then make a left. My bedroom is at the end of the second hall. Get in there while I get the food. Be naked when I arrive."

"Yes, ma'am," Megan said, her voice barely above a whisper. She left her skirt and panties where they had fallen. On wobbly legs that kept threatening to come out from under her, with head spinning dizzily, she somehow managed to follow Vanessa's directions, even though she had to reach out and steady herself on the walls from the time to time.

Chapter 23

About ten minutes later, Vanessa was coming down from her own orgasm, courtesy of Megan's expert tongue.

It had been quick.

As soon as Vanessa had come into the bedroom after leaving the Chinese food in the dining room, she had taken off her clothes as fast as she could, laid down on the bed, pulled Megan on top of her and then pushed Megan downward, wordlessly telling the woman in no uncertain terms where her head needed to be. When Megan started working her tongue around Vanessa's extremely wet center, Vanessa had known her climax wasn't far behind. Megan seemed to realize this and also seemed to not mind, for after taking a few tastes of the juices flowing out of Vanessa, Megan simply closed her lips around Vanessa's clit, pressed hard with her tongue and soon had Vanessa spasming intensely with release.

"That was amazing," Megan said as she settled herself next to Vanessa on the bed.

"Fucking amazing," Vanessa agreed, still catching her breath.

"It was the hottest thing to ever happen to me," Megan whispered. "The way you just took me like that. Do that some more in the future, please."

Vanessa grinned, remembering. It hadn't been planned, but when she had seen Megan standing outside her door, in that skirt which hugged those amazing legs, and in that fucking top! With no bra! A switch had been thrown and Vanessa just had to consume her.

"As you wish," she said.

"Are you quoting Boba Fett or Wesley from *Princess Bride*?"

"Definitely Fett." Vanessa turned her head to face Megan and just stared at her.

"What?" Megan eventually asked in a whisper.

"I want you to stay the night," Vanessa declared.

Megan beamed and Vanessa's heart went *boom!*

"I want to spend the night," Megan said. "I even packed for it, hoping."

Vanessa rolled onto her back to look at the ceiling.

"I almost texted you to suggest you do that." She paused, then continued. "I liked falling asleep with you the other night."

Megan moved closer, snuggling against Vanessa's side, her face in the crook of Vanessa's neck. Vanessa sighed with contentment.

"I liked waking up next to you the next morning," Megan said softly.

Vanessa wanted to stay like this all night, but her stomach growled.

"Good, now that we know you're not leaving, let's eat!" Reluctantly, she disengaged herself from Megan and left the bed. "Did you bring pajamas?"

"I did."

"Good, why don't you put those on while I grab my robe?"

A few minutes later she and Megan were unloading the food from the delivery bag in the dining room. Thankfully, the food was still warm. Vanessa brought out plates and silverware and Megan helped dish the food out of the containers from the restaurant. Vanessa produced a bottle of wine from the kitchen and like a sommelier presenting a selection to a customer in a five-star restaurant, held the bottle out for Megan to see.

"Gewürztraminer!" Megan exclaimed.

"Yeah, it was recommended to me by an adorable wine drinker I know."

Wine poured and food dished, the women began eating. Vanessa was happy to learn that Megan was the type who loved to share her food, which Vanessa considered a requirement when Chinese was involved.

"So…spill it about La Vida Mocha," Megan prompted. "What was the deal with closing so early today?"

Vanessa filled Megan in about her decision to alter the coffeeshop's hours temporarily, adding that she was going to give it three weeks before making any further decisions.

Megan smiled.

"Is it selfish of me to be happy that your Sundays are free again?" she asked, placing a hand directly on Vanessa's thigh through the opening in her robe. Vanessa felt heat spread from Megan's hand and settle between her legs. She took a breath before speaking.

"No, not selfish," she said, "I want to spend Sundays with you too."

"I sense a *but* coming."

"Buuuut...I need you to realize that I may not be up for doing much on Sundays. Most likely, I'll just want to enjoy *not* having anything to do on Sundays."

Megan's fingers were now slowly stroking Vanessa's thigh, almost absentmindedly. Vanessa wanted to chastise Megan, tell her that this was a serious conversation about Vanessa's one day off during the week.

"Keep going, I'm listening," Megan said innocently. But she slid her hand further up Vanessa's thigh.

Vanessa swallowed.

"Well, I was just going to say that on Sundays I might not be good company, that's all."

"Are you trying to keep me away?" Megan asked, pouting.

"No! Not at all! Of course I'd want to see you."

"To fuck?"

Vanessa waited a heartbeat before responding.

"Yes."

"Because that's all we're about, right?" Megan asked.

I don't know anymore.

Vanessa stared at Megan, not saying anything.

"Vanessa?" Megan prodded, quirking one eyebrow.

Vanessa nodded.

"Yeah, because that's all we're about," she said.

Megan nodded also.

"So, what's the problem?"

"There's no problem," Vanessa assured her with a slight hitch to her voice because Megan's sneaky fingers were now playing along the hem of the panties Vanessa had put on after getting out of bed.

"Keep going," Megan said. "What will you do with the rest of your Sunday after I've done what I want with you?"

Vanessa laughed.

"Have I told you how cute you are?" she said. "Anyway, I'd probably just veg out on the couch all day mindlessly scrolling through Pinterest or having a *Star Trek* movie marathon."

Megan's face lit up. "Oh my God, you've totally described my perfect Sunday," she said.

"Seriously?" Vanessa asked, chuckling.

"Totally! Or maybe a marathon of all those cheesy zombie movies Netflix has."

Vanessa laughed again. She looked at Megan and for a few moments was actually able to ignore the building pleasure in her center due to Megan's toying fingers.

She decided to take a risk.

"Spend Sunday with me," she said, hoping her voice wasn't betraying the nervousness she was feeling. "Let's relax together and have a movie marathon. Zombies or *Star Trek*, I don't care."

She was relieved when Megan beamed.

"That sounds amazing! Yes, I'll spend Sunday with you," Megan said. Then she narrowed her eyes. "Is it against the rules, though?"

Yes!

Vanessa shrugged.

"Probably. But, fuck it."

Megan beamed again.

"I agree."

Vanessa's heart started beating faster and it wasn't just because Megan's fingers were still teasingly playing on her thigh. It was also because she felt like her and Megan were now on a slippery slope towards something emotionally dangerous.

God, I need to talk to someone older than Chloë!

She made a mental note to call Angela and Desiree. William, bless him, was just not the person from whom to seek the wisdom Vanessa needed.

But that could wait because Megan's fingers were now rubbing the crotch of Vanessa's panties and Vanessa knew Megan could feel how damp the fabric was.

"Bedroom," Megan said.

Vanessa sucked her bottom lip between her teeth and then raised an eyebrow.

"But I haven't finished eating,"

With her other hand, Megan cupped Vanessa's chin and held her eyes with her own.

"And I say you've eaten enough," Megan declared, her eyes dark.

Vanessa felt her breath hitch. Megan scooted her chair closer and suddenly her fingers were pressing quite firmly against the crotch of the panties. Vanessa's nipples hardened and her center was positively leaking.

"Open your legs wider," Megan whispered, her lips less than an inch from Vanessa's.

But Vanessa decided she wanted to have some fun.

Let's see where she takes this.

"I haven't finished eating," she repeated.

Vanessa heard Megan groan.

"Okay," Megan said. "That's one."

"One what?"

"Open your legs wider."

"I still want an egg roll," Vanessa stated.

"That's two," Megan said and then leaned in for a kiss. When she pulled away, she said again, "Open your legs wider, Vanessa."

"First tell me, two what?" Vanessa whispered.

"Now it's three, because you still haven't obeyed. And to answer your question, let me put it this way: If you keep going the way you are, you might find it hard to sit tomorrow."

Vanessa almost came right then.

"Open your legs wider," Megan repeated.

"I'm not done eating," Vanessa said.

After all, three was nothing.

***

An hour later, Vanessa and Megan were laying side by side in bed, facing each other. Vanessa was softly playing with Megan's auburn hair while Megan was tracing Vanessa's jawline with her fingertip. Their legs were entwined and Vanessa couldn't help but marvel at how perfectly they fit together.

"Have you and Chloë ever had sex?" Megan asked.

"Good god, no," Vanessa said, surprised at the odd question.

"She's super pretty," Megan pointed out.

"She is, and she's a total sweetheart, and I love her to death, but no."

"And that cute girl in the coffeeshop the other day? Have you done anything with her?"

"Amy? No, we've never done anything together." The thought had crossed Vanessa's mind on more than one occasion, though, but she'd never attempted flirting with Amy due to Amy being a very loyal customer and Vanessa not wanting to risk losing one of those in case they did get together and it didn't work out.

"She's just a regular," Vanessa added. She tucked a lock of Megan's hair behind her ear. "What's bringing on all these questions?"

Megan smirked.

"You told me to remind you who you belong to while we're together," she said. "I'm just letting you know I'm aware of specific threats out there."

Vanessa laughed.

"Chloë and Amy are not threats."

Megan was silent for a while and then said, "You and Amy would make a cute couple. You know, whenever you decide to actually start dating again. Just saying."

Vanessa felt her heart tighten. She didn't want to be reminded about Megan leaving for New York, not tonight. She claimed Megan's lips for a kiss.

"I don't want to talk about who I'll possibly date in the future," she said after the kiss. "I'm having fun with you now. I belong to you now. I don't care about Amy because Amy isn't here in my house and in my bed. You are."

"Okay," Megan said softly.

"Talk about something else."

Megan moved in closer.

"My birthday is in ten days."

"What? Seriously?" Vanessa pulled away slightly so she could see Megan better.

"Number twenty-seven," Megan told her.

Vanessa grimaced.

"Oh god, so old! Sorry, my upper age limit on fuck buddies is twenty-six. If I want an old woman, I'll mess around with someone my age."

"You fucking bitch!" Megan squealed, laughing. She pinched Vanessa's nipple. "Smartass!" she added.

"Pinching my nipple is hardly a punishment, my sweet," Vanessa purred. "You'll have to think of something else."

Megan cocked an eyebrow.

"Wanna give me suggestions?" she asked.

Vanessa did indeed want to give her suggestions; deliciously erotic suggestions that Vanessa had an inkling Megan would like to explore with her. But that was a discussion for another time.

Instead, she asked, "What do you usually do on your birthday?"

"Have lunch with my family in La Jolla. It's a tradition. Every year, I take the day off work and they take me to a place called Marcano's. Have you ever been?"

Vanessa shook her head.

"It's one of the best steakhouses in California."

Megan propped herself up on her elbow again; it took her farther away from Vanessa and Vanessa instantly missed the closer contact.

"I was thinking of taking the next day off also, because that's a Friday," Megan said. "I have *sooo* much vacation time stocked up. And I was hoping you'd like to spend part of my birthday with me?"

"I'd love to."

"Good," Megan said, nodding. Then she looked away shyly, seeming to consider if she wanted to say something else.

"What's on your mind?" Vanessa prodded, rubbing Megan's arm.

"Promise me you'll tell me if you don't think this is a good idea. I mean, considering…"

"I promise," Vanessa said, intrigued.

Megan took a deep breath.

"I think I'd really enjoy waking up with you on my birthday. I'd like you to stay over the night before."

Vanessa pulled Megan back to her, cupped the back of her neck and kissed her. Then she pressed her forehead to Megan's and used her thumb to play with Megan's earlobe.

"Just try to keep me away," Vanessa whispered.

Chapter 24

Three days later, Megan was in her home office typing a follow-up e-mail to one of her co-workers when her laptop notified her that a Zoom call was coming in from Sophia, her boss. Megan answered it, Sophia's face appearing on her screen.

"Hey, Soph."

"Hey, Megan. You got a sec?"

Sophia was the Vice-president of Operations for BeachSoft. In fact, Megan was going to be BeachSoft's Sophia in New York: Vice-president of Operations for the East Coast. This, despite the fact that she was twenty years younger than Sophia. Even though Megan was supremely confident about her professional skills, there were times she wondered if she was too young for her soon-to-be new role in the company. But if the CEO, Lucy Whitaker thought Megan was ready, that was good enough for her.

"There are two things I need to talk to you about," Sophia continued. "First, has Lucy reached out to you, by any chance?"

Megan shook her head. "No, not yet. Why?"

Sophia pursed her lips.

"I'm just curious," Sophia said. "She had mentioned to me a few weeks ago that she wanted to start seriously planning for New York, but I haven't heard anything new."

"Oh." Megan felt a twinge in her chest. She knew that a couple of weeks ago, that twinge would have been pure excitement because she was jazzed about starting a new life in New York. She still was. But now, she knew that part of the twinge was sadness at being reminded that the end of what she was enjoying with Vanessa was still somewhere on the horizon. Nonetheless, she managed to put a neutral expression on her face and say, "Well, she hasn't talked to me about it."

Sophia shrugged.

"No bother. I'm sure we'll hear about it when Lucy is ready for us to hear about it."

"Okay."

"Have you started packing? You're not, like, living out of boxes and suitcases, right?"

Megan laughed.

"No, not yet. I packed some things I'm going to leave at my parents' house, but that's it."

"Good," Sophia said. "I hope Lucy doesn't wait too long to get the ball rolling on this. I got a friend on Wall Street and she tells me that because of how hard New York was hit with Covid, corporate real estate in the city now is *cheap!* We can get office space for a song. Well, a song if you're a billionaire like Lucy writing the checks."

Megan laughed. Lucy Whitaker was one of her personal heroes, a woman who had started her own software company and was turning it into a behemoth, even earning a place on the cover of *Time*. Lucy was proving that in the male-dominated world of I.T., women were no longer willing to just sit on the sidelines and settle for male CEOs to grant them high-level executive positions just to meet some diversity quotas. And it was Lucy who had personally recruited Megan to join BeachSoft.

"Anyway, young lady," Sophia continued, "stay ready. I'm your mentor for this and so be prepared to meet with me a lot over the next few weeks because we have a lot to discuss."

"Got it," Megan said.

"It's too bad we can't switch places, though," Sophia said.

Megan blinked.

"Did you want to move to New York?"

"Sure, one day. I'm from the Bronx, did you know that?" Sophia answered.

Megan didn't, though she'd always picked up on Sophia's New York accent.

"I came out here for college and ended up staying, raising a family. I've always wanted to go back, though. California is wonderful but I think I'm a New York girl at heart. But the main reason I'd go back now is because my parents live in Connecticut and they're getting pretty old. It would be nice to have a position back east again so I can keep an eye on them and help take care of them."

"You can't convince them to move out here to live with you?" Megan asked.

Sophia started chuckling.

"You have no idea how unbelievably stubborn those old fools are, Megan. My dad even fell on the ice last winter, broke his hip and still insists he loves winter. Anyway, my husband and I are both kinda over California, all this sunshine gets depressing after a while. I miss the culture and excitement back in the New York area, and he misses going to Yankees games. We figure we'll retire there, eventually. Find a nice brownstone in hipster Brooklyn to putter away in. Anyway, the main reason I called you is to talk about Trevor."

Megan managed to not make a face because her boss could see her. Instead, she plastered on what she hoped was a believable smile and said, "What about him?"

"How do you think he's doing?"

Megan knew Sophia expected honesty. This wasn't a time for diplomacy.

"It's been a struggle, Soph. Sometimes it's like I'm dealing with a child because he needs so much hand-holding."

Megan then spent some time recounting examples from the past few weeks

Sophia nodded contemplatively.

"Okay," she said. "I've heard a lot of grumbles myself from others and so I think it's time we cut our losses with him."

Megan's heart thumped, the implications of the conversation hitting her. It was very likely, after all, that she had just had a hand in someone losing his job. During a pandemic.

Fuck!

But then Sophia dropped an atomic bomb.

"Give him a call and tell him he's fired," she stated simply.

"Wait…what?"

There was a moment's silence. But then Sophia asked patiently, "What's bothering you specifically?"

"You want *me* to fire him?"

"You're his direct boss, Megan, so, yes, I want you to fire him. I don't expect you to enjoy it, but I do expect you to get used to it. You're about to be a VP and unless you're the luckiest VP in the history of VPs, you're going to have to fire people from time to time."

Megan felt like a silly schoolgirl.

"Of course," she said firmly. "I'll take care of it right away."

Sophia nodded, apparently satisfied.

"Good. Have a great rest of the morning." And Sophia ended the Zoom call.

Megan slumped back in her chair. She looked at the clock. It wasn't even eight-thirty; too early for the drink she felt she needed now. It was also too early to call Vanessa and talk about it; La Vida Mocha was still open for another ninety minutes yet. That was probably a good thing, now that Megan thought about it because Vanessa would probably think Megan was being a baby. Vanessa had probably fired lots of people when she had worked at that energy company. And Vanessa would sure as hell have no problem firing a sucks-ass employee from La Vida Mocha in order to keep her business running shipshape.

She took a deep breath.

She had promised Sophia that she would take care of firing Trevor right away, but *right away* turned into something closer to twenty minutes while she steeled herself to call a person she knew and tell him he was out of a job during possibly the worst time to be out of a job since the Great Depression.

She knew the only decent way to handle this was via Zoom—the closest thing to an in-person meeting she could have with someone nowadays. Taking a couple more fortifying breaths, she made the call.

When Trevor's face appeared on her 32-inch monitor, Megan forced herself to keep her expression neutral. He was about ten years older than her, she remembered, and had that kind of square-jawed handsomeness she supposed straight women simply melted at. Before they even had a chance to greet each other, Megan saw a young woman cross the room behind Trevor but not before running her hand lovingly across his shoulder as she passed. Megan suddenly recalled that Trevor had once mentioned a fiancée during a team meeting, that they were planning on marrying on New Year's Eve.

Fuck my life!

"Hey, Megan, what's up?" he greeted her as though he didn't have a care in the world.

Megan had decided before the call that, like Darth Vader in *Return of the Jedi,* she would dispense with the pleasantries.

"Trevor, I'm very sorry to have to do this, especially now, but I'm afraid it's been decided that it's best for you and BeachSoft to part ways."

She watched Trevor frowning as he processed her words. To Megan, it seemed to take a ridiculously long time.

"Wait...you're *firing* me?" he finally said, loud enough to attract the attention of his fiancée, who suddenly reappeared in the far background, standing in the frame of a doorway to watch this interaction.

This just keeps getting better.

"Yes, unfortunately, Trevor—"

"No, no, no...wait a minute! *You're* firing me? You. Megan."

"Well, I..."

"You're a goddam kid! How the hell do you get to fire me? Does Sophia know about this?"

Megan had to take a deep breath to quell an anger rising in her. First, what does her age have to do with it? She was still a rather high-ranked person in the company. Secondly, the insinuation that she needed Sophia's approval—as if Megan was a child who needed permission from Mommy—was insulting. Fine, Sophia had been the one to prompt Megan to fire Trevor today but technically, it *was* Megan's right as Director of Mobile App Development. But she'd be damned if she let Trevor know that.

"Of course, Sophia knows," she answered him, managing to keep her voice calm. "But I don't need her authority. Unfortunately, your performance makes me feel that—"

"Makes *you* feel like?" Trevor interrupted. "*You?* So, you're, like, what, one of the top dogs at BeachSoft? You're in all the meetings about how all us little people are doing?"

Megan finally had enough.

"You know what, Trevor? I *am* one of the top dogs in the company. Not only am I the *director* of your division but I'm about to be a *vice-president* of operations. You would have been better off keeping my role in mind while doing your work instead of assuming that just because I'm young and a woman that you could get away with poor performance. You can keep interrupting me all you want but it's not going to change the fact that you're fired. And you can call Sophia or any of my fellow *executives* and they'll tell you the same thing. You're fired."

Trevor sat there shaking his head, his face red, looking like he was nowhere near capable of having a rational conversation about this.

Finally, he blurted out, "Fired! By a fucking dyke!"

Megan gasped, feeling as if she'd just been slapped. Of all the ways she imagined this conversation going before actually calling Trevor, this had not been one of them.

She noticed Trevor's fiancée come running—no sprinting!—into the room Trevor was in and practically throw herself at the laptop. Megan caught a panicked expression on his fiancée's face before the woman severed the Zoom connection.

Chapter 25

"I am so bummed!"

Amy was pouting. Vanessa had to admit it was a cute look on her.

Her customer had just read the sign announcing La Vida Mocha's temporary new hours and had expressed her disappointment that her favorite coffee spot was once again going to be closed on Sundays, in addition to closing earlier throughout the week.

"God, I hate this pandemic!" Amy exclaimed. "And I get *sooo* mad now when I see people without masks on. I'm like, 'Hello! Don't you want things to return to normal?'"

"I know," Vanessa agreed, adding the frothed milk to Amy's cappuccino. "It's the paradox of being American. So many freedoms, including the freedom to be stupid." Vanessa didn't have to worry about making such a quasi-unpatriotic statement to Amy. Since La Vida Mocha's grand opening, when Amy started becoming a regular customer, Vanessa had learned that the brunette was no tight-ass, flag-waving citizen unable to stomach hearing a minor critique of American society.

"That's clever. You're funny," Amy said with a very direct smile.

Vanessa added the finishing touches to the cappuccino. This time it was her turn to pout because she had to put the drink in a to-go cup. It was 9:45 a.m. and since the coffeeshop was closing in fifteen minutes it made zero sense for Amy to drink her coffee in-house.

"I hate that you can't stay," Vanessa said, handing over the drink. "You need to come earlier next time," she added playfully.

Amy rolled her eyes.

"Well, if somebody had told me that you were closing at ten today, I would have."

Vanessa played along, rolling her eyes this time.

"Fine, Amy," she sighed in obvious mock exasperation, "I will text you each morning to remind you to get here earlier."

Amy's mouth fell open a bit and she held Vanessa's eyes for a few beats.

"Promises, promises," she said with a slight smile. "See you tomorrow?"

"Not until noon, though," Vanessa reminded her. She waved bye as Amy began walking out. Once the door shut, Chloë appeared by Vanessa's side.

"Getting Megan's replacement all lined up, huh?" she asked.

Vanessa's eyes went wide.

"What? No! What are you talking about?"

"Oh my God, Vanessa! You were so flirting with her!"

Vanessa's hands flew to her face.

"Oh God! Was I? Fuck! Was it obvious?"

Chloë shrugged and sucked in air through her teeth.

"I mean, look," she said, "I totally believe you if you say you didn't mean it…but I can also totally imagine Amy getting the impression that you'd like to take a shower with her."

"No! Fuck!" Now Vanessa completely covered her face with her hands, replaying the interaction with Amy, knowing that Chloë was right. "I am sooo clueless! Jesus, why did I do that?"

"Uh…because Amy is super cute and definitely someone most gay women would want to take a shower with?" Chloë answered.

Vanessa wondered if Megan's comment from last night, that Vanessa and Amy would make a cute couple, somehow subconsciously caused Vanessa to be flirty now with Amy.

Am I getting ready to replace Megan?

"Who do you think would win in a fight between Megan and Amy?" Chloë asked, smirking.

"Shut up! There isn't gonna be any fighting!"

"I think Amy would win."

"Fuck you, Megan would totally kick her ass!"

"Whatever you say, Vanessa."

"Shut up. In fact, you know what, whenever Amy comes in here, you make sure to serve her."

Chloë laughed.

"Oh yeah, ignore her!" she said, looking at Vanessa as if she was the dumbest person on Earth. "*That'll* turn her off! Have you ever actually *met* a lesbian? Or…*any* woman?"

"You are not helping!" Vanessa covered her face again. "Jesus!" After a moment, she dropped her hands and said, "Let's just start shutting down so we can get out of here."

***

Before she got into her Jeep after locking the back door of La Vida Mocha and waving goodbye to Chloë, Vanessa sent a text to Megan.

Closed! Heading to see Angela and Dee. How is ur day so far?

Megan's reply came as Vanessa was driving on the I-5, approaching the junction with the 78. Vanessa tapped "Read" on the infotainment screen and a second later the Jeep's female voice, which Vanessa had named Jessie the Jeep about three minutes after buying the vehicle, started speaking.

"Message from Megan," Jessie the Jeep began, "Tell them I said hi. My day is dramatic. I will tell you about it later. Stop by any time after three, if you want."

Vanessa frowned. *Dramatic?* She hoped everything was okay with Megan and she wished wasn't driving so she could send a follow-up text. She thought of calling but she never liked the idea of calling Megan during her working hours, not knowing if she'd be interrupting anything. In any case, she'd be at Angela and Desiree's place in a few minutes; she'd wait to text Megan then. And when she went over to Megan's later, she'd plan on spending the night because if Megan had had a bad day today, Vanessa wanted to be there for her.

Or am I just looking for any excuse now to spend the night?

So far this week, Vanessa and Megan had seen each other every day after Megan logged off in the afternoon. Also, so far this week, their long sessions of sex always seemed to begin with the assumption that they'd be waking up next to each other the following morning.

Way to become a lesbian stereotype...

She rolled her eyes. This is why she needed a chat with Angela and Desiree.

After parking in front of their house and firing off a quick text to Megan saying that she hoped everything was alright, Vanessa rang the doorbell.

"Girl, get in here!" Desiree said when she opened the door, a wide smile on her face. She pulled Vanessa in for a hug. "I know the CDC would have a hissy fit about me hugging you, but fuck them."

Vanessa laughed and returned the hug. When they separated, she fingered the cuff of Desiree's shirt.

"I love this. I could never pull off orange," she said, admiring the way the shirt's color complemented Desiree's caramel skin tone.

"Angela says the same thing," Desiree told her, then added in a conspiratorial whisper, "And she's right. Orange makes her look even more pasty white than normal. Come on in, we have the food set up in the dining room."

When Vanessa had asked if she could come by for some woman-to-woman talk, Angela had suggested that since La Vida Mocha closed at ten, Vanessa should come by for brunch. A few minutes after she arrived, she had a plate full of scrambled eggs, melon slices and even some smoked salmon with egg salad on a toasted baguette.

"This looks amazing!" She smiled at Angela, who Vanessa knew was the home chef of the couple. But Angela held up her hands in protest.

"Thank you," she said, "but my future wife here actually helped by making the eggs and the bacon."

Once everyone had sat down with their food and Vanessa had taken a couple of sips of her mimosa, Desiree asked her, "So who's the woman?"

Vanessa laughed.

"So, did you two know I've been spending time with Megan?"

"No!" Angela practically screeched.

Desiree shook her head.

"This damn pandemic," she said. "No one's hanging out anymore! We're missing all the juicy gossip."

"I *knew* I sensed a spark between you two when you were over here for the party!" Angela looked at Desiree. "Didn't I say something?"

"She did," Desiree confirmed. "But she's always looking for an excuse to play matchmaker."

"I am not! Anyway, who cares?" Angela put down her fork and leaned forward with her arms on the table. "Tell us details! How did it happen?"

"And don't skimp," Desiree warned. "Women love details."

Vanessa recounted the history of her and Megan, such as it was, from their first meeting at La Vida Mocha, to the two of them deciding on the night of the engagement party to have a little fling.

"Whoa, whoa, whoa!" Angela said, making a backing up motion with her hands. "Fling? That's all it is? What the fuck?"

"Ange, Megan is moving across the country, remember?" Desiree reminded her.

"And I've got my hands full with La Vida Mocha," Vanessa added. "A fling is all her and I could commit to."

"That's bullshit!" Angela said. She looked at Desiree. "Dee, tell her that's bullshit."

But all Desiree could do was shrug.

"So, what's the problem?" Desiree asked Vanessa, and Vanessa could tell by the look Desiree gave her that she knew what the problem was, and was feeling sorry for her.

"The problem is," Vanessa began, "that I've had flings before, ladies, but how I feel about this one is way different. I can see myself with Megan beyond a fling. I can imagine more than just sex with her. Even when I first met her it felt like suddenly a puzzle piece had fallen into place. I mean…the connection…holy fuck…it was unbelievable."

"Awww!" Angela said, grinning like a fool.

"I'm not trying to be sappy," Vanessa insisted, reaching down to scratch Barney the pug's ears. "If anything, I'm trying to be sensible and keep my head grounded. That's why I'm here talking to you two. Chloë—who I spend every friggin' day with—is great, but she's a toddler and I needed to talk to more seasoned women."

"Well, as a quote-unquote seasoned woman," Desiree began, "I think you just need to accept the reality of what this thing with Megan is. It's a temporary fling and you'll need to move on once she leaves for New York."

Vanessa nodded.

"Yeah, you're right," she said, somewhat glumly.

What had she been hoping for, coming here? That Desiree—who was the more practical and sensible of the Ang and Dee duo—would come up with some magical way for Vanessa to explore something deeper with Megan that would also allow for Vanessa to remain committed to La Vida Mocha *and* Megan to keep her dream job in New York?

"Thank you," she said to Desiree. "I think I just needed to actually hear someone say it like that."

Angela eyes were quickly flitting between Desiree and Vanessa, her mouth open.

"Oh my God, you guys are so unromantic!"

Desiree turned to her fiancée.

"Honey, it's not about being romantic; it's about being realistic. This isn't some silly rom-com. Vanessa has a business here in California which is everything to her, and Megan has a life-changing job promotion which is taking her across the country. It's sad but it's the reality of the situation."

Angela looked at Vanessa.

"Let me ask you this…do you think Megan feels the same way?" Angela asked.

Vanessa had anticipated this question and had thought about her answer as she was driving over here earlier. The fact was, she wasn't sure if Megan felt the same way. She knew Megan enjoyed her company beyond the sex, and the other night, when they both confessed to one another that they enjoyed falling asleep and waking up together…that seemed like it was charged with unspoken meaning. There was also the way Megan sometimes looked at Vanessa or touched her…

Vanessa shook her head, wanting to dispel any notions could really only be the result of wishful thinking. The truth was, Megan had given her nothing concrete to make her believe that she felt the same way.

"I don't know what Megan feels," Vanessa answered Angela.

"Then you should find out," Angela said. "What if she *does* feel the same way? You two would be amazing together!"

"And then what?" Desiree inquired, throwing up her hands. "Megan quits her job to make lattes? Or do you imagine Vanessa giving up the coffeeshop and starting over in New York?"

Desiree then looked at Vanessa.

"Here's another thing that's worrying me. And before I share it, I want you to know that I love you and I'm only doing this because I care deeply about you."

Vanessa was nervously intrigued but she nodded for Desiree to go on.

"Okay," Desiree began. "When was the last time you had regularly frequent sex with another woman?"

Vanessa blinked.

"Wow, I didn't expect that. Um…Rebecca."

"That long ago?" Desiree asked.

"I've been super busy," Vanessa replied. Her and Rebecca had broken up shortly before Vanessa decided she could finally move forward with plans to open a coffeeshop, which then kicked off a whirlwind string of months during which Vanessa's focus was solely on getting La Vida Mocha up and running. Then, of course, once La Vida Mocha was open, Vanessa hadn't even had time to think about finding a steady girlfriend. But Rebecca had been almost a year ago now.

Desiree gave Vanessa a pointed look.

"Is it possible, Vanessa, that these, let's call them *non-fling*, feelings you have for Megan are only because you're getting laid regularly now?"

"Jesus, Dee!" Angela squawked.

"No, she's right," Vanessa said, reaching over to squeeze Angela's hand. "Orgasms can fuck with a woman's mind." She looked at Desiree. "But I don't think that's it. I really don't. I genuinely like Megan for more than what happens between us in bed."

Angela leaned forward toward Vanessa; her eyes wide.

"Speaking of orgasms and bed, is Megan any good?" she asked eagerly.

"For God's sake, Ange," Desiree said. "She is not going to give us details about their sex life."

"I'm not asking for a play-by-play," Angela complained. "Just tell us…is she good in bed?"

Vanessa felt her insides flutter.

"So good," Vanessa sighed, taking a fortifying sip of her mimosa.

"Ooh, I knew it!" Angela squealed, clapping her hands. She turned to her fiancée. "Megan's young but, like, a mature young, you know? Plus, all that time she spends alone? Plenty of time to think and be imaginative."

Desiree cocked an eyebrow.

"Been thinking about this much?" she asked.

Angela tapped Desiree's arm. "Oh, stop! You know it's just a thing that I do."

Desiree rolled her eyes and then she reached over to place her hand lightly on Vanessa's arm.

"Look, I think the takeaway from this experience with Megan for you should be knowing better what type of woman you're looking for, when you're ready to look for a woman to settle down with. Maybe it will be someone like Megan, but I don't see how it can actually be Megan. Sorry."

Vanessa nodded and swallowed the rest of her mimosa.

Chapter 26

What a day!

Megan was downstairs in her condo, sitting on her couch, her feet propped up on the charcoal grey floor pouf she used as an ottoman. Even though it was now close to four o'clock and she had logged off from work nearly an hour ago, she was still dressed for the office in fitted black slacks and a white blouse. The only concession she had made to being off the clock was that she had unbuttoned two more buttons on her blouse, revealing the white bralette she was wearing.

She took another drink of wine, noticing her glass was almost empty.

Fuck it...

So, she downed the rest of the glass and refilled it from the bottle of Riesling she had propped up next to her on the couch. In a few moments, the refill—her third, she thought—was almost gone as well.

Her doorbell rang at a little after four o'clock.

Vanessa!

Megan hopped up off the couch to answer it, realizing instantly that that probably wasn't the smartest thing to do with three glasses of wine already in her system. She wobbled when she got to her feet and almost toppled over but somehow managed to stay upright.

"Fuck!" she said aloud.

She made it to the door without any further wobbles and opened it.

"Hi!" she greeted Vanessa, a little loudly.

Vanessa just stood there, cocking one eyebrow, an amused expression on her face as she looked Megan up and down.

Momentarily confused, Megan wondered what the hell, and then she looked down at herself, saw her wide-open blouse and said, "Fuck! Sorry!" She gestured to Vanessa to come in as she started re-buttoning her shirt.

"Oh, don't apologize," Vanessa said, stepping inside. "There are worse ways to greet me. In fact," she continued, taking hold of Megan's hips, "this is kind of sexy. Do you wanna be my boss lady today, because I can totally get into you reprimanding me if you're dressed like this."

Megan's hand shot to her face and her eyes widened.

"Oh my God, don't say that!" she exclaimed. She knew she should have been wildly turned on right now but Vanessa's comment hit a little too close to the mark to what was stressing her out.

Vanessa stepped away and Megan wished she had just kept her mouth shut. Mind-blowing sex on top of all that wine was something she could use right now to help take the edge off the day.

"Okay, what's wrong?" Vanessa asked.

Megan stepped past her into the living room. She tried to concentrate on walking normally but apparently failed because Vanessa noticed something off.

"And have you been drinking?" Vanessa asked, following Megan.

Megan plopped down on the couch and held up the half-finished bottle of Riesling.

"Yes. I've had a crap day and so I started without you."

Vanessa sat down next to Megan, turning to face her. She tucked a stray lock of Megan's hair behind her ear. Megan sighed, feeling comfort from that simple gesture. She was so glad Vanessa was here and, frighteningly, not just because Vanessa represented sex.

"Tell me what's wrong," Vanessa whispered.

"I had to fire someone today," Megan said without looking at her companion. Saying the words made her reach for the bottle again and refill her glass. She silently gave Vanessa credit for not stopping her.

"Wow, that sucks," Vanessa stated.

"Yeah, tell me about it," Megan agreed. "I'm sorry, where are my manners? I need to offer you some wine."

She started to rise so she could fetch a glass for Vanessa, but Vanessa gently prevented her from doing so by placing her hand on Megan's arm, keeping Megan seated.

"Forget the wine," Vanessa said. "Keep talking."

Sweet Vanessa. Why can't she be more than a fuck buddy?

Megan recounted the part of her conversation with Sophia that pertained to Trevor.

"Anyway, I had to call this guy and tell him he was fired. His fucking fiancée was even listening. And he totally deserved to be fired because he's a sucks-ass team lead who was not only a sucks-ass team lead but also a bit of an asshole. But it's also the middle of a fucking pandemic and I've never fired anyone before and it's all kind of fucking with me."

Megan took another sip of wine. Vanessa leaned in and kissed her cheek.

"And he called me a dyke," Megan said.

"What?" Vanessa said loudly.

"Yeah, after I told him. Said he couldn't believe he was being fired by a fucking dyke."

Megan could sense Vanessa tensing up, like a spring that's been pushed down, just waiting to be released. Vanessa was a woman of action, she realized, a woman who right now wanted to jump up, find Trevor and punch his lights out. It was fucking hot.

Too much wine.

Vanessa took a couple of deep breaths. Megan watched as the flush of anger slowly left Vanessa's face.

"It's okay," Vanessa said. "All of this is not a big deal. And like you said, the guy had it coming. Hell, I was worried that something serious was wrong."

Megan blinked.

Not a big deal?

She turned to face Vanessa; her jaw tight. A little voice was warning her that she needed to be careful considering how much wine she'd had, but she ignored it.

"I'm sorry I'm not more like you," she said. "But this is my first time ruining someone's life."

Vanessa pulled away from Megan. She even scooted a few inches further from her on the couch.

"What is that supposed to mean?" Vanessa asked, looking stunned.

Megan silently cursed herself.

"I just meant that you probably had to fire a bunch of people when you were a bigshot at that company you used to work for. Also, now that you own a business, you probably expect to have to fire one or two people eventually; so, you're used to it."

"It doesn't mean I like it," Vanessa said.

"God, I never said you did! I believe I only said that you're used to it."

Vanessa huffed.

"Actually, if you ever get *used to it*, you're a pretty shit person," she said.

"That's not…"

Megan let out an exasperated sigh.

How the fuck did this turn into what was sounding like a fight?

Megan reached for Vanessa's hand, relieved when Vanessa accepted it and even squeezed it.

"I'm sorry if what I said sounded mean," Megan said. "You're not a shit person and I didn't mean to imply that you are. I'm just…not completely myself right now." She used her grip on Vanessa's hand to pull Vanessa closer and then reached up, cupped the back of the brunette's neck and brought their lips together. As soon as their tongues started sliding against one another desire started cutting through the slight drunkenness Megan was feeling and she groaned as her nipples hardened.

When Vanessa pulled away, Megan leaned forward to chase her lips down, but Vanessa laughingly placed a finger over Megan's mouth.

"Wait, wait, wait," Vanessa said. "I have something to tell you that might cheer you up!"

Megan looked at her.

"You going down on me would totally cheer me up," Megan stated.

Vanessa laughed.

"I know, I know; but this will too. You know I went to see Ang and Dee, right? Well, they have an idea and I told them I'd run it by you."

Megan knitted her brows.

"Not some weird, like, foursome thing, right?"

"They said only if you're into it," Vanessa said.

Megan's mouth dropped open. After a moment, though, she smacked Vanessa's arm when Vanessa burst out into giggles.

"You suck!" Megan said with a pout.

Vanessa got control of herself and then said, "No, listen. They want to have, like, a girls' weekend to blow off some steam from all this pandemic shit. And they also remembered your birthday is next week and so what they want is for all of us to pitch in and Airbnb a beach house next weekend. You, me, them, Chloë, Abby and whoever else wants in."

Megan sat up.

"Huh!" she uttered. Usually, she wasn't much for schemes involving large groups of people staying in one place together. She hated communal living. She needed her own space and privacy and the ability to find quietude. But it would be awesome to get out of this condo for a few days. And since she couldn't actually travel anywhere that she wanted to go to now because of Covid, this beach house idea would be the closest thing to a vacation she could hope for.

And it meant spending an entire weekend with Vanessa. Megan wanted that. Badly. And, she realized, she wanted it not just for the sex but because there was nobody else she wanted to spend that much time with.

"I'd want our own room," she told Vanessa. "I don't want us sleeping on some fold-out sofa bed in the middle of the living room."

"I agree one-hundred percent," Vanessa assured her. "Anyway, they're already starting to look for a place." She smiled slyly and scooted closer to Megan, who felt her heartrate pick up. "And don't worry, I'll make sure it suits our own particular needs."

Megan waggled her eyebrows.

"Like making sure our room is soundproof?" she said. She was remembering specifically the very vocal cry of release she herself gave early this morning when Vanessa made her come hard just before leaving to go open La Vida Mocha.

Vanessa laughed.

"We are rather loud, aren't we?" Vanessa murmured, leaning in for another kiss.

"We are," Megan said. She licked her lips and pulled Vanessa close again. "Now, you've made me wait long enough, Miss Murray. I'm upset, horny and I demand release."

Vanessa bit her lower lip and said, "Well, maybe next time when I come over, you should just tie me down in bed after I walk in to make sure I do what you want."

Megan's clit stood at attention.

"Come with me," she ordered, pulling Vanessa up off the couch.

"Yes, ma'am," Vanessa said.

Chapter 27

Vanessa watched as Megan surveyed her handiwork.

Vanessa was spread-eagled on Megan's bed, completely nude, fastened to the bed at her wrists and ankles by some of Megan's scarves. Her heart was racing as she wondered what delicious torture she was in for.

Megan gave no clue, just stood there, eyeing Vanessa's form. Eventually, she came to sit on the side of the bed and turned to face Vanessa.

"Is this okay?" she asked.

"I'm fine," Vanessa assured her. Totally fine. Megan could leave her like this all night.

Apparently satisfied, Megan reached over and squeezed one of Vanessa's nipples and Vanessa groaned with pleasure.

"The safe word is cappuccino," Megan said, still rolling the nipple between her thumb and forefinger. "Repeat it so I know you're listening."

Vanessa got her lips working.

"Cappuccino," she gasped.

"Good girl."

Megan released the nipple and got up.

"I'll be right back," she said, and without waiting for an answer, left the bedroom.

Vanessa watched her go, confused, tantalized, anticipatory. She was loving how vulnerable she was, fastened to the bed like this. Yet she was also loving how safe she felt.

After a couple of minutes, Megan returned, holding a glass of white wine in one hand. She took a seat in a chair by the bedroom window, crossed her legs and started sipping her wine, like a woman who had all the time in the world. Vanessa watched her. Megan's long legs, encased in those hot power trousers, were so sexy, Vanessa just wanted to run her hands along the fabric of the pants before eventually unbuttoning them and then sloooowly pulling down the zipper. Meanwhile, Megan was simply allowing her eyes to roam Vanessa's body as she drank unhurriedly.

"I don't know where to start with you," Megan finally said, after another sip of wine. "You have no idea how wet I'm getting having you like this." She put her wine down and got up to come sit on the edge of the bed. She took hold of Vanessa's nipple again and Vanessa groaned as a mild pressure was applied to it.

"I bet so many women come into your shop wishing they could have you tied up in their beds," Megan said, increasing the pressure on Vanessa's nipple. "But they can't have you. Tell me why they can't have you."

"Because I'm yours," Vanessa said.

"Do you like being at my mercy?"

"Do I have a choice?"

Megan cocked an eyebrow. Vanessa thrilled at seeing a flash of domination flit through Megan's eyes.

"Answer the fucking question."

"Yes, I like being at your mercy."

"Good, because tonight feels like my birthday came early, and I plan on enjoying the fuck out of this."

Vanessa, her body feeling electric, suspected she was going to enjoy the fuck out of this too.

Megan smirked and then said, "You are going to come so much, baby."

***

Megan hadn't been kidding about Vanessa coming so much.

Currently, Vanessa was recovering from her fifth orgasm. Her still-bound form was trembling, her eyes were still closed and she was still nowhere close to catching her breath as her center continued throbbing, pushing out more of her arousal, adding to what was becoming a quite large wet spot on the sheets.

This particular climax had been the result of Megan's specialty: a slow-burn orgasm which Megan had stoked inside Vanessa's center until Megan—and only Megan—decided to let it explode, causing Vanessa to forget anything else existed in the world, yelling out with high-decibel screams as the waves of pleasure tore through her, writhing against the restraints fastening her to the bed. After what felt like an eternity, her body finally stilled and Vanessa managed to open her eyes to locate her lover, finding her sitting at that small table again, nonchalantly drinking some more wine and flipping through a magazine, of all things. After a moment, Megan looked up to see Vanessa staring at her.

"Has that one run its course?" Megan asked.

Vanessa nodded. Boy, did it run its course.

"Good," Megan said, putting down her wine glass. She came back to the bed, sitting by Vanessa's side. At this point in the night, all Vanessa wanted was to taste Megan. She knew the other woman must be soaked between her legs by now; in fact, she could smell it, and it was making Vanessa feel primal.

Megan took a glance at Vanessa's legs.

"Your thighs are trembling," she said, looking at Vanessa's eyes again.

Vanessa had to take a deep breath before being able to speak.

"Can you blame me?" she asked.

Megan started tracing lazy circles around Vanessa's right breast, slowly spiraling in towards the nipple. By now, Vanessa's entire body was one big erogenous zone and even this simple act by Megan was priming Vanessa for more.

Megan leaned forward and locked her lips with Vanessa's for an intense kiss, Vanessa tasting her own come mixed with wine together in Megan's mouth. After coming up for air, Megan slid down until she was once again between Vanessa's legs. Vanessa watched Megan's mouth drop open and a look of pure desire come over her features. Megan gasped and seemed to grow a little dizzy.

"Oh my God, baby," Megan whispered, "this is so beautiful. Do you have any idea how much come is leaking out of you?"

Vanessa had some idea, yeah. By now, her ass was basically resting in a puddle.

Megan lowered her head and started licking the juices coming out of Vanessa. She was gentle, obviously mindful of how sensitive Vanessa was down there now. Megan used slow, flat strokes with tongue, every now and then teasing Vanessa's opening by softly pressing against it as if she was about to penetrate, knowingly avoiding her clit which was now a live wire. Vanessa groaned at the build-up of yearning she felt growing again. She arched her hips upwards, trying to make even more contact with Megan's mouth. This kind of thing had never been done to her before: tied to a bed and made to have orgasm after orgasm. Vanessa couldn't believe this.

Why, oh why, does this have to only be a fling?

Megan, meanwhile, was humming contentedly as she drank, and hearing Megan's enjoyment was sending Vanessa into orbit.

"We haven't even gotten to the fun orgasms yet, babe," Megan eventually said.

"The fun ones?" Vanessa gasped. "These have been pretty fun."

But Megan shook her head.

"Wait right here," she said, as if Vanessa could, in fact, go somewhere.

Vanessa watched Megan go to her closet and pull out a leather tote bag that Vanessa had never seen before.

Megan set the bag on the nightstand and looked inside it. Biting her bottom lip, Megan appeared to be thinking quite seriously about what came next. Eventually, she looked at Vanessa.

"After Cindy and I broke up, I did some shopping," Megan said, lazily tracing Vanessa's jawline. "Do you want to see what I bought myself?"

Vanessa nodded. But Megan shook her head.

"Words," she ordered firmly. "Say, 'Megan, please show me what you bought.'"

Vanessa gasped.

"Megan, please show me what you bought."

"Better. First, there's this…" Megan reached into the bag and pulled out a stunning glass dildo. It was long with purple swirls of glass inside of it and pink nubs along its shaft.

"Oh, fuck," Vanessa whispered.

Megan held it before Vanessa's eyes like one of those models showing off a toaster on *The Price is Right*.

Vanessa licked her lips, her eyes wide, taking it all in, more desire leaking from between her legs. She wondered how much of that stuff her body could produce.

Megan rested the dildo between Vanessa's breasts and Vanessa could feel its weighty solidity.

Megan next pulled out a purple vibrator with a ridged head. Vanessa noted it was another long toy.

This woman doesn't fuck around.

Megan leaned forward to hold Vanessa's eyes with her own. "Do I have your permission?" she asked.

"Fuck, yes. Why haven't you showed me these before?"

Shrugging, Megan said, "I don't know. Wasn't sure yet if you'd be into it."

"I'm into it," Vanessa assured her. "Sometimes fingers just aren't enough. Get to work."

Megan raised her eyebrows and smiled.

"Kind of bossy for someone in your position, aren't you? I could put these away, you know."

After taking a deep breath, Vanessa said, "Please, Megan, get to work."

"Better."

Megan brought the two toys and herself back between Vanessa's legs and with no delay she began sliding the glass dildo into Vanessa.

Vanessa moaned deliriously. She was so lubed the toy slid in easily but it still made her gasp at how much it filled her, sending tingles through her core the entire way, those protruding nubs nearly making her come again right away. And Megan wasn't holding back, either; she slid the whole length in, making Vanessa take it all. Then, Megan switched on the vibrator.

"Oh my God!" Vanessa couldn't help but mewl at the sound moments before she felt the vibrator being slowly run along the skin just outside her pussy. Every now and then Megan would bring the vibrator close enough to the end of the glass dildo that the dildo would pick up the vibrations and transmit them deep inside Vanessa.

"Oh my fucking God!" Vanessa screamed out as she felt the next orgasm building up quickly.

Where did this woman come from?

Barely had that thought entered her mind when she could think no more because she was climaxing yet again.

***

"Cappuccino," Vanessa managed to utter nearly an hour later when she regained the power of speech.

Megan wasted no time. She hurriedly undid the bindings fastening Vanessa's arms to the bedframe.

"Are you okay, babe?" she asked, genuine concern in her voice as she moved to unfasten Vanessa's ankles.

Though now free, Vanessa still hadn't moved. She needed a few more moments while the remnants of that last climax still quivered her muscles.

"I'm better than okay, sweetie, I promise," she said breathily. "I just can't take anymore." She had to swallow and take a deep breath before continuing. "I have never come this many times in one night before."

Quick as a flash, Megan straddled her and brought her face close to Vanessa's.

"Do you mean that?" Megan asked.

It took a lot of energy just for Vanessa to nod.

"Yes, I mean that. No one has done this to me before, not even myself. I'm fucking worn out, sweetie." She had to gasp and close her eyes as a last tingle of pleasure shot out from her core. It was exquisite, but it just made her want to melt into the bed. Fourteen. She had actually come fourteen times. Sometime after the tenth orgasm, Megan had re-inserted the glass dildo and now Vanessa reached down and gently slid it out of herself, gasping at how empty she felt afterwards.

"Good," Megan said, obviously pleased. "If we ever get into a *huge* fight, you'd better remember this. Can I get you anything?"

"Water, please," Vanessa said, her eyes still closed. "And I'd kill for a cheeseburger. And fries. And a vanilla shake."

Megan laughed.

"You sound stoned."

"I feel stoned," Vanessa admitted. "And don't expect me to move. I think I'll lie here until next week."

Megan giggled and gave Vanessa a quick peck on the tip of the nose before getting off her.

"I'll get DoorDash working on that cheeseburger and fries," she said.

"And vanilla shake," Vanessa whispered.

"Right," Megan giggled again. "And vanilla shake."

"But wait!" Vanessa gasped.

Megan came back and sat beside her.

"What?"

"I need to taste you," Vanessa said. "I know how wet you must be. I've been dying to taste you. Please."

Vanessa saw desire overtake Megan's features.

"Fuck, I need you to," she said, standing again and quickly taking off those sexy slacks, along with her underwear. When she did, the muskiness of Megan's arousal penetrated Vanessa's nostrils and made her groan in anticipation.

Megan returned to the bed and straddled Vanessa, who felt Megan's dampness on her stomach. Megan then raised her hips and moved upwards along Vanessa's body until her center was positioned right above Vanessa's face.

"Oh my God," Vanessa moaned. Megan was soaked. Her upper thighs were slick and shiny with wetness and as she hovered her pussy above Vanessa's mouth, strings of her come were dripping out of her folds. Vanessa reached out her tongue to catch them, letting the liquid slide down her throat. It tasted divine.

"Megan, please," Vanessa begged, reaching up and taking hold of Megan's hips.

Holding onto the headboard, Megan slowly lowered herself down until Vanessa could lick, penetrate and suck properly.

Vanessa tightened her grip on Megan's hips. She wasn't going to let her go until she got what she wanted.

Megan's screams of pleasure as she climaxed and then climaxed again were probably heard out on the street.

***

When Sunday came, Vanessa emerged slowly from a deep sleep and stretched.

Day off!

She opened her eyes to look at the clock on the bedside table, knowing what it would tell her. And, yep, she was right.

5:43 a.m.

Owning a coffeeshop meant Vanessa's body had become programmed to wake her up early on any given morning, even on the mornings she didn't need to wake up early, so it was not unexpected that her clock was showing such an ungodly time. But because it was Sunday, Vanessa was now able to ignore the clock and close her eyes again.

She became aware of Megan's arm around her waist and the other woman's soft snoring. By turning her head slightly to her left,

Vanessa was able to bury her nose in Megan's ruffled hair and sniff the coconut-scented conditioner Megan used.

It was her day off and Megan was here with her.

And they could sleep in.

Vanessa smiled contentedly, placed her hand gently on Megan's arm and drifted off back to sleep.

When she woke up the second time, the clock told her it was almost nine.

That's more like it.

She frowned, though, when she realized she was in bed alone.

Getting up, she spent time in the bathroom freshening up before dressing in her favorite day-off clothes: old skater shorts that used to be red but were now more of a pale pink and an equally old *Doctor Who* t-shirt with a faded image of a Dalek on the front. She also pulled on a pair of green fuzzy socks and then left the bedroom.

"Hey!" Megan greeted her in the living room. Vanessa found her on the couch, reading on her Kindle, dressed much like herself in old shorts and a tee.

Like she belongs here.

"Hey, back," Vanessa said, lowering herself onto the couch and instantly snuggling with Megan who put down her Kindle and encircled Vanessa with her arms. "How long have you been up?"

"Close to two hours, I guess. Early riser, remember?"

"I feel bad. You could have woken me, if you wanted," Vanessa told her.

"No. This is your day off; you deserve to sleep in."

Vanessa sighed and held Megan closer. She could get used to this.

"But now that you're up…" Megan said. She reached for her phone which was on the coffee table and started tapping the screen. When she was done, she laid the phone back down.

"What were you doing?" Vanessa asked.

"DoorDashing us breakfast from that diner on State Street," Megan told her. "I already had the order set up; I was just waiting for you to make an appearance before pulling the trigger on it. We have scrambled eggs and bacon coming. We have French toast coming. And because I'm feeling particularly sinful, two cinnamon rolls are coming."

"Oh my God, you're amazing," Vanessa said, not caring about the calories that would be delivered to her door. It sounded perfect, better than yogurt and a fruit cup. She inhaled deeply as a new scent caught her attention. "And you made coffee!"

Megan smiled but also rolled her eyes.

"I did, but that coffee maker you have! Fuck, Vanessa, it's fancy! It took a while for me to figure it out and even when I thought I had, I didn't know if I was about to brew coffee or launch a space shuttle."

Breakfast arrived about thirty minutes later and they ate together in the dining room.

"Just so you know," Megan began, "I brought my iPad and my Kindle with me, so I have stuff to do to keep myself entertained, you know, in case you totally want to veg out uninterrupted."

Vanessa smiled, completely won over by Megan's thoughtfulness. She put down her fork and put her hand on Megan's knee under the table.

"I'm glad you're here," she said. "Seriously. If you weren't, I would have called you to invite you over anyway."

Vanessa noted how Megan blushed and then bit her lip thoughtfully as she held Vanessa's eyes with her own. To Vanessa, it seemed Megan wanted to say something, something she was debating whether to utter.

For her part, Vanessa knew that she wanted to say things. Things like how she hadn't slept as soundly on any given night all year long until she started falling asleep with Megan next to her; and like how when she found herself daydreaming about Megan, it was no longer just about sex.

After breakfast, they started their *Star Trek* movie marathon, beginning with *The Motion Picture* and then moving on to *Wrath of Khan*. Following *Khan*, they DoorDashed lunch from the same diner.

"God, are we two spoiled first-worlders or what?" Vanessa asked, only half-facetiously after thinking to herself how ridiculously easy it was to order food now. Pick up smartphone, tap this, tap that, tap this other thing and *bada-bing!* Food arrives shortly thereafter. And with the no-contact delivery option, it could all be done without speaking to a single soul. "What are we going to do if there ever is a zombie apocalypse and normal society breaks down?"

Megan scoffed.

"What are you worried about? You're an alpha lesbian. You'll create a whole new society of female ninja warriors who will conquer the western hemisphere for you and give you dominion over all its peoples."

Vanessa laughed so much her eyes watered.

"And what will become of you?" she asked Megan.

"I'm hoping you'll keep me alive to be your sex-slave-slash-tech-support person."

Probably because of lunch, they both fell asleep snuggling together on the couch while watching *Search for Spock*.

Before starting *Voyage Home*, Megan stated, "I want movie snacks! Kettle corn and candy."

"Of which I have neither in my house," Vanessa said with a pout.

They both looked at each other and after a second simultaneously said, "Postmates!"

Megan unlocked her phone.

"We are so pathetic," she said.

"You're right," Vanessa agreed. "We should get dressed and go to the store ourselves."

They both looked at each other again and after a second simultaneously said, "I don't want to put on a bra."

Postmates arrived less than an hour later.

After *The Undiscovered Country* they both agreed to skip *The Final Frontier* because each of them deemed it terrible. Besides, by then they were both in the mood for zombies.

They started with Romero's classic, *Night of the Living Dead*, moved onto the 2004 remake of *Dawn of the Dead*—both of them admitting to having a crush on Sarah Polley—and then watched three really cheesy and bad zombie movies on Netflix, which were nonetheless enjoyable because they laughed so hard at how awful they were. DoorDash interrupted a quality zombie movie, *28 Days Later*, delivering their dinner.

They finished the night with *World War Z*.

Vanessa noticed Megan's eyes getting droopy right around when Gerry Lane and Segen survived the plane crash in the movie. Vanessa was getting sleepy also. It was just after ten o'clock and she had to get up early tomorrow to open La Vida Mocha at 7 a.m. And she knew that Megan started her workday early also and was usually in bed by ten on weeknights.

"Come on, sleepyhead," she urged Megan, turning off the TV.

In the bedroom, Vanessa was struck by how easily they both went about their individual routines for getting ready for bed, without getting in one another's way. As she brushed her teeth, Megan was next to her at the bathroom's counter applying night cream to her neck, each of them sharing the counterspace without problem. When Vanessa finished brushing, Megan wordlessly handed over Vanessa's hairbrush because Vanessa always brushed her hair right after brushing her teeth. Similarly, while Megan was changing into her pajama set, Vanessa plugged Megan's iPad into the charger without being asked to.

It was as if they had been doing it for years.

In bed, with the lights off, Megan fit herself into a comfortable embrace with Vanessa and was asleep instantly. Just as Vanessa was about to fall asleep herself, she realized that her and Megan had spent the entire day together without once having sex. And it had been one of the best Sundays of her life.

Chapter 28

On Thursday, Megan was on the I-5, heading south to La Jolla to meet her family for her birthday lunch. She was dressed in gray boot-cut slacks and high heels and a dark green sleeveless cowl-neck blouse.

Twenty-seven.

As she did every year on this day, she mentally took stock of her life and decided, again, that she was doing okay. She had a dynamic career with a great salary and was about to be promoted to become one of the officers of a top software company; a fabulous condo that she owned and which was a five-minute drive from the beach; wonderful friends, and was now enjoying a summertime fling with an unbelievably gorgeous woman.

Megan smiled at the thought of Vanessa, and then smiled even wider as she remembered waking up with Vanessa today and how Vanessa had then given her a birthday orgasm with her lips and tongue, and then another birthday orgasm with her fingers, all before leaving to go open La Vida Mocha. Vanessa had jokingly suggested that she would try to make Megan come twenty-seven times today in honor of Megan's new age. For her part, Megan didn't doubt that if it was even possible for a woman to climax that many times in a single day, Vanessa would be the one who could make it happen.

So, at twenty-seven, Megan felt pretty satisfied at how things were going for her.

After a moment, her smile faded, to be replaced by a frown. She started nibbling her bottom lip.

Still, though...

At twenty-seven, she was still in the closet.

Every lesbian Megan was friends with was out and proud; some of them, like Vanessa, since they were in college, or even earlier. Hell, she knew women her age—sometimes even younger!—who were *married* to other women! Yet, here she was, one year closer to thirty and she still hadn't come out to her family. How long was it going to take? And more importantly, what was she waiting for?

Her parents were never going to become open-minded enough to stop looking at the entire LGBTQ community as a bunch of sinful, misguided and confused individuals who just needed to find a closer relationship with Jesus. This was especially true now that Megan's father had just been made deacon at their church and Megan's mother was contemplating a run for the La Jolla city council. It was a shame, Megan thought. A shame that her folks could be trapped in such backwards thinking. How oppressive it must be, she considered, to live a life believing that just because people were different, that they were somehow defective.

There might be a chance with Molly, Megan had often thought. The key word being *might*. The truth was, however, that Megan truly did not know how Molly would react to discovering Megan was a lesbian.

Which brought up the crux of the matter, really, Megan considered as she bore right to stay on the I-5 past where it joined up with the 805.

Was Megan willing to risk losing her family in order to be out and proud like her friends?

Megan loved her family, but she had also known for a long time now that she wasn't particularly close to them. Ever since high school she had realized that her and her parents had ideological differences on topics ranging from religion to science to politics to diversity. Megan had chosen to go to college all the way in New York City in part to put distance between herself and them, and even when she returned to California, she made sure not to settle in La Jolla. She only saw her mother once a month for their lunches and if Megan was honest with herself, she only put up with those lunches out of some sense of obligation rather than a desire to spend time with Audrey. And she saw her father even less; usually only on major holidays.

What all this was adding up to, Megan realized now, was the conclusion that it was downright stupid of her to not be out to her family. Sure, she hoped they'd accept her, even if that acceptance was given grudgingly; but if they didn't accept her being a lesbian then that was their loss, not hers. She had a responsibility to herself to live her best life, not a disguised life.

She suddenly thought of Cindy, but not in the way she had been thinking of her over the past several months since their break-up. Now, Megan felt an almost overwhelming surge of gratitude and…guilt. For two years, Cindy had patiently and without complaint allowed Megan to keep Cindy hidden from her family, even when it meant missing out on important things like holiday dinners and birthday celebrations. Throughout their two years together, Megan had often left Cindy at home while she drove to La Jolla to her parents' house, or met them somewhere nice for a meal—very often at places Megan knew Cindy would enjoy. And during their two years together, Megan made sure to never bring her parents over to her condo once Cindy had moved in.

An idea came to Megan just then and she checked the car's clock. She still had plenty of time. Traffic was surprisingly not bad today and she could still make it to Marcano's before their reservation.

She exited the highway at the next exit though she was still a good fifteen minutes from the restaurant and pulled into the parking lot of a Target. She didn't want to be driving and having this conversation.

Cindy answered on the first ring.

"Megan?" she said, the surprise evident in her voice.

"Hey, can we talk?" Megan asked.

"Of course, I'm just walking back from having an early lunch. Happy birthday, by the way."

"Thanks."

"So…what's up?"

Was that hope in her voice? Megan wondered.

"I wanted to apologize," Megan said after taking a deep breath.

There was silence for a few moments before Cindy asked, "Um…why are you apologizing to me, Megs?"

Now Megan was silent while she gathered her thoughts.

"Megs?"

"I'm apologizing for hiding you, Cindy. For not being out. Considering how in love we were, it wasn't fair to you. I excluded you from a lot of my life and I can only imagine how that must have made you feel."

"Oh, Megs…"

"I guess I'm also thanking you? For being awesome and understanding about it. I wonder how many other women in my shoes were as lucky."

"Megan, please, can I see you? There's so much I want to say. I'm still in love with you, Megs! I was so, so stupid and I've been miserable these—"

"Cindy, I'm moving to New York," Megan cut her off. "It's for work. I don't know when yet but it will be soon."

"Oh," Cindy said softly.

"And, I'm sorry, but even if I wasn't, I'm not sure I'd give us another chance. I wouldn't have been able to ever trust you again and eventually that would've driven us apart, don't you think?"

"Yeah, I suppose you're right." Megan heard Cindy blow out a breath. "Fuck. I blew it."

Megan couldn't argue with that, but the purpose of this call wasn't to beat a dead horse.

"Anyway, I just wanted to tell you how sorry I am, and how grateful I am. Despite everything, you deserve to know that."

"Thanks, Megs. I appreciate it. I'm not gonna lie, though…I wish I could change your mind about us."

"And I wish I could have a night of unbridled passion with Rachel McAdams."

Cindy laughed.

"Maybe Rachel has a place in New York," she suggested. "You might bump into her in Times Square."

"My luck is never that good," Megan pointed out, laughing also. "Listen, I gotta go. Take care, Cindy."

Cindy sighed.

"You too, Megs. Happy birthday again."

After ending the call, Megan returned to the I-5, anxious now to reach Marcano's.

She had decided she was going to give herself an extra special birthday present this year.

Chapter 29

Vanessa checked the clock on her living room wall. A little past eleven-thirty. Megan should be at that steakhouse in La Jolla by now.

She sighed, wondering what to do with herself now.

Stop being so down! What's the matter with you?

It was about the hundredth time Vanessa had chided herself, because *down* was how she felt, which was ridiculous. After all, she had gotten to wake up with Megan on Megan's birthday; she'd gotten to taste Megan before leaving for work; and Megan was due back from La Jolla by late afternoon, at the latest, to spend the entire rest of the day and night with Vanessa. Really, she had nothing to be *down* about!

Yet, she knew what was bothering her, even though she didn't want to admit it.

Spying her laptop on her dining room table, Vanessa decided to take her mind off things by focusing on work.

California's partial reopening was going well. Even though Covid cases continued to rise and fall depending on the region, on the whole the State government seemed to think that it was still okay for establishments like coffeeshops and restaurants to remain open as long as precautions were taken. As Vanessa and Chloë were cleaning up La Vida Mocha after closing at ten this morning, Vanessa told the younger woman that starting next week, La Vida Mocha would return to its regular hours. The announcement had made Chloë say "Yes!" with such exuberance that Vanessa had pulled her into a hug.

"But not until Monday, right?" Chloë had asked.

Vanessa confirmed that. She'd keep the coffeeshop closed this coming Sunday because this weekend was Beach House Weekend.

Angela and Desiree, two of the most efficient women Vanessa had ever known, had managed to find a remarkable-looking beach mansion on Airbnb just south of Carlsbad. Starting tomorrow, eight lesbians were going to be able to live like rock stars for a few days. The cost wasn't even outrageous once it was split eight ways, one of the advantages of a pandemic being that homeowners with listings on Airbnb were desperate to get any kind of bookings.

And because Megan's birthday was today, the Beach House Weekend was also going to be a de facto birthday celebration as well.

Yeah, Vanessa and Chloë would still have to run La Vida Mocha Friday and Saturday nights until eight p.m., but that still meant they'd have plenty of time to enjoy the mansion. And since the booking was until Monday, Vanessa and Megan could actually have the whole entire day of Sunday just chilling at the place.

Now, however, Vanessa had to make up the work schedules for La Vida Mocha for next week. Luckily, Luli wanted to come back. This meant that Vanessa wouldn't have to train a brand-new person from scratch. With three people available to run the coffeeshop, Vanessa could keep all their hours down to normal, even though she knew that she, as the owner, would still need to be there more than either of her two employees.

But once she was done making the schedules, Vanessa started feeling restless again. It truly was ridiculous, she thought.

She picked up her phone and called William.

"Oh. My. God!" William answered dramatically. "Does Megan have a cold? Is she out of the country? Did she decide she likes boys instead? Because I can't imagine why my best friend Vanessa would be calling me instead of being all lesbian with her new girlfriend."

"Shut up!" Vanessa said, groaning. "And she's not my girlfriend!"

Fuck, how many times did she have to tell people that? Including herself?

"I know I've been a bad friend but, well…Megan."

"No apologies necessary," William said. "Remember my little dalliance with that guy Warren a few years back? I saw you, what, twice in six months?"

"Have you had lunch? Can you get away?" Vanessa asked.

Twenty minutes later, Vanessa, wearing a mask, walked into her and William's favorite seafood place a couple of blocks from the beach in Oceanside, a spot they had frequented often back when they were living together. She spotted William at a table in front of a window looking out on Coast Highway. He already had two margaritas waiting on the table.

"Oh, you're a mind reader," Vanessa said after hugging him and then sitting down, removing her mask and taking a sip of the cocktail. A masked waitress made her appearance after a moment, asking Vanessa if she wanted anything other than the margarita.

"Just water, please," Vanessa told her. "And I think we're ready to order."

Her and William had been to this place so many times, they each had their favorite dishes: shrimp skewers and hush puppies for William; kale salad with a salmon fillet for Vanessa.

"Okay, spill it," William said when the waitress departed. He leaned forward, resting his arms on the table. "What's troubling you?"

Vanessa rolled her eyes and sighed in exasperation.

"Ugh!" she exclaimed. "I am just soooo bored! I have the afternoon off because of La Vida Mocha's new hours, but Megan is in La Jolla with her family for her birthday and I'm just so antsy! I didn't used to be like this! I've never had a problem with filling my free time. Even when I have nothing to do, I enjoy having nothing to do."

William motioned with his hand in a dismissive gesture.

"You're just horny," he said, leaning back in his chair and taking a long sip from his margarita.

"That's another thing," Vanessa exclaimed. "I'm horny, like, all the time now! I have *never* been in a sexual relationship like this before. Ever!"

William's eyes sparkled with curiosity and he leaned forward again, eagerness to hear more on his face.

"Ooh, do tell! But leave out all the disgusting descriptions about female anatomy, though."

"Shut up. All I'm willing to tell you is that I'm constantly thinking about sex with Megan and it's almost annoying."

"Almost?"

Vanessa blushed.

"Well, when I think about having sex with her, I come up with ideas and then I get to use those ideas on her later. So, there's an upside to it."

William made a face.

"Stop right there!" he said, holding his hands up before him. "I don't want to know."

"Anyway, what's been happening with you?"

"Finally!" William exclaimed. "Don't you know by now that when you meet up with me, I expect to be the first topic of discussion?"

Vanessa smiled.

"Sorry, being horny all the time has made me forget my manners," she said.

Their food arrived just as William launched into an update about all things William, which, not surprisingly to Vanessa, took them until they had both almost finished their meals.

Vanessa asked him about his thing with Tyrone. William shrugged and then said, "Tyrone and I are just messing around, having a bit of fun. I'm not really looking for love right now. But that's why I chose him; he's temporary."

There was that word again. *Temporary*. She and Megan were *temporary*. But why was William's *temporary* thing so different? If memory served, he and Tyrone have been *temporary* for over a year now! Why did William get to keep his *temporary* thing while Vanessa had to face hers going away? It was unfair and it was making her a little angry.

Their server came to clear their plates and they took the opportunity to order two coffees. Vanessa noticed William looking intently at her.

"What?"

"This is actually interesting to me," William said.

"What is?" Vanessa asked.

"Well, it's obvious to me that you have it bad for Megan. I've been waiting the entire lunch for you to finally admit it."

Vanessa felt the blush creeping up her face from her neck. But she admitted nothing.

"I don't think I've ever seen you have it bad before," William went on. "I mean, I know you kinda liked Rebecca but you weren't *gaga* over her. In fact, I had the impression that she was just filling a need you had at the time to have someone to wake up next to each morning. But any warm body would have done."

"Aww, don't say that," Vanessa whined. "I did like Rebecca."

"But not the way you like Megan?" William baited.

Vanessa pouted and suddenly refused to meet William's eyes.

"No," she finally muttered.

"It's actually nice seeing this happen to you," William said once the server returned with their coffees and left again. "You've always been a bit of a player."

Vanessa reached across the table and slapped his arm. She wanted to protest against the label. She even opened her mouth to protest against the label, but then shut it again.

Begrudgingly, Vanessa had to admit William had a point. Even though she would hardly have classified herself a *player*, her romantic history did not include a lot of long-term girlfriends, especially considering her age. But that hadn't been because she was channeling Shane McCutcheon. It was simply a matter of wanting to feel something that she'd been waiting to feel all her life.

Something like what she was feeling with Megan, a woman she first met twenty-one days ago.

And, God, it bothered her that she knew that number! What was she, sixteen-years-old?

Chapter 30

When the doorbell rang, Megan rushed to open her front door, excited, and this time it was not just about laying eyes on the gorgeous woman she knew was on the other side.

As soon as Vanessa stepped in, Megan pulled her close for a deep kiss, forcing Vanessa to drop the bags she was carrying.

"Looking for a repeat of that night I took you right at the front door of my place?" Vanessa murmured when they broke for air. "Because I can totally make that happen."

Megan smiled.

"Maybe later. Right now, I have some news to tell you."

"Oh?" Vanessa began. "Good or bad?"

"Definitely good," Megan told her. An idea came to her then. "Ooh! I should pour some wine!"

Vanessa raised her eyebrows.

"Oh, wine-worthy good news, huh?"

Megan felt like she was buzzing as she took Vanessa's hand and led her into the kitchen. A minute later, she had poured two glasses of white, handed one to Vanessa and took a deep breath.

"I came out to my parents today. Well, and Molly," she said.

Megan almost squealed with delight at the expression of pure surprise on Vanessa's face. It had been worth it to not text her the moment she left Marcano's and instead wait to tell her in person.

"What!" Vanessa exclaimed. "No way!"

"Way!" Megan confirmed, clinking her glass of wine with Vanessa's.

"Sweetie, that's...I mean, I take it from how bubbly you are that it's wonderful, right?"

"Totally!" Megan said gleefully. *Wonderful* couldn't begin to describe it, she thought. Ever since leaving La Jolla, Megan had felt like a new woman, a lighter woman, a *free* woman.

Vanessa pulled her in for a congratulatory hug.

"How did they take it?" she asked.

"They hate it!" Megan said, laughing.

Vanessa's face fell and her eyebrows knitted in confusion.

"Hate it? Then why are you so happy?"

"Because I don't care!" Megan said, which was one-hundred percent the truth. She filled Vanessa in on her ruminations while driving to La Jolla earlier. She then recounted what had happened at Marcano's.

Even before walking into the restaurant, Megan had decided she wasn't going to wait until her and her family were well into their lunch together before making her announcement. She might chicken out. Thus, after they had been shown to their table, Megan had said, "Mom, Dad, Molly, I'm gay. Always have been. Always will be. Thoughts?"

Her father had told her to stop being silly, no daughter of his was gay. Her mother had actually asked if she meant *gay* as in happy. And Molly had just sat there with a stunned look on her face not saying anything.

Megan had then said, "We can have this lunch together with you knowing I'm a lesbian and being fine with it, or we can *not* have this lunch at all."

"You're bluffing," her father had said then. "Because you know I'm not going to sit here pretending to be fine with what you just told me, but I also know you wouldn't break any family traditions like this one."

"And so, I got up and left," Megan now told Vanessa. "I *was* hungry, though, so I stopped off at a McDonalds to get something to eat, even though I have a lover who probably now thinks I'm disgusting because I ate a quarter-pounder."

Vanessa laughed and pulled Megan in for a kiss.

"I don't think you're disgusting, sweetie! In fact, I'm over-the-moon proud of you!"

"I'm proud of myself," Megan said, beaming. "I don't know why it took so long for me to do this. I guess I was always expecting that my family would start to show some glimmer of intelligence and human sophistication. Once I realized that was never going to happen, I said fuck it."

"Off-topic question," Vanessa began. "How many days has it been since we first met?"

Megan scoffed.

"Twenty-one. Everybody knows that," she replied. "Anyway, I wanna celebrate!"

"Well, it is your birthday, sweetie. We can do anything you want. Do you want your present now?"

"I do!" Megan said, before leaning in and cupping Vanessa's chin and giving her a mischievous grin. "And then I'll tell you what else I want to do…"

Vanessa raised an eyebrow.

"Maybe I want to hear about the what else first," she said.

But Megan shook her head.

"No, no, no…presents before sex, always."

They went back to the entryway where Vanessa had dropped her stuff when Megan had pounced on her. Megan saw that one of the items Vanessa had let fall was actually a Coach shopping bag. She looked at Vanessa, her mouth open in shock. With a tilt of her head, Vanessa wordlessly told her to go get it.

Megan picked up the bag by its handles and scampered into the living room, where she sat on the couch and reached inside it.

"Oh my God!" she gasped. "This is so awesome!"

This was a large Coach shoulder bag. Only, because of a recent deal Coach had made with the folks over at Disney, their traditional horse and carriage icon had been replaced with Luke Skywalker's landspeeder being pulled by a tauntaun, with R2-D2 and C-3PO riding in the landspeeder.

Megan looked up at Vanessa, who was standing against a wall watching her.

"Babe, this is incredible! I didn't even know Coach had a Star Wars line! Thank you so much! No one else I know has one of these!"

"And that *is* the important thing when it comes to handbags, isn't it?" Vanessa said, coming to sit down next to her. "Men think it has to do with having room to store all our stuff, but, nope! It's all about showing up the women we figure on seeing that day."

"This is too cool! Thank you, babe." Megan pulled Vanessa in for a real kiss now and it wasn't long before she wanted more. She slid her hands up Vanessa sides, just skirting the other woman's breasts, feeling Vanessa shudder in response. But Megan managed to pull away before things got too far.

Vanessa's face telegraphed her disappointment.

"I was kinda hoping *that* was what else you wanted to do today," she said.

"It is," Megan assured her, standing up while holding Vanessa's hand. "But upstairs. I need more space than a dumb old couch. Besides, your favorite toys are up there."

Vanessa quirked an eyebrow.

"And I thought it was *your* birthday," she said.

In Megan's bedroom, Vanessa had the birthday girl topless in moments and Megan was standing with her head tilted back, groaning at the sensations Vanessa's mouth was pulling from her nipples.

Then the doorbell rang. Vanessa pulled away from Megan's breasts.

"What the fuck!" Megan exclaimed. Then she remembered. "Oh, I bet it's Amazon."

With a smirk, Vanessa asked, "Bought yourself a little birthday present?"

"Always," Megan answered.

"Well, seeing as your half-naked, I'll go down and bring it in," Vanessa offered. "You, in the meantime…" she waved her finger in front of Megan's form. "Off with rest of these and don't expect to be getting dressed again anytime soon."

"Ooh!" Megan said, already starting to shed the offending clothes.

Chapter 31

Downstairs, Vanessa opened the front door not expecting to see anyone or anything except an Amazon package.

Instead, there was a cute young woman standing there. She barely looked old enough to drink. She had well-styled chestnut hair, was several inches shorter than Vanessa and was wearing a coral spaghetti-strap swing dress that was nice enough to be worn for a special occasion.

Frowning, Vanessa wondered if this was Cindy, the thought making her bristle inside. Her armor went up.

The woman seemed surprised and then confused at seeing Vanessa. She even took a look at the house number on the wall next to the door to be sure she had the right place.

Vanessa crossed her arms.

Yes, this is her house. And as you can see, she's entertaining a guest.

"Um..." the woman began uncertainly, "is Megan in?"

Vanessa was about to respond with snark and defensiveness but at the last second something stopped her. Something about this woman's appearance. Something about her eyes and the set of her jaw. They were familiar somehow. Vanessa was certain she had never met this person before, but she couldn't shake the sense that in some way she knew her.

"Megan's upstairs," she said in her normal voice. "Who should I say is calling?"

The woman was obviously quite nervous, but even her manner of being nervous was tugging at something in Vanessa. It was like Vanessa knew her, but didn't know her.

"I'm Molly," the woman answered. "Megan's sister."

Holy crap!

"Oh my God," Vanessa said, her earlier defensiveness now completely gone. "I'm so sorry! Um...come in, please!" She stood aside to let Molly pass.

"I'm Vanessa, by the way."

"Hi, Vanessa; it's nice to meet you," Molly said with what appeared to be a genuine smile.

Vanessa hooked her thumb in the direction of the staircase.

"Like I said, she's upstairs."

Completely naked by now, no doubt.

"I'll, um, go get her. Why don't you make yourself comfortable on the couch?"

"Thank you, Vanessa; I really appreciate it." Another genuine smile.

"Sure."

Vanessa took the stairs two at a time.

Walking into the bedroom, she found a totally nude Megan in bed, reclining against the headboard, those pert and perfect breasts of hers pointing right at Vanessa. Despite everything, Vanessa couldn't help but go breathless at the sight, her mouth dropping open.

Megan frowned.

"There's a disappointing lack of Amazon boxes in your hands," she said, pouting.

Vanessa blinked.

"What? Oh! No…it wasn't Amazon."

"Who was it?"

"Your sister. She's downstairs."

Megan sat up fully.

"Molly? What the hell?"

"I don't know what the hell, but she's downstairs. On the couch."

Megan scrambled out of bed. Vanessa picked up Megan's clothes from the floor where Megan had left them and handed them to her one at a time. As Megan started dressing, Vanessa asked, "Shall I just wait up here or…?"

"No! Come with me!" Megan pulled on her slacks, took Vanessa's hand and left the bedroom barefoot.

Back downstairs, Molly stood up quickly when Megan and Vanessa entered the living room.

"Hey, Megan," Molly said shyly. Vanessa completely saw Megan in her just then.

"Hey, Molls," Megan replied.

All three of them stood in silence for a while, Megan and Molly not meeting one another's eyes. Finally, Vanessa said, "Megan, I'm gonna go. I'll be at my place."

Megan turned to completely face Vanessa.

"What? No!"

Vanessa could see the hurt in Megan's eyes. She put her hands on Megan's shoulders.

"I'm five minutes away," she said, meeting Megan's eyes. "Your sister came to visit you, let her visit you. Call me when you're done and I'll be over here before your phone gets cold, I promise."

Megan smiled and then leaned in to hug Vanessa, which Vanessa readily returned.

In her Jeep, Vanessa admitted to herself that she was worried. She hoped Megan would be okay and that Molly hadn't come over just to make Megan feel terrible.

Chapter 32

"Why are you here, Molls?" Megan asked as soon she returned to the living room after seeing Vanessa out. Megan wanted Vanessa here, not her sister.

"Is that your girlfriend?" Molly asked.

Megan crossed her arms and stood with her weight balanced on one leg. Her power pose.

No, Vanessa was not her girlfriend, but Megan didn't want Molly to know that only because, probably due to their parents' influence, Molly most likely believed that gay people didn't have committed and lasting relationships. So, the last thing Megan wanted to tell Molly was that Vanessa was just a fling, someone to keep her company until she moved to New York.

With some defiance in her voice, said, "Yes, that's right," and then shuddered a little at how good it felt to claim Vanessa—even in a lie—as her girlfriend.

"She's beautiful," Molly said, in obvious awe, her eyes wide. "Like, wow! Like, fuck, she's gorgeous!"

Megan couldn't help a small smile picking up the corners of her lips at the way her sister was fangirling over Vanessa.

"Seriously, Megan, she's like a supermodel!"

At that, Megan burst out laughing. She couldn't help it. This was all too ludicrous.

When she got control of herself again, she said, "Sorry, Molls. I'm just finding it so weird that you're here drooling over Vanessa. Of all the ways I expected my birthday to play out, this wasn't one of them."

She saw Molly blush and look down at her shoes. Megan came over to the couch and sat down, pulling her sister down with her.

"So, why are you actually here, Molls?"

Molly took a couple of breaths before meeting Megan's eyes.

"You're not wrong about Mom and Dad," she said.

Not a news flash.

"But you are wrong about me," Molly continued.

Megan blinked.

"I know how ridiculous Mom and Dad are," Molly went on. "The truth is...The truth is I'm ashamed of them, in fact."

Megan gasped and reached out to take both Molly's hands in her own.

"Oh, Molly…"

"I know you've thought the worst of me," Molly said, looking down at their joined hands. "That I was just like them, but I'm not, I swear. I've just always wanted to try to be like a mediator, I guess, someone to bridge the divide between you and them and I guess I fucked it up because instead I made it seem like I was always on their side."

Megan felt her eyes watering. Her bottom lip started trembling.

Molly met Megan's eyes again.

"But the way they reacted today when you told them you were gay…I couldn't let that slide." She chuckled drily. "You missed me telling them off after you left. I gave them an earful."

"I bet it was epic," Megan said, sniffling. A hot tear ran down her cheek.

"It was. Totally." Molly reached out and wiped Megan's tear away. "I mean, how dare they treat you like that. Their own daughter!"

Megan couldn't wait any longer. She pulled Molly into a tight embrace, both sisters letting their tears run freely.

"I love you, Molls," Megan sobbed.

"I love you, dumdum," Molly sobbed back. "And I have no problem with you being a lesbian." She pulled back enough to look Megan in the face. "I've always known, by the way."

"You did not!" Megan said, swatting her sister's arm.

"Did too! I'm sure Mom and Dad didn't pick up on the little things like I did."

Megan wiped her cheeks and then cocked an eyebrow.

"Little things like what? Like how I never brought a man over to meet them?"

Molly shook her head. She reached into her purse and extracted a pack of tissues. She handed one to Megan and then used the other to dab at her eyes.

"No," she said. "It was…the way I'd catch you looking at other women. I mean, women are always looking at other women, it's what we do. But usually it's because we comparing ourselves to them or we like their outfits or their shoes. But when you did it…Like, if we were at a restaurant and our waitress was pretty. Or if we were out shopping and a cute saleswoman was helping us. You'd check her out."

"Damn! And I thought I was being subtle."

Molly chewed her bottom lip, thinking.

"But that's the thing. You *were* being subtle but maybe because I'm your sister, I was still able to see it when perhaps others couldn't. Does that make sense?"

Megan squeezed Molly's hand.

"Totally."

"I don't know what's going to happen with Mom and Dad," Molly went on. "I think we're both on their shit list together now." She chuckled again. "But I don't care. I just want my sister back."

"You got her," Megan promised.

"And Mom told me you think I should postpone the wedding until things get back to normal. I think you're right. I've been worried for a while now that I won't get to have the wedding I always wanted."

"What does Cole think?" Megan asked, referring to her sister's fiancé.

Molly made an *Are you serious?* face.

"As if I'm going to give him a say," she said.

Megan laughed.

"And just because you're a lesbian doesn't mean you get out of my wedding, whenever it is. I hope that's not what you were planning!"

Megan rolled her eyes.

"Yep, you caught me. All these years dating women was only done so I could have an excuse to be uninvited to your wedding. You're a regular Sherlock Holmes, there, sis."

They both laughed.

"Would you like some wine?" Megan asked.

Chapter 33

It was two hours later before Vanessa returned to Megan's, and when Megan told her of the discussion that she'd had with Molly. Vanessa couldn't be happier.

Even later, in bed, when they had both recovered from having hours of sex, and the various toys had been put off to the side, the two women cuddled together. They were both sweaty, tingling, sore, exhausted. It was pitch dark outside, though Vanessa had no idea what time it was and quite frankly, she was too tired to turn her head to look at Megan's clock on the bedside table. They hadn't even stopped for dinner. What's more, Vanessa knew she was going to have a hell of a time later untangling the mess her hair had become; not that Megan's was any better. Her auburn locks were now far from resembling anything that could be called a hairdo.

Megan was the first to speak.

"I knew when I first laid eyes on you that if I was ever lucky enough to have sex with you, that you'd be the best I ever had," she murmured, stroking Vanessa's arm.

"Is that the vibe I put out? 'Best sex you'll ever have?'"

Megan shook her head.

"No, not exactly. It wasn't a vibe, so to speak."

"What was it then?"

Megan bit her cheek and looked away.

"You're gonna think I'm silly," she said.

Vanessa tried not to smirk. Here was Vulnerable Megan again, making an appearance when not too long ago a very Domineering Megan had done things to Vanessa with a strap-on that had made Vanessa come so hard tears had run from her eyes. Not to mention the other things Megan had done that had made Vanessa's climaxes that much more intense. Vanessa was certain Megan's handprints would still be visible on her ass tomorrow morning. The woman knew how to spank.

"I won't think you're silly, sweetie," she assured Megan.

It took a moment, but finally Megan said, "It wasn't a vibe. It was, like, a message. It was like something telling me a fact, something detached from you. And…"

"And what?"

"And it wasn't just about sex," Megan continued shyly. "It was, like, I was being told I would so enjoy just being with you."

Vanessa felt her heartrate increase and warmth flood through her entire body.

"I know what you mean," she said softly.

"You're not making fun of me?" Megan asked.

"No, I promise, I'm not. I know what you mean because when I first laid eyes on you, I felt, not a message, but a boom."

Megan giggled and pulled away to have a better look at Vanessa, cocking an eyebrow.

"A *boom*?"

Now Vanessa felt like Megan was going to think she was the one being silly. Not to mention that this was a dangerous conversation to have. But it was too late to stop now.

"Yeah, a boom," she insisted, staring at a point beyond Megan's shoulder as she remembered. "I don't know how else to describe it, but it was like suddenly the air around me imploded. I swear it was something I actually felt. Like something was signaling to me that one day I'd find myself here in bed with you, or sitting on the couch, or out at the beach having a conversation like this."

"And that I'd be the best sex you ever had," Megan stated.

"Well, I mean, duh, of course!" Vanessa said with a grin, tickling Megan. The younger woman shrieked and struggled and somehow Vanessa ended up on top of her, staring down into her eyes.

"Ooh, topping me, Miss Murray?"

Vanessa grinned.

"Only to find out if you're as hungry as I am," she asked.

"Fucking starving!"

***

"By the way, I've been thinking," Vanessa told Megan the next morning.

"Uh-oh, we know how dangerous that can be," Megan retorted, earning a playful smack on the arm.

They were in Vanessa's Jeep, driving south from Carlsbad to the Airbnb beach house. Vanessa would have just enough time to drop off Megan and their things and maybe hang out for a bit before having to leave with Chloë to open La Vida Mocha.

"What do you think about hanging some of your artwork in the coffeeshop?"

Megan looked at her.

"What, seriously?"

"Yeah," Vanessa continued, "why not? Before I met you, I was thinking about reaching out to local artists to showcase some of their work in the shop anyway. Now, all of a sudden, I know a local artist! How perfect is that? And I love your stuff!"

"And if you didn't love my stuff?" Megan teased.

"Then we wouldn't be having this conversation," Vanessa admitted with a laugh. "What do you think?"

Megan took a moment before responding.

"I say, yes, but I'm so fucking nervous about it."

"What? Why?"

"I've never showed my art publicly. My website hardly counts, neither does posting it on Instagram. It makes me nervous that people will actually see it in person."

"Sweetie, your work is fabulous," Vanessa assured her. "People will love it."

"Just be prepared for me to be a wreck that day."

Ten minutes later, the Jeep's GPS guided the women to a gated driveway protecting a three-story mansion. Vanessa entered the code Desiree had texted her and pulled in.

"Chloë's already here," she said, spying the PT Cruiser. "So are Ang and Dee. You said Abby is coming, right?"

Megan nodded. "Yeah, and apparently she's bringing a plus one."

Getting out of the Jeep after parking, Vanessa heard the ocean that was on the other side of the house. It was going to be so nice falling asleep to that sound for the next few nights, especially with Megan next to her. She opened the back door on her side of the Jeep to pull her suitcase out, Megan doing the same on her side.

"Hey, what's that for? I didn't notice you bring that." Vanessa asked, looking at a blue fluffy pillow Megan had extracted along with her suitcase. Vanessa had seen that pillow at Megan's house on her sofa.

Megan smiled.

"It's a scream pillow," she said with a grin. "I felt safer bringing my own from the house, especially if my face was going to be buried in it."

"A scream pillow?" Vanessa repeated, confused. But Megan just cocked an eyebrow and then Vanessa got it and her own smile formed on her face "Oh…a scream pillow."

"You can feel free to use it, too," Megan said. "You tend to get a little vocal yourself, you know."

"That's a good idea, darling, but what if we both happen to need it at the same time?" Vanessa asked with a smirk.

Megan made a face. "Fuck! I hadn't considered that."

"First world problem," Vanessa said, laughing. "Let's get inside."

They found Angela and Desiree already in the pool which was on a deck on the second level. Each woman was on a floating raft and each already had a cocktail in hand, though it was only just past ten a.m.

"Finally!" Angela cried out upon seeing them.

"Happy birthday, Megan!" Desiree added, saluting Megan with her drink. "We brought a cake!"

"Your room is on the third floor," Angela said. "Across from ours. Try not to keep us up all night with whatever kinky things you two do."

Vanessa put her hands on her hips.

"This from a woman I happen to know owns a ball gag," she retorted.

But Angela didn't miss a beat.

"Exactly. Gag. Means quiet, so you won't hear a peep out of me this weekend. Right, babe?" She reached out and took Desiree's hand.

"TMI," Megan said, laughing. "Come on, let's find our room."

The second floor also contained the kitchen and that's where they found Chloë. She was with another woman neither of them knew and they were mixing more cocktails. Vanessa noted approvingly that Chloë was dressed appropriately for work in one of her cute dresses. They did have to get to La Vida Mocha in less than an hour, after all.

Chloë's friend, however, was in a black-and-white striped bikini. She was blonde, her hair pulled up into a messy bun. She was very pretty, had a few tattoos decorating her arms and looked to be about Chloë's and Megan's age.

Chloë was busy pouring ingredients into a blender and so she hadn't noticed Vanessa's and Megan's arrival. The friend did, however, and Vanessa definitely clocked how the young woman first licked her lips and then ran her eyes up and down Vanessa's form. It wasn't subtle.

Great! Megan is going to hate her.

"Ahem!" Vanessa said, to catch Chloë's attention.

Chloë turned.

"Hey, Vanessa! Isn't this a cool house? Hey, Megan!"

"Please tell me you haven't been drinking whatever it is you're making just before we go to work?"

"Relax, I only had a sip; just to sample that it was coming out right. I'm making these for Ang and Desiree. I think it's safe to say they'll be shitfaced before lunch. And for Sienna. Oh, this is Sienna, by the way! Sienna…Vanessa, my boss and Megan, her girlfriend."

Vanessa and Megan shared a look. Megan was smirking, a twinkle in her eyes, seemingly amused at Chloë's mistake. Vanessa was relieved. She also decided she wouldn't correct Chloë, even though she remembered telling Chloë that her and Megan were just having a fling.

Sienna shook Megan's hand first and complimented her on the Audrey Hepburn-style sunhat Megan was wearing. Then she shook Vanessa's hand. There wasn't a repeat of the earlier ogling and her smile and attitude seemed genuine, so Vanessa thought maybe the look from before had been just a one-off kind of thing.

"I don't have to work today, so can I get one?" Megan asked, nudging Vanessa playfully.

"Fuck yeah!" Chloë said. "There's more than enough."

"Oh God, are you going to be shitfaced before lunch, too?" Vanessa asked.

"Uh, hello! This is my birthday celebration weekend!" Megan teased.

"Yes, Chloë told me about that," Sienna said. "Happy birthday!"

"Thank you. I hope Chloë shared the recipe of what's in the blender because it looks amazing."

Vanessa started moving towards the stairs.

"We'll catch you later" she called back to the young women. "Chloë? No more sampling!"

Upstairs, she and Megan found their room. Vanessa rolled her eyes mentally at the cliché nautical décor. So obvious and safe. But it had a king-size bed, a private bathroom and a balcony which overlooked the beach. The roar of the ocean was so loud it was as if Vanessa had stepped into some kind of tranquility room in a luxury spa.

"Don't worry," Megan said now that they were alone, "I won't get shitfaced."

Vanessa, having left her suitcase by the bed, took hold of Megan's hips.
"Good, because I don't take advantage of wasted women. Besides, I don't want our beach house weekend to start off with me having to keep your hair out of the toilet while you puke your guts out."

"I promise I'll limit myself to only one of Chloë's concoctions. Although, that woman seems like she knows how to mix a pretty mean drink."

"Yeah, Chloë is pretty dangerous when you get her around bottles of booze. She turns into a mad scientist. So, what will you do while I'm gone?" Vanessa asked.

Megan shrugged.

"Hang out with the others a bit, especially once Abby gets here. Maybe do some drawing or some reading." She pulled Vanessa a little closer. "I think I'll also fantasize about how you were such a boss downstairs with Chloë. Yum!"

Vanessa then became aware of Megan's fingers unbuttoning her jeans. Vanessa grabbed Megan's hand to stop her.

"I don't have time!" Vanessa said, chuckling. "I need to leave soon and I'd rather not be a complete and total sticky mess down there when I do."

Megan pouted adorably but acquiesced.

"I guess you're right," she said with a sigh. "Let's go chill with the others a bit before you go."

Chapter 34

Abby arrived just as Vanessa and Chloë were leaving. She brought lunch, in the form of bags full of groceries that were intended for preparing to make a meal for everyone. She also came with the new woman she'd been seeing, Kat. Like Abby, Kat was butch, with an almost military buzzcut and a physique that made Megan think of a linebacker. But all Megan cared about was that Kat was as friendly as anybody she'd ever met and that she was really good at making Abby laugh.

Megan spent some time with them in the kitchen before deciding to let them get on with their cooking. She poured herself another one of Chloë's cocktails, forgetting her promise to Vanessa earlier to just have one, and went back out to the second-floor deck, expecting to find Angela and Desiree still in the pool, but finding only Sienna there instead.

"They went to their room," Sienna told Megan, floating on her back in the water. "Something tells me it wasn't to take a nap," she added with a grin. "You coming in?"

Megan did have one of the bikinis she brought for the weekend on, having changed into it after Vanessa left. She had even sent a selfie of her wearing it to Vanessa, being sure to have one of the top's spaghetti straps provocatively falling off her shoulder in the photo.

"Definitely," Megan answered Sienna, kicking off her flip-flops and stepping into the water. She had decided to not immediately close herself off to Sienna, who had made no attempt earlier to hide her desire for Vanessa. After all, Vanessa was an eminently desirable woman. Looking at Vanessa was fine, but Sienna was on probation and Megan would be watching her closely.

In the pool, Megan contented herself with just leaning back with her arms resting on the deck and letting her legs float out in front of her. The day was perfect, cloudless and not too warm. From her vantage point, Megan could look out beyond the deck at the beach and the ocean. The pandemic wasn't keeping people away from coming out to the sand and surf; the governor would have had to occupy the beaches with the National Guard to keep that from happening. Still though, Megan noted that people were putting more distance than usual between their beach blankets and their neighbors', and those who were walking along the shore were trying their best to make sure they didn't pass too closely to anybody else.

Eventually, Sienna floated over and did the same reclining thing Megan was doing.

"So, how long have you and Chloë been together?" Megan asked.

"We're not *together* together," Sienna began. "We have this friends-with-benefits thing going on and since we both happen to be between girlfriends right now…" She trailed off.

"Gotcha," Megan said. "But Chloë seems pretty nice?"

"She's fucking amazing," Sienna stated. "But we're not each other's type, you know? Not for a relationship, anyway. Besides, Chloë actually has a thing for older women."

Megan turned to face Sienna.

"Really?" she asked.

"Yeah, why does that surprise you? Vanessa is older than you, isn't she?"

"Well, yeah, but that's not why I'm…with her," Megan said, catching herself just in time from saying "dating her." They weren't dating, after all. They were…Well, Megan actually didn't know what they were anymore but it was too complicated to explain to Sienna.

"I would have…gotten involved with Vanessa even if she was ten years younger than me," Megan declared. "Okay, maybe not *ten* years younger, because that would be illegal, but you get my point."

Sienna laughed.

A thought suddenly occurred to Megan. Did Chloë have a thing for Vanessa? She made a mental note to bring that up to Vanessa one day. No, change that. She made a mental note to bring that up to Vanessa *tonight*.

"What about you and Vanessa?" Sienna asked.

"What about us?" Megan responded, hoping it didn't sound as defensive as she felt.

"Uh…How long have you been together?"

"Oh. Almost three weeks," Megan answered.

A perfect three weeks.

"Wow! Brand-new!"

Megan smiled.

"Yeah, it's been amazing," she told Sienna.

"So, how did you two—" Sienna stopped as a new sound became apparent on top of all the noises from the beach and the ocean. Megan had picked it up too. She frowned as she tried to first determine where it was coming from and then what it was. It seemed like it was coming from somewhere in the house…?

Both women realized what it was at the same time. They stared at each other for a moment and then burst into giggles.

"Told you they weren't taking a nap," Sienna said between laughs, the sounds of Angela and Desiree having quite loud sex adding to the soundtrack of the ocean's surf and beachgoers playing.

Megan took a glance over her shoulder at the house.

"God, no wonder we can hear them; their bedroom window is open. Oh my God!" she exclaimed as Desiree clearly called out Angela's name after first taking Christ's name in vain and then gave the kind of full-throated moan that could only come from a satisfying climax.

Megan blushed in sympathetic embarrassment.

Sienna mimed writing on the air.

"Note to self: close bedroom window before having sex tonight."

That started the two women on a new fit of giggles. For some reason, Megan felt, it also sealed their friendship.

"So, um…what do you do for a living?" Sienna asked, and Megan sensed her companion was trying to get her mind off the sounds coming from the third floor, and since Megan also didn't want to spend the next however-long-it-took-for-Angela-and-Dee-to-have-sex listening to Angela and Dee have sex, she gratefully gave Sienna a brief rundown of her job at BeachSoft.

"What about you?" Megan asked when she was done. "What do you do?"

Sienna sighed.

"I am an apprentice tattoo artist," she answered.

"That's so cool!" Megan exclaimed. Tattooing had never been anything she considered, career-wise, but she had always been envious of tattoo artists because they got to make a living creating artworks every day.

"Well, if it's any consolation," Sienna began, "you probably make a whole lot more money than I do. I have to hold down two waitressing jobs just to stay afloat until I can start taking tattoo clients on my own."

Megan nudged Sienna's shoulder with her own.

"You'll get there," she told her. "I'm just jealous you eventually get to be a full-time artist," Megan said. "And every day you'll be asked to create something different. It will never be the same day twice. How cool is that?"

Sienna laughed, blushing.

"You should switch careers, then," she said. "Give up the cushy I.T. salary and join the ranks of the almost-impoverished."

"No thanks," Megan said with a smile. "I like my cushy I.T. salary. Maybe someday I'll use some of it to open my own art gallery."

"Wow! Really?" Sienna asked. "Wait, so you're an artist?"

"I am," Megan told her. "In fact, I was planning on doing some drawing while I was here at the house this weekend."

"Nice! Will you show me your stuff?"

"Only if you show me some of your tattoo concepts."

Sienna blushed again.

"Okay, you got a deal." She turned around and pushed herself up and out of the pool. "I'm going to take a shower. Meet me in the living room in twenty minutes?"

"Sure," Megan said, also getting out of the pool. While Sienna scampered inside, Megan toweled off and then spent a few minutes at the deck's railing looking out over the beach, sipping her cocktail. She had been right, Chloë knew how to mix a mean drink. Whatever it was Megan was now drinking was potent stuff and she resolved it would be the last one she had, otherwise she'd end up breaking her promise to Vanessa to not get shitfaced.

"Hey, bestie! What's up?"

Abby had come out of the house, smelling faintly of garlic, and now stood by Megan at the railing.

"What's up is I'm starving!" Megan told her. "When's lunch going to be ready?"

"Keep your shirt on. Less than twenty minutes."

"So, I came out to my family yesterday," Megan stated. It was odd how Abby was only hearing about this now, Megan considered. Not too long ago, Abby would have been the first one

Megan called after such a momentous event. But that was pre-Vanessa.

"Whoa! Congrats!" Abby said, putting her arm around Megan and pulling her in for a squeeze. "How'd they take it?"

"I'm pretty sure I'm disowned, but I'm totally fine with that," Megan answered truthfully. "I gained a lot more than I lost, at least that's how I feel now. And it turns out Molly is fine with it; she came over yesterday to say so."

"Way to go, Molly," Abby said.

Megan beamed.

"Yeah, she was wonderful."

"Sucks about the parents, though. But as long as you're okay?" Abby said.

"I'm fine, really," Megan assured her. "Now, tell me about Kat."

"We're moving in together next week," Abby declared.

Megan's mouth dropped open.

"Nah, I'm just fucking with you," Abby said laughing, enduring a quick punch on the arm from Megan. "Anyway, it's been great with Kat. Her and I are…Wait, what's that sound?"

Megan listened and then rolled her eyes.

"That's round two," she said and then directed Abby's attention to the open third-floor window. "Sienna and I were out here trying to *not* hear them having sex just now."

A particularly pleasurable yell came from the third floor; whether it was Angela or Desiree, Megan couldn't tell.

"Wow, somebody is doing some good work up there," Abby said. "Kat and I didn't hear all this in the kitchen." Abby then got a devious look in her eyes. She started looking around at the ground and after a moment picked up a pine cone that had fallen from one of the trees landscaping the property.

"You're not!" Megan said, giggling.

"Oh, I am," Abby confirmed just before she chucked the pine cone straight through the open third-floor window with the expertise of someone who had once played college softball. Megan heard the pine cone strike something and then rattle around in the room, causing the sex noises to suddenly stop.

After a moment, a very confused Angela peered out the window, holding a bedsheet up to cover her chest.

"Oy!" Abby yelled, pointing towards the beach. "There are impressionable young kids out there who don't want to hear you two going at it like animals! Close the damn window!"

It took a moment, but Angela suddenly went white as the sheet she was holding and her eyes and mouth opened wide in shock.

"Oh my God!" she uttered, disappearing back into the room. A few seconds later, Desiree also gave an "Oh my God!" after Angela presumably told her about the window and the fact that Megan and Abby were downstairs and able to hear them.

Laughing, Megan and Abby saw an arm, and only an arm, reach up and push the window closed.

Chapter 35

What Vanessa wanted to be focused on was the two photos Megan had texted her. The first had been that shot of her in the bikini, with the one strap falling off her shoulder. The second had come in about an hour ago. It was a rather artsy shot of Megan's bare hip, with that same bikini, now off, draped across her thigh. When Vanessa had seen it, all she could think about was biting that hip, knowing the kinds of sounds Megan would make in response.

Instead, what Vanessa was focused on were numbers. Specifically, the numbers on the spreadsheet her laptop was displaying as she sat in the back room of La Vida Mocha. Things in the front of the coffeeshop were being handled easily by Chloë, who knew to shout out if Vanessa was needed.

The numbers were telling Vanessa that La Vida Mocha needed to do more business. The partial reopening of the state was helping, sure, and by all appearances, it looked to be permanent. As long as there wasn't another wildfire-like outbreak of Covid cases, Vanessa could expect to return La Vida Mocha to the operating hours she had established back when she had originally opened in January. Even now, with these shorter hours she had been running over the past couple of weeks, people were coming out in droves and patronizing the shop.

The problem was that there was a lot of financial ground to make up. The complete shutdown that had started in March followed by the take-out only restrictions imposed on restaurants and coffeeshops had cost a lot, and though Vanessa was not at risk of losing everything yet, she really needed La Vida Mocha to get back to paying for itself like it had been pre-Covid.

Sighing, Vanessa logged into her Chase account and transferred some more of her inheritance to her business account to give the shop an infusion of cash for the next several weeks.

Later, after the shop had closed and all the clean-up had been done, Vanessa and Chloë got into Vanessa's Jeep for the drive back to the beach house.

Pulling out of the parking lot, Vanessa said, "I want you and Luli to do me a favor when she joins us next week."

"Sure. What?"

"Ideas. I want ideas for coming up with some more income for La Vida Mocha. We gotta make up for all that time the state was on lockdown."

"Sure, I'll think about it," Chloë promised, "but I actually already have some thoughts about that."

They were stopped at a red light and so Vanessa looked over at Chloë.

"Really? Tell me!"

"Well…I know you said at the beginning that you didn't want La Vida Mocha to be this quote-unquote *lesbian coffeeshop*, but I kind of feel like you're missing an opportunity. I mean, obviously, we're not going to call it 'La Vida Mocha, the Lesbian Coffeeshop' but Carlsbad is the perfect place to promote the fact that La Vida Mocha is not only lesbian-owned but is an overall safe space for queer women to come and hang out in."

The traffic light changed and Vanessa started driving again.

"But I want La Vida Mocha to be a safe space for *anyone* to come to and hang out," she said.

"So do I!" Chloë insisted. "But there's nothing wrong with doing some subtle but focused advertising to our sapphic sisters. Take out an ad on Zoosk, get lesbians to have their first dates at La Vida Mocha. Link the shop's Facebook page to even more lesbian content, stuff like that."

"Those are good ideas," Vanessa said, thoughtfully.

"I'm not just a pretty face. Oh, and you should do something about the merch in the shop."

Vanessa looked over at Chloë really quickly before putting her eyes back on the road.

"What about the merch?" she asked.

"Like, in addition to our regular stuff, we should sell La Vida Mocha logo mugs with the Pride flag on them. Or, even better, the lesbian flag. Just order some, display them somewhere strategic and just let people notice them. See? Subtle; like, subliminal marketing. And I guarantee if you get some mugs or t-shirts with the lesbian flag on them, your wannabe wife Amy will be sure to notice, which would be awesome for us!"

Vanessa reached over and smacked Chloë's leg.

"Oh my God, you *cannot* say things like that around Megan! I will kill you if you do!" Vanessa knew Megan was susceptible to jealousy; in fact, Vanessa thought it was kind of hot. Despite the short shelf life of their relationship, Vanessa liked that Megan was possessive.

Thinking of the short shelf life…

"And, by the way," she began, "Remember, I told you…Megan is not my girlfriend."

Chloë looked at her.

"Are you sure?" she asked.

Vanessa blinked.

"Pretty sure," she replied. "We're just having a fling, remember?" She sighed because she knew she was going to have to explain it further, but she was getting tired of saying the same thing to different people. Especially because now she wondered if the bit that applied to her was still true anymore. "I'm too busy with La Vida Mocha to focus on a relationship, and Megan is moving to New York to start a new job."

"Oh," Chloë said and then fell silent. However, Vanessa felt Chloë still looking at her. "But the way she looks at you…" Chloë ventured after several moments.

Vanessa's heart pounded. Her mouth felt dry.

"What do you mean?" she asked.

"Vanessa, she's nuts about you," Chloë explained. "Some people wait their entire lives for another person to look at them the way Megan looks at you. Also…" Chloë suddenly stopped, seemingly unsure if she should continue.

"Also what?" Vanessa prodded.

Chloë sighed.

"Also, I see the way you look at Megan."

Vanessa's mouth dropped open.

Oh fuck! Has it been that obvious?

"It's why I assumed she was your girlfriend," Chloë said. "Can't you guys figure out a way to make it work?"

Vanessa bit her bottom lip.

"How?" she softly asked.

"I don't know. I mean, maybe you could try the long-distance thing?"

Vanessa shook her head and then admitted something to Chloë that she had never even uttered out loud until now.

"I thought about that just the other day," she said, still softly. "If she was moving up to San Francisco, maybe. But New York? It may as well be the moon."

"Fuck. I guess you're right."

"Yeah. Fuck. Anyway, change of topic: why would Amy noticing be awesome for us?"

"Because she'd definitely write about it in her blog!"

"Wait, Amy has a blog?"

"Yeah! A really good one. It's called *Lesbeing* and it's about being a lesbian in general but being a lesbian in Southern California in particular. She's got a ton of subscribers."

Vanessa was amazed. She should have had this conversation with Chloë weeks, if not months, ago. Chloë's ideas were good and Vanessa was wondering why she herself couldn't have come up with any of them but then decided it was because she was probably too close to the problem.

"Chloë, your ideas are great, I mean it. Thank you. Let's start implementing them ASAP."

Vanessa looked over to see a small and shy smile turn up the corners of Chloë's mouth.

"By the way," Vanessa said after about a mile, "I suggested that Megan display some of her art in the shop."

Chloë sat up straighter and turned to Vanessa.

"That's fucking perfect!" she practically screamed with excitement. "I mean, I'm not sure if you're aware of this, but Megan is a lesbian artist! If we hang her art and then hashtag the shit out of it on Twitter and Instagram…boom! Hashtag lesbianartist! Hashtag lesbianart! Hashtag queerarts! Whatever! Suddenly, La Vida Mocha is the place to come for coffee *and* to see art created by a lesbian artist. And, trust me, Amy will be all over it! She already mentions the shop in her blog anyway."

"She does? Like, what does she write?"

Chloë shrugged.

"Oh, you know…Stuff like, 'Sitting here at my favorite coffee spot, La Vida Mocha'; 'I really love the coffee and the vibe at La Vida Mocha'; 'I can't wait to marry Vanessa from La Vida Mocha.'"

"Chloë! I swear to God tonight is your last night on Earth!"

***

"Fuck, I missed you!" Megan said, throwing herself into Vanessa's arms as soon as Vanessa walked into their bedroom at the beach house. Vanessa had no time to tell Megan that she had missed her too because Megan had claimed Vanessa's lips in a passionate kiss.

When Megan finally let her go, Vanessa asked, "What are you doing up here? Everybody is downstairs chilling on the deck."

"I was down there until ten minutes ago when I realized you should be arriving soon and I wanted to be up here when you did."

Vanessa encircled her arms around Megan's waist.

"I like that," she said.

"I bet my poor Vanessa worked really hard today, didn't she?" Megan said.

"She did," Vanessa replied. "And you didn't make it any easier with those pictures you sent."

Megan wiggled her eyebrows.

"Wait until you see what I have planned for tomorrow," she teased.

"Well, tomorrow can wait. In the meantime…" Vanessa lifted Megan up, causing Megan to yelp in surprise and then yelp even louder when Vanessa lowered her on the bed, falling on top of her. "In the meantime, I've been wanting to do one thing and one thing only since you sent that last picture."

Megan's breath was ragged.

"And what is that?" she asked.

Instead of answering, Vanessa set to work unfastening the denim cut-off shorts Megan was wearing and then yanking them off along with Megan's panties. In anticipation, Megan spread her legs, but Vanessa shook her head and said, "Uh-uh" before using her hands to position Megan onto her side.

Vanessa licked her lips. There it was: that perfect right hip from the photo, with its absolutely flawless skin, just waiting for her. Vanessa's mouth salivated as her eyes took in not only the hip but the curve of Megan's ass. She brought her face down to Megan's skin and smelled the cherry blossom body wash Megan favored mixed with chlorine from the pool.

Vanessa reached out her tongue and ran it along Megan's flesh, eliciting a purr from the woman.

But that was enough foreplay, Vanessa thought. Time for the real action. She bared her teeth and then lowered her head.

Chapter 36

Megan had thought Vanessa was going to go down on her. Megan had *needed* Vanessa to go down on her because all day long Megan had been thinking about Vanessa going down on her. And when her shorts had been pulled off, Megan had spread her legs, ready for Vanessa to go down on her. But Vanessa had said "Uh-uh," forced her onto her side and surprised her with alternative plans.

The first nibbles on her right hip were gentle but then they got harder, more insistent. Megan gasped as her clit pulsed at the pain/pleasure Vanessa was causing, her center getting slicker and slicker until it couldn't be contained and she felt arousal leaking out onto her thighs. Vanessa kept biting, occasionally pulling with her teeth, occasionally sucking as she bit, occasionally just clamping down and holding Megan's captive flesh, the pain radiating out from the bite and going straight for her core. Megan felt her dark side awaken; the side Cindy never understood.

"Harder," she commanded Vanessa after a gentle nibble and then winced as Vanessa obeyed. Megan reached up under her shirt, to her own breasts which were still in the bralette she had put on after changing out of her bikini. She pulled aside one of the cups and pinched her stone-hard nipple.

"I'm marking my territory, Megan," Vanessa murmured. "You better fucking show these off; let everyone know you're taken."

Megan groaned, Vanessa's words turning her on even more.

At the same time that Vanessa moved from Megan's hip and started biting Megan's ass, Vanessa slid her hand between Megan's legs, found her swollen and wet folds with her fingers and pushed two inside easily.

"Oh God," Megan sighed as the fingers entered her and then curled, hitting her spot. She pushed against them, driving them deeper. She gave a little yelp when Vanessa's teeth took hold of another piece of her ass and clamped down hard, but she was delighted that Vanessa ignored the little cry and didn't relent, continuing to bite while fucking Megan with her fingers.

And so it went. Teeth and fingers; nibbles, sucks and thrusts. Pleasure wrapped in pain.

Eventually, Megan knew she was getting close. Her inner walls were beginning to squeeze Vanessa's fingers as the orgasm built. It was going to be intense, she knew it, and she increased the pressure on her nipple, wanting to hurt it too so that she had two sources of pain feeding the coming climax.

Vanessa's thumb then started flicking Megan's clit and Megan's eyes, which had been squeezed shut, flew open at the unbelievable sensations that was causing and that's when she saw the window.

Fuck!

It was wide open!

No! Fuck!

It was too late to stop what was happening to get up and close the damn thing. Vanessa was expertly bringing Megan to an amazing climax and nothing short of a nuclear attack was going to keep Megan from coming now.

She spied her scream pillow all the way on the other side of the bed and stretched out her arm for it, but her fingers could barely graze it.

"Oh fuck!" she couldn't help exclaiming in response to the building pleasure between her legs that was reaching its apex. She hoped the women downstairs on the deck hadn't heard it. That thought made her scrabbling for the pillow that much more desperate because she knew they'd hear what was coming next unless she got the fucking thing.

Miraculously, somehow, her fingers barely managed to clutch the very edge of the pillow at the same instant she felt the explosion of her orgasm. Desperately, Megan yanked the pillow to her and she was just able to slam it down on her face as her scream from coming hard escaped her mouth. Her pelvis thrusted violently, dislodging Vanessa's fingers and she kept screaming into the pillow, even managing to call Vanessa's name, not that anyone could tell; all that Megan could hear of her exclamations were muffled cries that were unintelligible.

She had no idea how long it went on for, only that she had temporarily lost motor control of her legs which spasmed the entire time her orgasm spent wracking her body. Finally, she had to lift her face from the pillow when her lungs started reminding her that they needed a little something called air.

"Oh my God, baby," she uttered, when she eventually came down from her high. She felt Vanessa's hand softly rubbing her ass and she tried to look over her shoulder to see.

"How bad is it?" she said, giggling.

"I certainly did a number on you," Vanessa said, and Megan could have sworn Vanessa sounded proud.

"Good, I won't mind showing off some sex bruises. Oh, those are hot!" Megan saw several purplish-red hickeys that had no chance of being covered up the side-tying string bikini bottoms she was planning to wear tomorrow.

Vanessa laughed.

Megan turned over onto her back and pulled Vanessa down on top of her, quickly bringing Vanessa's mouth to her own for a kiss.

"Do your friends know?" Vanessa asked when her lips were released.

"Do they know what?"

"That sweet little Megan has a dark side?"

Megan wiggled her eyebrows.

"I only show it to people I really, *really* like," she said, taking Vanessa's lips again for another kiss.

"Have you eaten?" Megan asked when the kiss broke.

"No, and I'm starving!" Vanessa stated.

"For taking such good care of me just now, let me make you something," Megan said.

"Make?"

Megan laughed.

"We ordered pizza earlier and there's a ton left. I'll heat you up a couple of slices."

"Well, you get dressed and do that. I need to clean up and change my underwear first. In addition to the occasional dirty thoughts I had about you while I was working, fucking you just now has made me soaked."

The thought of how wet Vanessa must be right now was priming Megan's center for some more attention. She reached down and cupped Vanessa's jeans-clad ass.

"Shall we...?"

Vanessa purred but then shook her head and got off of Megan.

"After I've eaten. I don't want anything distracting me while you have your wicked way with me."

Megan watched Vanessa open her suitcase to pull out clean panties and gym shorts. As Vanessa headed to the bathroom, she asked, "How was it hanging out with Sienna?"

"Oh, she's super cool!" Megan answered, getting off the bed and finding her own underwear and shorts. "I've decided we like her."

From in the bathroom, Vanessa chuckled and said, "I'm glad *we* like her."

"Oh, but she did tell me something interesting," Megan began. She went to lean against the door of the bathroom. Vanessa was just pulling on the shorts, her jeans crumpled on the floor at her feet. Once the shorts were on, Vanessa then examined her appearance in the mirror.

"What did she tell you?" Vanessa asked, finger-combing her hair a bit to neaten it back up.

"Oh, only that Chloë has a thing for older women."

"Mm, yeah, I know; Chloë told me," Vanessa replied, still fixing her hair.

"Well, I just want to make sure Chloë doesn't have a thing for a particular older woman. Especially one she spends all week working with."

Vanessa smiled, approached Megan and put her arms around her waist.

"I like your jealousy," Vanessa told her. "Maybe you want to put bite marks on my ass later?"

Megan cocked an eyebrow.

"And on your boobs, and on your thighs…just to be safe."

Vanessa gave her a quick kiss.

"I already told you; Chloë is harmless. She and I are so much like sisters now it would feel incestuous to even hold her hand for more than a second. Besides, if something was going to happen between Chloë and I, it would have happened a long time ago. Then there's the fact that as much as I love the little twerp, she doesn't really do it for me."

Megan gave her a doubtful look.

"She's, like, super pretty, Vanessa. And funny."

"Yeah, but she's kind of still getting her shit together, you know? And I prefer women who already have their shit together. Like you."

In her heart, Megan knew there was nothing to fear from Chloë, Megan having never gotten a vibe from Chloë that Vanessa was in her sights. Nonetheless, she at least wanted to hear it from Vanessa.

Of course, what difference will it make when I'm in New York?

Vanessa gave Megan another quick kiss and then took Megan's hand and started leading her out of the bedroom.

"You promised pizza," she said, "let's go. And don't worry about Chloë. Besides, I'm so glad nothing ever developed between us like that because I can't tell you how valuable she is at the shop. But I'm pretty sure she wouldn't still be working there if she was an ex. And she definitely would have turned into an ex," Vanessa added in a whisper.

Chapter 37

After heating up a couple of slices of pizza, Vanessa and Megan went out to the deck to join the others, who they found gathered in a circle around a fire pit that somehow looked like a piece of modern art. Everyone was paired up: Chloë with Sienna, Abby with Kat, Desiree snuggling against Angela.

Chloë had made more of her potent punch and a pitcher of it was on a nearby table. She poured Vanessa and Megan two cups of it. Vanessa took it with some trepidation; the last thing she wanted was to be hungover tomorrow morning. After taking a sip of it, she knew she'd have to pace herself.

The night had gotten chilly and it was Sienna who eventually got up from the group, ran into the house and then returned a few minutes later with an armload of blankets.

"I found these in a hall closet," she said, distributing them, one to each couple.

"Rock star!" Vanessa said, taking the blanket and draping it over her and Megan's laps in the loveseat they were sharing. Megan cuddled closer and Vanessa felt her heart swell.

After about half an hour, Desiree and Angela said they were calling it an early night because they wanted to watch the sunrise on the beach tomorrow, and both got up and left.

"Make sure the window is closed!" Abby stage-whispered when there was no chance of the departing women hearing her. Megan, Sienna and Kat all laughed, but Vanessa and Chloë shared a confused look and so Megan took it upon herself to fill them in about the incident earlier today, including the pine cone through the window.

"I'll say this, though, apparently Angela knows what she's doing," Megan finished with, bringing a fresh round of laughter from the women.

The conversation then shifted from topic to topic for a while. Vanessa was content to let the others do the talking while she simply sat back and relaxed, glad to be off her feet, enjoying being outdoors, being with her friends and enjoying how close Megan was. Underneath the blanket, Megan's right hand was resting on Vanessa's left thigh, her fingertips lightly playing along Vanessa's skin.

Vanessa realized that she was as happy now as she'd ever been. Okay, her coffeeshop needed to make more money otherwise it too would be a casualty of Covid like so many other small businesses, but tonight, here on the deck, with Megan next to her, Vanessa was feeling the type of optimism she hadn't felt in a long time.

Speaking of which, Vanessa realized that Chloë was telling the others about her ideas for generating more money for La Vida Mocha.

When she was done, Abby said, "Totally! Play up the lesbian angle, Vanessa. Carlsbad is only getting gayer every day, and it's not like we pay with Monopoly money."

"Chloë is brilliant," Vanessa said. "I'm putting her in charge of Operation Hashtag Lesbian."

"Coffee flights," Megan said simply.

Vanessa looked at Megan, her knitted brows demanding further explanation for the non-sequitur. The others were waiting also.

Finally, Megan went on.

"Well, you know how wineries do wine tastings by giving people wine flights? You could do the same with coffee. Offer three or four cups of different blends or roasts or whatever you call them for the customer to try. You could even put the cups on one of those flight paddles for presentation. Then you can explain what each coffee is like, where it comes from, what kind of flavors it has, et cetera."

Vanessa stared at Megan; mouth open.

Fuck, that's a good idea!

Megan continued, her brow furrowed the way Vanessa noticed it did when Megan was focusing on something.

"Maybe you charge ten or twelve bucks for it. Ooh! You know what you could do? You could pair each coffee with a piece of chocolate that you and Chloë think goes good with that particular roast. Or maybe some biscotti. Ooh! And then if someone likes a particular coffee, they could buy a bag of it to brew at home!"

"That's actually a really good idea, Vanessa," Kat said. "In fact, if you don't use it, I'm going to open my own coffeeshop and steal it."

Vanessa looked over at Chloë who gave her a wordless *Let's do it!* nod.

"Kind of beats my idea," Chloë admitted.

"No, it doesn't beat your idea," Megan insisted. "I think it complements it, in fact, because maybe once a month you keep La Vida Mocha open late one night specifically for a lesbian coffee-tasting club to meet. Give lesbians coffee and chocolate and you'll be nominated for sainthood. And if you could figure out how to serve them wine also they'll carve statues of you."

Chloë jumped in. "We could offer different coffees each month, Vanessa; off-the-beaten-path type stuff, you know? The kind people aren't going to find in their local grocery stores."

"Exactly!" Megan agreed.

Vanessa laughed and then took Megan's face in both her hands and kissed her deeply.

"Do you want to take over running the business for me?" she asked.

Megan made a *blech!* sound.

"Oh my God, that sounds boring. You do all that admin stuff and just let me and Chloë come up with all the great ideas."

"Deal," Vanessa said, giving her a quick kiss.

The conversation drifted to other topics again and when it did, Vanessa tuned out once more and let her eyes wander to the ocean. Being that it was after ten o'clock she could hear it more than see it, though every now and then some whitecaps would catch the light from the half-moon in the sky.

Suddenly, she became aware that she was getting wetter between her legs and realized that the hand Megan had on her leg under their blanket had moved up, her fingers now stroking Vanessa's inner thigh along the hem of Vanessa's shorts.

Vanessa turned her head from looking at the beach to looking at Megan but Megan was talking with Chloë and Sienna about something. Art, it sounded like.

Vanessa then had to suppress a surprised gasp when Megan moved her hand to cover the crotch of Vanessa's shorts. Megan pressed firmly against Vanessa's center through the fabric and then began rubbing her fingers in slow circles. Biting her bottom lip, Vanessa looked around at the others. Across from her, on the other side of the fire pit, Abby and Kat were engaged in a conversation about Kat's brother. Chloë and Megan, meanwhile, were listening to Sienna talk about the differences between the various styles of tattoo art.

Vanessa's clit was pulsing as Megan continued pressing against it and her panties were now damp. It was all she could do to keep a neutral expression on her face as the build-up of pleasure in her core kept increasing.

After another minute or two, Megan, as quick as a thief, slipped her hand under the elastic waistband of Vanessa's shorts, forcing Vanessa to take a quick intake of breath which thankfully went unnoticed. Almost of their own accord, Vanessa's legs parted under the blanket, granting easier access to the exploring fingers. In a moment, her panties were pulled aside and Vanessa began shivering when Megan's fingers now touched the slickness of her center and played, brushing gently against Vanessa's clit, teasing Vanessa's opening, promising to push inside and claim her.

Because she didn't think it would look natural if she just sat stock still like she was currently doing, Vanessa picked up her smartphone, turned it on and pretended to look at it, hoping that the fact that her hand was trembling would not be noticed by anyone.

Nothing to see here folks! Just a woman checking notifications on her phone and—oh fuck!

Two arousal-coated fingers had just gently pushed inside Vanessa forcing her to use more willpower than she ever had used before to not to moan in pleasure. Hot heat spread from Vanessa's pussy in two directions, down her legs and up her spine. Her climax started building and, in the meantime, she felt more of her juices flooding her inner walls, seeping out around Megan's fingers.

It was at this moment that Abby loudly called for Chloë's attention to ask about something. Vanessa had no ability at this point to comprehend exactly what Abby wanted, all she knew was that both Chloë's and Sienna's attention was now on Abby, not Megan. Vanessa took advantage of this and placed her free hand on top of Megan's. Megan whipped her head around to look at Vanessa.

Vanessa brought her head closer to Megan's.

"You're going to make me come," Vanessa whispered.

"And?" Megan asked in that no-nonsense voice she used when she expected obedience.

Vanessa had to shut her eyes and take a breath as her clit pulsed strongly at Megan's demeanor.

"And there are a lot of people around," she said.

Megan narrowed her eyes.

"Well then, I suggest you do it quietly," she whispered matter-of-factly. "In the meantime, let go of my hand. Now!"

Vanessa almost came right then.

She did as she was told and immediately Megan resumed gently fucking her. It was all Vanessa could do to keep her eyes open for another panicked look around the deck as her pussy teetered closer and closer to the brink of no return. Surely everyone knew what was going on, right? A woman could not give another woman this kind of pleasure without everyone within fifty yards being aware, right?

But no one was paying them the slightest mind. In fact, the four other women were focused on something Abby was showing them on her phone.

Megan brought her lips closer to Vanessa's ear.

"I wish I could take this blanket off," she murmured. "I wish I could show everybody what I'm doing to you. How powerless I make you. I want them to see the exact moment I. Make. You. Come."

And with that, Vanessa went over the edge.

Her entire pelvis trembled when the pleasure finally exploded. Her insides convulsed rapidly and her walls gripped Megan's fingers frantically. Her come streamed out of her and drips of it made their way towards her ass.

She had to fight to stifle the cries she wanted to release and in so doing forgot to breathe for about fifteen seconds. When she finally blew out the breath it weakened her even more. Megan, meanwhile, coaxed her through the orgasm by curling the fingers she had inside Vanessa and pressing the heel of her hand firmly on Vanessa's pussy, providing a surface for Vanessa to grind against while the climax expended itself.

Miraculously, Vanessa did not make a sound but her eyes watered from the effort and a couple of tears streamed down her cheeks. It was not lost on her, even in that moment, that this was the second time Megan had caused tears to fall from her eyes by making her come so hard.

This woman isn't human.

When she was spent and all that remained was her gently throbbing clit, she managed to whisper, "Oh my fucking God."

Megan kissed Vanessa's sensitive spot, on her neck, just below her earlobe.

"Good girl," she murmured.

Megan finally removed her hand from between Vanessa's legs.

"Now, look at me," Megan ordered quietly.

Locking her eyes with Vanessa's and making sure she had her complete attention Megan removed her hand from underneath the blanket and brought her come-slickened fingers up to Vanessa's mouth. She then rubbed one of the fingers first along Vanessa's bottom lip and then her top one until both lips were glossed with her own come. And then Megan leaned in and kissed her deeply.

Vanessa thought she was going to lose her mind.

Less than a month ago, Vanessa was not imagining spending a night like this anytime soon. Yet here she was, on a beautiful California night, on the deck of a beach house, cuddled against a gorgeous woman that not only had given her a great business idea earlier but had just given her a secret, thigh-quivering orgasm under the noses of their friends and who was now kissing her using her own come as lipstick.

This was living.

Chapter 38

"So, finish telling me about Kat. Is she the woman you were telling me about who winked at you in the grocery store a couple of weeks ago?" Megan asked Abby the next day.

She and Abby were out on the deck because where else would they be? The day was almost cliché Southern California in terms of weather and both women were in lounge chairs that faced the beach, deriving entertainment from watching a group of novice teenage surfers fail badly at mastering the tame Carlsbad-area surf. Megan was wearing one of her favorite bikinis, a stringy number that had made Vanessa talk seriously about keeping La Vida Mocha closed for the day when she saw Megan in it, while Abby was more covered up in cut-off denim shorts and a black tank.

It was just after lunch and Kat and Sienna had gone to the supermarket to buy ingredients for tonight's dinner that Kat planned on making later. Angela and Desiree were back upstairs in their room, the window closed this time. Megan and Abby had the deck to themselves.

Megan realized that lately, she hadn't had much chance to just sit and chat with Abby. Part of it was because of the pandemic, sure; she and Abby simply just didn't get together as often; but Megan also knew that most of it was because of what she had going on with Vanessa.

"The one and the same," Abby answered Megan's question. "So, after that first time I saw her, when she winked at me, I went back to Von's every day at the same time, hoping to see her again."

"Stalker," Megan teased.

"You bet!" Abby declared. "Four fucking days I went back until she finally showed up and when she did, I just happened to crash my cart into hers."

"Oh my God! So sitcom!" Megan said, laughing.

"Fuck, it worked," Abby said, raising the red plastic cup containing the vodka cranberry she was drinking in an apparent salute to the sapphic goddesses.

"Well, she seems nice," Megan said, meaning it. "I'm enjoying her company and I can tell you are too."

"Yeah, she's good people," Abby responded. "So, um, can I assume those bruises on your ass are consensual?" Abby asked pointedly, looking at the marks Megan's bikini bottoms could not hide, even though Megan was sitting.

"Totally," Megan assured her. "My roommate just could not control herself last night."

Abby rolled her eyes.

"Everybody thinks you lipstick lesbians are all nice and gentle and 'make love,'" Abby said, using air quotes. "But you bitches are the freakiest ones out there."

"Don't hate. Besides, Vanessa likes it when I get a little freaky." Megan briefly thought about the sex her and Vanessa had when they finally retired for the night last night. She had to cross her legs now just thinking about the new way the glass dildo had been employed.

They sat together in silence for a few minutes.

"So, I think I'm falling in love," Megan eventually said softly, no longer able to keep it in.

Abby looked over at her.

"Falling?"

Megan sighed.

"Okay, fine. I think I am in love."

"Think?"

"Fuck you. Fine, I am in love."

She had to take a deep breath after saying it because it felt so powerful and scary to say, especially to another person. The truth was, however, that Megan knew she was in love with Vanessa well before this beach house staycation. It was frightening. She had only known Vanessa three weeks! But Megan now could not imagine what a life without Vanessa would be like, nor did she want to find out. Ever since Vanessa arrived in Megan's world, Megan had felt a completeness that she had *thought* she'd had with one or two others but which she now realized she had never had. Not even with Cindy.

Megan had been doing a lot of thinking about Cindy lately. This time last year, after all, she was *so* in love with Cindy. Heck, just back in January she was *so* in love with Cindy and thus so devastated after finding out Cindy had been cheating on her.

But what had Megan thinking of Cindy so much lately was Megan trying to determine if what she had felt for Cindy was the same as what she was feeling now for Vanessa. The final conclusion?

Nope!

It wasn't even close. Yes, Megan had been in love with Cindy; there was no denying that. And Megan supposed that if Cindy hadn't cheated on her that she still would've wanted to marry her and build a life with her. Megan also supposed that in that alternate universe, she and Cindy would have been very happy together, and that in itself would have been amazing because it is more than most people get.

But the love she was feeling now for Vanessa...

It was Cindy times ten. Times a hundred. Being with Vanessa was like Megan had been given all of the answers to a test she didn't realize she was taking.

She completes me.

"I just want to check," Abby said, "that you're not just reacting to great sex, right?"

Shaking her head, Megan said, "No, I promise. This is beyond sex. But you're right, it's so quick."

"You haven't said it to her yet?"

"Nope."

Abby said nothing for a while. She just went back to looking out at the beach as if the answers all lay out there somewhere, in the endless Pacific. Finally, though, she said, "You've got a fucking big problem."

"I know," Megan confirmed.

"You're moving to New York."

"I know that too."

"Which is probably a good thing," Abby declared.

Megan looked at her best friend.

"Why do you say that?" she asked, genuinely wanting to know.

Abby shrugged.

"Unless you're about to tell me—which I don't think you're about to do—that you're going to turn down the promotion at work..." Abby let the thought hang unfinished. "You just need to enjoy this for what it is, a summer fling and then move to New York when the time comes. Why that's good is because you'll be three-thousand miles away which will make it easier for you to get over her. Besides, I'm sure New York has its own Vanessas, probably thousands of them. You just need to find one."

"I don't want a New York Vanessa, I want the California Vanessa," Megan said.

Abby looked at her.

"Too bad," she said.

Megan crossed her arms and huffed. Abby was right and Megan knew it. She may in fact be in love with Vanessa but she also wasn't going to turn down the VP job. So, did that mean she really *wasn't* in love with Vanessa? No, she decided. It just meant that the universe has a sick sense of humor.

"Just don't say anything to her about this," Abby advised. "Vanessa is one of those chicks that women fall in love with, like, instantly." She snapped her fingers. "Like, they see Vanessa serving up macchiatos or whatever and, boom! 'Oh, I love her! Oh, I want to marry her! Oh, I want to have babies with her!'"

Despite the seriousness of the conversation, Megan couldn't stop laughing at the funny, cartoon-girly voice Abby was using.

"Anyway," Abby went on, "you don't want Vanessa thinking that you're some silly little girl who blew a summer fling out of proportion, do you?"

Megan nodded. She definitely did not want that, especially if Vanessa was still considering this just a stupid and meaningless fling. But alarmingly, Megan had almost told Vanessa she loved her today, when Vanessa kissed her goodbye before leaving for La Vida Mocha. The only thing that stopped her was the fear that Vanessa would not say it back and Megan, being Megan, foresaw in an instant how the rest of her day would have developed from that point. Basically, she would have spent the entire afternoon in her room, sequestering herself from the other women here at the beach house, feeling rejected, listening to Adele and trying to come up with a way to text or call Vanessa to say something along the lines of, "Ha-ha, remember when I said 'I love you' earlier? Totally kidding! I was just goofing off!"

"I suppose you're right," Megan eventually said to Abby.

"So, change of subject," Abby began. "Have you heard from your parents?"

"Not a peep," Megan replied. "Actually, I haven't even thought about it much."

This was true. Since coming out on her birthday at Marcano's, things had been such a whirlwind, thanks to Vanessa.

Abby took a long sip of her cocktail.

"You'll get used to it," Abby murmured.

Megan reached over to give her friend's hand a quick squeeze. Abby had come out to her family a few years ago. At the time, Megan was still in New York, at NYU. Late one night, Abby, evidently forgetting the time difference, called Megan and explained that not only had she come out to her folks that day but that her folks had responded by essentially shunning her. And though Abby had tried—in typical Abby fashion—to sound unperturbed by it, Megan could tell, even over the phone, that her best friend was upset. So, Megan had emailed her professors, claimed to have strep throat, caught a flight to San Diego the next morning and spent two rather blurry days getting wasted with Abby before flying back east.

"I think I'm already used to it," Megan said, thoughtfully. "I mean, seriously, I'm not losing sleep over it. I look at it as their loss if they choose to cut me out of their lives."

"Same," Abby said. "Well, same now; back then I was pissed! Now that I'm an old woman of twenty-seven, I'm a lot more mellow about it."

Nodding, Megan said, "Anyway, Molly and I are meeting up for lunch next week. I feel like by coming out I got my sister back."

"That's awesome," Abby said. "And I'm glad the thing with your parents isn't fucking with you. It's like you said, their loss. I just want to make sure you're doing okay."

"I am," Megan stated, giving Abby's hand another squeeze in gratitude.

Chapter 39

Fuck! What a shitty day!

As she drove from La Vida Mocha to the beach house Saturday night, Vanessa wanted to stop the Jeep, drive onto the nearest beach and walk into the ocean to let the Pacific wash away the hellish day she and Chloë had just endured at the coffeeshop.

They had been slammed as soon as they opened. It was if all of Carlsbad had suddenly decided that today was the day to venture out for lattes and cappuccinos and mochas, and La Vida Mocha was the only place on Earth to get them. Vanessa knew she should be grateful for the business but, goddamn it…when it is just her and Chloë and half of the village comes in it is easy to get frazzled, especially when customers start to get impatient and act as if their coffee order is on par with being on the waiting list for a new kidney and then make faux helpful comments like, "You really should get more help in here, you know."

It was just one thing after another: parents coming in with ill-behaved children; couples getting into screaming fights with each other; people spilling their drinks; other people taking forever to order…

At one point, a customer approached the counter and asked for an iced mocha. With no chocolate.

"So, you just want an iced coffee?" Vanessa had asked, already annoyed at having to extend the conversation because there was quite a line behind this idiot.

"Nooo," the customer, a soccer mom type had said, as if talking to a recalcitrant six-year-old. "If I wanted iced coffee, I would have said iced coffee. However, I want an *iced mocha*, but without the chocolate."

"Ma'am," Vanessa had replied, "the only difference between the iced coffee and the iced mocha is that we add chocolate syrup to the iced mocha. So, what you're asking for is in fact an iced coffee."

The lady, apparently not appreciating the coffee vocabulary lesson, had pursed her lips and then said, "Miss, I want an iced mocha. No. Chocolate. Did you understand my English this time?"

Vanessa had been on the verge of personally escorting the woman out of her shop when she remembered that she charged a dollar more for an iced mocha than for an iced coffee. So, she had plastered on a fake smile, told the lady her drink would be right up and allowed the lady to give an extra dollar to the cause.

And was it a full moon today? Because Vanessa actually lost count of how many obnoxious men hit on her and Chloë at various points throughout the day and then would persist even after she or Chloë would tell them she was not interested and, when that didn't do it, that she was gay.

At about seven o'clock, with only an hour to go until closing time and Vanessa could see the light at the end of the tunnel, she overheard a guy tell Chloë as she was sanitizing a table for a customer that she's cute and that he wanted to take her out for a drink.

"Thanks, but I'm gay," Chloë had said.

"Gay, huh?" the guy had said. "Spend a night with me and I'll make you straight."

Vanessa had pounced. Considering how shitty the day had been up to that point, there was no way she was going to let this go.

"Oh, really?" she had said, loud enough for everyone in the shop to hear her. "Let me ask you something, then. How would you feel if a gay guy asks you out and then tells you that if you spend one night with him, he'll turn you gay? Would you take him up on it? Do you think that's how it works?"

The entire coffeeshop had burst into applause, providing the lone bright spot in the day, especially when Chloë's wannabe suitor's face turned beet red and he slunk out of La Vida Mocha, but not before turning at the door and yelling "Dykes!"

Now, just a few minutes from the beach house, Chloë was fully reclined in the passenger seat, silently watching the stars out the window while Vanessa was imagining taking a long, hot shower until she felt this crap day completely washed off.

Entering the beach house, Chloë spied Sienna in the kitchen and walked over to her with slumped shoulders, dragging her feet.

"Drink. Like, serious drink, dude," Vanessa heard Chloë mumble to Sienna. Vanessa herself headed straight for the stairs.

"Hey, babe!" Megan cheerfully squealed when Vanessa entered the bedroom. Megan had been reclining on the bed, obviously waiting for Vanessa to arrive, just like last night, and when Vanessa entered the room Megan hopped off it and ran to embrace her.

Vanessa inwardly groaned. The truth was, after the day she'd just had, she would have preferred to come upstairs to an empty room to have some time to herself before having to socialize with anyone, even Megan. Just an hour; maybe two. Nonetheless, she managed a wan smile as Megan brought her face close for a kiss hello which started innocently enough but which Megan obviously intended to take further when she pushed her tongue into Vanessa's mouth at the same time her hands inched down to grab Vanessa's ass.

On any other day…

But Vanessa reached down to pull Megan's hands away from her bottom and then managed to unlock their lips.

"Babe, what? I missed you," Megan whined, coming in for another kiss, claiming Vanessa's lips before Vanessa had a chance to object. This time, Megan's hands grabbed Vanessa's belt and possessively pulled Vanessa's groin tight against her own. Vanessa imagined that this is what it must be like for parents of small children, coming home after a hard day's work to kids demanding attention. She instantly felt guilty for equating Megan with a bratty child, but the truth was that Megan's forcefulness now, which Vanessa would normally get wildly turned on by, was having no effect on her. If anything, it was annoying her.

Don't fly off the handle!

Extricating herself a second time, Vanessa now held Megan at bay by placing her hands on the other woman's shoulders and stepping back until they were arm's length apart. Megan emitted a short scoff and frowned, her eyes demanding an explanation.

"Sweetie, listen," Vanessa began, "I like where your mind is going, I do, but I just need you to put on the brakes for now, okay? I had a really shitty day at work and I just need time to decompress before I do anything else."

Megan's features softened. She took Vanessa's hands off her shoulders and held onto them as she stepped closer.

"I'm sorry. What happened?"

Vanessa sighed. This was one of the facets of being a lesbian which experience had taught her was a minefield and if she didn't navigate the next few moments *very* carefully…boom!

She also knew that if she was straight and Megan was Max or Mitch or Matthew, she could simply say "I had a bad day at work" and most likely MaxMitchMatthew would say "Sorry to hear that, babe" and then go watch some sporting event on a ridiculously large TV. But Megan was Megan, a woman, and you simply did not tell a woman you didn't want to talk about your bad day yet and expect her to take it well. It had to be handled with finesse.

"Megan, I promise—I pinky promise—that I will tell you all about it later, okay? But right now, all I really want is to take a hot shower and then have some alone time to unwind a bit."

Vanessa could see Megan working on that in her head. It was, after all, already after nine p.m., early still for a Saturday night, but Vanessa knew Megan was wondering if Vanessa's need for some solitude would completely rule out any chance of hanging out tonight.

"How much alone time?" Megan asked.

"Not much, I swear. An hour or so. This is part of my process when I have a day like this. I missed you *so* much today and I want to make sure that when I hang out with you tonight that I'm not some grumpy bitch."

Megan smiled at that, thank god. She even closed the distance between them and gave Vanessa a hug, which Vanessa actually appreciated, drawing strength from it.

"Well, after your shower, I could just sit with you?" Megan said, still hugging her. "Maybe out on the balcony? I won't say anything and I can even give you a foot rub. I promise I won't make it sexual."

Vanessa kissed the top of Megan's head.

"And that sounds *amazing*," she said. "In an hour or so. Just give me that much time and I'll be right as rain."

Vanessa pulled away from the hug just enough to look at Megan's face. She could tell that Megan still wanted to convince her to let her stay but that she was also ready to concede.

It was time to seal the deal.

"The best part is," Vanessa began, "that I'm off tomorrow. We have all day here at the house together."

Megan beamed at being reminded of this point. In fact, it seemed to energize her. She gave Vanessa a quick peck on the lips.

"Okay, take a shower and relax," she said, heading to the bedroom door. "I'll be downstairs with the others. Just come down whenever." And with that, she left the room.

Vanessa let out a sigh.

Whew!

***

Twenty minutes later, Vanessa finally turned off the shower, her skin still tingling from how hot the water had been. She had purposely made the water that hot because only then did it feel like she was truly cleansing herself of what a shitty day she had had.

She stood there in the stall for a few minutes, leaning against one of the walls, her eyes closed, letting water drip off her while she took long deep breaths. Not for the first time since starting her own business, she considered taking up yoga. The breathing exercises and focus on centering oneself would come in handy on days like this. For the time being, though, this superhot shower and the long deep breaths was helping her feel normal again.

Once she had dried herself and put on her robe, she padded into the bedroom and stopped.

On the bed was a serving tray and on the tray was a single glass of white wine. Megan must have brought it while Vanessa was in the shower.

So considerate!

Taking a sip of wine, Vanessa decided to put off getting dressed for now. Instead, she crossed the room and stepped out onto the balcony with her wine glass, taking a seat in one of the Adirondack chairs and propping her feet up on the small round table in front of it. The balcony was around the corner of the house from the deck and Vanessa could hear her friends talking and laughing, though she couldn't make out any of what they were saying. She could also hear some music playing; Alyson Stoner, she guessed.

Drinking her wine, Vanessa once more ruminated on the day at La Vida Mocha. Now that she was at the beach house, showered and clean she found she could be a little more philosophical about things.

What it boiled down to was that days like today are the price of owning a service industry business, Vanessa considered. Whether one sells coffee, books, toys or iPhones, anytime you deal with the public, you're going to have days when it seems the assholes rule the world. But Vanessa deemed herself lucky in that so far, since opening La Vida Mocha's doors back in January, she'd only had three, maybe four days like today, thank goodness. And despite how crappy today was, the day's receipts were amazing. The shop had made a lot of money; enough to make Vanessa optimistic again that things would be alright.

Her phone chirped. A text from William.

You're spending the weekend at a beach house and I wasn't invited????

How did you find out?

Duh! I'm friends with Chloë on Facebook! She's been posting pictures! Address please!

Sorry, no boys allowed. We are planning the lesbian takeover of the world and can't have men ruining it.

You suck! Is Lover Girl with you?

Of course! In fact, she owes me a foot rub.

After typing that, Vanessa realized she wanted that foot rub now. Actually, she just wanted to feel Megan touching her.

Is foot rub lesbian slang for sick and perverted lesbian acts involving tongues and 12 inch dildos?

Vanessa laughed.

No. Foot rub means foot rub. Back rub means sick and perverted lesbian acts involving tongues and dildos.

Yuck! Anyway, I hate you for not inviting me to the beach house. Just be sure to invite me to the wedding. But only if it's at a beach house. Toodles!

Vanessa's mouth dropped open. Wedding?
She knew William was just joking, being a smartass, but she also knew his little crack was striking a nerve inside her, a not

unpleasant nerve, at that. Of course, Vanessa hadn't been thinking about marriage but she knew that she had to admit to herself that she had developed strong feelings for Megan. And so far, Vanessa had tried to keep those feelings in check because, really, what was the point?

Vanessa had fallen in love fast before…when she was younger, because that's what young women did, fall in love too quickly. Vanessa thought she had outgrown that, but if she was completely honest with herself, she was undoubtedly in love with Megan. And if Megan was staying in Carlsbad, Vanessa felt now that she would do whatever it took to combine her commitment to La Vida Mocha with the commitment needed to be the kind of partner and lover Megan deserved. She realized now that she should never have closed her mind to the possibility of romance because it never was a case of her needing to be so focused on La Vida Mocha as to exclude any chance of finding love. Instead, it turns out it was a case of simply finding the right woman to love; one that Vanessa wanted to devote herself to as much as she devoted herself to La Vida Mocha.

Fuck!

She shook her head and then finished the rest of her wine. Picking up her phone again, she typed out a text that would she knew would bounce around cell towers and maybe even an orbiting satellite or two only to end up reaching the phone of an auburn-haired beauty who was just downstairs:

I believe you said something about a foot rub?

Chapter 40

On Monday morning at the beach house, Megan and Vanessa woke up a little earlier than normal in order to have sex one last time in the mansion. Afterwards, Megan had to kiss Vanessa goodbye so Vanessa could leave to go open La Vida Mocha. Megan knew her lips were still flavored with Vanessa's come and that Vanessa couldn't help but taste it, especially when Megan deepened the kiss, eliciting a low groan from the brunette, who suddenly seemed like she couldn't care if La Vida Mocha opened today or not.

Once Vanessa was gone, Megan packed her stuff and then took her suitcase and her scream pillow—which had gotten a lot of use the past few days—downstairs where she found the rest of her temporary housemates assembled, getting ready to leave also. Megan gave Sienna a hug and they both promised to continue sharing their art with each other. Megan then said goodbye to Angela and Desiree, thanking them for arranging such an amazing weekend.

Abby and Kat then gave Megan a ride home to her condo.

Stepping into her home, she dropped the bags, went into the living room and flopped down on the couch. It had been a great weekend with lots of laughs, great food (mainly thanks to Kat's cooking) and mind-blowing sex. As relaxing as it had been, though, she was glad to be home among her things. Unpacking could wait...Right now she just wanted to sit here and chill.

But her phone pinged. It was a text from Sophia.

Hey! I know you're off today but Lucy wants to know if you have five minutes to chat?

Megan sat up, suddenly very alert. She texted back that of course she had five minutes for Lucy; just give her a few moments to go upstairs and login for the Zoom call.

"Hey, Megan!" Lucy Whitaker greeted her with a little wave in front of the camera when the Zoom connected. Lucy was in her forties and always looked stunning with her long blonde hair and piercing blue eyes that shone like sapphires. Even though she was dressed super casually in a Harvard t-shirt, she still exuded confidence, intelligence and determination.

"Hey, Megan," Sophia added from her Zoom window.

"Hey, Lucy, it's so nice to see you again," Megan began. "Hey, Soph."

"Megan, I am *so* sorry for intruding on your day off," Lucy said, "but I'm going to be incredibly busy the rest of the week and I didn't want to put this off any longer."

Megan felt her heart start thumping. She was certain the other women could hear it.

"You're going to New York, my friend!" Lucy exclaimed with a huge smile.

Megan's eyes went wide and she couldn't help her own Cheshire Cat-like grin from taking over her face.

"Really? When?"

"Okay, if possible, I'd like you there in two weeks," Lucy said. "I know that's short notice, especially since you have a place to sell here in California not to mention finding a new place to live in New York, but here's what I'm offering. BeachSoft already has a luxury apartment in Brooklyn that we use whenever executives travel to New York. You can stay there for as long as it takes to find a place of your own. Plus, if you still have to make some trips back here to California to deal with selling your house or other personal business, just expense the trips on your company credit card, no problem."

"Okay, fair enough," Megan said. It was a generous offer, after all, allowing her to handle all the logistics of relocating at a considerate pace.

"I am so excited BeachSoft is finally doing this," Lucy went on. "Having a presence in New York is going to be *huge* for us! Especially with all the future diversification plans we have. And you are definitely the person to head it up!"

"Oh my God, thank you!" Megan told her, feeling herself blush.

"I mean it, Megan. You may be super young still but what you've done for this company is A. May. Zing. And I knew—I just knew!—when I recruited you and convinced you to come work for me that we'd be having a conversation like this one day."

Megan didn't know what to say. She was feeling overwhelmed. This was Lucy-frigging-Whitaker singing her praises!

"Lucy, I can't thank you enough," she said, alarmed that her eyes were beginning to brim with tears. She willed them to stay where they were because, dammit, she was not going to cry in front of Lucy-frigging-Whitaker.

"Congratulations, Madame Vice-President," Lucy said.

The call ended several minutes later, Lucy promising to call Megan again next week. In the meantime, Lucy expected Sophia to mentor Megan in the fine art of becoming a vice-president of operations for BeachSoft. When Lucy left the Zoom, Megan and Sophia then came up with a pretty intensive schedule of meetings for the next two weeks to go over everything.

It was finally happening. Megan hadn't realized the relief she would feel at this news. Ever since being told that she would be heading up operations in New York, she'd been in a holding pattern of sorts: verbally promoted to VP but not actually being a VP yet; a future resident of New York City but having no idea when she'd be relocating. Having these matters settled at last felt as if she were now relieved of a weight she hadn't known she was carrying.

Her life and career were going through some momentous and exciting changes, she knew. Professionally, she could hardly ask for anything better right now. Vice-president of a large, cutting-edge tech company at the age of twenty-seven. Relocating to one of her favorite cities on Earth—and being able to afford to live there because her new salary, combined with the stock options, was outrageous.

So, why wasn't she more excited? Why hadn't she already told Alexa to play her Super Happy Playlist so she could dance around her condo like a silly teenager? Why wasn't she updating her social media with posts full of smiley-face emojis and pictures of the Brooklyn Bridge and the Empire State Building?

Vanessa.

Leaving Vanessa was not cause for the Super Happy Playlist. Just the thought of leaving Vanessa caused a pang of sorrow to stab Megan's chest, and the swirl of emotions which were now taking over her being was making her feel lightheaded and dizzy.

She went to the bathroom so she could splash some cold water on her face and hopefully get her mind centered again. How had she let this happen to herself? This was supposed to be a fling! A stupid fling! But, if she was completely honest with herself, she had known—known!—as soon as she walked into La Vida Mocha that first time and made eye contact with Vanessa that she had seen a part of the rest of her life.

Now, she was faced with saying goodbye to all that.

After drying her face with a towel, Megan looked around her master bathroom.

Vanessa's electric toothbrush was standing on the counter next to Megan's. Vanessa must have bought a second one, Megan considered, because this morning, at the beach house, Megan had seen Vanessa brushing her teeth with a different one. Odd how Megan hadn't noticed that Vanessa had even started leaving a toothbrush here. Thinking about it now, she knew she'd seen it here on her counter before. She even remembered looking at it one morning several days ago and wishing that she had found a pink one like it for herself because Vanessa's looked cute.

Megan looked into the bathtub.

On the shower caddy, three new bottles had taken up residence: Vanessa's body wash, along with her shampoo and conditioner. There was also Vanessa's pink and green bath pouf, hanging from a hook on the shower caddy, next to Megan's green one. And on the side of the tub, a second Venus razor now sat next to Megan's.

Megan thought for a moment, picturing the last morning she had woken up at Vanessa's, sometime before the beach house weekend. She remembered brushing her own teeth and then repacking her toothbrush, but she also remembered that the toothpaste she had used, her favorite, had come from a tube she now always left in Vanessa's medicine chest. Not only that, she also had a bath pouf, body wash and shampoo/conditioner in Vanessa's shower. She had brought those items over one night some time ago and just left them there without thinking of it. And—and!—she also had started leaving a pack of hair ties and some scrunchies at Vanessa's. Vanessa had even cleared out a spot in one of the drawers of the vanity for them.

And I have a razor over there too!

Megan stared at Vanessa's bath pouf, her pulse quickening. She liked that it was hanging there—no, she *loved* that it was hanging there! She loved that Vanessa had one day thought to herself that it would be a good idea to go to the store and buy a second bath pouf, just to leave here at the condo. And Megan *loved,*

loved, LOVED the idea that Vanessa hadn't even talked to her about it, that she had just done it! Same with the toothbrush, which Megan was now looking at. No discussion. No asking for permission. No, "Hey, do you mind if I start leaving a toothbrush at your place?"

Nor had Megan sought approval from Vanessa for the stuff she had left at Vanessa's. Megan had just purchased the items from Walmart one evening, brought the bag over to Vanessa's and, boom, just like that she had established a beachhead in Vanessa's place, to use a term her father—a World War II buff—often used.

Vanessa's cute pink electric toothbrush, standing on the counter next to Megan's black one, *belonged* there, but Megan was now faced with one day walking into a bathroom in New York and not seeing that toothbrush.

What do I do?

The only thing she could do now is make the most of the time they had left.

Vanessa was due to come over and stay after closing La Vida Mocha. The funny thing, Megan was thinking now, was that she was actually excited about just sitting and listening to Vanessa tell her about her day at the coffeeshop. This was the first day La Vida Mocha was opening back up to pre-pandemic hours. And that girl Lulu or LouAnn or something like that was coming back to work. Megan wanted to hear all about it. Before they fucked each other's brains out like always, Megan wanted to simply sit with Vanessa and hear her talk.

Megan suddenly felt short of breath and she had to sit down on the edge of the tub because her legs had gone wobbly.

"Oh my God," she whined. "What do I do?"

* * *

Vanessa arrived a little after seven. Megan, hearing Vanessa walking towards the condo, was at the door opening it even before Vanessa had a chance to ring the bell.

Raising an eyebrow, Vanessa said, "Eager, aren't you? I like it, but I desperately want to shower first."

Megan couldn't laugh. She simply stood there, holding the door open, looking at this woman whose toothbrush was upstairs in her bathroom. She was glad to be holding the door because her legs suddenly felt wobbly again. She watched as Vanessa's face morphed from amused to worried.

"Sweetie, what's wrong?" Vanessa asked, coming forward and putting her hands on Megan's shoulders.

"I need to talk to you," Megan said softly, pulling Vanessa in and closing the door. Holding one of Vanessa's hands, she led her into the living room. Both women sat close to each other on the couch, the worry on Vanessa's face more pronounced now.

"Megan..."

"I had a call from my boss today," Megan interrupted. "And by 'boss' I mean *the* boss. Lucy Whitaker."

Megan watched as Vanessa's face began transforming from worry to understanding. The woman was smart. It was one of the things Megan found sexy about her.

"Oh," Vanessa uttered.

Megan swallowed.

"When?" Vanessa asked.

After taking a deep breath, Megan said, "Two weeks."

Vanessa's mouth dropped open; her eyes went wide.

"Fuck..." Vanessa whispered.

"Yeah."

They both sat there in silence for a few moments. Megan's heart was pounding and her palms were sweaty. She didn't know exactly what she wanted to happen in the next few moments.

Vanessa stared at the floor.

"Doesn't give you much time," she said.

"No."

"All the packing and stuff."

"I know."

Finally, Vanessa cleared her throat.

"Well, we knew it had to end sometime, right?" she said.

Megan's heart deflated. Was that all she was going to get? Was this the evidence she needed that Vanessa *didn't* view what they had as more than a summer fling?

"Yeah, we did," she said, plastering on a fake smile.

More silence.

Megan was practically quivering from holding in all she wanted to say. But what could she say, really? She had gone into this thing with Vanessa knowing that it had to end because of New York, and also knowing that Vanessa had been upfront and honest with her, telling her from the very beginning that she was in no place to have a girlfriend because of La Vida Mocha.

But suddenly, Vanessa stood up. That was odd.

"What are you doing?" Megan asked, still sitting.

Vanessa seemed to be confused, like someone who had just suffered a blow to the head and now had no idea where they were or how they had gotten there.

"I'm going to go home," Vanessa said.

Megan stood.

"What?" she almost screeched.

"I'm going home," Vanessa repeated, moving towards the door.

"Wait!" Megan pleaded. Vanessa turned to look at her. "Why are you doing this? I thought we were spending the night together!"

Vanessa threw up her arms.

"We should never have started spending nights together, Megan!" she exclaimed. And did Megan hear Vanessa's voice crack? "It was stupid to start that! We should have kept what we did limited to fucking, each of us going home to our own bed no matter what the hell time it was."

Megan crossed her arms as she stared at Vanessa.

"Well, I certainly don't feel like fucking now," she said.

But I do want to talk!

"Fine," Vanessa began. "In that case, there's definitely no reason for me to be here. Even God took a day off if you believe that crap."

Megan felt herself start to tremble.

"Fine, go!"

"What do you think I'm doing?" Vanessa retorted, her eyes blazing.

Megan felt her blood boil.

"Just so you know," Megan began, "I'm going to be pretty busy the next two weeks so I don't know how much time I'll have for our little fling."

Vanessa shrugged.

"Okay," she said. "I'll just sit at home waiting for you to stop being important and call me."

Megan's mouth dropped open.

"If I call you," Megan stated.

Vanessa gave a dry laugh.

"Okay, fine. *If* you call me. Whatever."

Vanessa turned and put her hand on the doorknob but froze.

Megan's hopes went back up.

Please change your mind. Please change your mind.

But, instead, Vanessa said, "If I don't see you before you leave, good luck in New York."

Megan's heart fell.

Vanessa opened the door, walked through and closed it behind her.

Megan stood where she was and started crying.

Chapter 41

Stupid, stupid, stupid!

How did she let this happen to herself? Had she really been that lonely? Had she really been that hard-up for great sex? Enough to allow herself to fucking fall in love with a woman she knew right from the start that she couldn't have?

These thoughts and more were running through Vanessa's head as she angrily paced back and forth in her bedroom after arriving home from Megan's.

Megan's statement to her, *If I call you* was still bouncing around Vanessa's skull, causing her to hold her hands to the sides of her head in an attempt to somehow squeeze it out of her memory.

She groaned and then sobbed. She had been crying since walking to her Jeep from Megan's front door. In truth, she probably shouldn't have driven considering how blurry her eyes had been with tears. But she had made it home unscathed and had been crying non-stop since. But now these fresh sobs were forcing her to stop pacing and collapse to the floor beside her bed as her body was wracked with sadness and tears.

As agonizing as this was, Vanessa also knew that she had made the right decision by leaving tonight. Megan may want to just run out the clock on their meaningless fling, meeting up for sex right up until she left for the airport, but Vanessa couldn't do it. She had a heart to protect, her own, and so beginning her Megan detox now was the only sensible thing to do.

Her phone rang; it was still in her back pocket. From the ringtone she knew it was William. She debated not answering but, well, ride-or-die. With her luck, *this* would be the night William was being chased by Republicans.

Immediately after pressing the green button on the screen, William said, "Oh my God, what's wrong? I know something's wrong!"

Vanessa's mouth fell open.

"Wait, how did you—"

"Magic Rainbow Hotline," William stated, as if the answer was obvious, causing Vanessa to roll her eyes. This was one of William's pet theories, that gay people can sense when other gay people are in distress. "I felt a shiver go up my spine just now and knew something was wrong with you."

"She's leaving," Vanessa told him.

"Who?"

"Seriously? Who do you think?"

"Megan?" William asked, confusion evident in his voice. "But we always knew she was leaving, didn't we?"

"Yes," Vanessa confirmed, biting back a sob, "but now I know she's leaving in two weeks and I—"

"Oh, honey," William said. "You've really fallen for her, haven't you?"

Vanessa answered by letting him hear her cry.

"Honey, I'm so sorry. But we knew this was going to happen, didn't we?"

Again, Vanessa answered by continuing to cry openly.

"I'm on my way over," William declared.

***

An hour later, with William holding her on the couch, Vanessa was still unable to stop the tears, though she had managed to get the sobbing under control. To his credit, from the moment he arrived, William had said nothing. He just sat there, allowing Vanessa to cry as she huddled against him.

Eventually, though, he said, "So, what now?"

Vanessa sniffled and managed to say, "What do you mean?"

"I mean, what happens now? What do you want to do about this situation with Megan?"

Vanessa wiped her nose with a tissue.

"What am I supposed to do?" she asked. "Megan has given me no clear evidence that she feels about me the way I feel about her. I mean, I've *imagined* that she does but for all I know that was wishful thinking."

"Okay, but have you actually asked her if she feels the same way?"

"No."

"You could start there," William suggested.

"To what end?" Vanessa returned, fighting back some additional sobs that were threatening at William's line of questioning.

"Megan isn't going to give up the New York job and before you suggest it, I wouldn't ask her to. She's leaving and that's that."

"Are you going to continue seeing her until then, though?"

Vanessa took a breath. She wanted to continue seeing Megan. In fact, she wanted to lock Megan in her bedroom so they could do nothing but have sex and snuggle with each other for the next two weeks. Vanessa wanted to get her fill of Megan…

"No," she answered William. "I'd rather not; it's just going to make it that much harder when she leaves and it's already hard enough. At least now, I've basically started my post-Megan life. Anyway, this is all my fault. I'm the one who broke the rules of our dumb fling. I should have put a stop to the sleepovers; I should never have invited her to spend that Sunday off with me; and we shouldn't have even gone to that stupid beach house together."

And I sure as hell should never have fallen in love with her.

***

Three days later, Vanessa was in the back room of La Vida Mocha blowing out yet another frustrated breath while looking at her laptop's screen. The computer may as well be showing her gibberish for all Vanessa cared because she hadn't been able to focus on a single thing since she came in here.

Well, she had been able to focus on one thing.

Megan.

It was late morning and out in the main room of the coffeeshop Chloë and Luli had the place humming nicely as they dealt with the tail end of the morning rush. With those two handling things, Vanessa had come into the back to deal with some administrative stuff but then had gotten sidetracked with thoughts of Megan.

She hadn't heard from Megan since Monday night, nor had she reached out herself. What was the point, really? Megan was leaving and if it wasn't obvious already that she didn't have strong feelings for Vanessa, it was fairly fucking obvious now.

It was well and truly over, Vanessa believed, a fact which had made her cry herself to sleep every night so far this week.

She felt fresh tears beginning to form thinking about it now, but she refused to start crying because she didn't want Chloë or Luli seeing her upset. The three of them had a business to run. Vanessa's business. The one she had told Megan she was so super-focused on that there was no way she could get involved in anything more than a fling.

Just as well, really. There truly was too much at stake here for Vanessa to be getting her mind and emotions turned around by any woman. If she lost La Vida Mocha it meant starting over for her. Back to the corporate world, working for someone else. No, thank you. Nope. From now on, Vanessa was going to stick to the script: no relationships. And if she did want to have a fling again, she'd sure as hell be sure it was with the type of woman she could not possibly fall in love with even if that woman was the last one on Earth.

Chapter 42

"Let's call it a day," Sophia told Megan, that same evening.

Megan smiled wanly and nodded.

"Yeah, I like that idea," she said.

"Are you okay?" Sophia asked. "I know these sessions we have are a little long and boring, but…"

"Soph, I'm fine, really," Megan answered. She liked Sophia tons but they had never gotten particularly close during their time working together. Certainly not close enough for Megan to open her heart to the older woman about Vanessa. "I'm just a little tired because of all the packing I've been doing each night."

"Okay, if you're sure you're fine."

"I am. Thanks for asking."

The women said their goodbyes and the Zoom call ended.

And then like every other day so far this week, Megan burst into tears.

For each of the past three days since her split with Vanessa, Megan had had to bottle all her tears inside while spending what seemed to be endless hours on Zoom calls with Sophia going over what was needed in order to get the New York operations up and running. It was only after the calls ended when Megan allowed the dam to burst. And when it burst, it stayed burst. It was probably an exaggeration but Megan was certain that the only times over the past few days when tears weren't falling from her eyes were when she was fitfully asleep at night.

She'd not heard from Vanessa at all after Monday night and with each passing day it hurt more. But she couldn't bring herself to reach out to Vanessa either. Vanessa obviously considered what they had shared to be nothing but a fling and so what was the point in contacting her? To tell Vanessa she was in love with her? Oh, sure! And be laughed at? No, thanks!

But Megan knew Vanessa wouldn't laugh, that wasn't her style; she was far more considerate than that. Lovely and considerate. But she also knew Vanessa wouldn't just fall into her arms and profess a deep love for her either.

Not for the first time, Megan wished she was already in New York. Three-thousand miles, that's what Megan needed. Three-thousand miles of continent between her and the woman she loved instead of a five-minute drive that consisted of three lefts and two rights. But the thought of there ever being three-thousand miles between her and Vanessa just made Megan cry that much more.

And the dam stayed burst.

When she became aware of her surroundings again, Megan was shocked to realize it was dark.

Oh my God, what the fuck! How long have I been sitting here?

The clock in her home office told her it was after eight p.m.

Fuck, not again!

Yesterday following work, when the crying started, Megan had managed to make it downstairs to her sofa where she had simply sat, letting the sadness and sobs have their way with her until eventually she realized that hours had passed and she was now sitting in a completely dark room, starving because she hadn't eaten since lunch but having no recollection of that much time passing.

Now it had happened again. Crying. No sense of time passing. Ignoring her basic needs, such as food.

In a panic, she reached for her phone and sent a text to Abby.

I need help!

***

Abby was at Megan's in fifteen minutes. The first thing she did was order Megan to lay down on the sofa and cover her with a blanket. Then Abby raided Megan's refrigerator and somehow found enough ingredients to cook her an omelet that she served with an English muffin and some fruit.

After Megan had eaten, Abby poured two glasses of white wine and took a seat next to Megan on the sofa, letting Megan rest her head on her shoulder.

"Maybe she feels the same way," Abby eventually offered.

Megan, feeling much better now that she had eaten, shook her head.

"If she felt the same way, she wouldn't have left on Monday night."

"I get that," Abby said. "But maybe the fact that she left on Monday night actually means she *does* feel the same way."

"You're talking in riddles," Megan chastised, sipping some wine.

"Am I?"

"Yes! If Vanessa felt the same way she would have stayed on Monday night and we could have had a conversation about what to do about our situation."

"And what do you want to do about your situation?" Abby queried.

"I'm not having this discussion, Abs. It's like one of those stupid games people play like, 'What would you wish for if a genie gave you three wishes?' But there are no fucking genies granting three wishes; it's a stupid game and I won't play."

"Fine, fine," Abby said. "Forget I asked."

"Just let me sit here and be miserable."

"No problem. Do you want me to stay the night?"

"If you don't mind," Megan said with a mirthless chuckle. "After all, I don't want to wake up tomorrow and have another one of my crying blackouts and miss my morning meeting with Sophia. That wouldn't be very vice-presidential of me."

Chapter 43

At a little past nine-thirty, Vanessa was at home, in pajamas, legs curled up under her on the couch trying to watch a movie. She didn't even know which movie it was, quite frankly; but because she couldn't stand the silence of her empty house she had put on Netflix and clicked on the first movie which the service offered up. Some kind of war movie, and it had Sean Connery in it, that was all that registered with her. It didn't matter, she wasn't paying attention to it anyway.

Her phone rang. Picking it up she frowned at the Caller ID. *Abby?*

She vaguely remembered that she and Abby had exchanged phone numbers in prehistoric times, back when the world was still normal and she and Abby would be part of a larger group of women who would hang out now and then to go to lesbian bars or have backyard barbecues at someone's house or catch an indie girl band perform. Having the numbers of the various women involved in such outings sometimes made organizing them easier but Vanessa couldn't recall her and Abby *ever* actually calling one another.

"Hello?" she greeted tentatively.

"Do you love Megan?" Abby asked. It sounded like she was outside somewhere.

Vanessa's heart thumped.

"Well?" Abby prodded.

"I do," Vanessa croaked, tears beginning to well up again.

"Like, no bullshit, no fucking around love her?"

Vanessa cleared her throat so her next answer would be clearer.

"No bullshit, Abby. I love her so much."

There was a pause.

"I believe you," Abby finally said. "Now, here's what I need you to do…"

Chapter 44

Megan was wondering what was taking Abby so long.

They had both come upstairs to go to bed and had even settled in and turned off the lights when Abby had suddenly said she needed to call Kat and tell her goodnight, but that she'd do it downstairs. Megan had suspected that was because Abby didn't want Megan to overhear her being all lovey-dovey to Kat, which would kind of ruin Abby's reputation.

Megan had started drifting off to sleep when she heard the bedroom door open and then Abby get into bed with her. As she began falling asleep again, a smile came to Megan's face.

Why haven't I ever noticed how much Abby smells like Vanessa?

"Megan?"

Or sounds like Vanessa?

Megan's eyes shot open.

No way!

She reached for the bedside lamp, switched it on and then turned to her other side.

There in bed next to her was Vanessa.

"Oh, my fucking God!" Megan squealed, bringing her hands to her mouth, her eyes wide over them as she took in the vision of Vanessa in her bed. The other woman was dressed in jeans and a simple white tee, but to Megan's eyes, she looked angelic.

Vanessa, meanwhile, was looking at Megan uncertainly, as if afraid to speak.

Megan decided this was not a time for words anyway. Reaching out, she took hold of the back of Vanessa's head and initiated a slow and deep kiss.

When their lips parted company, Megan asked, "What are you doing here?"

"Abby called me," Vanessa said. "She let me in. Told me to come up here and get my woman."

Megan knew tears were falling from her eyes but she didn't care.

"Where is she now?"

"Said she was going home," Vanessa returned. She reached out and gently brushed some hair off Megan's face and then kept her hand on Megan's shoulder. Megan felt alive at the touch.

Vanessa stared at her.

"Megan?"

"Yes?"

"I did something wrong," Vanessa said. The intensity of her gaze increased and Megan now was sure the world had stopped spinning.

"What did you do wrong?"

"I fell in love with you."

Megan gasped. Yes, the world had stopped spinning. Time had stopped moving. This was the only moment in existence.

Again, taking a firm hold on the back of Vanessa's head, she pulled Vanessa in for another kiss. It was a deep kiss, her tongue penetrating immediately into Vanessa's mouth, her soft lips claiming ownership of Vanessa's. Vanessa surrendered to kiss completely.

When Megan pulled away, she saw tears streaming from Vanessa's eyes.

"I love you too," Megan said, sniffling. "I tried not to fall in love, I promise, but I couldn't help it. It was, like, from the first time I saw you I knew I was going to love you."

"I knew too," Vanessa told her. "Boom, remember? I saw you that first time and knew I could be in very serious trouble one day."

"Because you sensed I was a troublemaker?" Megan asked teasingly.

Vanessa laughed but then placed her hand on Megan's cheek.

"No, because I sensed I had finally found someone worth losing my heart to," she told Megan.

Megan struck again for another kiss. She wanted to keep kissing this woman until the next week or the next year. When this kiss ended, she said, "Oh my God, I love you, Vanessa. What do we do, though?"

Blowing out a breath, Vanessa shook her head. "I don't know."

"You're the older and wiser one, though," Megan said with a smirk, sniffling. "Can't you figure something out?"

"Okay, so, first of all, you're gonna pay for that 'older and wiser' crack," Vanessa said, tapping Megan's bottom. "Secondly, aren't you the tech genius? Can't you just write an app that helps us stay together?"

Megan giggled.

"You're silly," she said. "But, seriously…"

"I don't know what we do, Megan. But let's promise each other that we'll try to make this happen. Because I want this, Megan. I want you."

"I want this too, Vanessa," Megan replied. "I want you."

***

The next day, it was after four-thirty by the time Megan was able to log-off her BeachSoft laptop.

Fuck me!

She leaned back in her office chair and blew out a breath. The day had basically been another marathon session of Sophia teaching Megan how to do Sophia's job, since Megan was going to be BeachSoft's New York Sophia. The day had seemed even more exhausting because Megan had pretty much stayed seated in her office chair the entire time, getting up only to pee occasionally and to grab a quick lunch from downstairs.

Getting up from her chair, Megan winced at how tight her muscles all felt. She needed to get the hell out of the house and go for a nice long walk.

In her bedroom, she sent a text to Vanessa.

Done for the day! I need to get out of the house and so I'm going for a walk.

Having done that, she stripped out of her work clothes, chose cream-colored yoga pants and a pink racerback workout shirt to put on and then pulled her hair into a messy bun. Her phone pinged.

You should come by LVM! It's slow now and I miss you.

The message ended with a kissy face emoji and Megan melted.

She was actually super glad Vanessa suggested stopping by because Megan desperately wanted to see her, not only because she could never get enough of seeing the woman she was in love with, but because throughout the day—mostly when she was kind of zoning out during her sessions with Sophia—Megan had been trying to solve the problem of how her and Vanessa could make a relationship—a *real* relationship—work, and she thought she now had a plan. The tricky part was getting Vanessa to go along with it.

***

Despite her excitement at wanting to see Vanessa, Megan parked her car several blocks away from La Vida Mocha so that she could, in fact, get a little bit of walking in. She promised herself, however, that after visiting the coffeeshop, she'd also take a good brisk walk along the seawall.

When she entered the coffeeshop, she saw with relief that it was still not busy, with only two of the tables occupied by customers. Chloë was behind the counter, mask on, putting some clean coffee mugs near the coffee machine. A young Asian woman, also masked, was there too, opening a fresh packet of napkins. They both looked up when they heard the door's bell jingle.

"Oh, hey, Megan!" Chloë said cheerily. Megan waved back and approached the counter, the Asian woman scrutinizing her the whole way out of curiosity.

"Megan, this is Luli," Chloë said by way of introduction. "She used to work here when we first opened, before the world fell apart."

"Hi, Luli; nice to meet you," Megan said.

"Same here," Luli replied, her hidden smile also reaching her eyes.

"VIP customer," Chloë stage-whispered to Luli, pointing at Megan.

Megan's eyes went wide. Behind her mask her mouth fell open.

"Oh my God, no…I am *soooo* not a VIP," she insisted.

"Vanessa's girlfriend," Chloë stage-whispered again, with a smirk in Megan's direction.

Now it was Luli's eyes that went wide as she regarded Megan anew.

"Um…yeah," she said, "that pretty much makes you the Queen of VIPs."

"No! Chloë stop!"

Thankfully, Vanessa emerged just then from the back room wearing her Vader mask. Megan loved how Vanessa's eyes lit up when she saw her.

"I thought I heard your voice," Vanessa said. She surveyed the main room. "Still slow?"

"For now," Chloë answered.

"Do you want anything?" Vanessa asked Megan.

Just you.

"No, I'm fine for now," Megan answered.

Vanessa came out from behind the counter.

"I'm going to take a quick break," she told her employees. "But I'll be right over there," she pointed to a table near the window.

It was only once they reached the table and sat down when Megan and Vanessa both took off their masks.

Megan decided to jump right in since she didn't know how long she'd have Vanessa's undivided attention for.

"I want to suggest something to you," she said, taking Vanessa's hands in both of hers. "Something about how we could make this relationship really work."

Vanessa smiled, her eyes sparkling.

"Do tell," she prodded.

Megan took a deep breath.

Rip off the bandage time.

"Come with me to New York," she said. Now that her idea was out there, Megan suddenly felt afraid, as if Vanessa would tell her to fuck off.

Vanessa's eyebrows shot up in surprise, as if she had been expecting Megan to say almost anything other than what Megan had actually said.

"Wow!" Vanessa eventually exclaimed. But she didn't tell Megan to fuck off and so Megan went on.

"Hear me out," she said, squeezing the hands she was holding. "Let me present my case and then you can speak. Promise me," she added sternly.

Vanessa smirked.

"Only if you also promise to be this bossy later tonight in bed."

Megan felt relief wash over her. Vanessa had cracked a joke. That was good, right? It at least meant that she was willing to listen to what Megan had to say instead of automatically vetoing it. But she needed to dive in before La Vida Mocha got busy again.

"I know your whole life is here in Carlsbad, especially because you own this fabulous business." Megan made a gesture encompassing the entire coffeeshop. "But you can—*we* can—have a life in New York. I mean, yeah, *we* can, but *you* can separately, as part of *we* but doing your own thing as well."

Megan knew she was rambling. She felt her cheeks flush, partly because she was upset with herself. She had rehearsed this on her way over here. She needed to calm down. She took a deep breath.

"I'm probably not making any sense," she continued, "but here's the gist of it: you could come with me to New York and start another business. Another coffeeshop. Or a fitness studio—you'd be good at that. Or a whatever. Maybe you can even keep La Vida Mocha and just manage it from New York because that old ninja lady is right, something like that *can* be done remotely nowadays. But while you sort that out, we will be perfectly fine because as it turns out, with my new promotion, I'll be making a lot of money, babe. I mean, *a lot* of money. I can take care of you—shit! Not that you need anyone to take care of you! No, what I mean is, I can take care of *us* while you decide what to do in New York. You'll have time to figure it all out, which you'll need because New York is a fucking crazy place."

She swallowed.

"So, that's it," she said by way of finishing up, looking down at their joined hands on the tabletop. "I know it's probably sounds outrageously nutso, but I truly believe it's an option for us." Megan looked up again into Vanessa's eyes. "I don't want to be in New York without you."

There. It was out. Of course, she had sounded like an awkward pre-teen professing her feelings to a crush, but nothing could help that now. The only thing that mattered was that it was out there.

Looking at Vanessa, Megan knew she was seeing her future. The only question was, how would that future start?

"I love your idea," Vanessa said and Megan tilted her head back and blew out a breath she didn't realize she had been holding.

This was going to happen!

Then Vanessa said, "Buuut…" and Megan's heart plummeted.

"Sweetie," Vanessa continued, "I want to do the whole lesbian romcom movie thing right now and stand up, toss the keys to La Vida Mocha to Chloë, saying 'She's all yours now' and ride off into the sunset with you, but I need to think about all this, okay?"

Megan nodded slowly, trying to remain outwardly calm even though her insides were frothing with frustration.

"Technically, it would be riding off into the sunrise with me," she said softly. "Because, you know, we'd be heading east."

"Oh my God, you're such a nerd!" Vanessa said, laughing.

Vanessa's laughter made Megan feel less tense. Vanessa hadn't flat-out rejected the plan. And, after all, it made sense that Vanessa wanted to think about this, it was a huge thing to think about. And Vanessa was older, more sensible about things.

But, dammit, why couldn't Vanessa just toss the keys to Chloë?

"I totally understand," Megan said, and she was surprised when, after saying it, she realized that she was being honest. She *did* understand.

"Can we talk more about it tonight?" Vanessa asked.

Megan smiled.

"Of course."

"I'm not promising a decision, though," Vanessa warned. "This is going to take some time. I need you to be okay with that."

Squeezing her girlfriend's (*girlfriend's!*) hands again, Megan said, "I am, I promise."

"There's one more thing."

"What?"

"I love you, Megan Baldwin."

Megan felt she could just die from happiness.

Chapter 45

The next day, in the back room of La Vida Mocha, Vanessa was working on "The New York Problem" while Chloë and Luli ran things in the front.

Yesterday, she had told Megan she needed to think about Megan's idea of both of them relocating to New York. However, Vanessa knew there wasn't much to think about. In fact, that night she had gone over to Megan's and they had ended up in bed professing their love for each other, Vanessa had pretty much known that she might as well practice saying "cawfee" and buy a Yankees cap.

Megan was the one. No, Megan was The One, and there was no way in hell Vanessa was going to stand having an entire continent between them. It was going to mean a complete upheaval for her own life but wasn't love worth that?

Right now, Vanessa was in front of her laptop, looking at listings for storefronts for rent in any of the five boroughs of New York City, and, holy fuck, the rents were outrageous! Vanessa's jaw was hanging open as she scrolled through the listings of appropriately-sized and equipped vacancies that could become La Vida Mocha NY. Depending on location, some places were renting for more a month than La Vida Mocha took in during two or three months here in Carlsbad. And the vacancies that were somewhat affordable were either obviously so run-down and decrepit she might as well add Rat Shit Muffins to her pastry menu or were in neighborhoods which a quick Google search revealed were so crime-ridden she'd need to hire armed security to help pull espressos.

How on earth do people manage to stay in business there? Especially during a pandemic?

Megan's idea of keeping La Vida Mocha and running it from New York was an attractive option; but it, too, was ridden with pitfalls.

Chloë, whom Vanessa trusted, wasn't ready yet to take over day-to-day management, although, Vanessa had been delighted to learn that soon after their discussion a couple of weeks ago, Chloë had signed up for business classes that would start at the community college in the fall semester. But until Chloë was ready, Vanessa would have to find a capable and experienced person to run things here in Carlsbad while she was in New York.

"Is running this place from New York even possible?" William asked a couple of hours later, during another lull. Vanessa had called him to see if he'd be willing to come by because she desperately wanted someone to talk to about all this.

"I mean, yeah," Vanessa answered. They were sitting together on the sofa in the Lover's Nook, William sipping a cappuccino. "In this day and age, the technology certainly exists. If I find someone trustworthy to handle the day-to-day here in California, then I could just run the business remotely from anywhere."

"So do that," William stated, as if the matter could be closed.

"But do I really need that hassle? Running a business from three-thousand miles away? As it is, I'll have my hands full trying to keep a New York coffeeshop afloat. I swear, William, the more I look into it, the more it scares me. Opening a small business in that city is like committing financial suicide; and you know me, I'm not afraid to take chances, but, fucking hell, New York scares me. At least here in Carlsbad I feel like I have more than a fighting chance, especially now that some pandemic restrictions are loosening up."

"So don't bother opening up a New York shop," William stated, again as if the matter could be closed.

"And do what with myself?" Vanessa asked. "First of all, I doubt I'd be earning enough to be a woman of leisure, especially since I'd have to pay the salary of whoever is running this place. Secondly, even if I did earn enough, I can't just sit around doing nothing. I'll be in a strange city where the only person I know is Megan, I'll go nuts!"

***

Walking into Megan's condo after closing La Vida Mocha, Vanessa could sense how stressed Megan was. Preparing for her new VP job was taking a lot out of her, Vanessa knew. And Megan could apparently sense how stressed Vanessa was because after they kissed each other hello, a kind of pressurized energy passed between them and without any words being spoken, the gentle kiss hello turned into the hurried and frantic removal of clothes followed by hot and breathless sex in the living room, each woman instinctively knowing that her partner needed a couple of intense orgasms in order to open her tension-release valve.

Afterwards, snuggling on the couch, sweaty and still panting, it was Megan who spoke first.

"What's up?"

Vanessa shook her head.

"It's stupid compared to what you're going through getting ready to be a bigshot VP," she said. "I don't want you to worry about it."

Megan held Vanessa tighter.

"Babe, I love you so much," she said, making Vanessa's heart soar. "That means nothing is stupid if it's bothering you. Tell me."

"Okay. I spent an obscene amount of time at work today looking at starting over business-wise in New York and I did not like what's in store for me." She then spent a few minutes detailing what she had learned online and what specifically scared her about opening a new coffeeshop in New York.

When she was done, Vanessa felt Megan stiffen a bit. She knew what the next words out of Megan's mouth would be even if Megan didn't quite know them yet. It took a few moments, but eventually…

"You're not changing your mind, are you?" Megan asked quietly.

Vanessa kissed the top of Megan's head.

"I'm not changing my mind. I'll move with you to the Himalayas if need be."

"Promise?"

"Promise. Now that I've found you, I'm not losing you."

And Vanessa meant it. This woman she was now holding in her arms she intended to keep holding in her arms no matter where life took them.

Megan propped herself up on one elbow so she could meet Vanessa's eyes.

"I'm sorry in advance for how difficult this will be for you," she said. "For what it's worth, before I met you, this was a no-brainer for me but now I wouldn't want to move to New York without you."

"Don't say that," Vanessa insisted. "This promotion is a big deal. Do you realize that you will be an inspiration to all the little girls out there who want to have a career in technology?"

Megan made a face.

"You think so?"

"Absolutely! A female vice-president of a major software company at twenty-seven-years-old? As soon as we get to New York, I'm calling the *New York Times* to tell them to do a profile on you."

Megan giggled; it was still among Vanessa's favorite sounds.

"I just wish there was something other than me in New York to make it all worth it for you," Megan eventually said before chuckling and continuing with, "Too bad you're not Sophia."

Vanessa laughed and pinched Megan's hip.

"Oh, is that who you'd rather be with now?" she asked in mock indignation.

Megan kissed her.

"Of course not. It's just that Sophia has…her…"

Megan's voice trailed off and Vanessa watched as her brows knitted and her eyes got a far-off look to them, her mind obviously chewing on something.

"Sophia has her what?" Vanessa prodded.

"I wonder if…" Megan muttered.

"If…?"

Suddenly, Megan scrambled out of Vanessa's arms and up off the couch.

"Megan?" Vanessa asked, feeling alarmed now.

"Huh? Oh, sorry! I have to go make a phone call!"

And then, completely nude, Megan sprinted for the staircase and bounded up to the second floor, leaving Vanessa alone and utterly confused on the couch.

Epilogue
Six months later

Megan felt a tap on her shoulder. She turned to find the love and light of her life standing behind her.

"Guess what?" Vanessa asked. "Although I'm not sure you're going to like it."

Megan's heart began racing and her eyes widened in alarm. She wanted tonight to be perfect.

"What?"

"'*Anastasia Number Three*' just sold," Vanessa told her.

Megan gasped and her face fell.

"But that's my favorite!" she whined.

Vanessa laughed.

"Sweetie, most artists, when they open a gallery, *want* their art to sell."

"But that's my favorite," Megan repeated, this time with a pout.

Vanessa rubbed Megan's arms, bare because of the tank-style blue sheath dress Megan was wearing which fit her like a second skin.

"Then I guess you should have left it at home on our living room wall," she said with a smile and then pulled down her mask and bent forward to give Megan a kiss.

"Who bought it?"

Vanessa inclined her head towards the sales desk, manned by Sienna, where an older couple was in the process of completing the transaction.

"They said they'd like to meet you," Vanessa said. "So, be a good girl and go say hello. I need to check on things next door. Be back in a few." With another kiss, Vanessa went through the newly-added glass door which connected Megan's art gallery to La Vida Mocha. Biting her bottom lip, Megan watched Vanessa walk away. That little black dress Vanessa had bought especially for Megan's gallery opening was mouth-watering; so much so, in fact, that when Megan first saw it on Vanessa earlier tonight as they were getting ready to leave, she had been overcome with desire, guided Vanessa to the bed, laid her down and after pulling aside the black lace panties the dress concealed, proceeded to lick Vanessa to climax right there. Megan promised herself now that when they got home later tonight, she was going to do a lot more of the same.

It had been a whirlwind six months since she and Vanessa almost moved to New York. Even now, Megan still laughed at the memory of how she had run upstairs, completely naked, to call Sophia on Zoom, barely remembering to put a shirt on before Sophia answered. Then, Megan had breathlessly told Sophia the idea she had just had.

What if they switched jobs? Sophia could become the new vice-president of operations in New York while Megan took over Sophia's current position to become the new vice-president of operations here in California? Sophia would get to move back to her hometown *and* look after her parents while Megan got to stay in Carlsbad, with Vanessa.

After an initial shock, Sophia said she loved the idea, wondering why she hadn't thought to suggest it to Lucy Whitaker herself. The next day, they had both done exactly that, suggesting it to Lucy who fully supported it, especially after Sophia masterfully conveyed just how decrepit and helpless her parents in Connecticut were. For her part, Megan seriously doubted that the two people who created such a strong and dynamic woman as Sophia could ever be decrepit and helpless, but whatever worked was fine with her.

Convincing Vanessa took more work because Vanessa refused to be the cause of Megan giving up her dream job in New York. But after countless kisses and countless heartfelt assurances of how deep her love for Vanessa was, Megan got her to finally accept it by guaranteeing that it was the right decision because it was what she, Megan, wanted. True, she *had* been excited about living in New York but now that she had Vanessa in her life and by her side, Carlsbad felt even more like home to her.

It took a few months for Megan to fully settle into her new role at BeachSoft. The duties and expectations of her new position were demanding, but Megan proved equal to the task. The hours were longer, sure, and there were some nights when she just curled herself into a ball on the couch and snuggled against Vanessa not saying anything while they binge-watched something on Hulu or Netflix. But her contributions to BeachSoft's overall business strategy were proving tremendously valuable, so much so that Lucy

Whitaker started referring to Megan publicly as "my right-hand woman."

It wasn't until after Thanksgiving when Megan decided to give opening a gallery a go. The response to Vanessa hanging prints of Megan's art up in La Vida Mocha had been overwhelmingly positive, with many of them selling within days of being hung.

Turns out, the old lady with the Mr. Magoo glasses and the ninja-like super power of sneaking up on Megan and Vanessa, was the owner of the building La Vida Mocha and the vacant space were in. Vanessa had never met her before, only having dealt with the people at the property management company the old lady also owned. Her name was Ethel and she was quite the real estate mogul in Carlsbad. What's more, she had taken a liking to Megan and Vanessa, calling them the cutest couple she had ever come across. She gave Megan a great deal on renting the space and it was her idea to knock out part of the wall dividing La Vida Mocha and what was now The Baldwin Gallery.

Megan discovered that the weeks spent prepping her gallery for opening night was a great decompression tool from the demands of her job but now that it *was* opening night, she was nervous as hell.

The turnout, though, was great. Covid restrictions had been relaxed even more in Southern California and though facemasks were still required, at least people were able to show up and come in freely, and many of them were popping next door to La Vida Mocha for coffee. And Molly had just texted her to say that she and Cole were on their way.

More importantly, her art was apparently a hit. The opening officially started only an hour ago but she had already sold 5 works.

At the sales desk now, Sienna's face lit up when she saw Megan. Indicating the man and woman she had been talking to when Megan approached, she said, "Mr. and Mrs. Kleinmann, this is Megan Baldwin, the artist."

"I'm so pleased to meet you both," Megan greeted them cheerily, even though they were apparently taking away her absolute favorite graphite drawing, *Anastasia Number Three*. It was a poster-sized drawing of Megan's friend, Anastasia, who was an actual ballerina, in a dance studio, *en pointe*, doing an exquisite arabesque.

"You are so talented!" Mrs. Kleinmann stated, her husband nodding vigorously next to her. "And we love that you are so focused on dance art!"

"Our daughter used to be a dancer," Mr. Kleinmann added. "But thirty years ago, she had a skiing accident which really damaged both her legs. She never was able to dance again, not ballet anyway. She lives in Germany now with her husband; we hardly get to see her, especially now with the way things are because of the pandemic, but once we saw that drawing of yours, it reminded us of all those ballet practices we took her to ages ago."

Megan's heart melted.

"Oh my God, that is so sweet!" she said, meaning it. "I won't lie, it's my favorite drawing and I hate seeing it go, but I'm just so glad it's going to a good home!"

"It will have pride of place, I assure you," Mrs. Kleinmann said, and Megan was no longer sad that her favorite drawing was leaving her. Besides, the great thing about being an artist was that she could always draw Anastasia's arabesque again.

They spoke for a few more minutes and then Sienna needed the Kleinmann's to finalize the details of the delivery of *Anastasia Number Three* to their home tomorrow. Just in time, too, because Megan then spotted Abby entering the gallery with Kat. Megan squealed and rushed over to hug them both.

"Thank you so much for coming!" she enthused.

"Are we fashionably enough late?" Abby said, looking around.

"I tried to get her here earlier," Kat insisted. "But, no…she said we needed to be like the upper crust and pretend that time means nothing to us."

Megan laughed.

"I'm just glad you're here, you know that," she said.

"Where's the missus?" Abby asked.

Megan rolled her eyes.

"She's not the missus yet," she said, smacking Abby's arm playfully. "You should know, you're the best woman at the wedding."

"Jesus!" Kat exclaimed, looking at Megan's left hand. "Are you able to lift your hand with that rock on it?"

Giggling, Megan held her hand up for Kat to examine the ring, which did in fact have quite a nice-sized diamond on it.

"My woman did good," Megan said. Looking at it, she smiled at the memory of this past Christmas. That night, long after all their presents to each other had been opened, her and Vanessa were relaxing on the sofa in the beach house they had just bought, after spending the day with their friends at Angela and Desiree's place.

At one point, Vanessa asked, "Did you enjoy your Christmas, love?"

Megan had nodded and said, "This is honestly the best Christmas I've ever had. What about you?"

Vanessa had pretended to consider it for a moment and then said, "It was *almost* the best Christmas I've ever had. Almost."

Megan, thinking that Vanessa's statement was a prelude to a night of great sex, had shifted on the couch and started running her finger along Vanessa's cleavage, amply displayed in the V-neck sweater she had on.

"Oh, really?" Megan had asked, licking her lips. "And what, pray tell, would make it the best Christmas you've ever had?"

Even to this day, Megan had no idea where the box came from. Had it been stuffed between the cushions of the couch? Had Vanessa stored it underneath the couch but within reach? Whatever the case, suddenly Vanessa had produced a black velvet ring box and showed it to Megan.

"It'll be the best Christmas ever if you agree to be my wife," Vanessa had said.

Megan, after screaming "Yes!", then couldn't stop crying for a solid half hour.

***

"Oh god, you're not tired of showing that thing off yet?" Vanessa said, coming up behind Megan and wrapping her arms around her.

"Leave her alone," Kat said. "That's a ring worth showing off."

"Don't let her fool you," Megan said with a smirk. "She's actually super-proud of how bling-y this is. How's it going next door?" Megan asked her fiancée.

"Great! Chloë and Luli have it running like a well-oiled machine and a bunch of new people just signed up for the coffee tasting club. I'm going to have to add another day a month for that to accommodate them all."

The coffee tastings and coffee flights idea Megan had suggested months back had turned into quite the money-maker for La Vida Mocha. Vanessa had taken her time implementing it, though, because she had wanted to be sure to locate a variety of coffees from around the world that were not only delicious and responsibly-sourced but also not available in any grocery store in town. Now, the coffee flights were one of the most most-asked for menu items at La Vida Mocha, and the monthly coffee tastings were so popular that Vanessa and her staff were hosting them three times a month now, two of those being for women who love women because of Chloë's success with Operation Hashtag Lesbian.

"Well, speaking of coffee, I wouldn't mind one your five-thousand-dollars-a-pop Americanos," Megan said, turning around to face Vanessa.

Vanessa smiled.

"Seeing how business is so good, I think I can drop the price back down to around three bucks."

Megan quirked an eyebrow. Suddenly, it was as if everyone else disappeared. All the gallery visitors? Gone. Abby and Kat? Gone. The Kleinmanns? Gone. It was as if it was now just her and Vanessa standing here, all alone, together. Warmth burst inside Megan and spread throughout her body. She had never been happier. It still amazed her every single day that this gorgeous woman in her arms was hers and would one day be her wife.

Vanessa could charge her three bucks for an Americano, or five-thousand; it didn't matter to Megan. The price of a cup of coffee, the price of *anything* was nothing compared to finding and experiencing this kind of love.

She pulled Vanessa closer until her lips were millimeters from Vanessa's ear.

"I love you so fucking much," Megan whispered.

THE END

Thank you so much for reading *Nothing But A Fling*!
If you liked it, please consider writing a review! Reviews are so important to independent authors, and we love getting feedback from our readers.

Follow me on Twitter at *kanelesfic* for updates on the next novel in the series, which I am currently hard at work on. (Hint: it's about Chloë!)

Also, feel free to drop me an email at thekanemutiny@gmail.com

Made in the USA
Coppell, TX
26 October 2024

39237921R00164